Never-Ending

...by D.F. Williams

Published by Ember-Link International, Inc
Discerning Artists Division

First Edition, First Printing, September 2014

Note for Librarians: A cataloguing record for this book is available from Library and Archives Canada at
www.collectionscanada.ca/amicus/index-e.html

ISBN 978-0-9919688-1-7

Edited exclusively for Ember-Link International, Inc. Discerning Artists Division by Catherine B. Johns.

Printed in Canada
on recycled paper

www.firstchoicebooks.ca
Victoria, BC
10 9 8 7 6 5 4 3

BRITA BLACK

CHAPTER 1

When her husband started banging his head against the kitchen cupboard, Brita was thrilled. Without saying a word, she quietly snuck up behind him, put her hand on his wrist and took his pulse for a full minute. Seventy-eight and steady. Then, with her hand still on his pulse, she stood back and counted the head beats. Seventy-eight and steady. She wasn't surprised that heart-beat and head-beat were the same, or that they were perfectly synchronized, but she was very suspicious about the rate. Was seventy-eight as fast as his head could bang or as slow as his heart could beat or the other way around? Was there a rule for this sort of thing, or was everybody different? If everybody was different was seventy-eight a little different or a lot different? And, more curious yet, why didn't she have even the slightest bit of intuition about these questions when lately she had become a veritable fountain of intuition about all kinds of things? Could it be that head-banging husbands were outside the norm for intuition?

It was a curious question to be sure and as much as Brita prided herself on thinking up curious questions, an hour later when he was still at it, still keeping the beat at seventy-eight like an old vinyl record with a crack down the middle, she had had enough of curious questions and realized she had, for a change, some serious questions on her mind. Like what should she do now that she had him where she wanted him? Okay, maybe not exactly where she wanted him, but how would she finish the job? What didn't he need next?

She quickly decided the next steps would require some serious planning and the best place to do that was over a late lunch at Mario's followed by some window shopping, which was all she could afford since the head-banger had taken away all her credit cards and put her on that demeaning weekly allowance, completely spent on day one as usual. But that was his stupid mistake not to mention being in the past which she couldn't afford to dwell upon right that moment when she had more important things to think about. Like what to wear. Was it too soon to wear black? Could anyone fault her for that? Honestly, she was so tired of constantly worrying over what other people thought about the way she treated her husband. If she had known it was going to turn out like this, even fractionally like this, she would have worn a black dress to the wedding.

But all that worry was about to change, yes indeed it was and the thump, thump, thump echoing down the hallway was proof positive of that; music to her purse so to speak. She checked him from the doorway and thought about taking the wallet out of his back pocket but decided not to risk disturbing his breakdown. It was a totally out-of-place and odd thought considering all she had done to him but it made sense on some level so she put up a mental Do Not Disturb sign and turned her back on him like he was an old dog.

She was half way out the door when, without any warning whatsoever, another thought came into her mind from right-out-of-the-blue: 'Would he still be there when she came back?' She knew she couldn't ignore that question, couldn't ignore a thought from right-out-of-the-blue because lately that's where most of the things she did to him came from. No, she didn't dare ignore that thought and knew it right down to the soles of her $800 Jimmy Choo stilettos.

So she pondered the question for a while before positively deciding there was absolutely no upside for her if he got the wanderlust and she had to run around the neighborhood looking for him like an old lost dog. 'Eric, Eric, where are you? Come home, Eric'. Wouldn't that be embarrassing? And who in their right mind needs more embarrassing after being put on a weekly allowance? Seriously, who?

No, no doubt about it, Eric needed a good firm warning about any wanderlust plans that might be rattling around in that broken brain of his. She had to let him know that if he figured life was unbearable now, or however much unbearable his mind was currently capable of figuring, he had no bloody idea what was in store for him if he just up and wandered away. She had to send him a message, a good strong, unequivocal, *don't you dare even think about it Buster* message.

She approached him from the side and stared into the corner of his right eye, following it forward and back to the cupboard. She stared hard and mean until she was certain he got the message. *Stay put or else. Or else bad will get to worse on the fast track to horrible for you Buster. Trust me on this one because this time I'm telling the truth.*

Watching him eye to eye, back and forth, forth and back, made her feel like a vulture which, strange as it might seem, wasn't a bad feeling. In fact, it didn't even feel odd, so maybe it was perfectly normal. Normal? How could feeling like a vulture ever be normal, except to another vulture? One more curious question but not one she could take any pride in, vultures being the disgusting animals they are, forget even thinking how horrible their breath had to smell.

This seemed like another crazy thought until she remembered the lunch she had promised herself and then she made sense out of it. Vultures were always hungry, always on the verge of starvation and Brita had more hungers than she could count. Soon enough and she would finally get to satisfy them. Soon enough and no more window shopping for Mrs. Brita Black and that was just one of her unfulfilled wants, needs and lusts. But for the moment at least, all that had to wait, so she let out a big dramatic sigh of disappointment in the general direction of her head-banging husband before leaving him alone. Well, not exactly alone, he had that thing in his head, didn't he?

* * * * *

When she returned, he hadn't moved an inch, had stayed put like a good old dog and was still head-humping away at seventy-eight beats per minute. She tried to do the math in her head...seventy-eight times sixty minutes times four hours and twenty minutes. No, that wouldn't work, it had to be all minutes or all hours didn't it? No matter, it was probably a pretty big number. His forehead was looking pretty rosy and his eyes were glazed over but other than that, damn it, he looked fine. Just like the last time she had set him on the pathway to his self-destruction only that time, after eight hours of being paralyzed in front of a TV that was off, and a twitch in his chin that was on, he had found his way out of it, he climbed out of the hole she had dug for him and asked for more. Well, he got it.

She didn't think he'd be quite so lucky this time and even if he did get out of it, he damn sure wouldn't call it luck because she was just getting warmed up with his destruction. No sir, the best thing for him was to stay with the torment locked in his mind and not tempt fate by asking for another round of whatever came into her mind from right-out-of-the-blue.

Strange thought, she thought, then remembered she'd been having a few of those lately. Strange thoughts that is, not the other thing…what was that again? Oh yes, right-out-of-the-blue mind-shredding thoughts and all the different ways there are to drive somebody crazy when your allowance is spent and you have nothing better to do with your time. Just like drops of water wearing away a rock, she knew what she was doing. Just like the thump, thump, thump of his forehead against the cupboard was now starting to get to her. When would he ever learn? *Are you trying to drive me crazy? Is that what you are trying to do? Bad idea Buster.*

With that thought, she knew she couldn't tolerate his bloody thumping all bloody night and certainly didn't want to have to tiptoe around in her own kitchen for fear of interrupting him, so she decided it was best for everyone if he went outside. She pushed and pulled and body-checked him out the back door and onto the redwood deck then positioned him against the railing with his forehead a couple of inches from the garage wall. She gave the back of his head a little push, waited until he was back on track at seventy-eight and left him, slamming the door behind herself then locking it and drawing the blind. Now he could continue banging away, plodding down the pathway of self-destruction to which she had finally driven him without this whole nasty business completely ruining her evening. She was 100% committed to making this work and soon enough, so too would he be, literally, figuratively but most importantly, permanently, committed. That was the plan and it was a brilliant one, *if she did say so herself.*

Did she actually say that out loud or was it just an expression and she only thought it? Curious and hard to tell whether or not she had voiced it but whatever, it was perfectly understandable, really. All the mind games she had played on him over the last few months had taken their toll on her; she really needed a rest.

Somewhere sophisticated would be nice. Maybe St. Tropez, and this time at the Five Star La Bastide and not that cheap Three Star hotel down the street that he picked. Of course he claimed it was charming but that was really just a cover up for his insecurities about being with the rich and famous which is exactly where she belonged. Those were insecurities that Mrs. Brita Black most certainly did not have. Rich and famous not only suited her perfectly but as far as she was concerned anybody who wanted anything less than rich and famous was simply demonstrating the weakness of their character. Weakness she could no longer tolerate in anyone, let alone her husband, and that made the ruthless pursuit of her goal completely acceptable and if that wasn't what becoming rich and famous was all about then what was?

Brita knew her husband's weaknesses better than he did, she created most of them, and the head banging was nothing more than the culmination of months and months of mercilessly hard work and untiringly brutal mental manipulation. She deserved full credit for getting him started and although she wasn't absolutely certain why he kept at it or how it could be stopped, or even if it could be stopped, she didn't fault herself over those trivial questions. After all, she reasoned, if she knew those answers, what was to keep her from standing right beside him, both of them banging away like two kids on a teeter totter? Plus, it was completely irrelevant because she didn't want him to stop, if he never stopped that would be fine with her but for sure the whole convoluted mess in his mind had to stay that way for the few weeks it would take her to execute the rest of her plan. Just long enough to drop her into the plush and über expensive one bedroom suite at La Bastide all rich and famous with his money and then it wouldn't matter what he did or didn't do or think because then it would be too late.

With that happy realization, she decided to check on him because she really, really wanted to confirm her emerging reality by seeing him on the verge of losing what little was left of his. She peeked between the blinds and studied him. A distant neighboring light flicked on but she didn't worry about it. His house was on a large lot, practically an acre and this time she was glad it was like being surrounded by a jungle.

She had wanted to cut that jungle down and make a nice garden with a lawn and flowers and get some immigrant to look after it all, but he liked it wild. In truth, she would have bulldozed the house too but knew better than to mention that to him, especially after the poor reception she got to her gardening idea.

He had practically built the place with his bare hands and while she was okay with the ranch style, the rest of the place reeked of testosterone. Rough cedar siding-clad walls, a deep, wrap-around veranda with oversized furniture and river stone everywhere, like the whole thing came out of an old Western show like Bonanza. All surrounded by unkempt forest with very noisy birds, the only thing missing was a bunch of hound dogs scratching on the porch.

She longed for some true peace and quiet, the kind that came with tall ceilings, heavy drapes and servants but he wouldn't hear of that. Wouldn't hear of it then, but there's a new sheriff in town and his days of peace and quiet were over, that sun had set and if it ever rose again, it would be too late for him, for anyone actually, to turn back that clock.

The first domino had fallen and next one was teetering and after that it would be unstoppable, just like the head-banging. The long arm of the law and the whacko process for head-bangers like him would take over, she wouldn't even have to do anything. Even if it cured him, it would still end him because having something to fight doesn't mean a bloody thing if you haven't anything to fight with. His life would be basic as in basically over.

Hers would be starting. She would claim the bounty and begin the long, leisurely and wonderful process of satisfying a lifetime of pent-up, unfulfilled hungers. She reviewed her mental wish list and with each additional desire: clothes, jewelry, parties and travel, she became happier. She followed that with excesses of everything, until she had a perfect realization of her new life and with this came a serene sense of complete and utter self-satisfaction, a wonderful indulgent dream-like state of bliss. Better than any orgasm, she languished in the after-glow for as long as she could, until she realized she could no longer push the next thought out of her mind, which was becoming an increasingly annoying train of events.

Chain of events.

There, it just happened again. Right-out-of-the-blue, some stupid thought would enter her head and she couldn't avoid it, couldn't even really trace its origin. Sometimes the thoughts made sense, sometimes they were connected to what she was seeing or doing and sometimes they were helpful, interesting, even pleasant. But sometimes isn't all the time and then those thoughts were not helpful, interesting or even remotely pleasant. Maybe not even one of her own thoughts which is why she called them her out-of-the-blue thoughts. But how could that be? How could a person's thoughts not be their own? Jesus 'effing Christopher, was she starting to think like him? No way was anybody in her brain, no way, she told herself. That was his problem. Real or imagined it was his problem, not hers.

To regain control over her wayward thinking, she asked herself when she first started to hate her husband so much. It wasn't really a question worth answering but once a question was in her mind, it was her nature to work on it. She had always been persistent that way and nothing could stop her or stand in her way once she got started on something. He should have thought about that before putting her on an allowance. All that free time, what did he think she would do with it, and to whom?

When she couldn't trace the beginning of her hatred, she decided that maybe she didn't actually hate him; she had just grown resentful of having to act like she loved him, resentful of having to act out the hurt feelings, act out the disappointment, the betrayal, the faults and the crushed expectations. All that acting, all that thinking and orchestrating, all that drama and innuendo, the constant baiting and badgering, just to finally get what she so rightly deserved, maybe that was just too much to ask of one's self. Maybe it wasn't his fault at all, except for the stubbornness of course. That much was definitely his fault. If he had given her what she wanted right at the beginning or if he had given up earlier or even if he had given up easier, he could have spared both of them a whole lot of aggravation. No, except for the stubbornness, he wasn't completely to blame. Even the daughter couldn't be blamed for handing over the secret that ultimately pushed him over the edge. What a bulldozer of a secret that turned out to be.

Maybe nobody could be blamed, just like she didn't really hate him, maybe it was just bound to happen. *Of course, of course that was it,* she realized with sudden clarity. She had always lied to him. She had always intended to use him. Maybe not exactly like this but changing how you skin the cat doesn't change very much as far as the cat is concerned, does it?

She gazed out the window at her husband, deep in shadows, banging his head on the garage wall. It would soon be dark, the birds would go to sleep and except for the head-banger it would be quiet.

No one would hear him. Not even if he banged his head so hard that he killed himself, which would ruin everything but she didn't think he'd do that. No, suicide was definitely not in the plan. True, a dead husband was worth more than a divorced husband but that was nothing compared to what she would get for a crazy husband.

ERIC & TOOK A-LOOK

CHAPTER 2

Saturday Afternoon

"Jesus Effing Christopher, get out on that deck where you can bang your head to your heart's content. Get out. Get out of here Eric, you're starting to drive me crazy."

Wife is very competitive. If the contest is crazy, she'll play to win. Hardball all the way. No holds barred. Tell her she isn't crazy and she'll kill you just to prove it.

"Eric! I said get out of here. Now! Jesus Effing Christopher, all that bloody head banging is giving me a migraine."

Who is this Jesus Effing Christopher anyway? New guy? What banging? Oh yeah. That banging. No, no way that's stopping. Serious consequences to that and guess who gets the consequences. That's right, me. Good guess.

"Get out. I said GET OUT."

She is damn angry. Damn wrong too. She thinks angry and crazy are the same, just different volumes. Right, right and wrong in the first degree. Angry is radio; crazy is TV. Volume is just a side effect.

"Fine, good, now you can bang away to your heart's content, I've had enough. Enough I tell you. Enough! More than enough. You come back in this house and you'd better come back with explanations. You and that little shit in your fried head, Took A-Look, whatever, whoever."

She stomps away, her small feet making their biggest, angriest noise. They don't stand a chance. Not against that mouth. Stick to walking feet and don't let that mouth tell you where to go because all that means is more noise in a different place.

She is talking and walking as usual, but not to me, thankfully. Took A-Look can't get to his feet. Good. Can't let him stand up. Or else. And then some bigger or else, his specialty. Keep on pounding and shaking and moving so Took A-Look can't get on his feet. That's the plan, the only plan. He doesn't like it but he doesn't seem to hate it either. Then again, maybe he does. I really don't want to know. Remember who gets the consequences?

Slam goes the door behind herself and it's a relief to be alone, except I'm not really alone and never have been.

Sunday Afternoon

No more talk from her for a while, more or less. Mostly less and seldom more, that's the general rule for quiet. Who knows why but it's just a matter of time. She talks on and on and on, more and more, then stops for a second or less then starts again. It happens all the time. Never-Ending is one way to think it without saying it. Here she goes again. See what I mean?

"Didn't I tell you I've had enough, Eric? Didn't I tell you that?"

Yeah.

"Didn't I?"

Yeah again.

"Didn't I tell you this would happen?"

Whoa. What? What would happen? Maybe I wasn't listening, ever think of that? Too busy talking to think of that, maybe? Too busy talking to ever listen, that's for sure. What? What would happen? Okay, I'm listening.

"Didn't I tell you this would happen? Here they come. There they are."

Coming and going, that's another thing she does a lot. Like *where is* totally unimportant as soon as it becomes attached to *here* and then all of a sudden she has to leave it. Here and there. Must be a million miles between them. She has little feet. Lots of walking for you feet, so stick to your job, it's already a big one but let that mouth tell you where to go and not here to stay.

"Didn't I tell you this would happen? Here they are. They are going to take you away from here. Didn't I tell you this would happen?"

Guess so. Fine with me. Fine with me. Guess so, again.

"Hi Eric. My name is Marty. This is Steve. We aren't going to hurt you, Eric."

What happened to Jesus Effing Christopher? He finished banging her already? Oh yeah, head-banger, that's me. It's confusing to say the least or in my case, not to say the least.

Oh oh, Took A-Look is getting to his feet. Always happens when the banging topss, I mean, stops. Oh oh. Repeat oh oh. Took A-Look doesn't like the looks of this. He had a plan for her and this isn't it. This is her plan for him. He sure doesn't like the kooks of this, I mean the looks of this, maybe I do mean the kooks, hard to say, new day, new rules, not mine to say.

"We'll just put this nice, white, clean jacket on you, okay Eric? Lots of buttons and straps, very comfy, very secure, okay Eric?"

Oh oh, Took A-Look is tomming around back there, I mean stomning around bace there. Maybe its stomping aroung bck there. He's squishing the clouds all over the place, making sparks, smoke, colors; so many memories are colliding it's hard to know what's real, what's today. A whole year of university calculus just flew into a clock. He's sending bolt after bolt of lightning into the folds and valleys and peaks in the clouds of my brain like there's no tomorrow. Maybe there is no tomorrow, not for Took A-Look, that's always a possibility. He's seen tomorrow lots of times and knows all about them, repeats, most of them. Besides, with so many todays under his belt, what's another re-run of the past replayed as a tomorrow worth to him? Not much, I bet.

Making bets is about all I can do, all he will allow but lately I always lose and all that cloud squishing is getting me jumpy, twitchy, very tight and erratic so the betting window is definitely closed. He knows that but he doesn't care. I don't blame him because right now I don't much care either.

"How are you doing Eric? You okay? Steve, pull that strap a little tighter, he's got the twitches. Another notch Steve, nice and tight under the crotch. Got it Steve? Eric, you okay? Good. Good. Everything will be fine. Just fine. You'll see."

Took A-Look wants to see, kicks a big, white and pink sack away from his window, my left eye. It hurts like hell. He jumps hard on a cloud, squishing it with both feet; that hurts some more and a whole bunch of vocabulary leaks out the bottom of that cloud; I wonder if it was, what's the word for something you need? I hope it isn't lost forever, whatever it was.

He's angry all right. So much for the whether or not he hates it head-banging question. He grabs hold of a red cord in one hand and a blue one in the other, looks out the window, totally pissed off. Sees Marty and doesn't like him at all. Wait a minute, doesn't like him aren't the right words, maybe they leaked away. Took A-Look detests her but now all of a sudden Marty is the enemy, the only enemy. One single glance out the window and he absolutely hates him, who knows why and this time no sense in even trying to guess. He has too many yesterdays to even bother taking a shot at which one it might be.

To me, Marty looks pretty normal. Dressed in whites, not tall, not short, not fat, not skinny, clean-shaven with short, sandy brown hair, probably so no one can grab it. Kind of a long thin nose that goes with his long thin face which is a little rosy because of the exertion and dark eyes that dart around, paying attention to anything that might take a swing at him. Without the exertion, he would be pretty pale, not an albino but pretty pale, like somebody who doesn't get out much but where's the crime in that?

Obviously somewhere because Took A-Look hates him. Bloody strange isn't it, but that's the kind of day it's been and going downhill pretty fast by the looks of it but I won't say that out loud, thank you very much.

Marty doesn't see Took A-Look. Nobody sees Took A-Look if Took A-Look doesn't want to be seen which basically he doesn't. But that doesn't mean he's going to be quietly invisible. Not anymore. Peace has been undeclared. That's a bold step, even for him. And don't think that means there's been enough talk about peace because what it really means is there's been enough talk about everything altogether; that's what happens when peace is undeclared. No more talk, or else. Or else followed by you know what. More or else, his specialty, remember?

Steve isn't in the picture but he doesn't have to be because he is like the guy next door or the guy beside you on the bus. Totally average. Easygoing, not nervous like Marty and hair long enough you could wind your fingers into it. Also unlike Marty, Steve has got a fair amount of upper body strength to him. He's the kind of person who can be strong and gentle at the same time, which is pretty much this time. Took A-Look is pissed and thinking about sharing it with something rude. He knows Steve is in the fart zone and Took A-Look wants to gas him a fair and proportionate offensive response to the Tighter Under the Crotch invasion. All things considered, like this starchy, tight uniform which is cinched up pretty damn tight, that might not be such a good idea. That gas could be trapped back there for weeks then who knows who will get it?

Who knows? That's always a good question. No matter what the topic, that's always a good thing to ponder and a good question to ask. Who knows? A lot of knowledge is based on trust so getting an answer to who knows is a good idea unless somebody is making up the answers. Then it isn't.

"We're going for nice ride in the big, white ambulance with flashing lights. No siren unless you're good, okay? Don't move, this needle won't hurt a bit; it will make you feel relaxed. Okay?" says Marty and beside him Steve nods.

What's with the flashing light and siren remark? Is there a child around here someplace? Relaxed is okay. Also damn rare lately so maybe better than okay, maybe even all the way up to very nice. Who knows? Who cares? See how well that works? Sure, one question gets answered with another one, but at least you get to move on.

She has been quiet and unhelpful which is both unusual and usual at the same time. Oops, here she goes again. Did I tell you about the rule for mostly less, seldom more? Thought so. Quiet just isn't in her cards.

"I can't take it anymore, not for another second. He's driving me insane. I can't take it anymore. Take him away. Take him away, take him there right now, I can't stand being here with him."

She says that very convincingly. But it's best not to believe anything she says because it's impossible to tell the truth from the lies. I wonder if she can tell the difference? No point asking that. No point asking Who Knows either. All her answers are just more questions in disguise. That's the problem with liars, or at least that's one of their problems.

She will be alone. Not for long though, you can bet your mukluks on that. Not with Jesus Effing Christopher around. Not with here to leave and there to go, then back again. How she keeps that straight is anybody's guess. I never asked. That would be crazy.

Took A-Look wants to say goodbye to the wife, goodbye with his sharpest spear. Digs his feet into a cloud for a good toss. Hurts like hell but not for long because suddenly the blinds fall over the window like somebody cut the string. Snap and down they come. Took A-Look lies down and goes to sleep. Finally, some rest for both of us.

Marty wasn't kidding, it didn't hurt a bit, but I wouldn't exactly call it relaxing. More like numbing, right behind the eyes and into the brain cavity thing numm..m...b...ng.

Monday Morning In Bed At the Hospital

"Hello Eric, I am Doctor Marsha Coleman. Can you hear me?"

Oh oh, turn off the sound. Took A-Look is still sleeping. Very tired from Jesus Effing Christopher head banging and what not plus Marty slime all over the clouds. Keep the windows shut, let Took A-Look sleep. Play some nice music. Don't let him fall off his cloud and wake up. Hell to pay. Raging hell to pay, most likely. Sleep, Took A-Look, sleep. Listen to the nice music, harps and all the instruments you like. See Took A-Look, no sound from her, that's a huge bonus. Listen Took A-Look, listen, angel music all the way.

"When did this start, Mrs. Black?"

Oh foul and rotting dead fish on the beach, she is here, not there. Better not let Took A-Look know that. Miserable hell to pay on that count, the beginning of the end all over again, and again after that most likely. Can you two keep it quiet out there? Can you please keep it quiet, especially you-know-who with the big, nasty mouth?

"Two days ago, more or less, Doc."

Wrong, wrong, wrong!

"More or less? What do you mean by that, Mrs. Black?"

"It didn't happen all at once."

"It?"

"The head banging."

"What else has happened, what has your husband told you about this? Anything at all?"

Oh oh, Took A-Look is waking up. Nobody can sleep when she is talking because that racket always comes through, like a chainsaw in your ear. No music big enough to keep that noise out. Damn, now he wants the window open. Here we go again.

Without even getting up from where he fell down, he kicks the jelly sack away from the window. Ouch. Might as well raise the blinds and take a look myself. Might as well open an eye or two because I already know nothing else will move. Like being stuck in cement; the starchy white uniform must have hardened into a complete body cast.

Damn. I'm a statue. A whole lifetime of bird droppings to look forward to, crap anywhere and anytime you think about it. Not a lot different than being married to her so certainly not an improvement.

"Hello Eric. Are you with us now?"

Took A-Look sees Doctor Coleman but doesn't get off the cloud which managed to suck up all the vocabulary that leaked out of it before. Good. The word for something you need turns out to be important.

Maybe Took A-Look likes what he sees but that would be a lot to hope for. Can't see the mouthy one at all; you can bet your mukluks he loves that non-sight. Very good if it stays that way and she shuts up to boot. No such luck there, I bet. Not with Never-Ending a distinct possibility, as it always was, is and will be. Plus there's the more and less condition for quiet but we've been through that already and it's not worth repeating, unless you're her of course.

Windows wide open and Doctor Marsha is real close to Took A-Look. Eyeball to Window to Eyeball. Her pretty green eyes with little gold specks looking into his black eyes, tired with sleep but waking up pretty damn quick and not happy about being put down for a nap without anybody asking his thoughts on the topic. Is Took A-Look going to send a spear into one of those gold specks? He could. Better move Doc, this isn't the fart zone, you could get seriously hurt. Got medical insurance? Hope so. At least we're already in a hospital, that's a plus.

She moves back so Took A-Look can see all of her, very nice of her and she is nice looking too, not just the eyes. Not a bad idea to get out of spear range either. She smiles at Took A-Look, he doesn't smile back but he doesn't throw a spear at her either which is another plus. Maybe he likes her. He just rests on his cloud. I hope it stays that way. I also hope the mouth shuts up but know that's not going to happen. She never shuts up, it's just not in her to shut up. It never was; something I didn't hear before but now it's too late to do anything about it. She won't even allow not listening, that's her territory and she keeps it permanently pinned down with her mouth, like a dog with a squeaky toy. All chewed and slobbery, with absolutely no sharing.

"What has Eric told you about this, Mrs. Black?"

"Jesus Effing Christopher, how the hell would I know what's going on? That's your job isn't it? He just started banging his head against the wall and wouldn't stop. I told him he would end up here if he didn't quit so what do you think he did? I'll tell you what he did. Nothing. He didn't listen to a word I said. He just kept on with the head banging. And do you know why he did that? I'll tell you that too. Because he wants to be here; he knows he belongs here. He's right about that Doc, about the only thing he's right about but he's right about that. Make his dreams come true Doc, commit him, right here, right now, then you can figure him out, I'm done with it."

Jesus Effing Christopher is back. No surprise there, I suppose. She is lying, definitely no surprise there. She knows everything. She said so, over and over again. 'I know everything.' she says and then she says, 'Everything, I know everything.' just to make sure you're listening and you better nod, or else. Took A-Look hates that lie. He wanted to shut her up for good, but what he was thinking isn't legal in this century.

Oh oh. OH OH! Here comes the spear. Look out Doctor Marsha, sometimes Took A-Look's aim isn't so good. Close the window, close the effing window! Carnage is coming, bloody carnage is coming. LOOK OUT! At least duck, won't you?

"What has he told you, Mrs. Black, he must have said something? At this point, anything you can tell me is a help."

Damn, Took A-Look wedged his spear in the window and now I can't close it, not even for a blinking second. He's looking for the mouthy one but pretty soon he'll give up and Doctor Marsha will get it instead. He's concentrating on one of the pretty gold specks floating around in those clear green eyes but I don't worry too much about that. It's a long shot at a really tiny target. Still, he's trying to figure it out. He only has so many spears and doesn't want to waste even the little bent one. Not if she is around because he knows he'll need all his spears and then some for that revenge, that's for sure. She drives him crazy, and that's just the beginning of this whole mess, not the ending. With Never-Ending no longer in sight and peace undeclared it's anyone's guess what will happen next. Maybe nothing or maybe another Never-Ending. Who knows? Maybe nobody knows, that's always a possibility. Not a strong possibility but that's what maybe means isn't it, a possibility, not a certainty. Speaking of words, what happened to her, isn't it her turn to talk? Stupid question, she doesn't take turns, sometimes she doesn't even take a breath.

"Mrs. Black, can you tell me anything at all?"

Good move, Doctor. The gold specks are all gone. Just green, emerald green. Nice color. Very clever move. Keep her at bay. Don't let her ask the questions. Shut her up if you can. Even bigger job. Maybe mention there and see if she goes for it. Sometimes that works. Good luck.

"He just…one day…he just went there, to the head-banging thing. Maybe he's been under some stress or something. Maybe it's a chemical thing, maybe a hormone thing, he's at that age you know. I can't explain it, won't even try, you should tell me, that's your job, isn't it?"

She is lying again. Why? Took A-Look wants the window moved toward her but it's better to keep it pointed at Marsha. He'll never hit her from this distance. Besides, I don't think he really wants it moved. Doctor Coleman doesn't believe her and Took A-Look likes that. He could jump on another cloud and make the window move but he doesn't do it. Instead, he shoots an arrow into a tiny, whitish cloud that is minding its own business, way up high in the back, a very weak shot so the arrow falls out and a cute little seal sticks her head out the hole.

Good shot, Took A-Look. It's Marsha. He must like her. That won't last. Probably not once he gets to know her and for sure if she ever gets to know him. Head doctors just don't care for people like Took A-Look. That's common knowledge, wrong knowledge, but there's nothing anybody can do about it. It's their couch and they damned sure don't want to lie on it.

I said good shot, can't you even take a compliment? He throws a binding over a knobby little cloud and pulls it so tight my eyes bug out like a frog with a big bug stuck in its throat. I don't like bugs; he knows that.

Maybe Doctor Marsha notices because she says: "Why don't we discuss this in my office, Mrs. Black?"

"Okay with me Doc but I'm telling you right now I don't want to see any more of this and don't have much time to spare. I've got to be at the salon in less than an hour; it takes weeks to get an appointment with Jake and I won't miss it for this."

Doc Marsha moves close again. The gold specks are back in their green seas. She bobs a little in the waves and then twists her slender body sideways and dives out of sight, leaving a few bubbles on the surface for Took A-Look to watch. He pulls at the spear holding the window open and lies down again. Thank heavens. It has already been a not-so-hot, testy day and this is probably just the beginning of worse to follow, or is that to come? Any way you look at it, there's no point asking who knows when nobody cares.

Still Monday and Still in Bed.

"Hello Eric. Do you remember me?"

Marty.

"Marty."

I know but Took A-Look knows more. He hates you and you know why, I don't.

"You look good."

Liar. And don't give Took A-Look anything else to relax him like you did last time. All that slimy sleep makes him cranky.

"I'll be back later."

I'll be here. In case you hadn't noticed, I'm a statue.

Monday, A Little Later, Guess Where

"Good afternoon Eric. Good afternoon Took A-Look."

Oh sweet and sour whale blubber, she must have blabbed to Doctor Marsha about Took A-Look. She can't shut up. She tells everything. Didn't know that way back then but sure know it now and for a quite a while too. Took A-Look won't answer but that's not new. I won't answer her either but that's new. New day, new rules. Not mine to judge. Another new rule. Some things change, some things stay the same. Like next when she'll ask 'How are you today?' without even an introduction. Took A-Look doesn't like that and neither do I. It's one of the few things we agree on lately. No one seems to appreciate the meaning and importance of a nice introduction anymore. "How are you" can be a brutal question. Say you find yourself in a very unhappy, difficult situation and somebody you don't even know wants you to confess to it with just those three little words of introduction. Not to make it overly personal but think about it for a moment, how is a statue covered in bird shit supposed to feel? Think about that next time you ask a presumptuous, impolite and mostly insincere non-greeting, no introduction question.

She sits down on the side of the bed and looks out the window. She is trying, obliquely for sure, but trying nevertheless, to catch Took A-Look out in the open but he's hiding behind a cloud. She better watch out. One nudge from him on that particular cloud and something nasty could happen. That cloud has a black lining to it but that's not why he picked it to hide behind. Black linings don't mean a thing to him; he knows his clouds. Any second now and she'll ask that particularly rude question and all hell will break loose, I'm sure of it.

Come to think of it, I'm not so sure about it. Not at all sure that any kind of hell can break loose. Hell breaking loose might be a bad choice of words and not just an overused metaphor, which it totally is. The cement is gone but all the wires and rods which were in it are still here. Things move okay but they don't move far, like maybe an inch up or down or sideways and then snap, restraint kicks in, go no further. That's way too short for any kind of hell-breaking-loose unless you're a bug or a worm. Damn sure not enough room for hell-breaking-loose without a lot of imagination and that's not my department anymore. Took A-Look is thinking bear trap and he isn't too far wrong. Say what you want about him but he gets it right, most of the time. Traps don't care who they catch so you really have to remember where you put them or else you'll have to watch every step you take for a very long time. He knows that; he knows we are in a trap and he doesn't want a trap inside the trap, that's for sure.

"Hello again, Eric. I don't think we have been properly introduced. I am Doctor Marsha Coleman. You can call me that, or just Doctor or just Marsha if you want. I know you are Eric Black, you don't mind if I call you Eric, do you?"

Hell no we don't. Eric is fine and very polite. Good start.

"Should I tell you something about myself?"

Suit yourself.

"I have been working here for about two years. Of course you know this is a hospital and you have been here for almost a day now. The people here are very nice. Once you get to know them, of course."

The gold specks are dancing around again and Took A-Look can't help but take a peek at them from behind his cloud. It looks like he wants to shoot an arrow into the seal cloud but he won't take the chance that he'll lose his place in the dancing gold specks. He wants to get a good look at her and for sure he can't do that if she dives into the sea again. Then again, who knows? He isn't afraid of water, not even really cold water. In fact I think he likes it that way, the colder the better, but that isn't the point. He isn't afraid of anything, that's the point.

"Sometimes it's difficult to get to know people, isn't it?"

No.

"Maybe that's not completely true. Maybe the hardest part is letting them get to know us."

Maybe. Maybe not. Depends on Took A-Look. What are you doing back there, Took A-Look? She said us, didn't you hear it? Do want the windows open or shut? Stupid question. He can make the windows do whatever he wants them to do. He could make the windows close for good, if he really felt like it. Ouch. Sorry. I didn't say you would do that, just that you could do that.

"Still, this is still very different for me..."

No kidding, you should try it from inside a bear trap, with the bear. Different doesn't begin to do it justice. Make that different doesn't begin to describe it. Traps and justice are often inseparable.

"...so many years of going to school that it's hard not to be studying all the time but that's not what this is about. Studying that is."

The gold specks are looking somewhere else so Took A-Look has to leave the comfort of his black-lined cloud to get a better view. He wants to see what she is seeing. Say what you want to say about Took A-Look but when it comes to horizons, he's always curious about what is on them; it's in his nature. Only she better not try and catch him out in the open, that's all I can say. Seal or no seal, she better not try that.

He steps lightly on the clouds and sits down in front of the window. She doesn't move, doesn't try and catch him peeking at her. Smart lady. Took A-Look is a one-way street with tons of traffic on it, most of it heavy with lots of big steel wheels. One false step and ka-boom, smacked by a bus coming from the wrong direction. Every time, ka-boom, no warning whatsoever. Thump, thump, one wheel after another. Road kill, flat as a pancake. Took A-Look makes all the rules, that's why it's a one-way street but don't ever trust that sign or you'll get flattened from the opposite direction. Every time. No warning. Ka-Boom, thump, thump, thump. Believe me on that one. I'm an expert at it.

"Sometimes it seems like I'm still studying."

Good idea, Marsha. Don't give up on that studying. Just as sure as those pretty gold specks dance in those lovely green seas, some day there will be a test. Maybe not today, but sometime before Never-Ending. Trust me on that one and it will be one important test. Sooner or later everybody has to take that test and it pays to know something about the subject before that happens.

"We'll talk again later."

Actually, we won't.

She takes her gold specks away, but that doesn't say anything nasty about her. Took A-Look doesn't like that trade and rushes over to the cloud behind the black lined one and kicks it hard, producing an extra loud, combination greeting and goodbye from the fart zone. Very rude of him but all I can do is go along with it. Those are the rules, peace being undeclared and all that goes with it, or without it, depending on your point of view and who is in charge.

Tuesday Morning after the Crush, Out of Bed, Finally

"So, Eric, how about a little sunshine?"

Sure Marty, how about you and her take a long slow walk from here to there and don't forget how that works, there is there and never here. That will bring sunshine galore into my life.

Actually, probably not, it's probably too late for sunshine galore. Took A-Look has lost his sense of humor, he is so angry that not even sharpening spears will cheer him up. It's all my fault, I know that. I really should have picked a fight with her and not with him. He doesn't give up, not with her and not with me. And now here we are and he is in charge because I gave up, first to her and now to him. That's the rule of the day, or as long as it takes, not mine to say, not mine to judge. I just have to go along with it but don't ever think that's easy because it damn sure isn't.

Go ahead slime ball, push me out to the garden, I'm a statue and the birds need something to crap on.

ROLAND J. MASTERS, MD

CHAPTER 3

Anyone who thinks that five star hotels are all the same is someone who hasn't spent much time in five star hotels.

Roland J. Masters, MD learned that twenty years ago and now many of those grand old hotels were his mistresses. He thoroughly loved being surrounded by their luxury yet took nothing for granted. A good mistress is someone cherished, not someone owned.

In the back of his mind, the speaker droned on. 'Brilliant, innovative, a true visionary, a dedicated doctor, an orderly practical scientist and caring humanitarian, a man of the twenty-first century...'

He had heard it all before. It was his standard introduction and not only had he heard it before; he had written every word of it. It was a decent enough introduction, mostly plagiarized from his peers and contemporaries, all of whom were sending the same message:

'Behold the Genius.'

He didn't feel that way about himself but that was no more important than his introduction. His audience came to hear him, his introduction just gave them time to finish their private conversations before they had to shut their lips and open their ears.

Unlike others who believed in their own genius, and who frequently couldn't get past it and onto a topic of interest to anyone else, Roland only started on a pedestal because it dignified the subject and made his audience feel special. But he abandoned it for more human ground as quickly as he could, with neither apology nor explanation. Furthermore, rather than the mostly wild but always rich promises that his colleagues and competitors delivered like gems in the raw to anyone willing to pay for a peek at them, his message was one of hard work. Hard work and a relentless conviction to applied research which he delivered with all the sincerity and honesty that his considerable intellect could forge. According to market research, rich people expected their employees to demonstrate a hard work ethic.

Also unlike the speeches of his peers, contemporaries and competitors, his was a powerful, playful presentation. The recipe was simple: just enough facts for credibility without becoming boring, add just enough complexity for intellectual participation without becoming too challenging, then serve it all up with a little understated humor. According to market research, the rich expected to be flattered and entertained while their pockets were being picked.

He accepted their praise with modesty and when it was accompanied with generous financial support he accepted it with heartfelt gratitude. Both were sincere reflections of his true feelings because he considered himself to be little more than a well-dressed pan-handler with an education costing hundreds of thousands of dollars. Only he wasn't after a cup of coffee. He wanted the whole plantation and they knew it. According to market research, the rich took requests for outrageous contributions quite seriously, probably because it was so flattering to be thought capable of giving so much.

Of course market research was important but Roland really credited two letters, both consonants, as the reason why he was so much different from all the other pan-handlers and snake oil salesman who formed his competition. His business card said everything about himself that he wanted said about himself.

Roland J. Masters, MD

There were no PhD's or honorariums on his card, although the walls of his office were generously papered with his many credentials, diplomas and achievements all framed in dark rose wood. Rose wood, parchment and gold that proclaimed who he was: Physician, Healer, Medicine Man.

For him, it was as much pride to be a physician in the field of endeavor in which he practiced as it was an irony. He had never practiced medicine, never had a single patient after finishing his internship yet he felt neither inferior nor superior to his General Practitioner or Specialist Physician brethren. Simply speaking, they had entered the practice of medicine and he had continued learning. In fact, twenty-five years after he graduated with his first set of classmates, he was still working and learning as much as ever while they were cutting back on the hours, monitoring their investments and trying to trim another stroke or two from their single digit handicap.

Roland J. Masters, MD would never finish learning and he knew it. His specialty, his mystery, was just too big and too complicated for anyone with just one lifetime to dedicate to it and as a consequence of this personal article of faith, he was patient and humble. He was also driven, dedicated and hard-working but not because the field was extremely competitive or because he was getting older and running short of time. No, his motivation came from a much more practical source, a much more compelling source: he was getting closer.

He could feel it in his bones, as the expression went and that was as accurate a description as any could ever be coined. All he really needed now was one big break, one truly unique individual who held the key to the treasure chest and then the secret he had always known to exist would begin unraveling the greatest of life's mysteries, the mystery of life itself.

Intellectual life that is, because as far as he was concerned, the physics and chemistry of life were but mere stepping stones to intellectual life. The beginning, origin and development of intellectual life, the ability to reason, the one huge capability that set mankind apart from all other life forms on this planet, that was his quest. Not what we think we know but what we really know, that was the depth of his question, the object of his search.

For the speech he was about to deliver, his audience seldom varied. Rich and powerful individuals representing immensely rich and supremely powerful corporations, foundations or institutes. They were all part of the snake oil circuit and their mere attendance at this dinner was a guaranteed contribution averaging five thousand dollars, per chair, not including the plate charge, a mere thousand, all tax deductible. That was the rich and powerful part. Roland wanted them to add at least one zero to the number and was successful in achieving that objective with about 10% of them. That was the mortality part. According to market research the rich donated some of their money simply because they couldn't take it with them but they would gladly donate a whole lot more if they didn't have to go at all.

And, if they came to the false conclusion that they might not be forced to leave their gold behind, or even if that unwelcome event might be postponed by a few years, well, that was their business. Business as old as snake oil and pretty much unchanged since the first peddler stood on a rock with the elixir in one hand and a wooden club in the other. Roland was no more the first man to rattle that patter than he was the only one doing it. In fact, some of his competitors were damn near promising a get-out-of-death card and they weren't talking about cryogenics either. That fad had come and thawed. Life after death, even life after a minor suspension in the deep freeze was old, unworthy news. No, some of his competitors were actually promising to postpone the inevitable with bigger, better and longer postponements all fully guaranteed in the future by the inevitable march of science.

Genetics was the latest batch of snake oil, promising everything from a new liver to a new life. The market was huge; everybody needed something.

Show Time.

He took his time getting to the podium and wasted a few more seconds setting his papers straight. They needed to see his trim frame, his full head of grey hair, white teeth and lightly tanned skin. His blue eyes danced a little with the spirited anticipation he had developed over countless performances. Steady, practiced, confident hands moved the papers into order, adjusted the microphone, lifted the glass to his lips. According to market research, a Doctor's hands were his most important physical feature so he made sure everyone got a good look at them. Something they should also do with a pick-pocket in a train station, he thought with some irony.

"Good evening Ladies and Genes." The smile on his face radiated from his eyes and the room noticeably settled with their guarded approval of their first impression of him. That first thirty second impression, during which so many decisions are made, with so little real understanding of how those decisions were made but which are trusted to be right and are almost impossible to reverse. Belief, trust, comfort, attraction, fear, love or disgust, all mysteriously decided during the thirty seconds that the brain takes to make countless decisions, measurements, assessments and tests without even bothering to consult the owner until the verdict is delivered.

He believed this behavior to be one of several mysteries that originated in some animalistic state at the beginning of humankind. Some perception or knowledge that serviced such a crucial service that it became genetically incorporated in our intellectual state just like sight and hearing became genetically incorporated in our physical state. Thinking without words, perhaps even without thought.

That was Roland's mystery, his personal connection to the universe, to science, to medicine, to everything. He would find the origin of that intuitive knowledge, that unexpressed consciousness or he would die trying. It wasn't an even match and that's why he was standing in front of so much wealth and ability.

He looked about, smiled again and let them complete their second look at him and the humble disarming manner he had always possessed silently told them that he had taken the first step from the pedestal. *No snake oil today folks, just listen to me, make up your own minds, come to your own conclusions, it's your check, you decide what number to write on it. All you have to do is listen, no charge for that.*

"Does it make you wonder how a few billion cells, which for all intents but not all purposes are identical to every other cell in your body...does it make you wonder how those cells became so specialized that they can hear me? That's right, cells. The tiniest part of your anatomy is doing your listening.

"And meanwhile, a few trillion other cells are busy digesting or pumping blood because that is their job. Isn't it amazing that every single cell in your body has all the tools and all the skills necessary to do any job in your body? It could hear but it pumps blood; it could see but it thinks. Quite an accomplishment isn't it? It makes me wonder. It always has."

They wouldn't fall into that wonderment right away, it was far too early, but it would come. First they had to make certain he wouldn't get lofty and scientific with them when all they wanted were the important facts and a little help organizing them into the right questions. But when that was done, the wonderment would start, beginning with 'how does it work' which led to 'what if it stops working' and concludes with 'maybe I should add another zero to the number?'

"Before jumping into this fascinating mystery, which is you, I'd like to tell you what to expect. Of course you already know you are fascinating, somewhat mysterious and a whole more, but how much more, how much more is there to you?" He delivered the last part of the question with a little pause and a little uplift to his voice, giving it a hint of vaudeville.

"And what kind of more might you expect from, and for, ourselves?" he asked with hands raised at his sides, palms to the ceiling. With this posture he was rewarded with complete silence as every single mind in the audience recognized the question they had asked themselves again and again and again. How to get more. Latent potential of any kind but especially latent human potential wasn't a question of passive interest to this group of over-achievers, it was The Holy Grail. More was better and much more was best, amen.

"Today, I will talk to the mystery behind this question. Today I will suggest some things that might open a consciousness, a capability or a transcendence that we know to be there but which is, for the moment, locked and hidden from conventional thought." He loved making this promise and they loved hearing it. Who doesn't love a good mystery as long as it doesn't come with a trick ending? Who doesn't want an extrasensory power? Who doesn't want more?

"As is so often the case, the answers to age-old, difficult questions lie where you least expect to find them and the answer to the profound and enduring question of intellectual development is no exception. As you may have already guessed from my earlier remarks, the answer lies in the smallest living organism – the cell. Yes, everything we want to know about all human existence is in one tiny place, replicated trillions of times over. We are the answer to our own question. The irony of it is almost perfect, isn't it?"

Roland's eyes swept the audience as he spoke the last sentence. As strange as it was, either an audience got it or they didn't. This audience got it. Unlock that secret, read that scripture, set that force in motion and then tie a rope to it and hold on for the wildest ride of existence. This audience wanted to hear it all, they wanted the guided tour to the intimacy of their own existence, into the realm of being without words, being without time, pure unadulterated, single cell being. It was all there and if he explained it right, they would add zeros, it was in their eyes.

"The human cell is wondrous and fascinating. And almost perfect. Almost. Any more perfect and the human body would be a perpetual time machine. Just a few more genes, perhaps just a single gene or even a gene sequence and you might extend life by fifty or a hundred years. Not magic, it's no different than all the genetic adjustments which have been made since the beginning of time. Adjustments that added, among other things, longevity to the system. In that way, what we want, what *we all* want, is nothing new, it has always been part of the design."

Impossible, of course, and Roland could see who had smoked from that pipe dream by the pinched expression which came to their faces. Rich and powerful virtually guaranteed that snake oil had been sampled a time or two. That and dozens of other promises for cures, reversals, renewals and replacements. Every kind of human intervention from radiation to chemotherapy, holistic to invasive, shaman to shrink had been put to that everlasting test. Average age in the room was over sixty and collectively they had, in their lifetime, witnessed nearly every medical advance that was worth mentioning throughout the entire history of the human race. That and a few so-called advances that were not worth mentioning; they had been tricked before and weren't about to go down that path again with just any old snake-oil-medicine-man.

"Impossible, of course. Adding new genes or gene sequences to all the cells which make up a human being is, well, even beyond the realm of science fiction. And that assumes you could figure out what to add, where to add it and how to get it to express, how to get it to start working. No, it isn't that simple, never was and never will be. What you are today is the result of millions of attempts, millions of modifications and adjustments, some improvements, some failures, some patches on those failures and some patches on those patches. You are, your cells are, in effect, the entire history of your lineage, yet you are completely and entirely unique. Not only is it impossible to change that, but who would want to?"

The pinched expressions eased as he knew they would. Being unique was both good and bad. Unique made the ego feel good but the rational mind also had to accept some of the bully baggage that came with being unique.

"Or is it? Is it that impossible to change or are we just looking at it the wrong way? Maybe we aren't seeing something that is right in front of our eyes? Maybe the solution is hiding in plain sight."

The sincere question. The one which had driven him for years and which might never be answered. He knew it, just like he knew that the interested expressions which had replaced the pinched ones would quickly drift to other thoughts and topics. Thoughts like deciding on the minimum, socially acceptable number to put on the check, if he let them get that far. He wouldn't. He had a long, expensive way to go and no intention of making the journey on the slow boat with a four-figure passage.

"To even begin to give that question some serious consideration, we should start with what we know. To do otherwise would be nothing more than irresponsible speculation. Completely irresponsible speculation…but we'll get to that later." The murmur of approval for his slight humor and his candor came as if cued from off stage. Unlike most of the scientific community and even some of his medical brothers who cloaked their speculation as seriously profound theory and who completely downplayed their lack of methods to mask what they were saying, this audience was far more practical. But they were only practical as long as the boundaries between fact and speculation were properly disclosed. Then they would speculate because rich and powerful didn't get to be rich and powerful without some speculation, some snake oil in the bloodline. Rich and powerful knew all about snake oil, one way or another most of them were still in the trade.

"Let's start at the beginning, with what we know. We know, for a fact, that every cell in the body contains forty-six chromosomes. That's right, every cell, no matter where it is on the body or what function it performs, it has the same forty-six chromosomes as every other cell. And that means every cell has the complete and identical operating manual for every job in the body. Whether it is bone, marrow, muscle or brain, it has the encoded ability to hear or produce adrenaline or become skin. When it specializes its behavior, it simply operates with the set of instructions needed for the job it performs and ignores the rest of the manual.

This is why DNA testing works. It just takes a few dead skin cells or a drop of blood and the owner of those cells can be positively identified. Every cell in your body, no matter what it does, is a fingerprint to its one and only owner - you. Your cells and the genes within them are you. And if that doesn't provoke an identity crisis, what will?"

He didn't expect laughter, it was just an ironic ending with a little spiral of existentialistic humor for those who weren't already experiencing a new reality, a cellular viewpoint with all the attendant questions. If they are all the same how can one cell look different, be different, do different things? How do you reconcile being nothing more than a single cell, replicated a few trillion times in the primordial soup before being thrown out on the beach with fingers, ridges, spleens and nose hairs all neatly in place and doing their assigned job? There had to be more to it than that, didn't there? How could you even think the question? A single cell can't think a whole question, can it? Wouldn't that take millions of cells, all acting together? But how could they do that if they were all the same? Wouldn't one of them have to be the boss? Simple question my ass, this is impossible.

He knew better than to leave those questions in their minds for too long. "Let's come back to those questions later, when we have a little more information to work with." Heads nodded in agreement and in appreciation. No pedestal, just good old Doc Masters curing what could have been one awful migraine.

"We all know that genetics is the hottest scientific topic to reach the podium in all history. And why shouldn't it be? After all, as I said before, genes are the one, true, comprehensive and most complete library of life's entire journey. Everything which is needed, everything which was ever needed to sustain, protect and create life is resident in those genes and every last bit of it came from the past. All the information which is needed for every action, for every response, for every thought, for every substance which must be manufactured, from saliva to tears to adrenaline, is written in your genes. Everything. All the good things and sometimes, the not-so-good things too."

Good things were the bait. Not-so-good things were the hook. He took a sip of water while the minds in front of him played with the notion that the not-so-good genes, once detected, could be modified, mutated, eradicated completely or, at the very least, put into some kind of gene prison. "Not-so-good." he repeated as if those words weren't on every mind in the room when he knew full well it was the only thing on their mind. Good was fine, better was highly desirable but that not-so-good material was screaming for attention.

"But let's put that into perspective. Not-so-good doesn't always mean bad. At least not terribly, horrifically bad. Remember, there was a lot of trial and error in order to get you here today and many of the really bad mistakes died along the way. They might have reproduced for two generations or for twenty generations but in the end, that genetic material stopped being passed along because those who had it eventually died before they could pass it along. They became the end of that line, nature's last resort to correcting a mistake." Nothing like a little hope to keep people's attention; anybody who is still alive has a chance.

"Of course those had to be fatal mistakes didn't they? Fatal early enough in life that eventually the last owner died before the gene could be passed on. But that left lots of room for genes that fail late in life or even that begin to express, that is begin to perform, later in life. There are a lot more grey haired people today than there were in the tenth century, and a lot more aging diseases to go with them. We all know how much longer people are living now. Plenty long enough for untested, late cycle genetic material to start creating problems."

A little bit of fear never hurt anyone. One recessive gene might be okay but two of them could really raise hell. Some genes were time bombs, just waiting for something to start the count down. Everyone had an example on their minds. Cystic Fibrosis, Alzheimer's, Hypertension, Diabetes you name it, if their parents weren't already dead, they soon would be and that meant they were next. He confirmed their thinking. "The system isn't perfect, we all know that but what else do we know?"

He played the bait up and down, not allowing them to get too close to the mystery to see it clearly or get so far away from it that they would forget what they came to hear, even if they would deny that selfish intent with their last breath, the greatest motivator of all.

"I used the term library of human history to describe this wonder, and I'd like to talk about that for minute. It is a fascinating place to visit.

Imagine a cell taken from anywhere you like, ear lobe, liver, heart, anywhere at all, it doesn't matter because when it comes to DNA they are all identical. In that single cell is the nucleus which holds your own personal, unique library. A library with forty-six floors, one for each chromosome. How many libraries have you seen that are forty-six floors high?"

Some heads nodded, others looked up from the table where they were holding their single cell prisoner, still focusing on its not-so-good qualities.

"Each floor of this library is made up of rooms, one for each gene on that chromosome. That's where we will store all this information. Due to a lot of complications with defining and counting genes, the exact count isn't known, plus it is different between individuals anyway, but let's take thirty thousand genes as a generous count of the entire gene pool. That works out to about six hundred fifty rooms per floor of your own personal library. How many forty-six story building do you know that have six hundred fifty rooms per floor? And what is stored in those rooms? How about three billion DNA base pairs. Now imagine trying to find something as small as a fifty thousand base pair gene sequence in that forty-six floor, thirty thousand room library and try finding it with no instructions and no road map."

Rich and powerful appreciated math but it had to be simple and he had to be careful. Thirty thousand genes could easily become that many dollars. At one time or another most of the women in the audience had spent that much on a dress, so that was definitely not the number he wanted stuck in their heads. Three billion would be amazing but realistically speaking, he was looking for something in between, in the millions, the two figure millions from at least one of them.

"If only it was that easy, that simple, but…it isn't. It isn't enough just to be a cell. It also has to work, it has to include the complete reference manual, it has to know everything it is supposed to do, how to do it and when to do it, plus how to reproduce itself, plus rules for coordination with the cells next to it, not even to mention the external environment which it has to understand. The gene, or the gene sequence you are thinking about could even be affected by what you are thinking at this very moment. Like toes, you don't always feel them unless you think about them and then all of a sudden they have to be wiggled. Have to be wiggled because you think about them. So many instructions with so many options, so many variations, so many alternatives to consider and now compound that with the size of this library, the thousands of rooms and all that is stored in them."

They would think about that. It would begin the wonderment. Deaf, blind or with an extra toe, they all knew someone who had a problem in one of their rooms. Some of them were really messed up. Some of them were their sons and daughters.

"So, to carry on with the example we started with, let's say that on chromosome 35, that is, on the 35th floor of your personal library, in room 401 you will all find the information, or at least a good clue to all the information, for the cell you are thinking about. That is where and what makes the cell you selected behave like it does, do what it does every day. Wasn't that easy? Of course, I told you the floor and the room. Without those minor details, it could take you quite a while to open all those doors and sift through all the DNA stored there, wouldn't it?"

"And it must be sifted very carefully because what you are looking for is a very, very specific sequence which is the operating manual, but not necessarily the only operating manual, for that cell. Some of the pages in that manual are probably, no make that certainly, in some other room. In other words, that cell might be waiting for instructions from another cell, on another floor, in some other room before it even gets started. After all, the adrenal gland makes adrenaline because it is told to, because the eyes see something, the ears hear something or the brain thinks something and these little details just involved a whole lot of the library. Difficult doesn't begin to describe it, does it?"

Ten seconds was plenty of time for that exercise with this audience. They came to hear solutions, not write computer code or search through thousands of foot lockers looking for a sock with a hole in it. Ten seconds was more than enough time for them to answer the first question on their minds. No one could do it. No one could write the instructions for a toe or a finger let alone a heart or, the wonder of all wonders, the brain.

"Let's open one of the books in one of the rooms; maybe that will make it easier." They knew it wouldn't be easy but market research said they didn't want it easy. Especially if they were going to put their name on it.

"On the left page is a single letter, an A for adenine and on the right page is a T for thymidine, those two are always paired. On the next page is is a G for guanine and on the right of it is a C for cytosine, those two are always paired. And that is the entire alphabet. Tens or hundreds of thousands of pages with A-T's or G-C's, any number of pages of A-T's followed by any number of pages with G-C's. That is the manual. You can see why it is so hard to figure it out…it's like trying to find logic in in a pile of rice; four kinds of rice.

"These A-T's and G-C's are called nucleotides and every one of the thirty thousand genes in your cells is made up of them, each gene is a long and completely unique sequence which carries every instruction from the beating of your heart to the sensation in your fingertips or the tingle in the hair on the back of your neck. All that information is in every cell in your body, the entire library replicated, exactly, in trillions of cells. So, what do we know? What do we know for certain?"

The reaction was always the same, heads were down and staring at the table cloth. Each and every person wondering what floor, what room, in what books and on which pages were written the answer to the question in their minds. 'Is that where insulin is made and why mine doesn't work? How can I get in there and fix those pages, rip out the defective ones and get on with my life?' 'Is that my irregular heartbeat?' 'Is that my twitch?' 'Is that my memory loss?' 'Is that why I sweat so much?' 'Is that my ulcer?'

"In summary, unless we compare what we know to what we don't know, we know quite a bit. We know about the 46 chromosomes, we know about the 30,000 genes and we know the alphabet of the manual. We know there are three billion pairs of them, more or less, of course. That's a lot of A's, T's, C's and G's. We even know something about the language, that certain very specific arrangements of the A-T's and C-G's designate what is called the promoter region while other also very specific arrangements designate the transcription start, transcription stop or translation start or stop regions that regulate the process. These are the traffic signs and signals by which the gene functions to produce a hormone, to burn a fat or to convert a sugar, in other words, to do whatever that cell is supposed to do. We know a great deal, no doubt about it."

Barrier number one. Charted, mapped, listed, identified, processed all meant the same thing, namely, the hard work had been done. Now all anybody has to do is follow the map to see where it leads. Simple. This set of nucleotides equals left eyebrow, that set equals toe nail (small toe, left foot). Not completely untrue but by no means that simple. Not in the most naïve or optimistic view could it ever be called simple. Billions of tries with trillions of sequences had, as much by trial and error as anything else, resulted in life as we define it. Single cell bacterial life, that is. Human life was a whole different ball game, a whole different league.

"If you think that we know what some of those genetic instructions mean and what they govern, you are right. But some is not very much. What we know might tell us the color of a person's eyes, but we don't know which gene, or part of a gene, or parts of genes are responsible for dilating the pupil which is surrounded by the beautiful dark blue iris which had to come from grandmother. Where are those instructions? What floor or floors? What room or rooms? Which pages or parts of pages? And because those instructions are contained in every cell, not just the ones in the pupil, we can't just look at pupil cells for the answer. And to compound this problem, who is to say that the champagne you are consuming right now dilates your pupils because of a cell in the eye, or even the brain? Maybe it's a cell in the liver or stomach that starts that dilation. Maybe all three. Nothing like a tandem, multi-gene system under the control of single promoter to throw us off the track, is there? Amazing, isn't it? And we think we are smart?" He took a sip of water and knew that every eye in the room watched him and wondered, probably for the first time in their lives, how he possibly managed to take a drink of water.

"A single cell identical to any other cell but doing the job of a finger and not a spleen. One cell which senses heat but not sound because that is the job of the cell next to it. It could do it, but it doesn't. Surrounded with blood, taking in oxygen and manufacturing its own highly specialized product, on demand with damn good quality and quantity control. Wax for the ear, electricity for the brain, hormones, proteins, antibodies, the whole supermarket of life's requirements. Infinitely complex yet fundamentally simple and repeatable, all over the body. What a system.

We know..." Another sip of water, another precious second of life for the audience to return to the path he was clearing for them, his life passion.

"We know that some genes are always expressing, that is, always performing their function. Hearts must beat continuously.

We know that other genes are turned off until they have been stimulated to express. Like eyes that tear only when they get sand in them, or because of a cold virus, bacteria or simply because the air is dry and it's time to produce some lubrication.

We also know that it is very hard to find precisely where the brain can be stimulated with a probe in order to produce a tear but try finding that specific instruction in the genetic library. Yet the instructions are there, just like they are in the brain which can, somehow, send out a signal for a sad or a happy tear. The brain which is, according to some scientific lore and a little scientific fact, grossly underutilized.

You knew we would get to the brain, didn't you? You knew this topic had to end up there didn't you?"

Heads nodded instinctively. Instinctively. It always amazed him that that reaction was the same. Anyone who was paying attention, anyone who understood the basics of the mystery, nodded. Almost in unison and almost always with this question and with a single nod. Like birds in flight or a school of fish all turning in unison, all turning with a single brain to this question, this challenge, his mystery.

"Grossly underutilized." He repeated, knowing those words, in a room full of the rich and powerful was the psychological equivalent of getting a 10% increase in profits just by asking for it.

"Doesn't it make you wonder why, with all that is encoded in the genes, with all that they can do, why the brain is so underutilized?"

The concept of latent intelligent potential. A universe which was still substantially unexplained in spite of the fact that it was being penetrated and explored on a daily basis.

"Or is it?" Drill or knife, probe or camera, bullet or bat, the method didn't much matter if the right result could be discovered and patented. Increase brain utilization and both time and money had to increase proportionately, anybody could see that. Now things were getting interesting, now the contribution was providing some spinoff benefits, some cash flow. This thing could pay for itself. Tax deductible too.

"But that is what we know, or a snapshot of what we know or believe we know, today. Tomorrow or in the tomorrow's to come, the blanks will be filled in. This gene or gene sequence will perform this function and that gene or part of a gene will do something else. But that topic is unworthy of speculation for it is a certainty, it is reported on a weekly, if not daily basis. That's not what you came to hear, we both know that."

It was true. You couldn't pick up a paper without some reporter's gross exaggeration of scientific speculation that this or that gene was responsible for hair loss, weight gain or liver spots. Snake oil is in aisle four, third shelf, organized alphabetically by cure.

They had waited patiently for the speculation he had promised them. Like every other time he had given his talk, they had waited and with each speech he had refined and improved his timing. If he talked too long or with too much scientific detail, the financial contributions decreased, indirectly proportionate to their boredom and frustration. If he understated the magnitude of the permutations and combinations or overstated the complexity of genetic interaction, the contributions went down even more. Rich and powerful people had everything they needed to get simple answers and they didn't have to put another zero on his check in order to get it. For that he had to give them something they couldn't get anywhere else. That was the deal.

"In the past while, I have mentioned a couple of things which I would now like to repeat. Of primary importance is that the Human Genome, which is defined as all the genes in all the chromosomes...the Human Genome is the evolutionary roadmap of our development as a species. It has developed and changed and been passed down from generation to generation, it contains everything that has been kept, whether currently in use or not. Of secondary importance is how much we understand of its structure, of its alphabet, but how little we currently understand about how it actually works. These two facts, when twisted around each other like the double stranded DNA helix, open the arena for some reasonable, prudent, interesting, speculation."

Speculation. The right word. Market tested, carefully mated with other market tested words like reasonable and prudent. End result: Wall Street, not Off the Wall.

"There are two significant, intriguing gaps in our understanding of the Human Genome. Gaps which are so large that there are only two or three possible explanations for their existence. The first gap is within, that is inside the construction of most genes, construction which we understand very well, after all, every A-T and C-G has been written out, even if we don't know what they do.

"Here is the puzzle. Embedded within most genes are hundreds, but most times hundreds of thousands of nucleotides, A's, T's, C's and G's which, in the best reckoning of the best minds in the genetic community, have no specific purpose for being there. They are present in some individuals but not in others or they differ significantly between individuals, even related individuals. At first glance, these excess or redundant A-T's and C-G's appear to be nothing more than a biological dumping site for discarded genetic material, so-called junk DNA.

So little conformity exists in these regions that it is reasonable to assume these nucleotides are redundant or obsolete. Naturally...and I use that word intentionally, naturally, there are also some skeptics who assert that these nucleotides are part of a bizarre and complex multi-gene function that will never be understood. Any way you look at it, there is enough surplus genetic material to build an elephant and that introduces another explanation for this surplus. Inventory. Spare parts. After all, nature wanted to encode something, some response to a threat, some learning or map like the one encoded into the Monarch butterfly's DNA which allows it to make a journey of thousands of miles to a virtual pinprick location in Mexico without ever having travelled that route before. Perhaps this inventory, driven by a catalyst we don't know, creates memory like that, memory that can be passed from one generation to the next. The knowledge behind fight or flight, the knowledge that can make unconscious choices, our own personal legacy to evolution.

Or, perhaps these are just pages of filler which make the gene unique, like adding more numbers to the bar code of supermarket packaging when only a few numbers are really needed to identify the product and the extra numbers are there simply to remove any confusion. This is a reasonable explanation, isn't it?

Or maybe all this material is leftover from a mistake, an evolutionary attempt at something that didn't work out. It didn't do what it was supposed to do but didn't do anything bad either, so it was just left there. Nature, we have to remember, isn't always a good housekeeper and when it comes a little nucleotide flotsam and jetsam, why should she bother? A few million nucleotides don't take up much room and space is not at a premium. Why should we expect nature to clean up her basement when we don't clean up ours?

So, to summarize, what we have here are a few hundred million nucleotides, more or less, that may be part of a multi-gene function under the control of single promoter, inventory for future generations, encoded randomness to guarantee uniqueness or some biological refuse of failed evolutions, to name just four possibilities." Translation, not very interesting and only speculative for those willing to play the long odds that anything useful would be found there.

"I mention this today because people are selling this research without even mentioning the needle in the haystack which is the odds of a discovery, any discovery in these areas." Under his breath, Roland counted to five. Long enough for those who hadn't bought that research to congratulate themselves but short enough for those who had bought it to get over their disappointment and think about betting on a winner this time. It was time to introduce the mystery.

It was time for them to think about something they had never thought about before. Maybe one of them might even make the connection and think something that they had always known to be true but that had never seen the light of conscious thought.

Maybe this time, nature would favor him with an answer, not a secret.

CHAPTER 4

Brita knew from a very young age she was a very talented little liar. Other kids excelled at school subjects or piano or baseball but for Brita, lying was her special talent. She knew it and she worked at it just as hard as the other kids worked on their gifts. She was always trying to improve the delivery or the credibility or the intrigue of her stories. At least that was the way it was when her lies were just fun and games. That was the way it was before step-father Albert became part of her life. After him, her lies weren't fun and games anymore. Then they became the currency of life, a matter of survival. No doubt about it, Albert was the wake-up call; he was the first game-changer in Brita's little life.

It was a time that some people call a defining moment, maybe even an epiphany because Albert moved her along the liar scale from passively casual all the way to pathologically compulsive, a quantum leap to be sure. That's when she realized that every lie had to serve a purpose because if it didn't, you were just lying to yourself. Of course that took all the fun out of it but there was no way out of that deceitful mousetrap.

It took a lot of time and effort to discipline her fertile imagination against making up stories just to see what might happen, who might be tricked once, twice, three times but in the end it was one of the best things that happened to her. Not that Albert deserved any credit for it because even if he started her down that path, or pathology if you will, it was little Brita, as usual, who had to do the hard work.

When Albert first came onto the scene, he set out to isolate Brita because, as far as he was concerned, she was unwanted and unnecessary baggage that came with the mother. What he didn't know then and never fully understood until it was too late, was that Brita was already isolated and that included isolation from her mother. Albert wasn't the first man to put his boots under that bed, probably not even in the first hundred. No, Brita learned where she stood in the pecking order from experiences so early in her life she couldn't even remember them. Couldn't remember the experiences but would never forget the lesson they taught her. Little Brita didn't belong to anyone except herself and she didn't want to belong to anyone because no good ever came from being owned by someone. The first 99 men to own her mother were ample proof of that fact, so try isolating that kettle of fish, Albert.

And that was where her defining moment began, if she wanted anything she had to lie to get it and if she didn't have to lie to get something she usually did anyway, just for the practice. Lies told to Albert were denied by lies told to mother. Other lies told to mother complimented a truth told to Albert resulting in the perfect lie, the lie they told to each other if they wanted anything to make sense. Lies for school books, lies for money, lies about teachers, friends, parents of friends and friends of parents. Lies to boys about boys and lies to girls about boys and about other girls. All kept together in Brita's unique mind and memory and by the fact that every lie served a purpose and that was the key. Without purpose or plan it was impossible to keep anything straight, just ask any chronic liar. Or maybe not, what would be the point? Maybe just think about how much harder it is to keep random, senseless lies all moving together in a straight line than it is to keep structured, purposeful lies all moving along, hand-in-hand to this or that final destination. Great overlapping circles and swarms of lies designed to fulfill all Brita's wants, needs and desires, that was her epiphany and that was to become her life's work.

But sometimes, even Brita had to admit, it got messy. Sometimes people who should never have met, accidentally found each other. Sometimes they compared lies when they weren't supposed to and sometimes Brita couldn't cover up fast enough or convincingly enough to keep the web of deceit from becoming unanchored in one corner and that started the inevitable collapse of the whole damn web of deceit. Then months of work collapsed and stuck all over her, trapping her in one big, sticky, complicated mess.

But that was before.

She was 36 when she experienced her second defining moment. She couldn't remember the moment it happened, or if there was a triggering event, or if perhaps it was the connection of previously unconnected lies or logic like puzzle pieces that finally came together and created the astounding learning which was to change her life, again.

It was as if she woke up one morning, maybe from a dream or something and a switch somewhere in her brain that was always off was now on and she was completely different. Not a different person of course, but different, like they say people who have a near-death experience are different. Or like people who become parents for the first time suddenly realize that they are mothers or fathers and just automatically change, just automatically become what they never were before and start nurturing a new life. They never look back or wonder where that Mom or Dad person came from or if she/he was there all the time, just waiting for the baby to take its first breath so they could do the same with their brand new identity.

What she did know about her epiphany was that it happened soon after the first time she slept with Eric. It wasn't the next morning, or even the day after but the next time she saw him, a few days later, she was a changed woman. She had emerged from her cocoon, spread her wings and was ready to fly. For a while she thought she must be in love; she had never felt so good, so confident, so much in control, so unpossessed.

Except it didn't make sense for her to be in love, in those few days nothing had changed about Eric or his money; those two concepts were as logically inseparable as they were emotionally united. Or so she thought until she realized how her lies had suddenly become so convincing and her acting so incredibly perfect that sometimes even she didn't know the difference between fact and fiction, cause and result, victim or victor.

What a gift, what a wonderful gift and it was only to get better over time.

For a while, she thought her metamorphosis was one of those cellular cosmic things that are programmed to happen, maybe to different degrees, or on different wavelengths, to everyone. Like hair that turns grey or some big event occurs and changes a person's life path forever. Something in the genes or an awakening, freaky nature, quirky fate, that sort of thing, but she asked around and no one admitted to having an epiphany so profound, so astounding or with such consequences as hers. And they couldn't lie to her because that was the other amazing part of her new-found self; she could spot a lie in an instant, sometimes while it was being formed in the person's brain, an unspoken, unborn untruth. It was quite amazing how she could read the eyes, the body language, the tilt of the head or a slightly raised eyebrow and then hear the voice suddenly but subtly change tone or cadence or volume that could only mean one thing. Another naked lie had wormed its way into the world. Even the liar's skin betrayed them as the pulse quickened, their blood pressure increased and the hue and texture made the skin look like it was being illuminated from the inside. Of course she had to be touching the person to feel the minute electrical surge which accompanied the lie but with all the other evidence she had at her disposal the only time that came in handy was at night, in bed. But it did come in handy. Some pretty big lies are told in bed; everybody knows that.

Yet becoming a state of the art lie detector was barely half her epiphany and certainly the least important half. The best part was that none of those rules, behaviors, reactions, symptoms, call them what you want, applied to her. Everything she said came out like the complete truth. If she said the sky was falling, people looked up.

It was a wonderful gift and so easy to use. Of course she always knew that most men were easy to fool for a while but she soon discovered they could be fooled indefinitely when you could lie so perfectly and keep it all in perfect order.

Eric didn't have a chance.

Her newfound ability changed everything. The stakes went up. Slow and steady became fast track. His vulnerabilities were exposed and she was invulnerable. It was like seeing the future only better because she was making it to suit herself. It was like she was born to be the consummate liar and now it was completely natural and totally real; she had arrived. And there was no chance of getting caught because she knew how to keep it all in a straight line. Her second nature had become her first nature.

She rewrote her past and he believed every word of it. She proclaimed the innocence of her intentions, her desire for companionship and sharing, her awe of his mind and he believed every word. She displayed her devotion, caring, love and friendship. She laughed at his jokes, made love to his body, was fascinated by his stories, his interests and his beliefs. She created their future and he fell right into the part she created for him.

She gave her vows at the small, private ceremony in the living room in front of the massive, river stone fireplace, and everyone cried at her sincerity, her love, her lies. It was the perfect beginning to his end.

It was perfectly planned and brilliantly executed. A pre-nuptial agreement she couldn't get around but at that time his net worth was more than enough to keep her in the style to which she wanted to become accustomed. Eventually he would stray because all men eventually did, with or without a little encouragement and then a good lawyer could renegotiate the pre-nup settlement into something more worthy. Maybe get her twice as much, maybe more if he did something really embarrassing. But that was then. That was when she would have been satisfied with a share of his wealth. Now she wanted all of it, because now she knew how to get it.

The funny part was the way it happened. With a little help from Arlene, Eric's mousy, overly protective, pre-nup loving daughter, it looked like a messy, expensive and definitely risky divorce could be completely avoided. Arlene truly turned out to be the gold miner's daughter. It started so innocently, just a few little lies which were intended to anchor some really devastating untruths on the way to isolating Daddy from Daughter and connecting Brita with the rich and famous.

With just a few little lies about Eric's periodic absent-mindedness, his occasional withdrawals, some made-up anxiety symptoms and yak, yak, yak girl talk, Arlene spilled the beans to Brita, her newest best friend.

The family secret was out in the open. Dear old dad had an imaginary buddy living in his head. Not another personality, not a figment of his imagination, but an actual person, like a little leprechaun or a dwarf or some such creature drifting around in the folds and crevices and clouds of his brain. That's exactly how Arlene described it, Took A-Look, was his name. So weird it had to be true. Arlene said she had met the little intruder, had talked to him and he had talked back to her. Sometimes, she said, it wasn't clear who was in control and that was why dear old dad had his moments. What a confession! What a bulldozer. Who wouldn't want to pick that scab?

A TV soap opera gave Brita the rest of her plan. Get Eric declared mentally unfit, get him committed to some back-woods asylum and have some back-woods judge appoint her conservator of the matrimonial property. She would get it all and not even have to run away, not even have to fight. The judge would believe her because everyone believed her and she wouldn't even have to lie very much, not that it mattered. Then came the best part, the ironic part; she would use his own money to hire the lawyers to keep him broke and broken. Brilliant, plus sweet revenge, see how he likes living without credit cards. Best of all, how hard could it be to drive somebody crazy when they already had another person inside their head?

It happened so fast, it took Brita by surprise. She had been sowing her seeds of discontent for months, building the pain then backing off, creating the uncertainty then resolving it, blaming then forgiving, exposing every lie or mistruth until he was naked and vulnerable. She was softening him up for the deal when Arlene gave up the keys to the family bulldozer and the TV show gave her a lesson on how to drive it. The first time Brita confronted Eric about his imaginary brain mate, it was like she stuck a boning knife in his guts.

Fantastic. So fantastic that she couldn't leave it alone, she kept on picking and poking and he kept backing away and withdrawing and getting more and more messed up. Then one day he completely withdrew. Eight hours of staring at a blank TV before he got out of it. So she left it alone until she got this crazy thought right out-of-the-blue. She followed it; she called Took A-Look a scared little shit because he wouldn't come out and fight and that did it.

Whatever fight Eric had left in him, he took to the kitchen cupboard. It was like reducing a child to tears; it was exactly like that. Maybe even better than that, maybe more like reducing a man to a child and then to tears. She knew, without knowing how she knew, she had triggered the ultimate conflict. Took A-Look vs. Eric. Winner by default: Brita. Brilliant.

Perfect, and now just a few more days, a couple of weeks max and her new life would be off like a jet plane. First class all the way; she could practically taste the champagne.

CHAPTER 5

Thank-you for seeing me today Mrs. Black. I hope you are feeling more relaxed. Your hair looks very nice."

"Sure thing Doc. How is he? Is he worse?"

"No change. It isn't reasonable to expect change so soon."

"That figures."

"Does it?"

"It does. The man is doomed and he's going to take his time about it."

"Perhaps you can explain what you mean by that."

"His brain is mush, oatmeal, ground beef. What more can I say?"

"How long have you been married?"

"Too damned long. I want you to sign these papers, certifying that he is a hopeless vegetable and is staying here or wherever you want to put him. I can't look after him and I wouldn't if I could. That's the whole truth."

"I can't do that Mrs. Black. I haven't finished my assessment."

"Well I have and if you won't sign these papers then my lawyer will put you in front of a judge. She'll make mincemeat out of you. She's a mean son-of-a-bitch. The meanest lawyer you've ever met, believe me."

"So you won't try to help me understand what is happening with your husband?"

“What’s to understand? He’s a vegetable, a moron, an idiot, one flake left. Give him mashed potatoes and he’ll stare at them for ages. I told you all this yesterday, weren’t you listening?”

“I thought you said this happened suddenly, in the last couple of days. Isn’t that what you said?”

“Jesus Christopher Doc, I don’t remember everything I said yesterday but sure, yeah, probably. I was under a lot of stress. I told you about him and his fantasy friend, Took A-Look, didn’t I? What more do you need? He’s done in this world. Sign the papers and let me get on with my life.”

“What was he doing on the deck?” Marsha had read the report and wondered then how the patient ended up on the deck or more importantly, who made that decision?

“You think I could sleep with him making that racket in the house? You think I felt safe? Sign the papers Doc. You fix him, I’m finished with him. He’s damaged goods now, he’ll never be the same, no matter what you do and you know it. I have got to get on with my life. You have to understand my position here. I’ve suffered enough.”

“Tell me Mrs. Black, has Eric been in therapy before? Someone who might be able to give me some background on his condition?”

“In therapy? Not that I know of. Jesus, what would people think? It was all I could do to keep everyone from finding out about this. Lucky we don’t have any neighbors close by, what a sight he was. What a mess. Just sign the papers, make it easy on yourself. Seriously, make it easy on yourself.”

“I won’t do that, Mrs. Black. When my initial assessment is complete, I will then, and only then, determine the correct path for his therapy.” Definitely not the words she wanted to hear but there wasn’t any point in trying to avoid the obvious with Mrs. Brita Black. She had her guns loaded and if she couldn’t nail her husband, some other poor soul was going to get it just for target practice. Like the poor soul sitting right in front of her who was refusing to commit her husband.

It was all but over and somewhat absentmindedly, Marsha shook her head as she wondered how two people like the Black’s ever found each other and when they did, why they decided to share a life together. It wasn’t the first time she had wondered that, it happened from time to time, but this was almost bizarre. Or maybe it wasn’t bizarre. It’s not like she knew him, was it? But she had a feeling, an intuition, a flash of understanding that she couldn't quite put to words yet had to acknowledge it as genuine regardless of its source. It might turn out to be nonsense later but it shouldn't be dismissed right now. Where it came from, she hadn't a clue, but it wasn't the first time she had experienced the feeling of profound knowing without cognitive understanding and she smiled in recognition of the state and the extreme sense of presence that came with it.

"Bad decision Doc, see you in court."

The slammed door didn't surprise Marsha. Slamming a door in your mind is not physically the same as really doing it but there are lots of similarities. Definitely not a surprise in this situation.

Right from the first conversation when her husband was admitted but not committed, the wife's motives were clear. She didn't want any part of the problem and provided just enough information to pour the cement over him, let it harden, and now the real agenda. Just a little over a day and she wanted her freedom. Her freedom along with everything else she could grasp with her professionally manicured, ivory-painted fingernails. A pure and simple attempt to take legal control of the marital assets as conservator; a soap opera script. It seldom worked but when it did, the only thing Eric Black would keep would be his name, unless she wanted that too. It was an obvious strategy with illusive but destructive tactics, many of which had already been played on the victim.

Obvious and illusive, that also described Brita Black. There was plenty of logic to believe she was lying, at the very least that she wasn't telling the whole truth, but the woman was totally convincing, totally real, completely believable. Whatever she said, Marsha had to shake her head to clear the image and mentally repeat the words she heard. Then she had to void those words of any emotional attachment and assess what was left for a single grain of truth. The woman simply didn't leave any of the telling clues that she was lying and that baffled and bewildered the senses. Marsha had never met anyone who didn't tell some lies during committal, especially husbands and wives who had already lied about the illness for so long sometimes even they didn't think they were lying. But that didn't include Brita Black, she had her own agenda and wasn't about to share it with anyone, in a lie or otherwise.

The woman was straightforward and calculated to the point of brutality with no hint that she was telling anything other than the truth. Little wonder Mr. Black was in the state he was, after her he didn't need a therapist, he needed an exorcist.

And how she knew about Took A-Look was also a curiosity. Not exactly dinner table conversation for two people who were obviously not very close or trusting but she wasn't wrong about him. He was in there all right. It was in the eyes. Strange. Quite strange really. But weren't they all? Or aren't we all?

Strange, Marsha repeated the word out loud and then wondered how curious got promoted all the way up to strange?

As if to answer that, she knew, or sensed, or both, that something very unique was happening or was about to happen. It was always that way when she found herself on her own couch, questioning her own thoughts, interrogating her logical connections as if they belonged to someone else, just like she was trained to do.

At least she wasn't hearing the answers, not yet anyway, so she smiled to herself as a kind of reward, an old habit that signaled it was time get off her couch and as she did, she summarized her own diagnosis.

How little we sometimes know, especially about the one person we think we should know the most about.

CHAPTER 6

Roland felt the same trepidation he always felt when it was time to ask the question which was burned into his mind so deeply that it replaced almost every other question in his vast body of knowledge. Of course, unfortunately and ironically, the question was also the source of so many other questions that it couldn't stand alone and couldn't be worked on alone even though eventually that was how it would be answered.

For instance, lots of people had been tricked by their own genetics yet all but a handful had been blessed with more than just a fragmentary third-party history of themselves. A past they couldn't ignore and couldn't re-shape or enhance because it wouldn't let them? A past that they were born with? He started the questioning, as he always did, with enthusiasm.

"And now I'd like to get past the science of DNA and introduce another mystery, an evolutionary odd duck. A duck which is much more interesting and with a great opportunity for the speculation I so carefully avoided before. This duck is called, affectionately by some and with unbridled disdain by others, the Legacy Gene. That's right, a new, unique, rare and as you have probably already guessed, a very, very curious gene.

We aren't talking about a few misplaced nucleotides anymore, about junk DNA. No, we are talking about a whole gene, a complete apple from the original garden. Actually we are talking about approximately 300 of these apples which have been discovered to date. Not very many when compared to the 30,000 we all share but that isn't what makes this duck so odd.

Plus, very likely, there are a few more Legacy Genes that have not yet been discovered because the person who has them didn't contribute DNA to the Genome Mapping Project." He paused to bait the trap they were all dying to step into.

"Perhaps, not very probable I will admit, but definitely possible, someone in this room has an undiscovered Legacy Gene in them, a piece of living history, a true global survivor, in their genetic make-up."

Individual reaction to this possibility covered the spectrum of emotion but which could only occupy a single position of logic. The owner of that gene was exceptionally unique. Owning that had to be worth a lot because if they didn't have at least one undiscovered Legacy Gene in them then they most certainly had a dozen or so of the already discovered ones. That simple piece of math explained a lifetime of uniqueness; it explained every thought and feeling which was different from everyone else. A language spoken by only one person.

"Legacy Genes are the evolutionary odd duck, the platypus. Some people have fifteen or twenty of them and some have two. Some Legacy Genes show up more often than others. That is, the occurrence of a specific Legacy Gene might be as high as twenty-five percent of the population; one out of every four people will have it. The least common Legacy Gene is, by genetics standards, quite rare, like one person in ten million. You can bet that all the people who have that gene, whether they like the idea or not, are closely, indisputably related somewhere in their past."

Not that anyone in the room would necessarily get excited about that possibility, in fact, most would prefer to deny it. Their family trees had been researched, documented where expedient, re-written as needed and sometimes carefully pruned of offending ancestors. No way would they want to graft the murderers and other miscreants back onto the stumps of the branches from which they had been so painstakingly severed.

"To repeat the basic law, one last time, there is only one reason that a gene is randomly present in only part of the population and that is because the gene itself is neither harmful nor essential. At least, not essential for life as we know it today. Obviously, it once had a purpose and is now blocked from expressing, from performing its once vital purpose. But, what purpose could that have been?"

By default, it had to be a good purpose, at the very least a protective or defensive purpose. Really bad genes didn't make it through the evolutionary gauntlet, right? At the very worst, a benign purpose, an attempt which might not have succeeded for one challenge but which might be good for another. He took another slow, studied sip of water, reinforcing the unconscious connection of each and every human thought and action to a string of letters inside a cell that tell the brain it was time for a drink, time to consider thirst as an immediate priority. As usual, a fair share of the audience reached for their water glasses. Oddly enough, of those who did, women outnumbered men, two to one.

"Some think that Legacy Genes, like the filler nucleotides in a gene sequence are just genetic mistakes which have been left in the system. Why not? They don't do anything terrible so they weren't removed through the process of extinction. Others think that these genes were developed for some purpose which has, itself become extinct. Like in response to a bacterium which no longer exists so the gene is simply dormant, waiting for that bacterium to return and initiate the start sequence so it can begin producing the antibody that is its sole purpose, its design. That would explain why some people have it and others don't. That particular defense mechanism was only developed where it was needed, say in Egypt, so only the descendants of those Egyptians who survived that plague would have it."

He paused for a moment. Just long enough to allow the emotional bond for the Legacy Gene to strengthen. If that bloody bacteria ever came back, an absolute certainty with all the tombs which were being opened these days, that Legacy Gene, or at least the antibodies it produced, would be damn useful and people would pay anything to get it.

"Then again, perhaps the Legacy Gene holds the instructions for other capabilities, capabilities which have gradually become less dominant, less mandatory for survival. Maybe they are the key to unlocking acute senses such as a reptile's ability to see infrared wave length or a shark's ability to sense bio-electro-magnetic impulses. Of course no one agrees on this. Nor can anyone refute it because most human genes are also shared, in some form or another, with the animal kingdom. An eye for eye, so to speak."

He was building to the climax, they knew it and were waiting for it. Waiting for him to say out loud what they couldn't say in public but found irresistible in the privacy of their own thinking. Maybe they could unlock that gene and all its power, deliver all those acute senses on command. What a gift that would become.

"Who knows, perhaps the Legacy Gene will activate parts of the brain which are dormant, which are unutilized or underutilized? Perhaps unlock ancient secrets. And what would be discovered if that were to occur? What mystery might then be solved? What perception might be realized? What Michelangelo might emerge from the gloom?"

With an audience of slightly more than 140 people, he knew that would approximate the number of answers to his question. Each of them, just like he did, had their own, unique, bothersome mystery. Something that could not be seen or tasted or heard or felt except through that primordial, wordless state, a sense which came without language because it preceded the spoken word, the first intelligent grunt.

"Ladies and gentlemen, it is time to speculate. To speculate where few in my field want to go – into the past. I cannot tell you what your reward will be, all I can say is that it is our legacy to discover it. As I am sure you realize, the potential is vast. These genes could unlock human potential unlike anything else in the genetic toolkit. Skills, senses, communication and language, learnings from the beginning of time. The wisdom of our ancestors, a consciousness that has either been lying dormant or operating in the background of our brains for tens of thousands of years. That is the quest. Not to engineer, not to alter and not to construct but to explore the universe by examining the past, your exact past, something that is waiting inside you, waiting to be unwrapped. Perhaps we will even discover the beginnings of thought, or intelligence by finding a clue that is stored in a legacy gene and conveniently wrapped up in words like instinct and intuition."

He had never received a standing ovation and never wanted to receive one. That was the correct response to a performance, but entirely inappropriate for the initiation of a quest. The Master of Ceremonies would be quick with the conclusion. On each face was written a question and Roland J. Masters, MD was expected to legitimize it. Not answer it, but legitimize it. 'Yes, that is possible' and those words might be enough to add a zero to the amount. They couldn't wait for the mingling to begin. Snake oil or not, everyone wanted a case of it. If it unlocked all that potential, unraveled the greatest of all life mysteries or if it simply put some fears to rest, who could resist such a challenge?

CHAPTER 7

Tuesday Morning,
Statue in the Garden,
No Birds Yet

Her little feet are doing the double-quick march. Radio angry, 150% TV crazy. That's a lot of percents but I told you she was competitive, didn't I?

She didn't come to see me, that's for sure and sure nice of her too, for a change. Took A-Look loves the hear-sight, he's dancing on a happy cloud. Sunshine all over the place. Bright and warm and light streaming through the trees, a smooth little breeze making bow music with the branches and fluttering the leaves like little baby snare drums being brushed. Rustle, rustle, rustle. Nice tune, Took A-Look. Bet Doctor Marsha had something to do with that. Don't kick that fart cloud at her again, okay?

Of course I know who is in charge.

Fine go ahead and kick it anytime you want.

No I'm not giving you permission.

Yes, I know who is in charge.

I know all that but I can still talk to you can't I?

Well can't I?

Talk about cranky.

"So then the teacher tells me that Lawrence isn't working up to his full potential. His full potential, she says, like she has a clue what that means. She doesn't of course. You know what I mean, Eric, do you know what I mean?"

No.

"Of course you do. Such good listeners as you always know things like that."

No I don't. And I don't want to know. Neither does Took A-Look. He'd put your little Lawrence in a leaky boat and shove him out to sea with a broken paddle. And a bucket with a hole in it. In a raging storm. Wouldn't you Took A-Look?

He isn't listening that's for sure but his reasons for quiet are different than mine, that's also for sure. He is busy thinking about her as he follows every clack of her stiletto heeled shoes echoing down the sidewalk from over the wall. Angry as hell she is. Slams the car door. She is a door slammer, always was, always will be. Any kind of door. Coming in, slam. Going out, Slam. Never-ending slamming, that's her trademark. Just like the mouth, she slams it open and slams it shut. It's damn startling if you don't see it coming or are trying to have a nap, which is almost impossible whenever she is here and not there.

"It's nice of Mister Sorenson to put us together like this, isn't it?"

No. It sucks. Sorenson is an ass, first class. Hold on, rephrase. Sorenson is complete ass, he has no class.

"It's so nice of you to listen. You are such a good listener. Do you know what the teacher said after that?"

Let me guess? She said that Lawrence was a day dreamer and that he needed more discipline at home.

"She said my Lawrence was a day dreamer and he needed more discipline at home. Can you believe that?"

Yeah. Too bad she didn't say anything about a leaky boat and a stormy sea. Bet she didn't say anything about Lawrence setting the house on fire while his Momma was having a nap on the couch either. Sorenson told that story on you, Mrs. Reynolds. See what can happen with a poor introduction. It makes a mess of everything right at the very beginning when you can least afford to have a mess. How do you ever recover a conversation that starts from almost being burned alive by your own son?

Right Took A-Look? What are you doing? Having a nap? Sharpening spears? Wanna talk? Wanna bet Lawrence never comes to visit his Momma?

"He doesn't come to visit me you know."

I win.

"His father comes once a week, on Wednesday at five o'clock. That's tomorrow. He talks to Dr. Marsha and then he visits with me until six o'clock sharp. That's supper time for us self-feeders you know. Wednesday is meat loaf with mashed potatoes, second choice is spaghetti with meat sauce, ragu, you know. Never anything that needs to be cut up. If it needs to be cut up, it's already cut up."

Hey Took A-Look, you die of boredom back there? The windows are open if you want to see what Mrs. Reynolds looks like. Or do you just like to listen to her? He fires a dull little arrow into a cloud but it doesn't stick and falls out harmlessly. A parrot sound comes out the hole. Not the loud squawking parrot noise but the incessant jabbering, cooing parrot sound which is much more endearing. Guess he's already seen her. She's pretty colorful with a dandy beak on her and lots red hair tied up in a knot on the top if her head. She looks like someone who would make a better grandmother than a mother. When did you do that Took A-Look? When did you take a look at her?

He isn't talking and that's not good. She must have reminded him of something. Like maybe she is where and he is here. If it was up to him, she would be under ground. That's what he wanted and no amount of discussion about what is permitted in this century could change his mind. Sometimes the strength of one person's convictions is the weakness of the other person's. For sure that's one thing that happened but like all contrarian things, knowing about them doesn't end it.

He isn't happy about anything, that's for sure and I feel pretty bad for him. I can't help it; it isn't his fault peace was undeclared even if he did the un-declaring. He didn't have a choice about that so now I get the consequences, that's what happens when the time for talk is over. Undeclared peace is not an easy state for anybody. Unless of course you are a parrot because for parrots the time for talk is never over; for them it's a noisy world but a peaceful one.

"I really do miss my Lawrence. More than anything. He is a quiet boy, a good listener. Like you, Eric, you are good listener too. Not like his teacher, she doesn't understand him at all. She doesn't see his good side and just won't listen to someone who does."

And vice versa right Took A-Look? Honestly, what can you say about that?

"What an idiot." It flowed into the air space in front of my mouth before it could be stopped. It didn't come from Took A-Look and that left only one other choice.

"Oh Eric, thank you. Thank you so much. You have no idea how much that means to me. Please call me Julia. I do so like to be on a first name basis. I'm so glad you decided to talk to me. We will be great friends, I know that. And you are so right about his teacher, you are so smart about that. I'm sure you are so smart about everything, not like me. I do wish you could meet my little Lawrence. Would you do that? Would you meet him? Would you talk to him? I just know you would make a difference. I am so sure of it. I have this feeling that you of all people can talk to him. Would you do that for me, for him, Eric, would you talk to him?"

Oh oh.

Please change the subject.

I hope nobody else heard that accidental idiot comment, especially you-know-who with the hyphenated name. Bad things happen out loud. Peace is undeclared and the time for talk is over. That's the rule and I broke it but it was a mistake, an honest mistake. Truly. Everybody talks to parrots, it can't be helped, like talking to puppies only more upscale. Sorry, Sorry, Sorry.

Oh oh.

Took A-Look isn't buying the everybody-talks-to-parrots upscale explanation and now it's too late for apologies and far too late to get him off balance because all of a sudden he's crazy as a mating muskox and starting to kick clouds, left, right and center, up and down probably on the way.

Crap, oh crap! That hurts! So does that. And that one too. He knows his clouds like nobody in their right mind knows their clouds and he's just getting warmed up. Unhappy is about be transcended. He's still taking aim but that won't last too long, no doubt about that. Random, orchestrated chaos is on his horizon and he's completely focused, his black eyes just tiny specks on a horizon he can't see over but wants to.

Crap. Oh crap! Not good! Not good at all! He's warming up faster than an ulcer in smoking chili oil. Fire! FIRE!!! Fire burning all over the place. Three engine alert! Ouch, ouch, ouch. Faster and faster. He's not taking aim anymore, he's all warmed up and he's not about to stop.

Oh Oh. Bad, very bad, and much worse is on the horizon and coming to town in a fearsome frenzy with crazy wobbly wheels going downhill, gaining speed by the second. A crash is coming but that won't stop anything because a worse crash is coming after that but it won't stop anything either.

Damn, damn, extra damn. Here and there and everywhere, lightning bolts are flying. No sparks yet. Just one big, loud CRACK after another and the wet, smoking sizzle left behind. Nothing's hit either, not yet anyway.

Oh oh. Now the clouds are crashing into each other, that's bad, that's really bad going to worse heading for much worse and it can't get worse than much worse without finding new words and metaphors and there's no time for any of that right now. Clouds are crashing faster and faster like they want to destroy each other in cloud warfare. Fog Alert! Fog Alert! Fog Lights, Fog Horn, SOMEBODY QUICK - Oh Oh, somebody's messing with the windows, now its blinding light with fearsome dark flashes in between.

Man oh man, the windows are opening and closing like crazy, things are twitching and jerking and spazzing all over the place, worse than a wet dog team all shaking themselves dry at once getting each other all wet and starting all over again. Oh boy, as if it couldn't get worse, here comes whatshisname.

What is his name? Gone. Squashed flat as a bug between two rocks. Here comes the other one. Steve. Average Steve, that's him but not looking too average and in a big hurry to prove it coming right at me. Oh Julia! Oh Julia, dear Julia Parrot, look what you have done to me. Just look what have you have started. Ka-Boom, the storm cloud thunders so loud I can't even hear my own voice. Where did the lightning go? That's what I want to know at this exact moment, where is that damn lightning? There has to be lightning, so where is it?

Oh man, oh man, oh man!!! Took A-Look is kicking the ever-lovin' crap out of the wind cloud. Both feet pounding on it like a little tin wind-up toy.

He's kicking it again and again like a little steam puffer train gone wild and berserk, racing downhill so fast it can't possibly make the corner at the bottom. Can't possibly turn, can't possibly stay on the tracks. Wreck coming! Wreck coming up, look out! Run for your lives. Look out below, above too!

"TAKE IT EASY, ERIC! Calm down! Breathe normally for Chrissakes! CALM DOWN ERIC. Stop all that panting and puffing, you're going to hyperventilate yourself. Jesus Christ, HOLD HIM DOWN STEVE!"

"HOLD HIM DOWN??? Son-of-a-bitch Marty, stick him with that needle before somebody gets hurt! Hurry up! Like now, for chrissakes, NOW!"

"HOLD THE ARM STILL!"

"YOU HOLD IT STILL! I'm sitting on top of a freaking earthquake!"

Took A-Look is furious, absolutely furious, and damn fast too. Hands and feet are flying, lightning bolts happening all around him. Lightning and thunder and a huge howling, freeze dried wind. I can't keep track of anything. Steve is right, somebody is gonna get hurt. Hurt bad. Soon too. One good kick in the wrong cloud and something is gonna get busted, something that Steve is sitting on or that Marty is holding down. Maybe something of theirs if something of mine gets a decent swing at it. Or maybe not. Who knows but this is not the time to ask that question regardless of what I said before about the importance of who knows.

Was that a loud, mean thunder clap or the sound of something breaking? Hard to tell, hard to know, hard to think, impossible to feel anything. Crap oh crap, can't inhale any more, the wind cloud is all pooped out. Out of gas, out of wind, no air, NO AIR. Aaah-ooo-Gah, Aaah-ooo-Gah, submerging fast, nobody yelled dive but somebody should have. Close the ever-loving hatches, I'm drowning down here.

"He's turning blue, he's going cyanotic!"

"DAMMIT STEVE, gimme a hand here. SHIT! He's wrecked his arm on something. Blood everywhere, maybe busted. DAMMIT. I'm getting soaked, he musta got an artery. Dammit all to hell, I hope this sonovabitch doesn't have anything contagious in him."

STICK HIM. STICK HIM ANYWHERE! For Chrissakes Marty, stick anything that isn't moving."

Took A-Look has his face right up to the window which is jumping up and down like car lights going over speed bumps very fast, up-down, up-down, up-down. Personally I can't see a thing between up-down, damn dangerous to drive like that but he doesn't seem to care. He's got his biggest sharpest spear, trying to take aim on Marty. The one with the walrus tusk point. Up-down, up-down, up-down, like on a boat, quite a challenge even for him. He's getting ready to throw it. LOOK OUT, WINDOW!!! His arm goes back and back and back some more. Way, way far back and then he's kinda suspended in space like an old time slapstick movie when the film gets stuck in the projector. Picture stuck on the screen with the projector still running, whirring away like everything is okay when it's not okay at all and the celluloid is burning crisp and noxious. Then by some Hollywood miracle the film catches again and Took A-Look looks like he is starting to throw the spear but instead he falls face down real slow, like gravity got him right in the chest and pulled him down like a fish diving under the boat trying to fight off the hook but can't. Ker-splash, Took A-Look. Ker-splash you get a bath.

Starts off being funny enough to laugh out loud which would be a real mistake but then the walrus tusk tip tilts up in his falling hand and rips a huge hole in a big white cloud, real high up and the white stuff starts falling all over everything.

Really big, furry flakes that keep getting bigger and bigger, more and more peaceful every second. No wind or anything, just the white stuff... what's the name for it? the cold stuff made of flakes?...white and cold and furry?...no, not furry, flurry maybe but what's the name for lots of cold... but white cold not colorless cold...what's it called again?...

CHAPTER 8

"Do you have an explanation for what happened in the garden, Mr. Sorenson?" Marty Sorenson was one of the few people who Marsha had disliked from the very first moment she met him. Plus, he was the only person she had ever met who managed to grow that dislike a little bit every time she met him. He was at least 15 years older than she was and had worked at the hospital for twenty years compared to her two. She was fairly certain that had something to do with it. He figured he had twenty years of solid experience while she figured he had one year repeated twenty times.

"He had a seizure and cut his arm." Marty had seen all kinds of them come and go and Doctor Marsha Coleman wouldn't be any different from the brain drain she replaced or the brain drain who would, sooner or later, preferably sooner, replace her. Nobody stayed at the state hospital for very long unless they were completely incompetent, alcoholic, drug addicted, or with their own mental health issues. The patients in those categories usually got out before the doctors who mistreated them. Of course, she wasn't defective in any of those ways, but once she got some solid experience and published a paper or two she'd go to the big money clinics just like all those before her had done.

The truth of it was, and the truth of it would always be, the orderlies ran the hospital. That's the way and the only way. Just like Marty Sorenson worked for the Head Orderly who was The Boss until Marty Sorenson became Head Orderly and now he was The Boss. The woman should just accept it and get over it. Sooner or later she would leave her precious cases, so why make such a fuss over a dozen stitches in his arm. Really, compared to the broken brain in his head, really what's the big deal?

"Start at the beginning, Mr. Sorenson. I am trying to understand his behavior."

He knew she was impatient but couldn't decide whether it was better to prolong the game and bring her frustration to the boiling point or give her an answer which would produce the same result only faster. What was the question? Oh yeah. I'm not a bloody doctor so how the hell could I possibly know a seizure when it's blowing blood, crap and corruption all over the place? Starting at the beginning, too. He decided to stonewall her for a while. He could always drop a bombshell later, if he felt like it.

"I took Mr. Black out for some sun as we always do for everyone, including new patients. I put him out in the garden near Mrs. Reynolds where we could keep an eye on him which was a good thing because, not even ten minutes later, and he goes completely ballistic." How's that for a totally non-therapeutic answer? Ballistic, did you like that?

"Did he say or do anything?"

Do anything, say anything? A catatonic? A schizoid? A mute negativist? Whatever. Like I should spend my time watching a pot of porridge which is going to erupt, without warning, the very second I take my eyes away from it? Get real Doc, these ones don't do anything, don't talk, don't do anything no matter what you do to them, you should know that. "No, he didn't say anything."

"Did you ask Mrs. Reynolds if she saw or heard anything?"

No, I'm here talking to you instead of listening to that neurotic woman rationalize her contribution to the world. Precious bloody Lawrence. The light of his mother's eye, and the darkness behind it as well. Believe me on that one, I know something about that kid's life. Knew it the first time I looked in the little cretin's eyes. "No."

"Why don't you do that?"

It wasn't said like a question even if the words made it a question. Marsha didn't even try to keep the authority out of her voice. How can one person create so much conflict, so quickly, out of so little and for absolutely no apparent reason? What on earth motivates such extreme, antagonistic behavior?

"Sure, if that's what you want." Waste some more of my time why don't you?

"Right away Mr. Sorenson."

"Sure."

"On your way out, ask Gail to come in here, please."

"Sure thing." Bitch. On his way past the secretary's desk he put his hand out like a hitchhiker and poked his thumb a couple of times backward. No eye contact needed. Just another dumb bitch that would tell him what do if he gave her a chance, so he didn't. Screw both of them. Steve can talk to the Reynolds woman. Sooner or later and even the high and mighty Doctor Coleman will figure out what goes on around here and then she'll have to let the status quo rule the roost. Probably at exactly the same time she understands that patients get better or they get worse and one treatment is just as good as another. Especially patients like the Eric Blacks of this world. Those ones are like cheap baseball cards of first year wannabe's who never make it off the farm team. They don't get any better and can't be traded for anything worth a nickel.

For what seemed like the thousandth time in two years, Marsha pushed Marty Sorenson out of her mind. She had tried communicating with him, she had tried listening to him, she had tried coaching him, she had tried everything in the book and then tried it all again. He was a rock and would forever be a rock. It happened. Truth to tell, in a place like this, it happened a lot. Staff put up as big a wall as some of the patients did. It was a basic survival instinct, although she suspected that he had come with that wall and not built it on the job. She consciously pushed that thought from her mind too; no point in looking for more work when there wasn't enough time in the day for the patients she actually cared about.

Gail stuck her head around the corner of the door, her eyes bright and happy. Very cute and very intentionally so. "Hi."

"Hi yourself. Come in."

Slightly over-weight but not at all conscious about it, her Admin sat down, completely comfortable in spite of the hostility which was still hanging in the air. Hostility she had heard through the open door as Dr. Coleman had once again confronted the extreme pain-in-the-ass Head Orderly, Marty Sorenson. She sat in the chair facing the desk, nearest to Marsha. It was a comfortable chair in a personal but professional office. Not at all like Marsha's predecessors who seemed to think that the office had to look like everything else in the hospital, all grey, right angled and perfectly suited for obtuse impersonal theoretical conversations about people having extremely serious personal problems.

Gail had helped Marsha decorate the office and that was when she first knew her opinion was valued. They both agreed the old gun-metal grey desk with the mismatched credenza and tinny bookshelf behind it needed to be replaced. Gail found a modern teak desk with a return and a matching credenza with bookcase in a used furniture store. It wasn't what you would call elegant but it had nice simple lines, was the right size to fit the small, rectangular office and was more feminine than masculine. When Marsha wanted to load the bookcase with text books and studies, Gail suggested she use at least half the shelves for other titles, books that Marsha had read and liked. Just enough to break the Doctor Stereotype without becoming too homey or personal and it worked, visually and psychologically, better than either of them imagined.

Marsha gave her so much praise it was almost embarrassing when really it was an obvious choice. Simply make the office reflect the person and Marsha was a thoughtful, interesting, straightforward person so follow that path and the result is easy. At least in her case it was easy because she was human and not afraid to be known that way, unlike some of her predecessors who used their desk as barbed wire and the medical books as a No Trespassing sign.

Because the office was small, after the desk and credenza were added, there wasn't a lot of decorating left to do. Marsha found a nice black leather arm chair, quite modern, which she liked but which Gail returned. It was too big and imposing so Gail picked out a three-quarter manager's chair, in ox-blood leather with bronze studding that cost more than the rest of the furniture combined. It was perfectly proportioned because it centered Marsha in the chair and in the room like a portrait that has been professionally framed for the singular purpose of enhancing the subject. Marsha loved it.

For the patients that Marsha saw in her office, which was about half of them, and for consultations with family members, Gail had two matching wing-back arm chairs done in a light tan fabric. They were very comfortable and because her guests could curl up between the arms or huddle against the wings, very protective emotionally. The chairs were close enough to the desk that it served as a table for the lukewarm coffee or tea which was served in plastic cups. No knickknacks, for obvious reasons. No pictures, just Marsha's degrees and certifications; they both agreed on that.

Bad day?" Gail asked, trivially. If the discussion with Brita Black hadn't already condemned the day then the one with Sorenson certainly should have finished the job. Not to even mention poor Mr. Black and his injured arm to go along with all the problems in his head. It wasn't even eleven o'clock and Marsha was already behind one session. Not that that patient would mind. Or maybe he would. It was always difficult to predict how a paranoid would take something because everything was against them, regardless.

"Not a good one, Gail, not a very good one." Marsha smiled, half out of relief to be talking to someone without having to be constantly on guard. She knew why she called Gail into the office but chose to delay it for a while. Gail was a peaceful person so it was nice to be around her, just for that. They were almost friends but would never cross that threshold and both of them knew it. Gail's quiet acceptance of the things she didn't understand or couldn't change was rooted in faith. It was her source of peace and a significant difference between the two women. Marsha's beliefs were scientific in nature and that forced her to try and understand what was hidden from her and she believed that she could, eventually, make a change for the better. They understood each other's viewpoint and in that way contributed to each other's well-being, but it was a big enough difference that both of them knew they would never be friends in conventional terms.

"Good news, Marsha." Gail timed her intrusion carefully. Marsha could get pretty intense and sometimes even good news needed the right moment for a successful launch. She sensed that she was ready for the news, just as sometimes she called her Doctor Marsha while at other times it was Doctor Coleman or like now when it just plain Marsha. There wasn't any real rhyme or reason for it, it just made sense at the time.

"Good news?" Marsha said with undisguised but slightly sarcastic curiosity.

"Eric Black's daughter called. When you were meeting with - him. I've set up an appointment for tomorrow, at ten."

"Ten?"

"I've rescheduled..."

"That is good news, Gail. What..."

"She found out from somebody that her father is here. She's none too happy about it."

"No?"

"No. She wanted to know who committed him. Wanted to know who had the right to do that. She was extremely upset and very angry."

"And that's good news?"

"She cares, Doctor Coleman. She's concerned about her father. That came through loud and clear - mostly loud."

Marsha noticed the switch from first name to her formal title and understood the reason for the change. Most of the time Gail held her opinions to herself, particularly her opinions about patients, but that didn't mean she was afraid to say what was on her mind. Nor was she afraid to be wrong with her opinion. Gail believed that it was better to say things out loud and be wrong than to keep everything inside and not be any help to anybody. 'Better to be wrong than useless', she would say, usually after voicing her thoughts, as a way of apology or justification even when none was needed.

Both of them knew that when it came to dealing with the friends or family of patients, Gail was right a lot more often than she was wrong. This was one of those cases where she knew she was right although she didn't quite know why she felt so strongly about it. Something had touched her, déjà vu perhaps, some sixth sense, common sense, who knows? Anyway, where it came from didn't much matter because she knew that Marsha wanted to hear her opinion. Friends and family were generally a lot less complicated than the patients but sometimes doctors treated them the same way and needed to be reminded that they shouldn't do that. Friends and family weren't the ones who were committed, even if occasionally they should have been. Let sleeping psychosis lie, everybody has a pet phobia, that sort of thing. Gail could see and accept that as being perfectly natural when Marsha's intellect and compassion often tempted her into looking deeper.

But at least she was different from the other doctors because she didn't make that mistake intentionally. She didn't make a head game out of everyone she met. To her it was more of an occupational hazard, unlike most of the other doctors for whom Gail had worked where it was part of their huge ego. Whatever psychiatrists learned in university or experienced in practice, few of them could apply it personally so most of them were somewhat weird, to put it nicely. Head games, like they didn't play them when most of the time they were the ones who wrote the rules, got them started and then kept score in their bank account. Gail knew she was being a little harsh on them but she really did like Marsha and really didn't like them so if that was harsh, screw it, she was entitled.

"Did you pick up anything other than her anger?"

"Not much, Doctor Marsha. It was a very quick call. After I explained 48/48 to her, she did the math and asked for an appointment, you-know-when."

Marsha hated that part of the system but it was something that was beyond her control. The rule of 48/48 was her right to hold someone, without consent from anyone, patient included, for 48 hours for evaluation. The next 48 hours were a nearly automatic extension at the discretion of the physician in charge and a ten second review by the Administrator. After that, somebody had to sign for longer term commitment and that could be the patient, a direct family member or, in the worst case, the physician in charge. Worst case for the physician because that was typically when things got ugly. That was when if somebody decided to fight commitment, then along came the lawyers and hearings, contrary expert opinions, human rights, civil rights, animal rights and generally a three ring circus with tons of clowns and no ring master. It was the sledge hammer approach to not fixing a broken watch.

Aside from being a complete waste of everyone's time, at least everyone who wasn't billing somebody else, the patient usually got the brute end of the hammer because their mental competency was determined, judicially, in a contest between two sides with the patient in the middle, like they were a piece of property, not a person. Some really sick people were set free and then some truly innocent person would end up paying for that mistake. More often though, without treatment, even a little bit of treatment, escaping commitment usually produced an outcast who was victimized and abandoned, ending up on the street, destitute and homeless, keeping only their problems, another life lost.

Eric Black was heading right into that circus and for all the wrong reasons. Brita Black didn't want to be the one committing him because that would put her so-called conservator tactic, the English translation for which was property grab, into legal limbo for a year or ten. Judges simply didn't like the idea that a wife or a husband, including their own wife or husband, might commit them to an asylum and then spend them into servitude if not bankruptcy. A voluntary commitment by Mr. Black would be just about as bad for the wife because it would put some reasonable doubt in the judge's mind. Anyone who was well enough to commit themselves might eventually get better and that would put the brakes on catapulting the matrimonial nest egg over the wall and into Mrs. Black's outstretched arms.

With enough money and the right lawyers on both sides of the fence, it could go on for years. So, Mrs. Black wanted Marsha to do the dirty work, commit her husband and set the judge's mind at rest. But that trick had been played before and Marsha wouldn't allow herself to be pushed too far or too fast. It wouldn't be the first time that a spouse gave their partner an unhealthy dose of a heavy duty psychotic and blitzed his brain into oblivion while doing the same thing to the bank accounts. Rare, but it happened and that was the only time the 48/48 rule worked. Just enough time to sort out the cause of the problem before someone's life was completely destroyed from the outside before anyone had even a half a chance to figure out what was going on inside.

"Was the daughter surprised her father was here?"

"Not so much surprised as she was angry. I think she saw it coming but hoped it wouldn't." answered Gail. She knew Marsha would ask that question even before she had hung the phone on the daughter.

"Situation normal." mused Marsha.

"Should I have the extension drawn up, just in case?"

"Please…and thanks for your help Gail. I'm going to look in on Mr. Black."

Marsha was half way out of her chair and had to rewind her thoughts to the beginning, something else had got into her head and distracted her to the point she couldn't remember what she originally wanted.

What the dickens was it that she wanted Gail to do?

Right, draw up the extension papers.

And what was the other thing?

There was another thing.

Positively there was.

But whatever it was, it was gone, submerged somewhere and while she didn't remember what it was, she didn't expect it back.

CHAPTER 9

Could be Tuesday Afternoon; Statues Don't Give a Damn about Time.

Took A-Look is having a major problem staying on his feet, somebody oiled all his clouds. He's slipping and sliding all over the place. Doesn't hurt though because he can't stomp and every time he tries to kick, he falls over backwards.

You're kinda funny, Took A-Look.

He doesn't think so.

You might as well forget about it, Took A-Look. We aren't going anywhere. That asshole strapped us down but good.

Good idea Took A-Look. Crawl to the window and check out the ceiling. Looks like snow, doesn't it? You like that? No? Too bad. No, I can't move the window. No, you can't move it either. Oops, fell off another cloud, did you? Too bad.

I know. I know. Eventually you'll get even but right now it's my turn. In case you hadn't noticed, I'm a little upset over that last cloud kicking incident.

Well hello Doctor Marsha.

See Took A-Look, it's your favorite seal. She's brought her gold specks and green seas to visit us. Isn't that nice? You'll never make it to the fart cloud so forget about it and stop being so contrarian, you like her and you know it.

"Let me see about that arm, Eric. Is that cast too tight? Mmmm. Not too bad. Once the swelling goes down a little it should be fine."

Doesn't she have a nice touch, Took A-Look? Yes, very gentle. See, it doesn't kill you to be a little agreeable.

Forget it. You'll never stand on that cloud. It's covered with Marty slime. You'd better be careful, you fall off that one and you'll go straight down the tube and get trapped in the big, black abyss for ages, just like before. You know that don't you? You like her, don't you? Sure you do. Go ahead, crawl over to the window and take a peek.

He wants to but because I suggested it, he won't do it. I'd remember that obtuse, button-hook strategy for later but what's the point? That's no longer my department. Took A-Look gets the clouds and I get the consequences; that's the arrangement. But he can't stay away from those gold specks forever, he can't wait to see his seal again, I know that. Pretty soon he'll forget whose idea it was and then he'll think it was his idea and crawl over for a peek. Here he comes. He just can't resist his horizon curiosity and he loves seals. Walruses not so much but that's entirely understandable from any point of view except from one walrus to another. Even then sometimes they try to kill each other.

"You were hurt pretty badly, weren't you?"

Who is she talking to? It was just a scratch, a few stitches. Is there somebody else in the room?

Oh, I see. She's talking to Took A-Look. Staring him right in the eyeball too. It sure would be nice if Took A-Look made a friend but that's not his style. Not even with a seal. Go ahead, Took A-Look, say something. He won't. He could, but he won't. Especially not now when he's all covered with Marty slime from slipping and sliding around the clouds, his own clouds to boot; what an outrage for him.

If Took A-Look has anything to do with it, and he pretty much has everything to do with it on account of peace being undeclared, Marty is in for a bad day, a dreadful day, and that will happen a lot sooner than Never-Ending. It might not change anything but that's not Took A-Look's problem. That's Marty's problem and if he doesn't believe that, then he isn't paying attention, he isn't thinking about the Never-Ending test. Sort of like I wasn't paying attention with the wife but that's spoiled milk from another time which is largely irrelevant at the moment. I should have made her irrelevant long before it got to this point but like I said, nobody plans spoiled milk.

"Feeling a little groggy back there?" she asks very sincerely, like she'll accept any answer and not just words. It's pretty clear she knows how to talk with or without words and isn't really hung up on who she is talking to either.

Took A-Look tells me to open the windows a bit more and I do.

"It wasn't very nice what happened, was it?"

Oh Oh, Is she blaming Took A-Look for that? That's no way to make friends, no way at all. Seal or no seal, he gets the clouds and I get the consequences, that's the arrangement. Don't open that forgotten can of smelly old bait. Not unless you want a harpoon in one of those pretty gold specks. He's watching them, wondering why they aren't dancing like before but it's obvious. She is one sad seal, even I can see that. She knows that being hurt on both sides is a real demonstration of sincerity.

"I am so sorry this happened." She said as if to make like we were having a real conversation.

Me too. It sucks. Right, Took A-Look? He nods, which is unusual for him. Not nodding which he does quite often but agreeing with somebody other than himself which is rare lately. And unusual because he is usually right which is why he is in charge these days, no matter how much that hurts. No point resisting that, things just get wrecked which doesn't bother him but it sure bothers me. He's the brave one, not me, but I'm sure you know that by now.

"Are you comfortable enough?"

No.

"Do you want anything?"

Yes.

"Is there anything I can do for you?"

Yes.

Somehow she understands and puts her hand on Took A-Look's roof. Then on one side of the wall, then on the other side. Very cool and extremely gentle. Very seal-like, when they aren't in a playful mood, which goes without saying. Playful is rough and tumble.

Curious. Why do people say goes without saying when they've already said it? Which makes me wonder, did something happen to the curious cloud?

No, Took A-Look, I'm not talking to you.

No, Took A-Look, I don't know who I'm talking to, maybe myself, okay?

Fine, go back to your own thoughts, sorry to have bothered you.

He pushes on the jelly sack in front of the window and lets a little of his own light escape. Just a tiny, thin, fast beam of it. No way could she see it.

Come on Took A-Look, give her a break. You like her, admit it. We could use a friend in this place, why not her?

"We'll see." she says like she is following our private conversation and maybe knows somebody who would make a good friend for Took A-Look. I hope not. That's one person I'm not sure I want to meet.

Took A-Look giggles with the thought. If he made a friend, that could be a problem. It's more than enough trouble to deal with his enemies and that doesn't even include the her who created this whole situation of undeclared peace. Ranting and raving, here and there, slam, slam, slam. I could take it, but not Took A-Look, he got fed up with her. He's the brave one, that's why I get the consequences. All in all though, it's not such a bad trade, at least all her aggravation stopped.

Oh oh. Just like I didn't want this to stop, Marsha gets up and with a pat on my shoulder, she leaves.

Too bad, we were both enjoying it and it's been a long, long time since we've enjoyed anything together.

See you later, Marsha.

She looks over her shoulder like she is saying goodbye and maybe she is but I'm pretty sure it isn't to me.

CHAPTER 10

"Mrs. Arlene Mallory is here to see you, Dr. Coleman."

"Thank-you Gail, please tell her I will be with her in a moment. Could you come in for a second?"

"Right away, Dr. Coleman."

In spite of the fact that Gail had greeted dozens, hundreds actually, of family, friends, lovers, authorities and every other variety of interested and disinterested visitor, only Marsha had ever bothered to ask for her opinion before running head first into an ugly confrontation which could easily be avoided. Then again, all the other doctors she had worked for had been men and most of them seemed to relish confrontation because they couldn't lose. The system was set up that way and while there were some good reasons for it, mostly it made them into petty gods and totalitarian dictators.

Gail closed the door behind herself, pushing it firmly until the latch clicked solidly. It was an act of complete professionalism and it was intended for Arlene Mallory's ears. As if to tell her that authority wasn't just behind the desk but in the doors and walls and hallways and she had best be careful with her behavior while she was in this hospital.

She placed the file containing Mr. Black's commitment papers on the desk but didn't sit down. Marsha would check the paperwork first, as she always did, but that wasn't an insult.

"Very good, Gail. Thank-you." she said after reviewing the documents a little more thoroughly than usual.

Marsha was always quick to compliment and to Gail it was just as much a compliment to have her work checked as it was to hear the words. She hardly ever made a mistake but Marsha didn't take that for granted any more than she would skip the compliment. She always wanted the best for everybody, but for some reason or another, Gail knew that Mr. Black was more than just anybody and she had checked and cross-checked the documents herself just to be positive there weren't any extra spaces between the words let alone an actual error.

"What am I in for, Gail?"

"Good news, Marsha. The daughter is really concerned. No resemblance to Mrs. Black, attitude-wise or otherwise. I think she's good people. Not likely a happy story but not the enemy either. She knows something but I don't think she wants to talk about it."

"Thanks again."

Marsha's smile began to fade. If Gail had anything else to say, she still had a second or two left to get it out in the open but she didn't and left before the smile had completely disappeared.

She opened the door, smiled and nodded at Eric Black's daughter. That was all it took for her to stand and start for the office but Gail didn't give way at the doorway. On the surface she became an unintentional road block. Not enough to give offense but enough that she wasn't looking at Marsha when she entered the room and that gave her a brief moment to study her visitor.

It was a move which one of Gail's former bosses had taught her and no one had ever told her to stop so she still did it. Of course that old boss was obsessed about a lot of things but that particular tactic made sense; it gave the doctor a quick, uninterrupted, unchallenged moment to make their first impression without confusion from the other person doing the same thing. Sometimes it was the visitor who needed committing and not the patient. Exactly what happened to Mrs. Reynolds when she brought in her son Lawrence after he had set fire to the couch, while she was having a nap on it and thought that made it all her fault.

"How do you do, Mrs. Mallory. I am Doctor Coleman." She stood and extended her hand but stayed behind her desk. First impressions told her she should keep her distance.

The handshake was accepted and complete before the daughter finished speaking. "How is my father, Doctor? I would like to see him right away."

First impressions were correct. Straight to the point, spoken by a woman who knew what she wanted and usually got it. She was trim, neat and dressed for business in a blue skirt suit and a white open neck blouse. A gold chain was draped perfectly around her thin neck. If she wasn't a lawyer herself, she had seen one pretty recently, probably that morning. She knew her rights.

"Please sit down Mrs. Mallory, I am hoping you will help me understand what is happening with your father." We'll see if Gail is right, thought Marsha. Somebody is the enemy, who is it?

"Help you?"

"Your father is seriously ill, Mrs. Mallory. I know that can be hard to believe but he isn't here by accident. He is very seriously ill."

"Not Dad. He's never been sick in his life. What are you talking about? Seriously ill is ridiculous. This is all part of her plan."

Gail was right. Her plan could only mean Brita Black's plan. That had to be sidelined as quickly as possible, if possible "Mrs. Mallory, your father is very sick and we don't have the slightest bit of useful information to help us understand why. Not the slightest bit. I need your help and, more importantly, your father needs your help."

Marsha turned her eyes to the file containing the commitment papers, opening some space between them. Space in which 'not even the slightest bit of useful information' could be internalized and the blame shifted to the real enemy, Eric Black's psychosis, before Dr. Marsha Coleman was honored with that unwelcome distinction, throw in Brita Black for good company.

"What could possibly be wrong with him? I can't believe this. This is not happening. It's just not…not…"

"Please sit down, Mrs. Mallory."

"Thank-you, Doctor…"

"Coleman."

"Coleman."

"Your father is…as far as we know right now…somewhat catatonic. Do you understand what that means?"

"He has withdrawn…" She couldn't finish her definition as her brain suddenly realized who was being called that ugly name.

"Something like that. Unfortunately, even today, the physical or psychological sources for the disorder are poorly understood. We understand the symptoms like mutism, stupor, excessive motor activity and so on but the cause of the condition is still more of a mystery than it is a known."

"Can he talk, does he understand what is going on around him?"

"At the moment, probably yes to both questions, although he hasn't said anything yet. But that can change, and change as quickly to the negative as the other direction. I have to tell you that. He is in a very fragile position. What we do now is very important, and urgent."

Marsha held the daughter's stare. Longer was always better and to prove it, the daughter started her questioning almost immediately.

"Are you telling me that he going to get worse before he gets better? Is that what you are trying to tell me? That you know him better after two days compared to me who has known him all my life? I won't listen to psycho-babble, doctor. This is all wrong. This is all her doing, I know that for a fact and you are falling right into the trap she has set for him. I won't allow it. Not for a minute, I won't."

And you want to take him away from here as soon as you can because you know better. Right? Like I've never seen this before? Marsha's thoughts preceded her words and she hoped the conversation would stay that way long enough for it to come to the best decision for her patient.

"Maybe it is wrong. Maybe I am wrong. Maybe the world is wrong. But that doesn't matter. Your father needs your help. You can either believe me now or I can take you to him and you will see for yourself. If that's what it takes to convince you, fine but…and understand this to the depths of your soul, Mrs. Mallory, that could be the biggest mistake you have ever made. That could result in his undoing instead of your understanding. He is very fragile, very much on the edge of his own existence and you might just become the force that pushes him over that edge."

Arlene Mallory didn't give a flying twist for the ultimatum she had just heard but she damn sure paid attention to it, a lesson learned from her father. 'Ultimatums precede action. First comes the warning which grows to a threat that finally distills itself to an ultimatum which might, or might not, announce action. Ultimatums rarely work but they always signal that action is coming, perhaps the one stated but not necessarily so. And for that reason, an ultimatum can be more dangerous to the one who gives it than the one who receives it. So pay attention, Arlene. Use the information provided, heed the warning, then decide what to do and do it fast.'

Arlene took a long, hard look at Doctor Coleman and cleared her mind for the sole task of assessing the danger which she presented or represented, she wasn't sure which. Also a tactic she had learned from her father. 'Take your time Arlene, go at your own pace, your own way. Control the negotiation. Study your adversary.'

The woman was almost pretty. No, actually, she was very pretty, but either hiding it or neglecting it. Facial structure which would not only hold up over time but improve with age. Not careless with her appearance but not particularly caring about it either. Nondescript, dark brown hair that could easily be colored into attractive, beautiful hair if cut properly. She should have her eyebrows shaped at the same time.

Wide spaced, green eyes with gold specks but not almond enough to be bedroom sensuous. A little more eye liner and some eye shadow would do wonders. Skin tone that held secrets of its own. Some olive to it and something else too, a touch of red, no, more like native copper. An almost pretty package that anyone else would have turned into exotic. Then, with the right wardrobe, that shapely body, hidden underneath that lab coat, could, with the wave of a hand or the turn of a hip, easily transcend exotic to erotic. Probably not a good idea, considering the nature of her work.

Her voice was another thing completely. Refined and controlled but with an undertone of authority and seriousness. It went with the eyes. Green with gold specks. Eyes as captivating as a fine porcelain vase, an expensive one made by a master craftsman, long since gone. Strange or natural, she couldn't figure but for certain, everything came back to those eyes.

"Will you help me?" Marsha had used the twenty seconds to complete her second impression. A mouse of a woman. Size two at best but she wore the right clothes, well cut and well sewn. First impression was intended to be delivered with seriousness; combat ready and unafraid to throw the first punch.

Careful with her blonde hair so that it didn't resemble the straw which was probably its early morning appearance. Just the right length to be manageable and just the right cut to fit the 25 to 30 age group to which she belonged. Blue eyes like her father but with an intensity he had lost and with which she was struggling for control.

Arlene's analysis of the doctor hadn't helped her decide. Usually that was all she needed but in this case it wasn't nearly enough. She wasn't surprised. Doctors were good at hiding their thinking. Especially these kinds of doctors; they have their own motives. "I want to see my father."

So much for the threat, the guilt and the logic. "I don't advise it."

"I'm not asking for your advice."

"Then I won't permit it."

"Tomorrow you won't have a choice, I know how it works."

"You won't help me?"

"Tomorrow, Doctor Coleman. Tomorrow and I will take my father away from here. Do you understand me? This is not a negotiation."

How could anyone not understand that? How could anyone not understand the depth of that fear? Who on earth has never imagined, or tried not to imagine, what was now a reality for the poor woman? The mystery that is the human mind. A mystery too compelling, too powerful, too absorbing to resist questioning. Even more irresistible when that mind goes astray and then anyone and everyone has an opinion but no one really knows; sometimes not even the person who should know best; the person whose mind has gone.

Arlene Mallory was facing the ultimate denial shackled to its inevitable reality. Her sanctuary, safety, reason and logic were all standing behind bars, guarding the illusion of free thought, but something unforeseen has gone completely amuck and the worst of fears have escaped. Mom or Dad, brother or sister in an insane asylum. There are no gentle words for such a thing, no words at all, not really. Everyone wanted to deny that reality, escaping that horrible reality was even more important for the person outside it than for the one trapped in it.

Marsha decided to issue a challenge, to respond to the daughter's force with counterforce. "You know Took A-Look, don't you, Mrs. Mallory?"

The response was instantaneous and undeniable. It was written on her face, displayed in her posture and sounded on her breath as she gasped. Marsha knew.

So did Arlene. No way was Took A-Look the problem. That bitch step mother had used that secret to get her way and the doctor was falling for it. No way was Dad sick because of him. No way in the world. It was as clear as it ever was, it was just too damn long living with that bitch of a wife, that witch of a person. She could drive a saint to murder, God knows Arlene had had those thoughts herself. The ultimatum was a sham. Dad might be fragile but who wouldn't be in a place like this? Get him out and he will be perfectly fine, no doubt about it.

"Doctor, I will be back tomorrow at exactly two o'clock. Have him ready to go because I am taking him with me and no one, not you and not that bitch Brita will stop me."

CHAPTER 11

Look, Took A-Look, mashed potatoes and meat loaf, it's Wednesday already.

Time flies, right? Isn't that what makes Never-Ending? Ha Ha Bad joke.

Not talking, Took A-Look?

Or not listening?

Same question right?

See Marty over there? It's a long shot but want to give it a try? Maybe waste a cheap one? Like that one you made out of the bent twig with that piece of sharp river stone and too much leather binding? Who would have thought the leather would swell up so much? Who would have thought? Go ahead, chuck it at him. Aim high and let gravity do the rest.

C'mon Took A-Look, talk to me. What are you waiting for? What's your problem? You don't have to say anything in particular. No one is listening. Say anything, I don't mind.

Fine then, I'll talk. So, here I am. Old and cold, waiting for what I already know absolutely and positively is going to happen but like there is a single chance in a billion that it won't. Just waiting for yea old prehistoric, before God was invented, Medicine Man Shaman to come dredging his sorry ass up into the light to tell me how wonderful everything is now that I am a statue. Yep, that what's I'm doing, that's the problem of the day. C'mon Took A-Look, let's talk. Nobody's listening. Isn't that what you like?

C'mon.

C'mon?

C'mon!

C'mon!!!

No?

Oh, Oh. Don't come over here! For effing Christopher's sake, wife banging notwithstanding, Never-Ending absolutely included because there isn't any other choice, don't come over here, Doctor Marsha.

Oh oh, just like I didn't ask for it, here she comes. Just as sure as Moses went to the Mount, here she comes. This is a very bad time, Doctor Marsha. Very bad. Took A-Look won't even talk to me. He is demanding silence. Don't mess with that. Please don't mess with that.

Please watch out. It's one thing to be around Took A-Look in a hospital bed and another thing altogether different to be around him when he isn't all strapped down. Don't take a chance with your pretty gold specks and lovely green seas, he's not in a seal mood, that's for sure.

Check out those mashed potatoes Took A-Look. Ummmm…your favorite picture…Ridges. Contrast. Little creamy mountains. Nice color. Shadows too. I can send some smell back there if you like.

Where are you Took A-Look? Damn it. Where are you?

Well I'll be. She walked right by us. Who would have thought? You missed it, Took A-Look. You missed your favorite seal because you don't want to talk to me. What do you think she thinks about that, about you? Aren't you the least bit sorry? Aren't you even the least bit curious? How about sad, surely you have some of that.

* * * * *

There has to be a way to get through. There must be a reason. Mrs. Black was right about the mashed potatoes. How much more does she know?

I suppose we've released patients into family care and custody who are in worse condition than Eric. He seems to be managing his supper.

But it won't last, it can't. Mrs. Black and her mean son-of-a-bitch lawyer will make certain of that. They'll make mincemeat out of him just as she promised to do to me and then I'll have to say he should have been committed but I didn't do it.

And why?

Because of some stupid feeling, some wayward thought without real substance, something so unscientific I couldn't even whisper it to a judge without getting kicked out of court.

But if I do commit him, his wife will run away with his wealth and his daughter will be after me with even greater vengeance.

Me, me, me.

What does that matter?

He is the one who will pay, as if that hasn't already started when somehow it's my belief it is also ending.

Belief, lots of times stronger than fact but a completely unreliable witness in the courtroom.

What is he thinking?

Who is Took A-Look and where did he come from?

And why, why does this all seem so familiar?

CHAPTER 12

Sons will be sons until they take a wife, daughters are daughters all their life.

In the final analysis, lousy choice of words, Arlene realized, there really wasn't much choice. Maybe something was wrong with Dad. She had replayed the conversation with the doctor over and over. She had memorized the look, the tone, the body language and it always came back to the same result. Marsha Coleman simply wasn't the type of woman, or doctor, who would kid around about her father's condition. And there was something else, something which Arlene couldn't ignore, something that told her Marsha Coleman already had a special relationship with her father. It wasn't a certainty by any means but Arlene could sense the fine hairs on her arms waving in their own little electric current and that meant something was up.

At the very least, before taking his fate into her hands, she should listen and the more she thought about it, the less the ultimatum was an ultimatum because she had to admit, she wasn't really paying proper attention at the time. No, it was more like an opinion, a professional one, and, if the doctor was right, it was Dad who would suffer. Plus, there was the minor issue of Took A-Look. Dad hadn't said anything so that left only one other source for that bottom drawer family secret, the Step-Mother Devil Brita. And she wouldn't go away, she wouldn't let go of that secret. The fight was on and Arlene needed somebody in her corner and maybe that somebody was Marsha Coleman.

The night had been pure torment, the morning wasn't any better or any brighter and the meeting with her lawyer capped it all off like the only cure for her headache was a bullet to the brain. Without actually admitting it, the stupid lawyer spent most of the time explaining his own incompetence by insisting that she should go to someone who specialized in matters of mental competency. As if that wasn't enough, he also wouldn't listen to a damn thing she tried to get him to agree with. Like, specifically, her father's mental competency wasn't the real issue and the Step-Mother Devil Bitch Brita had no right to commit him so she could steal his money. She was the enemy, so earn your retainer and go after her with your writs and torts.

No wonder people think lawyers are so useless. The whole point of the meeting was to protect Dad, not help Brita commit him and all the lawyer could say to that simple logic was that Arlene should, at all costs, keep the doctor from committing him even if that meant she had to do it herself. It was crazy, the bloody lawyer belonged in the hospital and her father belonged at home.

Crazy and not a single ray of hope anywhere. Not a single decent choice in the lot. When the two o'clock appointment finally rolled around she felt like she was being swallowed up in her own grave.

The secretary showed her into the office, precisely on time.

Precisely at the time Doctor Coleman decided it was time to stop beating around the bush. "Tell me about Took A-Look, Mrs. Mallory."

There wasn't any doubt about who was in command. She wasn't going to give anything until she got something. Committed or not committed wasn't open for discussion until Arlene delivered the goods on Took A-Look, which, for the first time that day, actually made some sense.

If she really didn't think Took A-Look was bad, maybe she shouldn't be afraid to talk about him and Took A-Look wasn't bad, at least he never used to be. What the hell indeed, she had nothing and everything to lose; not very often that happens simultaneously. Truth time. Bloody hell. Then again, what the hell she thought, look around, it fit and it wasn't a loss either. She didn't give in because she had to, it was her only choice.

"I don't exactly know Took A-Look, Doctor Coleman. I can sense him, but I don't know him, not like you know another person." The words tumbled out of their own accord. Hours and hours of thinking and questioning had left her tired and confused. All the explanations and all her rehearsed words were obliterated by Marsha's direct and straight to the point 'Tell me about Took A-Look' introduction. That was not an ultimatum.

So she resigned herself to the fact and let it come out in any order it wanted to come out. Perhaps, that way, she might even learn something about it herself. The doctor listened attentively and didn't interrupt.

Marsha wasn't about to stop the flow. Whatever she heard was more than what she knew and she would take anything and everything as long as it was there for the taking. The daughter gave up her thoughts like she was handing out Halloween candy, little tricks and treats with every memory that came to her front door.

At least that was something, at least she was talking. Probably too late, with every passing day it seemed like Eric Black was slipping deeper and deeper into another world. Every day? The garden episode was not even two days ago and last night he couldn't take his eyes off the mashed potatoes. When she checked him earlier in the morning, he was banging his head against the side of his bed. What kind of a world was he entering?

Arlene's story was interesting, so was the way she told it. Like it had happened to someone else.

Before her birth mother died, Took A-Look had never been mentioned. She was six when Mom, real name was Shelley, had left her little daughter. It was so long ago that both Mom and Shelley were just names. Not persons, just names, just shallow, shadow vestiges of personae nondescript for a young woman who only really knew or thought of herself as a daughter through her father's eyes. Mom, Shelley, whoever, was just a photograph in an album scarcely ever opened.

It was Took A-Look who had, on a lonely, dark and scary night, explained the death of the woman in the photograph. She was a little girl, lying on her bed, crying her heart away, when he came to her.

'Don't be afraid. Not for your Mom and not for yourself. People die because that is the way. It has always been the way, a way as old as the rocks themselves. There is nothing to fear, you will understand it, if you try. Everything and everyone is part of Never-Ending. You are part of it and so is your mother. She is with you and will always be with you. She may speak to you or she might not but she is with you. Never-Ending, believe in it daughter, it will make your life worth living and your death without fear.'

A comforting hand and a warm hug; tears shed on his shoulder. She pretended, at that moment, it was her father talking yet knew then and even more so over time, she knew it wasn't Father or Eric or Mr. Black or any of the other names by which he was known. But to her it was just another name and there was always peace, always harmony so she was no more afraid of another name than she was of any of the others. She accepted it because what a little girl doesn't fear can't be wrong and because belonging and acceptance go hand in hand with loving and being loved. It made perfect sense for a little girl.

After that, she didn't think about who was who for a long time but she knew her father's special friend was always there. When she was teased at school for being small or when she was confused by a world at war with itself, he was there. When she tried and failed or when something in her world was falling to pieces, he was there with his wisdom and his strength. Eventually, she asked his name and with her father's voice she heard: 'I am Took A-Look'. What a funny name, but what a perfect one.

And it all seemed perfectly natural because she had grown up with him. Took A-Look and Father, Eric, Mr. Black and Dad. All dimensions of the same person, all seeing with the same eyes but seeing things slightly differently and not afraid of holding, or expressing, differing views.

For all the time she could remember, it made sense and then, when she tried explaining it to Brita, to make things better for everyone, she made a huge mistake. Trusting that woman for a single second was a mistake. That was the undoing. Brita couldn't, or wouldn't leave him alone. She kept on picking and picking, like Took A-Look was a scab and not a person.

She had lost her mother and now she was about to lose her father and that caused a tear to drop and her story to stop.

"How did your mother die?" Marsha asked absently.

"No one ever told me. All they said was that she passed on."

"Were you ever asked about it? By a physician for your medical background?" Someone must have asked that question, it was inconceivable that they hadn't. Marsha sensed something dark in the way Arlene avoided the question and as if to confirm it, her hostility returned.

"Of course I was asked. And I told them just what I told you, she passed on, natural causes. For God's sake this isn't about me, it's about Dad. I want to see him, if I can't talk to him or be with him, at least I want to see him."

"I still don't recommend it. Your father is..."

"Tortured by that gold-digging bitch of a wife of his. That's what he is and that's all he is. I intend to take him away from her just as much as I intend to take him away from you. Now, doctor, I want to see my father NOW." It all made sense. Took A-Look had never been bad for Dad before and he wouldn't be bad now. She shouldn't have told her step-mother about him and the doctor probably didn't deserve it either. Away from both of them and everything would be fine.

"Mrs. Mallory, how can I make you understand? Your father is withdrawing from us and the further he withdraws the more likely it is that he will never come back. You could be the cause of that. Is that what you want?" Anger had to be countered with determination and logic, loaded with guilt. It was a dirty trick but she had to get the woman's attention while she still had the chance. There was absolutely no doubt in her mind that if Arlene Mallory walked away again, they would be on opposite sides forever. Opposite sides fighting for the same thing with no winners and Eric getting the worst of the worst.

Arlene Mallory's hostility turned to anger. Anger which lasted mere seconds and she couldn't vocalize a single word in order to keep it going before it was flooded into submission with tears. She was damned determined to do the right thing and figured that the only thing she could do, had to be, by default, the right thing. She had to get her father away from this dreadful place and tend for him as he had done for the little girl who was still inside herself. It was a heartbreaking moment and one that took all Marsha's strength to resist comforting. She had to resist the transference of that pain. She needed strength, not sympathy. A lot of strength and unfortunately, in all likelihood, it might be needed for a long, long time.

"Mrs. Mallory..." she started but was interrupted.

"Please call me Arlene, doctor. I don't know what to do. Please help my father. Please let me see him." came through the sobbing and tears which ebbed and flowed as quickly as her own thoughts could break free from the emotion. She knew she had made a decision, her words had said as much but her heart was everything except committed to what her mind had already accepted.

Marsha knew there would be more to come and not just today. Arlene Mallory had much more on her mind than what had spilled out of her.

How couldn't she have? The sobbing was dying out more quickly than it should; pain was turning into despair. Please, please don't go down that path. Despair is so passive. Fight it. Fight it, Arlene.

"I should have seen this coming. I should have done something. I should have known. I should have known what was happening. They…the two of them…didn't always agree but I thought that was normal…that they would work it out like everyone works out issues, like a marriage of sorts." More tears, more sobs, more unhappiness than a loved one would ever want to give or see taken. Marsha handed her a tissue, then another.

"There is no sense in blaming yourself, Arlene. You are not responsible for this." She said it sincerely, to make up for the guilt she had induced but could not honestly admit. "But you can help us now. Help us understand what is happening and help us to make certain that your father is safe."

"I will, Doctor Coleman. I will do everything I can. Believe me, I will. But can I see him? Just for a moment. My heart is breaking. I have to see him."

Of course she has to see him just like she knows she shouldn't. She wants to know he is alive but is terrified by what she might find. She wants to see something which will confirm that he is still there, still her father. In the face of all that is unreasonable and unreasoning, she wants a reason for hope. She doesn't want to be devastated, but that's what will happen. That's what always happens in meeting a person familiar who has become a complete stranger, a catatonic. If only we knew why. Why does it happen? Chemistry, biology, psychology, physiology. All combined like flavors in a soup made of sweet, wholesome ingredients that somehow turns to poison.

"Two things, Arlene." She waited until the woman's mind had grasped the words and joined them together to form a life raft out of the debris floating around her.

"Two things? What two things?"

"First, we need you to sign the commitment papers. Then, you can see your father. You cannot talk to him and he cannot see you, but you can see that he is…safe."

"She hasn't already committed him?"

"No, she hasn't. For…let me say…strategic reasons, she wants me to do that. Your father has not and, at the moment, cannot, commit himself. But you can commit him and that might just hold his legal world together long enough for him to get well or at least keep her from taking everything else away from him."

"Where do I sign?" Arlene suddenly understood the 'strategic reasons' as the bafflegab her lawyer had spewed out so endlessly that morning. That was the connection, that was why she had to do what she didn't want to do. She felt a hot rush of hope flush through her veins with the realization that if the doctor could help her father then she could also do something positive, like throw the biggest legal wrench in the world into her step-mother's greedy plans.

She signed the papers without bothering to read them, an act of trust that would not be repeated with the papers she intended for Brita Black. The fight was on; there were no rules and no safe territory. Arlene would and could fight that fight until the end of time. Thanks to her father's planning and generosity she had all the resources necessary to do it and that wasn't even a fraction of her war-chest compared to her determination.

Brita Black was in for a surprise and this time Arlene would keep all her options open and all her cards hidden. There would be no ultimatums from Arlene Mallory, just one preemptive strike after another. Unrelenting and Never-Ending.

From hating lawyers a few hours ago she now knew differently. However many lawyers Brita Black had, Arlene would have just as many. For defense. The rest of those wolves would tear her apart.

CHAPTER 13

"Hello Eric. Do you remember me?"

Marty Slime Bucket.

"Marty."

Slime Bucket.

"You look good today."

Arm-crushing liar.

"Let's get you back to the garden for a little fresh air, you'll behave today won't you?"

It's not me you have to worry about.

Same scene, new day, eh Took A-Look? How are you feeling?

Me too. Still a little slippery back there is it? No? Good. Want the windows open some more? Maybe a little music? No, I haven't seen the seal lately, why? Did you want to see her?

He walks over, a little unsteadily, and gives the fart cloud a big boot, producing a dandy one. After the cloud-kicking incident and all that came with it, he's pretty much back to his old self. I'm happy for him.

He's happy too as he strolls over to the window, yawning like Rip Van Winkle and looking around like it was a brand new world which maybe it is, still not mine to say, not mine to judge.

No seal though, too bad.

I can't stay mad at him forever even with a never-ending guarantee, parts and labor included. Sooner or later he will declare peace again. It's in his nature. Like rocks are rocks until somebody turns them into a statue, but they're still rocks and will be again. That's the whole major point of Never-Ending. It's not magic even if sometimes that's the only way to completely understand it.

* * * * *

Arlene may have got what she wanted but she certainly didn't feel victorious about it. From Dr. Marsha's office on the second floor, in a wing of the hospital which was mostly administration, it looked like any other hospital until they left for the ward.

She passed through a secure door and listened to Marsha announce their departure from safe and secure to vulnerable and unpredictable: 'Marsha Coleman and Arlene Mallory, daughter of Eric Black, supervised visit.'

The door closed behind them and locked automatically, ominously, thought Arlene. After that, it didn't look, feel, smell or sound like any other hospital Arlene had ever been in. She shivered but it had nothing to do with the temperature and she knew it was because her self-defenses were taking over and she was suddenly ashamed of herself. Poor Dad was stuck in this chaos and she felt responsible for it even though logic told her she wasn't. She wondered if logic worked at all on this side of the door.

The moment was not made any easier as she walked in silence beside the doctor who seemed to be completely comfortable, smiling and occasionally waving to patients and staff. Lots of people were milling around; it looked like the accommodation part of the facility, a hallway of metal doors each with a small rectangular window at eye level and strong lever-operated passage sets that could be locked from the outside. Half way down the hall, they came to a wide, open staircase that wound up to the third floor and down to ground level. They went down and continued in the direction they had been travelling. An elevator was opposite the stairwell and although she had never been claustrophobic she was glad they didn't use it.

She could smell food but it was an institutional smell which didn't invoke hunger or even curiosity. It was just slightly stronger than the smell of bleach, laundry, stale coffee, unwashed human beings, the faint smell of cigarette smoke and a few other unique but unidentifiable odors. A minute later and they turned into another hallway, this one short and opening into a large room with windows to the outside and the smell of fresh air carrying a scent of cut grass. There were twenty or thirty people in the room, about half of them turned to look at them; the others were either preoccupied in conversation or held captive by their own thoughts.

Marsha took her by the elbow and guided her across the room to a window that looked out onto the garden. When she saw it, she adjusted her opinion, garden being vastly overstated for an area which was mostly concrete pathways intersected by a few thin grassy patches all bordered by some low shrubs planted against the high wall that surrounded everything. No gate or other opening to the outside. For reasons she couldn't quite understand, her second impression of the garden was dedicated to figuring out how to escape from it. She concluded it wouldn't be easy, especially with the obvious presence of the staff who were well-positioned and watchful.

"Your father is over there, Arlene, sitting in the shade of that tree by the wall." Marsha said quietly and noted that Sorenson did what he was told to do and kept the poor man isolated. Head orderly or not, disobeying that order would have had consequences that even he was smart enough to know would be swift and non-negotiable.

"It's so far away. He looks terrible. All bent like that. Has he said anything? He looks awful. Why does he look like that?"

"It is very difficult to control the response of a patient's adjustment to this place and the body often reflects what the mind is experiencing. It often reflects that inner conflict or anguish. Some people find it easy to adjust and others have a more difficult time. Your father is about in the middle of that range. He will adjust to his new surroundings over time and then he will look more…more natural."

"What happened to his arm?"

"Unfortunately, he had an uncontrolled motor episode and he injured it." With a little interference from staff, Marsha thought and looked for Sorenson who was, as she expected, nowhere to be seen.

"He broke it? How…"

"Not broken actually, we put a cast on it to help it heal and keep it from being re-injured. It happens sometimes. Even under restraints they have more than enough strength to seriously hurt themselves. In a sense it is the opposite of what he is doing, or more correctly, not doing now; it is pronounced motor immobility instead of excessive motor activity."

"But why is he sitting like that?"

Probably because Marty Sorenson positioned him like that. Because sometimes the staff treated patients like they were mannequins. Positioning them, when the patient allowed it, like bizarre statues or when the patient couldn't be manipulated, they put the rigid, resistant body in a corner or hovering over a desk or something equally inhuman. All for their own amusement. Of course it could also be a not so subtle message to Marsha about who gives orders and who executes them. But that was a fight for another day.

"It is symptomatic of the illness, Arlene. I'm afraid I can't give you a very clinical explanation for it."

"What has he said? What has he told you about what is happening to him?"

"Nothing Arlene. Your father hasn't said a word." True but not the complete truth. Steve, on Marty's orders, had talked to Julia Reynolds. Julia had several stories to tell about the garden episode. 'His teacher is an idiot' were the words she chose to remember.

Then the excessive motor control incident and while those two things had to be related the only person who could explain how they were related wasn't talking.

"This is much worse than I imagined, in every way, it is much worse." Arlene said quietly but with clear distress.

More than anything else in the world, she just wanted to hug her father and be hugged in return. She imagined that he had to be in great pain and it hurt her as much to think about it as she imagined it hurt him to feel it. If only she could reach him, just for a second, just long enough to tell him that she loved him. How many times had she thought that? It reminded her how very close they were, how sometimes they could carry on a conversation like it came from a single mind.

It was hard to leave and Marsha could feel Arlene's conflict with deciding the lesser of two lousy options: hard to leave but impossible to stay.

* * * * *

I feel it too, Took A-Look. What do you think it is?

He threw the bent twig, broken rock, too-much-leather-wrapping-spear into the seal cloud and out she popped. He'll get the spear later. Took A-Look is a lot of things but neat isn't one of them and if I've said that before, it's still true.

I don't think so Took A-Look. Maybe though, but I can't see her, can you? You want the window moved? You'll have to do it, it's stuck. I'm tired too. Personally I'd rather listen to some music. What do you think?

He gets up and looks around and around. Who knows why? It's not like he doesn't already know every square inch of every square inch back there. It's not like there is anything new, anything he hasn't seen thousands of times before. Absolutely nothing gets past him, not even when I am sleeping. Still, he looks around, maybe searching for the source of his boredom or perhaps looking for things that would answer an unasked question or explain a mystery only he could know about.

Then Sorenson walked past the window and distracted him. Sorenson and Took A-Look will always be enemies. Sorenson doesn't have a clue what he has started. Never-Ending is a word with more consequences to it than anyone can imagine. Flattened on a one way street is just a minor detail compared to a Never-Ending battle with somebody like Took A-Look. He's the brave one, remember?

* * * * *

Arlene felt like she carried all the uncertainty, unpredictability and fear from the ward right through the security door which moments before had represented the border between sanity and insanity.

"It's very likely that he will never be the same again, Arlene. One day he may be able to live on his own, but no one is ever the same after an experience like this. It is impossible to say when that will happen, or even if it will happen."

"I want the best for him, Doctor Coleman. The very best you can do. What can I do? How can I help?"

Good, she's a fighter. Let's hope it's in the genes and let's hope she got it from her father. Marsha explained the process.

She needed to complete her assessment. All kinds of measurements and tests. Maybe there was a physical cause, a vitamin deficiency, an excess of this metal, an imbalance of that hormone or this mineral or anything that can be measured which is damn near everything. Unlikely to be the cause but that was the place to start. After that, drugs. Some mild and some deadly. This dosage with this affect and those side effects, a different dosage and a different response; some good, some lousy. The distinct possibility of temporary or permanent damage to the neuro-receptors which could be beneficial or could be harmful. Long-term or short-term improvements or setbacks, completely unknown most of the time. Psychotherapy if the drugs work and she can get a response from him or even if she can't. She didn't pull any punches because optimism and hope can do more damage than anything else and not just to Arlene.

What she didn't say, but which she sensed Arlene already knew, was that somehow she had to find a way to talk to Took A-Look. He was the shortcut to all the therapy in the world. He had to be. She knew it, something was telling her that. Something, like something inside herself, maybe it was that feeling she hadn't been able to shake ever since she laid eyes on him. 'Laid eyes on him' - such a strange but accurate expression, a fast beam of bright light coming from a dark, mostly black place in Eric Black's pupil.

Gail set up appointments for the daughter and gave her the appointment card on her way out. Once a week for the next six weeks, one hour sessions. Poor Marsha. Her case load was already busting at the seams and now this. Why the hell don't they get some more help in this facility. It's all ass-backwards. Like everyone is satisfied because they have measured the problem and know that it is getting bigger only so budgets can stay the same or get cut less than planned. More people on the streets or in their homes with more and deeper problems. All they ever bloody approve is more drug testing because the drug companies give it out for free and it would be a bloody outrage to test them on criminals first.

She updated Marsha's calendar and closed it like a secret diary. It didn't have to be treated like that, but it was habit learned from Arbuckle, two bosses prior to Marsha. He was a heavy drinker and would cross out the appointments he couldn't remember and insisted that no one ever saw his appointment calendar. He hated going to court because he had to be sober.

As if cued by the thought of going to court, Brita Black came marching through the door, heading straight for Marsha's office, combat ready and not needing any provocation to fire the first shot. Gail picked up the phone pressed seven and said loud and clear, "Send security to Doctor Coleman's office and tell them to bring a straightjacket and sedation. Code Fifty"

Whatever Code Fifty meant stopped Brita Black in her in her tracks but it didn't change her attitude one iota. "I want to see Doctor Coleman, right now." she said with undisguised contempt for the lowly secretary she had once been herself. Once but never bloody again would she kiss ass like that. Now it was their turn and she wouldn't make it easy for them.

"See this button, Mrs. Black. It's called a panic button. If I press it, you will be in more trouble than you care to think about and make no mistake about it, they are already on their way and this will just ensure they do something to you that you don't even want to think about. Believe me, we know how to deal with people who break the rules around here."

Brita was used to making threats and knew the secretary wasn't bluffing. "Don't tell me that I need a bloody appointment. Jesus Effing Christopher, don't tell me that. That's all I've got to say to you, your little power trip is over, hear me? I know my rights. Is she in there? Do your effing job."

"And I know your rights as well as my own, Mrs. Black, and you are over-stepping them. Sit down and I will see if the doctor has time to see you." Calm in the presence of fury, the only way to deal with it.

"Jesus Effing Christopher." She muttered to the wall and tried to hide her frustration by sizing up which of the two chairs in the small waiting room might be more elegant or advantageously positioned than its identical twin. "How can you people make something so simple so bloody complicated? You bloody belong here, all of you." spoken to the chairs and not to the bloody secretary who, for the moment, had the upper hand which was still way too close to the bloody panic button for comfort.

Gail didn't move until her opponent was seated.

Poor Mr. Black. Poor Marsha. She decided it would be better to see Marsha in person and not talk to her on the intercom so she went to the closed door and knocked on it gently a couple of times before opening it enough to stick her head through the crack. She gave Marsha a 'what do I do?' look and waited.

Marsha had heard everything including the code fifty. She was also expecting Mrs. Black. In a way, she was looking forward to it and allowed herself a slight smile even though she knew she was prejudging the woman and that wasn't very professional. Nor was it very subtle, Gail caught the smile, understood the reason behind it, and let some brightness into her own eyes. Marsha frowned at herself in admonishment. Gail caught that too.

"We're all human, you know." Gail whispered.

"We don't say?" Marsha whispered in return.

"No, you're right. We're not." Gail pointed to the waiting room. "Do you have time?" She hoped for no but knew the answer would be yes and then realized what she really regretted was not being present to witness Mrs. Black getting a chunk torn out of her ego or wherever Marsha chose to start slicing. Marsha wasn't exactly what you'd call a fighter but she didn't back down and could more than hold her own in any kind of cat fight with any amount of emotion.

"Bring it on."

Interesting choice of word. 'It,' not she, Gail reflected.

"The doctor will see you now, Mrs. Black." As usual, Gail partially blocked the woman's path so Marsha could get an early read on her visitor's mental state. It worked too, Mrs. Black was livid as she pushed her way past the secretary and into the office.

"You know why I am here, Doc. Have you committed my husband? You'd better say yes or I'll personally take the moron straight to my lawyer and get him certified hopeless. She's a mean son-of-a-bitch. Trust me on that one."

"Gail, stay here, please." Marsha pushed a button on the machine beside the telephone. "Mrs. Black, this conversation is being recorded."

Two statements which produced the expected result as Mrs. Black tried to figure out if the game was still the same or if someone had changed the rules and failed to inform her. They did have to kiss her ass, didn't they?

Gail took a couple of steps into the office and stood behind one of the two chairs facing her boss. It wasn't the first time she had been asked to witness a discussion between a doctor and family or concerned who-evers but it was the first time Marsha had ever asked her to do it.

Mrs. Black was obviously planning her next move. Tape recorders and witnesses had put her on alert. She started toward the vacant chair.

"Don't bother sitting down Mrs. Black, you aren't going to be here that long."

Gail had never seen Marsha quite so intense. Completely and utterly determined. It occurred to her that the reason why she thought Marsha wasn't much of a fighter was because she always won before the fight started. Brita Black was in for a thumping and however quickly it happened, she would probably be swallowing her loss for a lot longer than the fight lasted. Marsha didn't give her a second to gather her wits or start an offense.

"Mr. Black has been committed…"

The wife turned triumphant. "Why the hell didn't you call me?"

"…by his daughter."

"What? Jesus Effing Christopher, how the hell did Arlene…Juanita, Jesus Effing Juanita, damn her! That 'effing taco bell is so fired."

"You, Mrs. Black, are not allowed to see or talk to your husband. Nor will you be allowed to send him letters, cards or messages. Absolutely nothing. Not even flowers. Do you understand what I am telling you, Mrs. Black? Do you fully understand what I am telling you?"

If anything, Marsha was getting tougher and tougher by the minute but that didn't seem to matter to Mrs. Black.

"What? You can't do that. He's my husband, I can do anything I want to do to him."

"Wrong. He's my patient. You aren't going near him."

"Like hell I'm not."

"Talk to your lawyer, Mrs. Black. Better yet, listen to your lawyer, because if I see or hear of you coming to this facility again, you are going to need that mean son-of-a-bitch like you've never needed anyone in your life. Did you get that message, Mrs. Black? Do you understand what I am telling you?"

"Damn you. Give me those commitment papers. I want him back. I have a right…"

"Wrong again. You have nothing. Eric Black is my patient and you are leaving this facility right now."

She was seething. "I'm not finished with you, Doctor Effing Coleman, don't you ever believe that."

"Escort her from the facility. If she opens her mouth, tape it shut. Under no circumstances is she to be allowed within sight or sound of Eric Black. If she comes back to this hospital, restrain her, sedate her, lock her in protective custody and call the police. Charges will be laid."

Mrs. Black didn't understand what was going on until she turned around and saw the two orderlies behind her, the same two who had taken her husband away. She was bewildered until they came up to her, one on each side. She tried to shrug off the hands on her elbows but they just got tighter. "That hurts. Stop it you son-of-a-bitch, that's goddamn assault. You'll pay for this, you'll pay big. My lawyer will have you morons for breakfast. She's a mean..."

Marty Sorenson put two wraps of tape over her mouth, all the way around her head. Steve gave him a curious look for a taping job which usually only covered the mouth, ear to ear at the very most. Getting that tape out of her hair was going to take a while, she'd be damn lucky if she didn't have to cut it but that didn't seem to matter to her. Having her mouth and jaw taped only served to increase her fury and she struggled some more so Marty twisted her arm a little. Not enough to hurt her but enough to tell her how quickly that could change.

In all of his twenty years at the hospital, it was the first time he had ever ejected a visitor. He remembered a few who came for a visit and got injected but never this. But more than anything, it was the expression on the doctor's face and the look in her eyes that he would remember. Make that better not forget.

Doctor Marsha Coleman was giving orders like she was in command and that was a bad sign. The doctors never ran the place and they never would. Sooner or later she would have to learn that lesson, and in her case sooner would definitely be better. Sooner as in right now, if only he could figure out how to do it. That was what motivated the extreme tape job which he thought she'd protest but didn't. If anything she actually seemed to approve of it so obviously anything he did to Mrs. Black wasn't going to work.

As soon as they cleared the office doorway Brita gave up the struggle. Marty gave her arm a little squeeze, hoping to get her fired up again and maybe buy some time to figure out how he could get Steve out of the way. He had heard the orders about keeping the woman away from Eric Black and wasn't about to swim up that stream but it was exactly the lesson which Marty had in mind for Doctor Marsha Coleman. Exactly the way to teach her who made the rules and who got to break them. He had seconds to figure it out, seconds to find a way to put A and B together and not get blamed for it.

Mrs. Black didn't respond to the arm twist. She was probably too busy thinking about taking revenge to notice anything he was doing. Just exactly like he was thinking about revenge and both of them were targeting the same skirt. "Are you going to co-operate with me Mrs. Black?" he asked. With a little luck she would think that the squeeze he had given her and was just a nice way of testing her co-operation and not an expression of his authority and control, his first choice.

She nodded but her eyes said no. No with a lot of effing adjectives surrounding it. Too bad he had taped her mouth all the way around her head because now there was no way he could get it off without ripping out half her hair. So, she wouldn't be able to shout or scream at her husband and that severely limited the remaining options.

"Okay then, we'll release you but you must stay between us. Doctor Coleman doesn't want any contact between you and your husband. Understand?"

She nodded. He looked her square in the eyes and she nodded again, this time she definitely understood his lie. Now all he had to do was give her the right signal without giving it to Steve at the same time. Eric Black was in the day room leading into the garden and with her hands free, she wouldn't have a problem getting to him as long as she was really quick about it. She might even be able to pull the tape off her mouth, but that would depend on her pain threshold and how much she liked her hair.

"Just so you know what could happen if you disobey the Doctor, we'll take you through the ward so you can see for yourself where you could end up, see what it's like. Steve, let's take the stairs, not the elevator." Marty hoped that decision would distract Steve's attention away from the fact they would be walking right past the day room where they had left Eric Black. Using a security card from his pocket, not the one on his belt, the three of them passed quietly through the security door leading to the stairway.

He released her arm, Steve did the same, both of them giving her a little more room between them. Not very much, she would have to be very quick, but she looked like she had the legs for it. In fact she was in pretty good shape all the way around. Kind of a socialite type with a little too much make-up for the time of day and the bright yellow dress definitely belonged to some other occasion. A little over-dressed for afternoon tea but a little under-dressed for a cocktail party. Then again, maybe it was the perfect outfit for a husband commitment celebration. Main point being the dress was loose enough that she could easily sprint a dozen yards or more if she was given half a chance.

They were down the stairs and walking toward the corridor that led to the day room and garden when Mrs. Black came up with a way for Marty to communicate to her without arousing Steve's suspicions. With her arms free, she started tugging at the tape on her mouth, trying to peel it back. No way would she be able to unpeel enough to speak but she must have known that within the first couple of seconds. Just as she must have known it would give him the opportunity he needed to tell her what he wanted her to know.

"Not yet Mrs. Black. Not until you are far enough away that Mr. Black can't hear you. You heard *her* orders. Not until we are past the day room and through the doors at the end of this hall."

She was looking him square in the eyes and he was looking straight at the hall leading into the day room and garden. She read him like a road map. A road map with a thick black line indicating the most direct route between A and B. Steve was staring dead ahead, pretty much unconscious of what was being communicated or perhaps only hearing what he wanted to hear, Doctor Coleman's orders being repeated in his head like some kind of comforting mantra that also delivered his bi-weekly paycheck.

She put her hands down like a little school girl who has been caught primping her hair instead of doing her lessons. No doubt about it, she got the message and was taking long, deep breaths through her nose, building up her oxygen reserves.

When they were about fifteen feet from the hall leading to the day room, she slowed her step, not quite coming to a stop but slow enough that both of her guards were suddenly a pace in front of her, then two. Marty stopped to allow her to catch up and Steve followed suit, as usual. Steve was on her left, so was the day room. She came up between them with one long stride, followed by two more long and very quick strides that put her out of arm's reach before she broke into a dead run heading straight for the day room. Her surprise was complete, capturing Steve for a bewildered, confused second while he tried to figure out what she was doing. Not that he hadn't had patients who had run from him before but those were patients and when they ran, most of the time they ran just for the heck of it, not with a purpose.

Besides, never before had a visitor actually tried to break into the day room and Marty watched Steve's struggle to understand what was happening by trying to figure out why it was happening. Until that very moment, Marty hadn't really considered how much conflict this would create; just how beautifully the perverse logic of the ward would operate in the runner's favor. It was one of the first lessons an orderly learned. Just because something was running didn't mean it should be chased. Far from it. The rabbit couldn't escape and sometimes the rabbit actually planned on getting caught because it wasn't a rabbit after all, it was just acting like one. Then the orderly got a big surprise, a surprise that usually hurt for quite a while.

Steve came to the conclusion that Mrs. Black was a rabbit at exactly the same moment Marty came to the conclusion he didn't want to miss a second of what she was planning to do when she got to her husband. By then, Brita had a full head of steam, a good lead on Steve and nothing short of miracle was going to stop her from getting to the dayroom with plenty of gas left in her tank.

CHAPTER 14

Hey Took A-Look, what are you doing back there? Sharpening spears maybe? Are you having fun? This is a pretty nice place don't you think? They call it a day room.

What, no Never-Ending joke about being in a day room?

Fine. Be that way.

Took A-Look has been quiet for a while which isn't anything new nor is it good news or bad news. Sometimes he just wanders around and around even though he knows every square inch of every square inch and what he is really doing is taking cloud inventory. It's a big job and he takes it seriously in spite of the fact that hardly anything ever changes back there. But when it comes to cloud kicking, not only is he fast but he's damn accurate and that comes from supreme cloud knowledge not blind luck.

Lots of planning too if it's going to be perfectly coordinated, like a ballet dancer with an extremely complicated routine to some very fast music with lots of other dancers who might get in the way.

No, maybe not exactly like that. Maybe more like a conductor with a really, really wild piece of music, going absolutely frantic trying to get every last horn to toot at exactly the right time but not all-together. I didn't used to understand how the orchestra ever kept up with such crazy, arm-swinging, stabbing, twitching, hair-flying conducting performances until Took A-Look gave me a first-hand demonstration. That's serious stuff, and he doesn't even have an orchestra. Can you imagine the music he would produce if he had a little help?

Don't forget about the arm, okay, Took A-Look? She said the cast would feel better when the swelling went down. She was right, wasn't she?

He already knew that because he'd checked those clouds several times over but I was hoping that the mention of his favorite seal would divert his preoccupation with cloud inventory. It didn't. Not even a glance at the seal cloud.

Plus, lately, he has been quite interested in everything outside the window which is very odd. Way too much interest from somebody who basically disapproves of everything that is going on out there. It doesn't take a genius to figure out that sooner or later interest and disapproval are going to collide. Sooner or later somebody is going to get a spear up the ass and I can't keep him off balance forever so no point in even trying. He knows it too. He can wait and wait and then I get the consequences. Spear up the ass may be his department but sometimes he forgets who ultimately ends up getting the consequence.

Want me to check out the parrot? You know, Julia? I can hear her but can't see her.

Apparently not.

Fine then. If you're not too damn busy with cloud inventory, would you take a precious second out of your schedule to un-stick the window and turn it a little bit so I can at least watch something? Public enemy number one parked us in the corner and I can't see a thing except for this puke green wall which by now even you must know doesn't have anything going for it. I feel like I'm surrounded by slime.

Thank you. That wasn't such a big deal, was it?

Yes I do appreciate it. Talk about being in a bad mood, like that was such a big deal when you know perfectly well it wasn't.

Fine, go back to your work. Sorry for asking.

Talking to myself, that's what.

And I'm also checking out the parrot over there, not that anyone cares. Nice outfit. Very colorful. All sorts of reds, blues, greens and yellows like a calypso dancer with balloon sleeves. She's talking to the stick man with the bald head. Lollipop, that's a good name for him. Lollipop isn't much of a talker himself but he's a good singer. Innovative too. He can take the words from one song and sing them to the tune of another.

Like an hour ago when he took the words from Tina Turner's Private Dancer and sung them to the tune of Neil Diamond's Cracklin' Rosie. I couldn't remember all the words to Cracklin' Rosie if you paid me a million bucks but when he sings Private Dancer to that tune, I remember every single one of them.

The men come in these places	Ah Cracklin' Rosie get on Board
And the men are all the same	We're gonna ride til there ain't
You don't look at their faces	no more ago, takin' it slow
You don't think of them at all	and Lord don't you know...

Or something like that. Lollipop drools some of his words plus some have to be shortened or extended to match the new music. Try it, it's tougher than you think.

If Lollipop ever gets out of here, the music business is in for a real change in direction. No doubt about it, nobody will ever have to write new words or tunes for a long, long time.

But he isn't singing right now and not because the Parrot is jabbering, I bet. When it comes to self-expression, Parrots have it easy, Lollipops have it tough. But he's thinking, that's plain to see.

Julia Parrot is still on last night's topic. Meat loaf with mashed potatoes. Second choice, spaghetti with meat sauce. What's that called? Ragu. If it needs to be cut up it's already cut up. Of course that's not the topic. Wednesday is the topic, Ragu is just what keeps the topic from being Tuesday. Wednesday is when the Parrot's husband comes to visit. That's the topic. First with Marsha and then with the Parrot until the husband is Ragu and he can leave but she can't. It takes about half an hour, the husband-to-Ragu part, at least that's what she is saying and I have no reason to disbelieve her.

But make no mistake about it, that parrot sure can talk. She must have sixteen million ways of staying on the same topic. Lawrence has the worst of both worlds. A mother he loves to death but who he can't get to. He isn't doing very well, not according to her pre-ragu husband. Lawrence is failing everything. That can happen to dreamers. No doubt about it. Dreamers don't have a big part in the real world. Complete assholes who are full of themselves and create their own reality have a bigger part in this world and if that isn't a crime, it should be. Dreamers are important. Everybody dreams when they sleep and that should be a clue about the importance of dreaming but most people miss that fact completely. Lawrence's teacher is an idiot, but I've said that before and won't make that mistake again. Lawrence really needs help. His dreams are turning into nightmares, with flames.

Lollipop looks like he is about to sing. I'm hoping for something by Peter, Paul, Mary, Stevens, Young, Cosby and Nash or vice versa. It's a wild shot and you can just imagine the complications with paying the royalties.

False alarm. He gets up and leaves the Parrot. Poor Julia. She looks at me but doesn't come over. There's no way I can tell her it's okay, that Took A-Look is busy with his cloud inventory and she wouldn't be a bother to him. She can't find anybody else so she talks to herself. Too bad, all of us could use the company.

I wonder what's for supper. Something colorful would be nice. Except for the parrot, it's pretty bland around here. Various shades of dull, like the faded greens, blues and pinks of everybody's pants and shirts. No matching required. Pink shirt and blue pants or green pants with pink shirt. Totally optional but anybody who can dress themselves gets to decide. Anybody who can't dress themselves wears the same color, top and bottom. That's how they tell the dressers and non-dressers apart. Today, I'm green, like the wall.

Jimmy doesn't help with this decorative catastrophe but he could. He's the only painter we have but he only uses black paint and only does lines which you could argue is drawing and not painting but he does use paint so it's anybody's call. Truth is, you have to be very meticulous to be a good line painter and Jimmy is an outstanding line painter. Too bad he isn't allowed to do floors, walls and ceilings. He has a real knack for perspective. I'll bet he could make a square room look like a sphere or make a hallway look like it goes on and on forever, like in science fiction movies. Maybe even turn it into a vortex. Maybe that's why he isn't allowed to work on anything except paper. It would be too confusing to the staff if the hallways turned into vortex's or if he turned a window into a door and somebody accidentally walked off the third floor into the parking lot.

Yeah it's a neat picture, isn't it Took A-Look? Hey, what are you doing up here? Bored with cloud counting already? Sure those lines could be icebergs. Yeah, a lot of icebergs. You're in a pretty good mood all of a sudden, aren't you? No it's not a crime. Let's not get in a fight, okay?

Holy shit, look what's coming through the door like a downhill freight train with no brakes?

Hot Damn! HOT DAMN TWICE!!! Look at her come.

Holy shit Took A-Look, do you see what I see??? DO YOU SEE THAT, TOOK A-LOOK? THAT'S HER. Hot Damn! Hot diggity-damn, she's back in the crazy contest! I told you. Excellent, fantastic, awesome. C'mon. C'MON CRAZY ASS! We're rooting for you! Always room for one more.

No kidding, I didn't hear her first either so good point. First time ever that she's shut up. Somebody should get the Nobel Peace Prize for that tape job. Two wraps, all the way around. Damn fine, damn fine. C'mon wife, jump in, the water's tepid.

Oh oh. Look out, LOOK OUT JIMMY. A fearsome vortex is heading your way. Whew, close call! Close call Jimmy and lucky for you, those fingernails are damn sharp, good thing she cornered on the table and not your neck.

She's coming our way Took A-Look, she's a-coming to the mountain. Go figure. Think she still loves us. Ha Ha. Think she wants us back?

I know, I know, Took A-Look, you thought of taping her up a long time ago. I know, I know, it should've been done then. But isn't it great now? MARVELOUS you say? You bet it is! C'MON Crazy Ass! Come and get us.

WHAT? What the hell is that?

Is that Steve on her back? It is isn't it?

Totally amazing and pretty damn good riding too.

RIDE'er STEVE, RIDE'er hard and put her away wet!!! Use the spurs! Whip'er up Steve. Whataya think, Took A-Look, is this exciting or what?

Very funny Took A-Look, hilarious in fact. He would have to be a very, very horny muskox to try that, wouldn't he?

C'MOM STEVE RID'ER INTO THE GROUND.

Watch out! Watch out! Mind the Parrot, for crying out loud. Turn'er left, Steve, No, No, No, LEFT, the other LEFT for Pete's sake. Close call, close call, Julia.

Oh oh, LOOK OUT! Look out Steve. Look out cowboy! She's taking another corner, a tight one. Don't let her throw you boy, HANG ON! Hang on for dear life! Ride'er Cowboy, Rider her 'til she's hot then put her away cold.

Isn't this the most excitement ever, Took A-Look? You bet it is. YOU BET IT IS! She's looking right at us, barreling right down on us like a mean old bull. C'MON STEVE, C'MON Brita! Don't nobody give up, no quitting, you hear?

Ah, you're right. She's slowing down some isn't she, Took A-Look? Think she'll make it all the way here? Neither do I. What do you think she wants with us? I agree, who knows and who cares?

ATTA BOY STEVE, GRAB A HANDFUL OF HAIR. Get your hand under that tape like bull rider. Hell yes you can grab a hooter if you have to. Don't worry about it, don't even think about it, that's within the rules, sure it is, sure it is!

Very funny again, Took A-Look, but I really don't think she wants us back that badly. I bet Steve didn't think she was that tough. He better watch the knees, that's all I can say.

C'MON MARTY, CATCH UP, CATCH UP QUICK! Atta boy, ATTA BOY. Yahoo, again but she's tiring. Bring her down Steve, c'mon Steve, bring her down. She's sweating good, she's sweating up a storm.

JUMP HER Marty, c'mon, JUMP HER. THAT'S IT, THAT'S IT, C'mon Marty, Go, Go, Go! Pile on! PILE ON! I told you…PiiiiLL-LoonnnNNN!!!

I don't think Marty really wants to help but eventually he'll have to, won't he Took A-Look? She ain't no quitter, is she Took A-Look? She might just throw Steve yet. Wanna bet, Took A-Look, Huh, Wanna Bet?

You do? Okay but if she tosses Steve after Marty piles on, the bet is off. That's only fair. C'mon Steve, hang on, don't let her toss you. C'mon crazy ass, you can do it. He's only a couple of hundred pounds, you can do it! C'mon, c'mon, C'mmmonnnn!

Oh, oh. she's running outta gas. Oh oh, she's teetering. Teetering real bad.

TIMMM--BRR!!!

Damn, I thought she'd make it. How'd you know, Took A-Look, how'd you know she couldn't do it?

Good thinking Took A-Look. It never occurred to me that she used her mouth for breathing. Sure you still won.

Finally, here comes Marty to the rescue. Think she has enough gas left in her for a good kick to the balls? Wanna bet? Whataya mean you pick her? So what if you hate Marty more than me, why do you get her? I didn't hear you call first pick. Okay, okay, you can have her, she's all yours. Ha ha.

C'MON MARTY, C'MON. Watch those feet. WATCH'EM! WATCH'EM. Watch'em like your whole future sex life depends on it 'cause it does. Watch'em, I'm telling you!

Oh oh, don't look her in the eyes, Marty, for Chrisakes don't do that. You'll get it for sure if you do that. Don't look there I'm telling you, those eyes never tell the truth.

Now that she's not carrying Steve around, she has plenty of gas left in her doesn't she Took A-Look? That's right, full of gas. Oh, oh, don't let her get on top of you Steve. She's gonna do the alligator death roll on you Steve. Don't let that…oh, oh, too late. Poor Steve. GRAB HER MARTY, C'MON, GRAB A HANDFUL OF ANYTHING. SURE YOU GRAB THOSE, WHY NOT? C'mon. Grab her from the back, Marty. Good job, now pull her off Steve. Pull hard, she's plumb choked with gas. Oh damn. Maybe that wasn't such a good idea.

No, Took A-Look, Steve's balls don't count. The bet was Marty not Steve. I know Marty helped by pulling her up but the bet was Marty's balls. You can do a lot things but you can't change that.

Boy-oh-boy, is Marty pissed or what?

TIMMM—BRR, Again!!! Good move Marty, I didn't think you'd end up on top. Watch the knees, watch the knees. It's over Took A-Look.

Whataya mean it isn't over? Not 'til they get her out of the room? Okay. Okay!!! GRAB HER STEVE, GRAB HER GOOD. Best you should grab those legs, Steve, and be quick about it I tell you. QUICK for Pete's sake.

Don't let her get that knee up! No, no, no, not that knee, the other one, the other...OH DAMN, hot damn, I bet that hurt.

Not very funny Took A-Look but you're right, I know that hurts. It's worse when you're not expecting it though. She's definitely out of gas now, wouldn't you agree to that? Yep, the show's over. There she goes. She's giving us the stink eye. Do you care, Took A-Look, do you care about a little stink eye?

I said, do you care?

He isn't listening. Not that he has to listen but I've never seen him so happy. He's probably never been so happy, not in a million years. He's dancing the light fandango back there and it's coming straight from his heart. Absolutely perfect. Feet hitting all the right clouds, just the right way. Hands swooping and dropping and flying like hummingbirds with little electric wings. Better than wind music in the leaves by a long shot. Light, sound, color and sea breeze, a little bit of sweet flower scent on it. Boy, does he know his clouds or what. I'm really, really proud of him.

Too bad it won't last. It can't. It's another thing we agree on. Never-Ending simply won't allow it to last.

CHAPTER 15

For a lot of people, Marsha's office was a sanctuary from their own persecution but a lot of people didn't always include her. Sometimes this was where her self-persecution began and this was one of those times. She had to reason it out and if there was blame to be had, she had to suck it up.

Some people can't help it; some people can't be helped.

She always believed the first part but she could never truly accept the scientifically proven, logical corollary. Not truly accept it even though in the back of her head, she knew it was true, she knew that some people, some minds, were beyond salvage. Every now and again she would admit it, but never out loud and then only when her conscience was at the breaking point. Like it was now because she knew all along that Marty Sorenson would find a way to break her orders but she never imagined it would unleash such a dangerous reaction from Brita Black. Unfortunately, Marty Sorenson couldn't really be blamed for underestimating the woman, who could ever predict such extreme behavior, so Marsha had no choice but to pronounce herself guilty. That woman was a terror, no doubt about it and she wasn't sure which woman she was thinking about at that moment.

Having quickly accepted the blame for setting the wheels in motion, Marsha sat back in her chair and moved onto the next question on her mind. Was it worth it?

She started with the facts.

An orderly in the day-room, Ruby Jackson, gave Marsha a very detailed report of the action. Noticeably absent from that accounting was any action from Ruby herself. Being a woman probably had something to do with her decision to abstain until the last moment; two against one were already pretty tough odds for a size six, white girl against two orderlies. Being middle-aged and a little out of condition for what she described as 'steer wrassling' might also have factored into a decision which made Ruby an observer and not a participant. Being a generally kind and caring person might also have had an influence but in the end there was really only reason why she didn't try and help. Steve and Marty were getting the shit kicked out of them and Ruby's only real regret was that Mrs. Black's mouth was taped shut and she couldn't get enough air to either fight harder and longer or take a good bite out of somebody's private parts or any parts for that matter.

"She put up a good fight, Doc. She's a regular scrapper. Those boys are walking like they've landed real hard on a too-soft part. Yep, bow-legged, butt up and slow as cold molasses. She got'em both real good and came out without so much as a scratch to herself. Helluva fighter, fast too. Unpredictable as a roach; you can't tell a thing by the eyes. Looks left, fakes right, goes straight ahead. Confusing as hell."

Marsha let the orderly enjoy the moment all over again. Ruby was a good, honest, caring person who was so far on the outside of Marty Sorenson's orderly circle that she was practically invisible to them. How she managed to summon up the courage for another day of being shunned and ignored and treated like she was invisible was a mystery. Maybe because she was black and being frozen out of petty, self-righteous, obsessed little cliques didn't matter to her but the answer to that question wasn't important to anyone, especially Ruby, at that moment.

"I see. Ruby, did you notice any reaction from Mr. Black?"

"Not really, Doc. It happened pretty fast and caught me by surprise before I could see anybody else on it. Fair to say it caught everyone by surprise." Ruby said quietly. She wasn't in the habit of answering a question directly. Not even a question like two plus two. She had long ago come to the conclusion that she wouldn't learn anything by giving quick answers. Not that she would ask too many questions herself but she knew if she could get the other person to ask enough questions at least she had a chance of figuring out what they were truly thinking, what they really wanted to know or what they really wanted to hear. Like whether or not the question was truly important or if the person just wanted to gossip, or if maybe they were just trying to find someone else to blame. Of course Doc Coleman wasn't like that but she was still a doc so it just plain made sense to be sparing and cautious with choosing words.

"Before it all started, Mr. Black was sitting in the corner of the day room. Sorenson had positioned him against the wall, not right dead in the corner 'cause I would've changed that, but at an angle where the patient couldn't see very much unless he turned his head." Ruby paused for a breath and some confirmation that Doc Coleman had heard enough about where everybody else was sitting or what they were doing. She didn't get it, she was silent, listening and thinking, like she was trying to imagine the situation.

By implication of the silence and her intense concentration, the Doc's interest in Eric Black became obvious. Ruby hadn't really thought of him as different because they were all different but she knew, right then and there, that Doc Coleman had a special interest in this patient. In an odd way, it also made her feel more important, like what she had to say really mattered. She was happy she said she would have taken him out of the corner; it was an unnecessary detail but an important one for her and even more important now. Details suddenly were easy to find.

"Before it all started, he had turned his head, very slightly, but definitely turned it and he could see everything in the room. He watched the whole thing. No doubt about that, his eyes were glued to it." She waited for the question she believed was inevitable. Why did she notice Mr. Black's behavior in the midst of all this chaos? In other words, are you making up this story because you think you know what I want to hear?

"So Mrs. Black went straight for her husband, no surprise there. I wonder what she was thinking?" Marsha said, mostly to herself.

Ruby's suspicions vanished with the informal, almost intimate turn in the conversation. And it didn't hurt that she had figured out, by herself, why Ruby had seen Mr. Black's reaction. Once the initial shock registered, almost everyone in the day room looked at Eric Black. And not to see his reaction but to see what, or who, was provoking Mrs. Black's furious determination.

"She was thinking something mean and evil, that's for sure." Ruby said offhandedly, following the exact tone of the questions she was answering. Call it equality or maybe humanity.

"But why, why would she want to do what she did?"

This time the question was directed to her and Ruby felt the flush of inclusion from someone important asking for her opinion and putting it on an equal basis with all others. "Because she can, Doctor Marsha, because she's whipped him before and they both knew it. Only this time he didn't care what she wanted to do to him, it didn't matter."

Marsha figured that made sense until she realized she was simply reinforcing her own thinking. She had wanted a confrontation, not quite on the scale which was delivered, but a confrontation, an ice-breaker. Everything she had seen and heard from Brita Black and that had been confirmed by the daughter, it all pointed in the same direction. If she hadn't induced her husband's condition then she triggered it and that kind of power had to be challenged, stopped and if possible outright reversed.

Julia Reynolds started it. She had, inadvertently, proved that there was still a spark of resistance left in the man. Something which might reverse his deteriorating cognitive state and drive the coma-like consciousness thieves into retreat. But that would only happen if he could see some hope for the future. A direct confrontation to the power which she held over him seemed, at the time, like a good idea. Show him that she couldn't hurt him anymore, maybe even be defeated and perhaps give him some hope, that was the whole, imperfect, plan. Something, anything that would put a halt to the catatonic slippage.

"So she just had to prove it to him again, to reinforce her absolute power?" It made sense. The last thing the wife needed was a healthy, and therefore wealthy, ex-husband.

"Uh-uh, sort of. Only it was a just reminder for him but it was really a lesson for you. He's been whipped before, he'll never forget that. It's instinct for him. She was trying to teach you a lesson, that's what she was doing." Ruby blurted out her thoughts too suddenly but didn't regret it for but a second or two. Doc Coleman had a way of getting through to her so she just accepted it.

"Instinct?"

"Uh-huh. Like two puppies, brother and sister are getting along fineand equal until one of them decides to be the boss. After that nothing changes. Instinct takes over and nothing else matters, that boss will be the boss. I know you doctors don't like instinct."

"We don't?" Marsha challenged Ruby with a straight face but a teasing voice. Everybody has an opinion on everybody else, sometimes that was the only thing which kept the place upright. Like sometimes she needed to be treated like a doctor because at least that meant something, because it provided a basis for communication and other times she needed to be treated just like any other person. What she couldn't fathom was how anyone could completely shut out every kind of communication, how they could shut out everything like Eric Black was doing. For a short time, sure, that made sense, everybody likes their solitude but to shut it out completely? And everything? How can anyone retreat so far from the world around them and still be alive? And where do they go?

The teasing was an invitation Ruby couldn't refuse. It didn't happen very often, and Marsha was the only doctor who had ever offered to be lectured by an orderly but this was even more special than any time before. Plus, Mr. Black was a new patient and because of that Ruby actually knew more about him than she did.

"Instinct, Doc, is when people do things without thinking about what they are doing. Technically speaking, Doctor, they have pre-determined the outcome, what we in the business, call in so many fancy words the desired end state, in advance of, what we call in so many other, completely different fancy words, the cognitive action required to achieve that state."

Ruby was dead serious. Marsha put on the most puzzled look she could manage but it wasn't easy.

Ruby saw the conflict and waited until she was sure her Marsha was in control of her emotions. "Instinct is not very well understood, I'm afraid to say. Not very well understood at all and...and...having said that twice you can begin to appreciate just how a great a mystery it truly is. Uh-huh, it is a mystery, which is, by definition, something we don't know much about. That's instinct for you, technically speaking, of course."

Marsha nodded unconsciously. A serious question was hiding behind Ruby's banter and both of them knew it. As convenient as it was to place the blame on chemical imbalances, hormones gone berserk, the seemingly random appearance of a protein-based catalyst or a mutant bacterial or viral life form lurking somewhere in the background until conditions were just right, all that reasoning was nothing more than a convenient excuse for denying the unknown. The truth, the reality, the actuality of Eric Black's condition had eluded scientific light. Unexplained physiology taking the blame for inexplicable psychology.

Ruby wasn't quite done: "Everybody has instinct but some people are closer to it than others. Like my two sons, James and Earl. Both of them play with the same puppy but only one of them gets nipped. Why do you suppose that is, Doc?"

"Instinct?"

"Very good, Doc."

"So which one has the instinct, James or Earl?" Marsha asked. It was an interesting question, and always would be.

"James wouldn't hurt a fly. Earl got bit. The dog's got instinct."

Marsha laughed, maybe even a little too loud. It had been a testy day and she needed the relief of something that, for a change, was dead serious.

"And Eric Black, what do you think Ruby, does he have instinct?" The serious question: 'was the gamble with Eric Black's sanity worth it?'

Ruby figured it just like she had figured it all along. "Oh he's got instinct all right. His eyes were dancing with stars. That lady made a big mistake, she went too far and got herself whipped. She woke up the big dog. Dumb don't count."

Marsha reflected on the only remaining paradigm. Some people can't help it; some people can't be helped but everybody can help themselves, if they want to.

Maybe the paradigm wasn't solved but at least it was tested.

CHAPTER 16

T.G.I.F.

Morning comes with such chaos that you have to wake up early or it will crush your whole day. I know that now so as soon as the first little bird opens her mouth, I'm awake. It's the most peaceful time of the day and not even Jeffrey, my loud-snoring roommate in the bed next to me can ruin it. Jeffrey is wrecked, just like his snoring, but Took A-Look likes his company. He was up all night sharpening spears. Something is going to happen, maybe we're going hunting today and unless your name is Sorenson, hunting would be a very nice change of pace from undeclared peace.

Took A-Look is sleeping by the window, the only clean place there is back there, sleeping like a baby, but that's not something to take for granted. One false move and he'll be on his feet throwing spears or kicking clouds like there's no tomorrow.

Who knows, maybe he got the name Took A-Look because he is always vigilant and so curious with horizons although there's probably more to it than that but what's more than horizons and vigilance, I can't even guess. After all, in the grand scheme of things, horizons and birds and seals all belong together, sometimes they are all together, sharing the same air but not many people see it that way. Except Took A-Look, of course. One day when he's in a good mood, maybe I'll ask him about his name. Then again, maybe I should ask myself whether I really want to know because some of the things he says, I'd rather not hear.

Right now, it's too peaceful to think of such things. Sometimes maybe is the most satisfactory answer there is. Completely unlike Never-Ending which isn't at all satisfying, no matter how many ways or how many times you look at it. Unfortunately, it seems like unsatisfying is a Never-Ending quality and the more you think about it, the more unsatisfying Never-Ending becomes. Maybe that's why Never-Ending doesn't have any adjectives or adverbs, they become obsolete and redundant from being repeated Never-Ending.

Jeffrey is pretty big guy, maybe 250 pounds, but he isn't very tall, maybe 5'7" so he's very fat around the middle and in the face. That probably accounts for him being such a dandy snoring machine. His chest doesn't move much but his belly moves a lot and so do his cheeks.

Like me, he doesn't talk. Who knows what his excuse is. Unless your name is Julia Reynolds, it's extremely impolite to ask those kinds of questions.

The day starts in total gloom which sounds depressing but it isn't because that is just a start, not a forecast. Little by little the gloom gets chased away and the shadows which collected in the open spaces have to move into corners and other places like behind the bed or along the light green door moldings. With every extra ray coming their way, the birds pick up the tempo, like if they didn't sing, the rays would stop coming. Birds know more about horizons than any living thing on earth. Maybe that's what they are singing about. Part of Never-Ending yet with a horizon to separate it from Not-Never-Ending has to be something, or somewhere worth singing about.

Jeffrey is snoring up a storm and Took A-Look is sleeping, what more could you ask for? Not breakfast that's for sure.

Breakfast is 100% pure artificially simulated unreality. The tastes and smells have been sucked out of it. The juice is orange but it isn't orange juice. The stuff in the bowl looks like porridge but just tastes like wet. I usually eat the toast which looks like today's toast but can't possibly be. Nicely browned with a glistening sheen on it which looks like butter but it isn't, just like it looks crisp when it's on the plate but turns all limp and soft when you pick it up. Like it was porridge yesterday and today it's toast but no one bothered to put the crisp in it. No taste unless you put some jam on it. Red jam or orange jam, they both taste the same, sweet but not the way sweet tastes, more like the way sweet sounds. Simulated goes a long way in a place like this. The birds are real but I'm sure somebody is working on that problem.

When the crush starts, the orderlies will start at the end of the hall and open the doors, one after another, like a train coming into the station. Somebody will shout. Somebody else will cry. Maybe the person who shouted will curse the one who cried but somebody will curse. That's the beginning and from then on, the volume goes up and around like a spiral staircase, all you can see are the stairs in front of your face. That's the day. Crazy noise that doesn't have any purpose, any character or any reason to be because when rules aren't important, when rules aren't followed, crazy jumps in, no discussion required. Except for Julia Reynolds of course, she has to find someone to listen to her. No break for parrots, not even in the simulated scheme of things.

It's pretty easy to become accustomed to the chaos which is both a blessing and a curse. No one wants chaos but boring is problematic. Spiral staircases should have told you that.

Jeffrey isn't firing on all cylinders any more. He's spluttering in between snores like an outboard motor with water in the gas. And the snores aren't ending with a big whistle of out-wheezed air either. Like the snore's tail has been chopped off. Snore, splutter, pause. It goes like that, no big whistle. The pauses will get longer and longer until they completely surround the snores and squeeze the sound out of them. After that, there's just the sound of air moving. In and out of his lungs, a little quicker each time until that sound stops and he's completely awake, sitting up and silent as a statue for the rest of the day. Pretty soon and the crush will begin in earnest; pretty soon it will open the door. I'm not looking forward to it. I'm really, really not looking forward to another crush.

Hey Took A-Look, what are you doing up already? You look like a big pile of muskox droppings. You're welcome. I know you were busy all night. I can see that from your pile of spears, what did you do, sharpen all of them? No kidding, even the little bent twig one with too much leather wrapping. That's a pretty big night of sharpening. What? And all the arrows too? No kidding? What's the occasion?

All sleepless things considered, he's in a pretty decent mood but it wasn't a whole night of sharpening arrows and spears that did it. Not by a long shot.

Wasn't that a grand fight with the wife? Yeah, I know you won the bet. After what she did to them, I really didn't think they had the balls to get her out the door but they did, didn't they? It was pretty smart of them to tape those ankles and knees together wasn't it?

You're right, really smart would have done it a lot sooner.

He's thinking about an instant replay but decides against it. Later probably. We'll need it. Jeffrey's awake. Doors at the end of the hall are getting closer. The crush is getting louder, more chaotic, drowning out the birds.

What are the plans for today, Took A-Look? No, I don't think she is still here. Yeah, that's too bad. First time you ever wanted to be together with her isn't it? No, I'm not trying to tease you, it's just an observation.

Sure, I bet she'd win again today too. I know we can't both bet on the same thing. I know she isn't here. Fine, have it your way, I agree with you. Is that better?

So much for the decent mood theory but I really can't blame him. He doesn't like it here and if you know him at all by now, you also know that's not an earth shattering revelation. There's only one place in the whole world that he truly likes and we are so far away from there that it might as well be a dream. All things considered you wouldn't think, at least I would never have thought, that a hospital like this would be so boring but it is. A tiny bit of anything which makes sense is much more interesting than a whole lot of nonsense. Nonsense doesn't go anywhere, in circles maybe, but a tiny bit of something which makes sense has infinite possibilities. Bent grass, a puff of wind carrying a scent, a vibration coming up through your feet, you can't ignore that. You have to deal with it just to get past it. That's being alive, this is just living, just existing, just breathing, just Jeffrey, poor guy.

Hey Took A-Look, where are you going with all those spears, you call off the hunt?

I can see that, but why are you taking them over there?

Took A-Look is a lot of things but neat isn't one them and that makes this behavior curious. He takes a big armful of spears and dumps them in a corner and then does the same thing with a whole armful of arrows which he dumps in another corner. That's his idea of cleaning up, just moving the mess from one place to another. Spear shavings, bits of bone, rock and leather are all over the place but that doesn't matter to him, that doesn't need to be cleaned up. He sits down in front of the window but at least he sits not jumps or flops or any of his usual, uncaring, careless, behaviors. Something is up, definitely.

You want the window moved? No? How come? I know you've been thinking, I saw you back there. About what? Okay, fine, not about what, about where, like I couldn't guess that for myself.

Anywhere but here, I know you don't like it here, you think I do? So where do you want to go? There? You want to go back there? Fine with me if that's what you want. No, I'm not saying that to agree with you. Yes, that means I agree with you. How much do I agree with you?

Okay, it's much better than fine, but why do you want to go there so badly? Sure you can tell me later. But are you sure, it's a long, long trip? No, you don't have to say it twice. If that's what you want then that's what you want. What do you mean now I've said it three times? Never mind Took A-Look, why don't you go take a nap? Yes, I'll deal with the crush. Yes, I'll take of it. Yes, I'll take care of that too. Yes, I know what to do. Now who is repeating themselves? Good morning muskox droppings yourself.

In case you missed it, Took A-Look just declared peace. The spears and arrows are back where they belong. He is saying good morning. Trust has been restored; respect is being returned. Change is in the air and for that I am exceedingly happy which is something you can't say for everybody, especially Jeffrey who is getting more and more tense as each door opens, each voice adds to the chaos. The crush is almost here; a couple doors down I would guess.

She would never make it here. Not a single door slams. Every one of them has an automatic pneumatic closing device which makes them impossible to slam but you can still hear them hiss open and shut, like now, a little sooner than I thought.

Well I'll be. What a pleasant, and timely, surprise.

I wonder if she will feel the same way.

Your favorite seal is here Took A-Look, how about that? No, I won't say hello from you, how on earth do you think that would help anything? I know it's polite. I know you like her. Fine, I'll think about it. We are sharing aren't we? Well aren't we? Thank you.

"Good morning Eric."

"Good morning Doctor Coleman."

"Please call me Marsha. You don't mind if I call you Eric, do you?"

It was a very surprising moment that came with an overwhelming sense of calm and peace unlike she had ever felt before. And there was no betrayal of that peace in his eyes, in fact, that seemed to be the source of her feelings, like he radiated peace, like he declared it to be and so it was. And there was something else about those eyes. The faded blue, almost cloudy iris of day's past was now bright, dark and defined with deep grey, almost black flecks. Like something you would see on the horizon of a calm sea, like small boats or perhaps a pod of whales, surfacing. Now why would she think that? He broke it.

"I'd prefer it, actually…Marsha. How long have I been here? Eye-to-eye and she might be looking for Took A-Look but with peace declared that was fine. Whatever she saw would be between the two of them but peace had been declared and she deserved a look at it.

He's looking right back at her, totally absorbed in her beautiful gold specks. Are you in love, Took A-Look? Oh, you are in awe. That's nice.

"A little less a week. You don't remember anything?" She knew what he would say but she asked anyway. He remembered everything but would lie about it. Whatever chance she had of understanding what he had experienced was gone because the only way he would get what he now wanted was to deny everything. If he had learned anything from this experience he had learned what he needed to learn and becoming her case study wasn't an option, wasn't part of the bargain, that much was obvious.

"Vaguely. Very vaguely. I feel like my brain has been blitzed." He lied and knew she understood both the lie and reason for it. Like close friends sometimes protect each other by skirting the truth. Strange but completely natural. Yes Took A-Look I know that strange and completely natural don't normally belong together but don't forget where we are. In here, strange and natural are the same, aren't they?

"Disoriented?" she asked. Strange but completely natural. Of course he would lie but that wasn't the reason for the question. They were becoming oriented to each other and she wanted to continue, wanted to see where it would lead and for that she needed his participation. So she asked: Disoriented? Then he would decide how close they would become.

"Sort of. It's like I'm searching for something, something concrete and real. Something outside of myself. It is very hard to explain but I feel okay. I feel okay with not being able to explain everything right now. Perhaps one day it will be more clear."

She moved closer and felt the swelling under his cast, then patted it like it deserved a reward for good behavior.

She knows about statues. Took A-Look nodded in agreement or maybe just because he felt like it, but in awe for sure. He is arranging some of the fog around the seal cloud. That's curious because like I said, he isn't much of house keeper and fog is the absolute least of his concerns.

"You had an episode." She said to keep the channel open. The words weren't important. She sensed change but couldn't find anything concrete to say about it, to introduce it or to conclude it. But change was there in front of her, she saw it shrouded in fine, shifting, billowing mist. It was making her eyes water a little. She was understanding something but couldn't exactly put words to it yet it felt okay. Isn't that what he just said?

"An episode?"

Took A-Look shook his head a little but kept moving the mist around, making little sparks where he was tearing it apart. Now that peace has been declared, I can't feel the sparks but I can see them.

"It's called an uncontrolled, excessive motor activity episode."

"Like a fit?"

Thanks Took A-Look, thanks for declaring peace again. No you aren't bothering me, do you want to be left alone? No, you are enjoying this too aren't you?

I figured he would make a move on the seal cloud but when I look for it I can't find it. He's moved it and put another one in its place, hiding the seal cloud behind some mist, probably. Then certainly as he pulls the mist back a little bit and there she is, Doctor Marsha. That's nice Took A-Look, that's a lovely arrangement.

"Something like that. How are you feeling now?"

"Kind of groggy. And hungry too. This is a mental hospital isn't it?"

Sure, Took A-Look go ahead and lie down. Yes, if Doctor Marsha mentions you, I'll say something nice. Yes I'll tell you everything later.

"It is. Do you remember coming here?"

"A little." Another lie but this time an important one. It was time to build the bridge. The bridge to the outside and that meant it was time to tell some truth. Never travel on a bridge built entirely on lies.

"Do you know why you are here?" She felt him creating distance and was surprised to find that she also wanted it that way. Maybe because she knew that a relationship with Eric Black inside the hospital would only compromise a relationship with him outside the hospital. The feeling she had was one of destiny, absolutely impossible to describe but absolutely recognizable by the way air goes into your lungs, light enters your eyes, sound fills your ears and your skin tingles with anticipation. In the right way, under the right conditions, that feeling is destiny, it can be no other and can only be intentionally, willfully mistaken for something else.

"I'll bet my wife had something to do with it. We haven't been getting along very well lately."

"What did you fight about?"

"The same thing as always. Our marriage is over, but not ended if you know what I mean. It never was a marriage, I know that now. But with her it was almost impossible to know what she really meant, impossible not to get carried along with the tide she created. I know how stupid it sounds, a grown man being manipulated like that but she has ways of turning things upside down."

"Custody issues?" Marsha asked absently while thinking about his statement. '*Impossible to know what she really meant.*' She repeated it silently and then confirmed that it was indeed accurate, she had felt exactly the same way about Brita Black. The woman could create confusion out of nothing, completely baffling a person's senses and destroying their logic.

"No, we didn't have any children together. The problem is much more mundane than that. It's money. We had a pre-nuptial agreement but she wants more, wants everything I expect." he said absently then quickly added: "Am I free to leave, Doctor Coleman, sorry, I mean, Marsha?"

"No, I'm afraid you can't leave, just yet. You have been formally committed so there are a few procedures…"

"Committed? By her?"

"No, by your daughter."

"Arlene? Oh my God. I hadn't thought about that. She must be worried sick. Is there a phone I can use? I really need to let her know that I'm okay."

"There is, but..."

He interrupted: "But?"

"Eric, Arlene is coming to see me this morning...in a couple of hours. Why don't you wait and talk to her then. Use the time to get cleaned up and prepared. I'm sure that would be better. It won't be too long." Marsha was giving him good advice but it was advice that would take this whole experience away from herself and it wasn't easy to give.

He saw it. "Of course. You're right. Better to do it in person, that way she'll know that I'm fine. Then we can leave together." He wondered if she would argue but sensed she wouldn't. At least not yet and probably not unless he showed some weakness, some indecision with his life and that would probably be her next question. He knew who he was, he knew where he was, did he know where he was going?

"Where will you go, Eric? What will you do?"

"I'll go to Arlene's for a few days. I'll see lawyer and he will sort out the divorce. After that, we'll see."

"I see you have thought this through which is good but Eric, I urge you, take your time...I don't mean to say you should do anything different, just take your time with it." She wasn't sure exactly what her own words meant because his last words were stuck in her mind. 'After that, we'll see.' Plural. Eric and Took A-Look. How did that work? Who was in charge? How long would it last this time?

"That's good advice, Marsha. I'll take it. Thank-you." he said sincerely while thinking that she was probably a very good therapist. Empathetic for certain, but more than that; probably her sense of humanity which was governed by dignity and respect. It made her the kind of person you wanted to be with.

"I am happy to see you are feeling better...I really am."

"Thanks again. I appreciate that, I really do. To tell you the truth, it feels a little strange to be here. I hope you aren't too insulted that I want to clear out as soon as possible."

"I'm not insulted at all. Actually, we usually celebrate occasions like this. I'll call you after I've talked with Arlene."

"I'll be ready."

The crush had come.

I can see it in Jefferies's eyes.

He is afraid to look into mine.

I know the feeling and look away.

CHAPTER 17

"Mrs. Mallory is here for her appointment and Mrs. Black's lawyer has called for the third time. She's holding on line two." Gail's secretarial intuition told her that Marsha would see Arlene Mallory right away but the lawyer didn't have a chance.

She waited for an answer, only her head through the office door and while waiting figured that something was happening. Exactly what was happening she couldn't guess but it was obviously a good something. Marsha was relaxed but pensive, rocking gently in her leather chair, legs crossed and drumming on the armrest with her fingers. She was working on her game plan, Gail knew it would be a friendly game – her lab coat, her armor, was hanging on the coat rack.

"I'll see Mrs. Mallory, Gail. Tell the lawyer to pound sand."

"The lawyer says she'll call the Director if you don't talk to her this time."

"Fine. Give her the number."

Gail smiled, nodded and turned into the small ante-room which she shared with patients, visitors and a small but healthy bay laurel tree. All plants had to be edible. The room was divided in half by the path from the hallway door to Marsha's door. Gail and the bay laurel had the real estate on one side of the path and on the other side was the reception with two chairs, one of them occupied by Mr. Black's daughter.

The rapidly blinking light on her telephone was the only sign of urgency that Gail allowed in the room and her desk was neat. She liked it that way and so did Marsha. Most of her other bosses preferred the complete opposite. As if more paper and files on the secretary's desk had to mean the doctor was absolutely buried with work and that just might explain his crazy behavior or pathetically deficient interpersonal skills. She eyed the blinking light.

Billable time for the lawyer, she thought, no sense in prolonging that if at all possible. Mrs. Mallory could wait a moment longer and wouldn't regret the inconvenience of listening to her step-mother's lawyer get a lesson in who could push their weight around and who couldn't.

"Hello?...I'm sorry but Doctor Coleman is very busy and can't take your call...No, I can't say when she will have time, maybe next week...No, I can't tell you that either...No, I don't have that information...Yes, I told her that...The Director's name is Doctor Fielding, do you have his number?... Good. Have a nice day."

She disconnected the lawyer with one button, waited for the dial tone and then pushed another button. Whoever was on the other end of that line must have been waiting because the response was instantaneous and there were no formalities on either end of the conversation.

"Betty, the lawyer's name is Higgins-Mersh. That's right, Higgins-Mersh. Thanks."

The lawyer was in for a rough day. Doctor Fielding had been the Director forever and had spent about as much time in court as he did with the politicians who controlled his budget. At least with lawyers he could show his detest and for as long as anyone could remember, he had yet to meet the lawyer who knew even half as much mental competency law as he did. Most lawyers dug themselves a big hole before they realized Doctor Fielding was more than capable of filling it in, on top of them. Higgins-Mersh was about to receive a lesson in offensive legal tactics she could never get in law school, regardless how prestigious.

"Please go straight in, Mrs. Mallory." Gail smiled warmly but stayed behind her desk. Marsha didn't need a quick read on Arlene's state of mind; she was good folks.

Arlene was impressed with the show Gail had put on and smiled warmly in return. The idea of having her father transferred to a private clinic had been on her mind from the first moment she walked into the state facility and it had been a futile battle with irreconcilable realities from that moment on. She was absolutely certain that her father would get a better environment at an expensive private facility just as she was absolutely certain he would get better treatment from Marsha Coleman. Somehow or another, he just had to put up with his surroundings and take Doctor Coleman seriously.

"Good morning, Arlene."

"Good morning Doctor." She took the chair in front of the desk to which she was waved and used it as an excuse to avoid eye contact. Preparing for this meeting, God forbid that it turned into a head-shrinking session, had become another exercise in futility. She didn't want anyone poking around in her head any more than she wanted anyone poking around in her father's head.

"Would you like coffee or tea?" Marsha asked but suspected she would be refused. Arlene was in for a good day but didn't yet know it.

"No thank-you." she answered as Marsha passed behind her. The door closed with the same muted click as before. Authority. Control. Position. Power. It had started. Undeniable and inescapable, it had finally started. Years of living with the fear she now had to confront came frothing to the surface with a single, dull, metallic click. She had promised herself she wouldn't burst into tears again and wondered how long she would be able to keep that promise. She was feeling shaky.

"Very good news, Arlene. Your father's condition has improved, improved quite dramatically, actually." Marsha hadn't planned or rehearsed the message but it came out as well as she could have wanted. She really didn't have a choice in what to say or when to say it so that part was pretty straightforward. Atonal, optimism and pessimism in equal parts, exactly how she felt. Dead center in the middle of the road. Happy to see his improvement but sad with her lack of understanding of that improvement and because of that mystery, afraid it might not last yet almost certain that this time, for this patient this one time, it would last, who knew why?

"What? Oh, thank God. How? What…?"

"It happens sometimes…"

"But what exactly do you mean?" Arlene interrupted. "Is he better, has he recovered? Can he go home?"

"Better, Arlene, not necessarily well. There is a difference. We can't be certain this will last. Anything..."

"Can I see him? When can I see him?" Of their own accord, her tears had started but she didn't care. Tears of joy didn't count against the promises she had made to herself. It was amazing but it also wasn't. She should have known better, she should have believed more strongly. Maybe Dad wasn't normal but he sure as hell wasn't sick, not that kind of sick.

"You can see him this morning, after we have talked, we'll sit down together." Marsha's schedule would be wrecked but that wasn't anything new. Eric Black's sudden change in reason and coherency was definitely new, and definitely more important than her schedule.

"I really want to see him now. I just want to take him away from here before she...before she can do any more damage." The tears were streaming down her cheeks, tears which had started with joy but which were now being sourced with an overpowering feeling of relief. Everything she had feared, including and especially having to talk about it, had been postponed, side-tracked, rendered mute and taken off the agenda, possibly forever.

"In a little while, Arlene. I can't guarantee that your father will be able to leave with you."

"What? What do you mean?"

"Just that we will see. But it looks very promising. Let's just take it one step at a time, okay? Try not to worry, this is really good news, I'm not trying to take it away from you."

"Doctor Coleman, nothing is more important to me than Dad, he is the only family I have. I can't take any chances with leaving him here all alone. You must understand, I just have to do something."

"I do understand Arlene. We both want the same thing. We both want this to last, you have to believe that is important to me too. Do you believe that, Arlene?" Marsha was completely sincere but that didn't surprise her because sincerity was her norm, almost her trademark. What surprised her was the depth of her feeling. It reminded her, yet one more time that Eric Black was more than just a patient and that while she didn't know exactly why she felt that way she knew the feeling and depth of it belonged together. And moreover, she almost knew that he felt exactly the same way about her, just that nobody was putting feelings into words, or was it the other way around?

Arlene nodded. The words were as true as the honesty with they were spoken and because of that, she felt her bond strengthen with both of them.

"Just a few questions, Arlene. Do you think your step-mother might have given your father some drugs, something that could have triggered this episode?" Marsha had several questions like that one. All with the same purpose in mind. She had to open a dialogue with Arlene even if it was on a subject which held little interest to her compared to where had he been, what had he seen and how did he manage his escape from that awful state of denial when so many others had failed? All questions which Arlene couldn't answer but for which she might provide a clue with which to pursue the mystery.

Arlene seized the opportunity to send the whole Took A-Look episode into deep space. "I wouldn't put it past her. She is an evil woman who wants only one thing, his money. She doesn't give a damn about anything, or anyone, except herself. If you want my opinion, she would do anything, anything at all to get what she wants."

"When did you first sense that she was after his money?" It wasn't going to be an easy task to open up the past but she had to start somewhere and at least Arlene was prepared to talk about this part of it.

"It wasn't right away, at least not before the marriage or even for a little while after it. Not that I could see anyway. Brita was so believable with everything she said and did that you just couldn't help but trust her, you just couldn't help but think she was genuine. At least until she started to say one thing and then do the opposite. It is very difficult to explain, it is such a contradiction. I mean at one time, I honestly thought we were friends. Can you believe that? She tricked me so thoroughly and I still don't know how she did it."

"I believe you Arlene. I only met her for a little while but she is definitely convincing, definitely capable of real deception and that can be terribly destructive when you don't see it coming, don't know what to fight against. Can you tell me a little more about when you saw these changes happening?" The question was vague, as intended. Hopefully Arlene would choose to talk about her father, the real subject of interest.

Arlene judged that the topic was safe, maybe even better than safe. The doctor had hinted, more than hinted, she had actually said 'dramatic improvement' and that meant everything could be wrapped up very, very soon. Plus, it would be a lot better for him if he left with a clean bill of health, something which would give that money-grabbing bitch of a wife and her greedy lawyer a well-deserved panic attack. And, there was also the minor detail surrounding the commitment papers. Who knew what it would take to reverse that problem? She never should have signed them without reading them first. She had to play along and she wanted to play along. It just made sense.

"Dad met Brita a couple of years ago and as far as I'm concerned she had him picked and plucked from the first hello. She was all sweetness and joy, just as nice as you can imagine, she fooled everybody. I mean everybody. They were married within three months and things stayed pretty much the same as the beginning, at least as far as I knew, for a few months after that. She was probably content with what she was getting; they had a pre-nuptial agreement, did I mention that before?"

"You did. Did the troubles start all at once?" Marsha coaxed.

"Not right away and not at all obvious about her real motives but she had it all planned out, you can bet on that. She just started spending more and more money, like she was trying to find out how much she could get away with. Like she was trying to figure out whether or not she could get everything she wanted without him telling her to stop."

"Did he? Did he tell her to stop?"

"He must have. Pretty soon there was nothing but fights and acrimony. Not enough to drive him away but enough to keep him, oh I don't know how to say it…keep him like a hostage. In a constant state of tension, swinging one way then another. She did everything she could to keep him off balance but it didn't seem like it was that bad, not like physical abuse, I just don't know how to say it. Like somehow everything became his fault and maybe sometimes it was. But mostly it was a lie, her whole life was a lie and he was the one who got trapped in it. Trapped in a big sticky web of deceit."

"What do you mean, she did everything?"

"Embarrass him in front of his friends, argue over the smallest details, contradict everything he said, order him around, nag, flirt with other men, accuse him of infidelity, you name it, she tried it. She was trying to drive him crazy but not get caught at it."

"Like chipping away at a stone?"

"Exactly. Not enough to fracture it but enough to wear it down."

All the words which Marsha expected to hear. Erosion wasn't nature's most powerful force but it was the most relentless. Everything, eventually, gives way to it. It was one of the first things that every therapist learned, followed by the fact that treatment was seldom successful if the wind and waves causing the damage weren't stopped. Maybe her temper tantrum in the day room did the trick, exposed her vulnerability. But so quickly?

Arlene used the pause to re-introduce the conclusion she really wanted to hear. "Do you think she drugged him? Do you think she pushed him over the edge?"

"It has been tried before. There are some very powerful, psychotic drugs which will do that and which, unfortunately, aren't all that difficult to obtain."

"That bitch. Can you prove it?"

"No. As you know, we did a complete set of blood tests, looking for any kind of chemical imbalance. Very complete and the results were quite normal but that doesn't rule it out. We can't test for everything and sometimes the residual amounts are so small they can't be detected.

We still have more tests to do, but those are for biological agents, like bacteria, and not chemicals, not drugs, but still capable of being intentionally introduced." It wasn't what Arlene wanted to hear but it was the truth. Not what any lawyer would want to hear either, if it got that far. One would have to argue that normal results were good and the other would take the opposite view. The court reporter would go crazy with psycho-babble from expert witnesses, nothing would be resolved and the case would eventually be settled, out-of-court. "Tell me, Arlene, what did, or what does, your father do for a living? Anything that could result in that kind of exposure?"

"He was, is, a geologist." she answered without realizing the topic was changing to her father.

"A geologist? Did he work for a mining company or something like that?"

"Most of the time he consulted, sometimes he was independent. Think of him as a prospector from the good old days."

"How does that work? What I know about earth sciences and mining isn't very much." The good old days, when there were some, was always safe ground. Arlene seemed quite secure in them, happy, even proud.

"When he free-lanced it would be for a mining company or a speculator. Basically they would have some mineral rights somewhere and he would pack up his gear and go prospecting. You know, live in a tent, take rock samples, map features and so on. Surface geology to start with and then if he got a show, a trace of something valuable, then they would pit mine or drill for samples to prove it up."

"So he looked for gold?" Another image of Eric Black, this time with his back-pack, rock hammer, compass and whatever else he needed to wander around in the jungle or the mountains, free and undisturbed, entered her mind.

Another image? No. Not really. Not like so many other patients where the healthy image was in such contrast with the one she knew. He was different, both images were the same. But why? What sixth sense was sending the message that the man she knew and the one she didn't know were the same? What sixth sense was completely content with the way things were when logic couldn't confirm or deny what the other five senses were reporting?

"He wouldn't ignore it if he found it." Arlene laughed. She had always been proud of her father's work. None of her other friends had fathers like hers. He was always doing something way far away and bringing her the most interesting gifts. She continued.

"There were all sorts of different situations and all sorts of different minerals. Like if a company already had a show, they might ask Dad to prove it up before some other company could get in and claim beside it or counter-claim. Or it might just be bare bones prospecting where he would go into a remote area, somewhere that hadn't really been explored before, and evaluate its potential. Sometimes, but not very often, he would go into a developed mine and map extensions or evaluate recovery methods. He was very good, really good with anything to do with rocks and getting the minerals out of them."

"Is that how he made his money?" A risky question because it could bring the step-mother back into the conversation, but a gap that needed to be filled in. The daughter didn't seem to mind, perhaps because of her pride in his success.

"More or less. He usually charged a fee for his work, kind of a daily retainer. Whenever he could, he negotiated a percentage of anything he found, sort of a partnership share or a royalty. About seven years ago he hit a big one in northern Canada, lead-zinc with a good silver show. When the mine was developed, it takes a long time to develop a mine you know, the money from his royalty started to come in. A trickle at first, then quite a bit. He's got millions and it just keeps coming. And it will keep on coming for years to come."

"Is that where he usually worked, Northern Canada?" Another risky question with Took A-Look lurking in shadows of it. Assuming the name had any connection at all to what it sounded like.

"Northern Canada and the Arctic during our summer, then places like Indonesia or the Philippines in the winter unless it was Australia or half a dozen countries in South America. Lots and lots of different places. He's been everywhere, really."

Marsha wanted to say that Arlene must have had a damn lonely childhood but knew what kind of reaction that would produce. Those absences must have had a devastating impact on a young girl who had lost her mother. "Did you ever go prospecting with your Dad?" she asked in subterfuge.

"A few times. Not to the really remote places or jungles where there was a lot of sickness or...or...tribal revolt." Arlene realized what was going on. The doctor was prying where she had no right to pry. That was private land and it was time to hang out the 'No trespassing' sign. "Doctor Coleman, I want to see my father. He can answer these questions better than I can."

"That's a good idea, Arlene. Why don't we spend a few minutes with your father and after that you can tell me what you think. It will also give us an opportunity to talk about any follow-up care or treatment? Okay?"

Marsha received a nod to her question but it wasn't a very convincing one. Arlene's agenda was, once again, set in stone. She was taking him away and that was both the beginning and the end of the discussion. After that, if he wanted treatment, he could afford to do whatever he wanted.

In other words, the patient would diagnose, prescribe and heal himself; it never worked.

"Gail, would you have Mr. Black come and join us, please?" she spoke to the phone while trying to think of a way to re-open the conversation. Arlene's body posture and concentration told her not to bother. Like it or not, it was over. She could be obstinate and refuse to release him but that wouldn't last for more than a few days. Not if Eric Black continued to be coherent and reasoned. Not even his wife would want to keep her husband committed against his own free and logical will and the Director would be even more insistent on his release. Keeping so-called healthy millionaires in a state facility against their will was bad for his budget regardless of how entertaining a legal battle might be at the other end of it.

Enjoying the silence and the prospect of success, Arlene decided that she actually liked Doctor Coleman. It had taken a while to get over her stereotypical expectations of a psychiatrist in a state hospital but when she did, she found a caring, reasonable person sitting across from her. All in all it was a good experience and she vowed to learn something from it. "How long will it take, Doctor?"

"Just a few minutes, Arlene. I'm sure your father is ready."

CHAPTER 18

"Good morning Mr. Black. Do you remember me?"

"I remember you Sorenson."

"That's right. You're looking better today. How do you feel?"

"You can cut the chit-chat, orderly. You're way over your head and don't know half of what you think you know."

"Yeah right, look who's talkin'. You're wanted somewhere else. This way." Marty Sorenson knew when to back off. Twenty years of experience had taught him the stupidity of getting into a pissing contest with patients, regardless of winning, losing, right, wrong, empty or full. Just giving them a chance was the equivalent of giving them a free hand to do whatever came into their loony heads. No, that was not how to win the game, it was much better to wait. Eric Black, like so many others before him, would be back. Then he'd see who ended up with wet shoes and there were lots of ways for that to happen.

"Go right in, Mr. Black. They are expecting you." Gail's first look at the patient who had so completely captured Marsha's interest met with her complete approval. Very trim and rugged looking but not rough or crude, he was every bit what her mother used to call a 'wash and wear man.' He was probably younger than he looked because his wrinkles were deep and distinct but not ridged, sort of like he had been born with them and not earned them the hard way.

Clear blue eyes with dark grey, almost black specks, intense like the daughter's but with a command and control behind them that she lacked. Freshly shaved with his hair combed and parted to the side but not fashionable or arranged like a business man going into a meeting. He was in the pinks, top and bottom, a man not afraid of the color. Not afraid of anything by the looks of him. What the hell was he doing here in the first place? No wonder Marsha was fascinated. Talk about being in the wrong place at the wrong time, Eric Black was the walking, talking and very confident description of that.

"Thank-you." he smiled at Gail and walked straight into the office as if he had been there a hundred times before. Not that there was a choice of doors other than the one he came through but it was his step which caught her attention. It was the step of someone who has done a lot of walking on uncertain, uneven ground. It was solid and assured, like an animal that has a way of moving through brush or trees without looking at their feet, without breaking a twig, without rustling a bush, without being noticed.

"Dad!"

Arlene was on her feet and in her father's embrace before he had taken two steps into the room. With the daughter's back to her, Marsha couldn't see her expression or what passed from her eyes to her father's but she could see his reaction from the moment he entered and throughout the embrace. Happy and a little embarrassed but clear and completely possessed of his intellect and reason. The look of well man, better than well, the look of a complete man. Sometimes it happened, she told herself in spite of the fact she had never before personally witnessed the miracle.

"Please make yourself comfortable, Eric." She said when father and daughter broke their embrace. It was obvious they were close and while he might have shown a little embarrassment when he entered, it was now gone. Marsha sensed that whatever secrets the two shared, they weren't ashamed of them and to her that meant one thing and one thing only. Took A-Look was as real to them as they were to each other.

It figures, she thought, and then questioned herself. Why would that figure? Because he is real to me too? She couldn't argue that feeling in spite of the fact she couldn't empirically defend the source of it. She couldn't really find the source of it, or could she? *Didn't I see him? Didn't he see me? My God, I should be on my own couch!*

"You look good, Dad. Lost a few pounds but we'll take care of that right away." Arlene stated with humor tempered with relief. The storm had passed and there wasn't even that much damage to show for it, to clean up after such a severe tempest. Marsha watched Arlene staring straight into her father's eyes. Something else was being communicated and whatever it was, Arlene looked a little angry then started to blush and then produced a small, girlish giggle before looking away.

Marsha felt a sudden spike of jealousy which should have surprised her but didn't. She knew exactly what caused the feeling and wasn't ashamed of it. Sometimes her job was too lonely for words and the words which weren't being spoken in front of her were a consummate definition of that loneliness. That and something else which was very intimate. No, she corrected herself, not something else, someone else and she wanted to be part of the exchange, the sharing, the peace which she was watching in front of her.

"We'll see what the good Doctor has to say about that Arlene." He winked at his daughter and turned to Marsha. "What is the procedure, Marsha? Do you have some ink blots for me?"

Serious but not too serious, cooperative but in complete control and not a single indication of being controlled. "No, no ink blots, Eric. More to do with what has happened recently and how it might affect you in the future." It was her turn to look into his eyes and this time she was captivated by them. It sent a primordial shiver down her spine.

"In other words, will I relapse?"

"That is always a concern."

Not to mention what is going on at this very moment. It was a déjà vu feeling that she traced back to the moment she spent with him just after he had hurt his arm. No, not he, not him, not Eric...that was Took A-Look.

"I intend to deal with that right away Marsha. With your help, if possible. Perhaps you could recommend a therapist and provide the background, test results and so on for this...unfortunate occurrence. Assuming of course that you can't help me yourself...which I would certainly prefer..."

Marsha was confronting a well thought out plan and she knew it. Eric Black had all his bases covered and was answering questions which hadn't been asked. No, he had never been in therapy before so he wanted a reference. Yes, he knew that his physical and mental condition needed further attention. No, it wouldn't be here. Yes it would be prompt, just like his release.

"Thank you Eric, but no I can't offer treatment beyond this facility... meaning you must be a resident patient here which I'm sure is not what you want, not what any of us wants for you. And I can't recommend anyone either, your personal physician will have to do that. Who would that be?" If Marsha had a choice, make that a chance, she preferred to release a patient into the care of a physician, not a family member. Chances of that happening were usually lousy and not because of the patient or the family. Most patient-physician relationships were simply too weak for the physician to agree to such a thing. Even a good relationship wasn't a guarantee, the cost of malpractice insurance made certain of that.

"Are you thinking about releasing me into my Doctor's custody?"

"You don't have to do that." Arlene pounced on the question. "I'll take the responsibility. I signed for the commitment so I can do this." As far as Arlene was concerned that issue wasn't open for negotiation. She knew what was best for her father and no one was about to get between the two of them.

"You committed your own father?" Eric joked lightly and watched Arlene's blush rise before realizing his mistake. "You did the right thing, Arlene." But it was too late to put the brakes on his daughter's runaway emotions.

"This never had to happen. It's all her fault. That bloody woman, it's all her fault." she said with a thick, heavy voice.

He took his daughter's hand to comfort her. "Don't worry about it. It's all over and it won't ever happen again."

His words had an ominous ring to them. Ominous? Or was it just the brutal, naked contrast of witnessing someone under the absurd control of an unseen force and then seeing the same person suddenly restored to complete control over their own thinking and destiny? Does anyone actually have absolute control?

Marsha realized that she was seeing a tiny, reflected light in his eyes and had the sensation that she was being watched. Not the foreboding, skin-crawling sensation which horror movies try to imitate but the pleasant, familial feeling of being admired or watched by a loved one. It was as if that light was shining toward her with outstretched arms the way a child sometimes sees the love in a parent's face, in a parent's eyes. The loving face combined with the security of a tight embrace, human warmth, peace.

"Really Dad, really? Is it over, finally over?" Arlene asked.

"It's all over, Arlene. I'll take care of it. Believe me, I'll take care of it."

Interesting choice of word. It, not her or Brita, but it.

It sounded like he was talking about taking out the garbage. Detached. Cold and detached. In complete contrast to his other behaviors, particularly with his daughter. Then again, the wife didn't endear herself to anyone, she probably didn't even deserve what she would ultimately get. With that thought, Marsha realized that she had made up her mind. Eric Black was already working on his future and she was doing the same thing with him. The doctor, the lawyer, the butcher and the baker. Life went on. Interrupted with chaos, tragedy, luck or happenstance, it went on and it didn't seem to matter if you answered all the questions or left them alone for another day or another year. Life went on but so too did her questions and she had to ask at least one of them.

"What can you tell me about Took A-Look, Mr. Black?" Without thinking about it, she shifted to his formal title.

Arlene seemed to whiten a little with the question but Eric's response was smooth and flowing.

"Took A-Look is, well, you could call him a metaphor for inner strength. He is...was...like a...medium...a guide. He helped Arlene cope with the death of her mother. Sometimes the strength we need must come from somewhere outside ourselves, objective not subjective. Like faith, you have to trust."

"Faith?" You could also call that a damned convenient metaphor.

"Faith in ourselves, Marsha. It's what allows us to bear something which we don't think we can bear. It a way of getting past our problems by believing we can get past our problems. It's knowing that the future will arrive and our problems will be diminished."

He was answering the unasked questions again. His problems were in the past and whether he dealt with them directly or left them alone it was up to him...or up to them, depending on which version of his subjective/objective reality you picked. The past was there to be forgotten or remembered, depending on the circumstances, depending on good or bad. She had her own experience on that topic. No more and probably not much different than anyone else who has triumphs and regrets but nothing that had brought her to her knees, to the brink of non-being like had happened to him. If Took A-Look was alive and well in the back of his head, what was he thinking? And after that, what about after that?

Then nothing, she suddenly realized. Everything was all right. She was the outsider, the odd one out. She was the one who didn't understand, she was the one who built a reality that denied another person's reality. The only thing keeping her from believing in him was herself. Herself and a few dozen textbooks, but what did they know? What do any of us really, really know for certain? She pushed the button on her telephone.

"Gail, please prepare Mr. Black's release papers." She hesitated for a second but not because she hadn't made up her mind. The hesitation was an offer, an opportunity for him to explain or comment further.

Offer rejected by virtue of silence, as she expected it would be and then added: "No conditions for the discharge."

"This will only take a few minutes, if you would like to change clothes and return here, the papers will be finished by the time you get back. Mrs. Mallory, you may wait outside if you like."

"I will, thank-you Doctor."

Arlene and her father were already standing when Marsha turned in her chair and got up to say goodbye. She shook hands with Arlene and then extended her hand to Eric, who took it warmly. His words of thanks came to her like they were from a movie, a movie being played in the background of her mind, not right in front of her.

A realization was dawning and she was concentrating on it. Took A-Look and Eric had made a deal.

"Good-bye Arlene. Good-bye Took A-Look" she said, without realizing her error.

MARTY SORENSON & GUT VIK

CHAPTER 19

In the beginning, Marty Sorenson decided he wouldn't forget Eric Black but that soon changed and when it did, he discovered that he couldn't forget Eric Black. There was something about that man, and it wasn't just his final words, words which were insulting enough not to be easily forgotten, but it was the way they went into Marty's consciousness that made them unforgettable and inescapable. Those words were like bullets passing through a wall and finding the person who thought he was safe hiding behind it.

No, he thought, it wasn't quite like that. It was more like an arrow when you see the shaft stuck in your chest, know the point is coming out your back and realize that something in between has been skewered and is about to stop beating. Yes, that was it, but not an arrow, it was a spear, definitely a spear, a spear with a white bone tip. A spear that had been applied with a lot of force by an experienced hand. Right to the heart of the matter, just like the words: "You can cut the chit-chat orderly, you're way over your head and you don't know half of what you think you know."

For the first few days after Eric Black was released, the words echoed in Marty's brain, over and over again, at the oddest of times. When he wasn't even thinking about the man, when circumstance or environment were totally alien and there wasn't anything to explain those words being sounded in his head, they would just pop in and start playing. For a few minutes, if he was lucky, but at other times they lasted for hours and hours. Just like some stupid supermarket radio jingle worms its way into your brain and almost anything can set it off but nothing can stop it.

When he wasn't thinking about those words, or wasn't being consumed by their endless repetition, he thought about Eric Black's return. Most of them came back at least once, especially when they were as catatonically fucked-up as Eric Black. Then the High and Mighty Mr. Black would discover who was top dog and who was lying on their back begging for mercy. Then Marty would take his revenge for the insult and the persecution of those words; he had done it plenty of times before and it was too sweet not to think about getting even.

Foolishly, he became so busy planning this revenge that he didn't bother thinking, for even a moment, about what those words meant and that they very well might be true. Not once did he think that.

Not once did he think that, as day after day fell out of the calendar, until he finally realized Eric Black wasn't coming back and there wasn't going to be any revenge so he stopped planning it. Strangely enough it was just about that time that the words also started to fade. They weren't there as often and they didn't stay as long but it wasn't because the insult had cooled or the feeling of a spear stuck in his chest had gone away. No, unfortunately that wasn't the case; he couldn't put that insult in the background of his mind like other insults he had suffered, and harbored, and let smolder, and then revenged later at his convenience. It wasn't that way at all. Fact was, and a lousy fact it was, Marty began to understand that he was no longer in complete control of all his thoughts.

Every time he tried to figure it out he kept coming back to the same result: Eric Black was in control. He was inside Marty's blood and brain like an evil virus with an agenda all his own and that was when he finally understood why he only knew half of what he knew. The other half was streaming into his mind from somewhere, or from someone, else. After that, all thoughts of revenge were replaced with blind hope. Hope that this was a temporary thing which would eventually fix itself or even just go away, he didn't care where.

Sometimes when the words faded into the background of his brain, a background that was becoming increasingly more chaotic, they were replaced with an image. Eric Black's face when he put on his street clothes as he prepared to leave with his daughter. Something Marty had seen more times than he could remember and with so many different faces and cases he had learned to stop thinking about them as soon as the door closed on their backs. If they returned he would remember them easily enough and if they didn't come back, they were outside his world and ceased to matter, ceased to exist. There was simply no point in trying to figure out what they were thinking when they left the hospital because there was nothing to be gained by doing so. But Eric Black was different, he couldn't be forgotten. No matter how hard he tried, that man's words and his image just couldn't be pushed away, pushed outside. They came and went as they wanted to and there wasn't a thing he could do about it, especially the eyes.

The eyes were the worst part and that was both completely irrational and entirely logical. It was irrational because Eric Black's eyes seemed to see everything, outside and inside, from all angles, magnified, like he had some extra-terrestrial x-ray vision that could see flesh, thoughts, memories, everything. And it was logical because Marty was beginning to see the same thing in his own eyes except for one major detail. When he looked in the mirror, he wasn't sure whose eyes were looking back at him, they weren't Eric Black's and they weren't his own, so whose eyes were they?

It was a walking nightmare that was getting worse, day after day, week after week. Like when he was shaving and his eyes held his mirrored face steady as the razor went from side to side until he accidentally made eye contact with a stranger looking back at him. How could that be? How could the one doing the seeing not be the one being seen? Worse than that, the stranger's eyes were eyes that you wanted to run away from. But your own eyes? How do you deal with that? How do you run away from that? How can you stop thinking about that? Now he knew he didn't know as much as he thought...certainly not half as much, maybe not even a quarter as much. One thing for sure, if Eric Black came back, Marty Sorenson would actually be glad to see him but obviously, he knew what was going on and even more importantly, he was free from it.

It was starting to make sense, which was really terrifying. Eric Black's eyes had looked into his mind with the exact same penetrating awareness as the shaft of the spear which was buried in his chest. Eric Black's dark blue eyes with black specks penetrated his brain with an unnerving and unerring sense of command and control. Those eyes saw everything and it wasn't an act or a projection. It was the real thing, it was real seeing, right to the core, right to the heart of the matter and now Marty knew why the image kept returning and couldn't be pushed away.

It was the eyes behind Eric Black's eyes which made that realization occur, which made no sense at all for a long time but which was now completely logical because it happened to him every time he looked in a mirror and saw the stranger's eyes looking back at him. Whatever he was becoming, Eric Black already was, which was troubling but with one major difference: he was in command and control and Marty was losing both with little hope of recovery.

The eyes which emerged from the chaos that had become his mind and his life were cold, cruel, light blue eyes from somewhere or someone in the past. It was a past without a memory to go with it, but it came with recognition so strong that he knew there had to be a memory sourcing it, it was just shrouded in mist. It was fearful. Anyone in their right mind would fear that mist, that swirling dank cloud that kept the face from being seen clearly but which allowed those eyes to see out, to watch him.

Then, as if all this wasn't bad enough, the talking started. Talking which he tried to deny, then tried to justify by reason he had always talked to himself and that it wasn't any different than anyone else so no problem, right? For sure lots of people at the hospital talked to themselves, especially Julia Reynolds, who had made such a fine art out of it she could keep both sides of a conversation going for days on end. Everybody talks to themselves, don't they?

Sometimes they blurted out an observation when no one was around to hear them. Like he caught Steve talking to an empty hallway. 'Jesus, that woman can talk. It's like she's trying to drill a hole into your head with words.'

Sometimes they chastised or complimented themselves. 'Damn, I forgot the towels.' or, 'That wasn't luck, that was genius.' Everybody talked to themselves, whether they said the words out loud or not. Just like some people mouth the words when they read and some people don't but they were all doing the same thing in their heads, just like Marty was doing. Completely normal, right, sure it was.

Just like carrying on an actual conversation with yourself was normal, right, who hasn't done that? Like working out a problem with two sides to it, or two options to choose from, and arguing both sides with yourself. 'If I do this I will enjoy it.' Opposed by: 'If I get caught doing it I won't like the consequences.' Lots of people did that. Playing the devil's advocate, the good Marty on one shoulder and the bad one on the other shoulder. Completely normal, right? He even confirmed it with some of the other orderlies. Sure they did it, if there were two sides to an issue, why not mentally pit one side against the other? Why not take both sides and argue them against each other? Everybody argues with themselves, right?

But what if they weren't your own words, then what? Was that so normal? What if there were three sides and one of those sides always came as a surprise?

Fortunately for Marty, topics like this were easy to discuss at work. No one paid any attention to it or looked too deeply into the reasons behind his interest in the topic. They were all amateur psychologists anyway. It was one of the first weaknesses Marty exploited with a new orderly. What they thought about others told him everything he needed to know about how they reasoned and what their values were. People who talk too much about themselves don't seem to think about what they are giving up, what they are exposing, Julia Reynolds excluded. Her constant, on-going banter could disguise anything forever.

It's called Never-Ending.

Never-Ending, that's when he got really worried. That's when it occurred to him that he wasn't talking to himself and that he wasn't in control of both sides of the argument. Somebody else, with their own unique agenda was coming up with answers and observations, compliments and criticisms. Lots of criticisms, just like mother, bless her for dying so soon after the old man bought the farm. Both of them too young and too self-involved to be any help to him now. Oh yeah, and too dead.

Maybe that was it. He was 43 years old, unmarried with only a couple of completely superficial relationships in his memory and a fair amount of baggage from his youth which was still seeking its final destination. A little young for a middle-aged crisis but considering the blistering pace of his life, his rapid accession to the apex of his career and some of the other shit he had done but for which he had never been caught, it made sense. He was simply realizing his accomplishments and entering another stage of life, trying to break free of the past, so to speak. He was becoming this new person, a painful process but he was used to that. Mostly on the giving end of the pain but so what? Nothing lasts forever, right?

Never-Ending.

Screw off!

Never-Ending. Get used to it.

Finally, he denied his denial and admitted that he wasn't growing up. He was growing something all right but he wasn't growing up. And it wasn't a very nice something which was growing steadily, uncontrollably, in the back of his head. He couldn't turn it off and he couldn't out-smart it. It? It? The sonovabitch had a name.

Gut Vik.

Jesus, what kind of a name is that and where did it come from? Had he made it up? He didn't think so. It sounded bloody Norwegian, didn't it? Gut Vik, what a name.

It's a been around for a lot longer than you have, you should fear it.

Screw you!

You will learn. Just like all the others, your eyes will be opened in a way that you cannot imagine.

Marty's next move was one of sheer self-defense, he knew it but what else could he do? Once he knew he wasn't talking to himself, he knew he had to stop talking. Not completely but as much as he could get away with and with as few words as possible when a nod or a shrug wouldn't do the trick. There weren't a lot of ways to do that without giving up some of his control over the other orderlies but that sacrifice had to be made so nod by nod, grunt by grunt, he had to give up his power because without words, he couldn't maintain outside control any better than he could maintain inside control with them. It wasn't great but at least he was still an orderly and not a patient.

"You are such a good listener, Marty. Now, where was I? Oh yes, Lawrence is such a good boy, he really is. He's twelve now, he had his birthday last week, but I've told you that already, haven't I? Of course I have, where is my head?"

Good question, he thought. You should try answering it sometime, no one else can. Silence, he realized, had some sarcastic benefits and that helped his concentration.

"Lawrence doesn't come to see me, you know? You know why he doesn't come to see me?"

Because your husband doesn't want Lawrence to know that his mother is a basket case?

"Because of my husband."

Thought so.

What do you mean Gut Vik, it's her own fault? For Chrissakes I've got twenty years of experience with these idiots. Everybody outside is ashamed of everybody inside, fault is secondary.

"He is ashamed of me. He doesn't say so but I know that's what he's thinking. That's what he has always thought. The big businessman with the talkative house-wife, like that's a crime. It isn't you know? Of course you know, you are such a good listener Marty, you really are. Just like my Lawrence was a good listener until my husband turned him against me. 'Don't you ever shut up?' he would say, over and over again until one day Lawrence said it too. Can you imagine how that felt? Can you imagine that?"

"Yes, Julia."

"Oh I do so love it when you say my name. I used to be Julia Bloomquist which has such a nice sound to it. Much better than Reynolds, don't you think? Bloomquist sounds much nicer and it was even better when I was young and pretty. I was quite pretty once, I really was. I'm sure that's what attracted my husband to me. He hated everything else about me, not right away, but eventually. 'Don't you ever shut up?' What an awful thing to say but that's what he said, over and over again until Lawrence picked it up and said it too."

Never-Ending.

Screw off with the Never-Ending. You hear me Gut Vik? Screw off with the Never-Ending. Why don't you go back to where you came from? What do you mean, me first?

"Husbands shouldn't do that. That shouldn't be allowed. One minute it's all hugs and kisses and the next minute they hate you. It shouldn't be allowed. I don't want Lawrence to grow up like that but he probably will, just like his father and all the other men in his family. It's hereditary, you have to believe that. You do believe that don't you?"

"It's true and always will be."

What? Don't you put words into my mouth, Gut Vik.

I'm living proof of it? Screw you. Screw you Gut Vik. Go back to hell where you came from. Nobody tells me what to say, what to do. You hear that you fucking asshole. What do you mean, you'll show me a thing or two?

NO! NO! NO! Don't do that, for Chrissakes don't do that! Stop it! STOP IT! I take it back! I TAKE IT ALL BACK! Jesus Christ, Stop it! No, no more.

FOR CHRISSAKES GUT VIK, STOP IT! YOU'RE GOING TO KILL HER, YOU'RE GOING TO KILL JULIA. STOP HITTING HER. Please, please.

Oh Jesus, now we're in for it. Look what you've done. Holy shit. Her broken teeth, my fist cut up, blood everywhere, undeniable, probably even on video. Shit, shit shit, we're in for it now. You heard me Gut Vik. I said we're in for it now. For Chrissakes, why did you do that? What the fuck did that prove?

Oh shit, here they come, five of them.

"Steve, Steve you gotta believe me. Jesus, Steve, it was an accident. Honest man it was an accident. Don't give me that, you don't have to give me that...don't stick me with that stuff...no drugs, no drugs please...I won't do anything...I'll be good...you don't have to stick..."

* * * * *

Marsha was sitting in her office when she heard about the orderly's attack on her patient, Julia Reynolds. It occurred at 12:10 in the day room and she heard about it at 12:19. She was one of the last to know.

Fielding, Chief of Staff and Administration was in the day room five minutes after Sorenson had been subdued and he had already decided that Marsha would be the contact point for all the legalities to follow. Two reasons: first it was her patient and second she could be trusted to take a fair and logical approach toward quickly concluding the investigation. He would have preferred three reasons but knew that Marsha could not be manipulated into making him look good so he had to settle for two.

It was an unreasoning, brutal attack without any warning whatsoever and like the incident itself, everything moved quickly after that. Sorenson was sedated, the police were called and they took him away, good. The first thing any manager learns about a crisis situation is to maximize distance as soon as possible.

Obviously the police felt that way too. Within hours of being dropped into a holding cell, a detective was appointed and before Marsha went home that afternoon she was informed by Fielding's Admin, Betty, that she could expect an interview the next morning at ten o'clock, so plan for it. In the meantime, Marsha looked after Julia who was badly beaten and scared witless.

As usual, Director Fielding was more concerned about what happened outside the hospital than in it and couldn't be found anywhere.

* * * * *

Except for Julia Reynolds, the next day started like most of the days before it. Marsha visited with her patient and was pleased, or as pleased as she could make herself believe, that things were not as bad as the day before. No broken jaw, one tooth missing and two others that would need some work, cuts around the mouth that took a few stitches but which shouldn't scar and two very black eyes. How her nose missed the attack was anybody's guess and there wasn't any point in asking Julia that question because she was heavily sedated and would like stay that way for a while to come.

After a brief examination, Marsha walked the ward and saw a couple more patients before her ten o'clock appointment with the police. Her mind wasn't completely on her work and she knew it. Not that she had any premonitions to occupy her thoughts, it was actually quite the opposite as she decided her absent-mindedness was because she didn't have any real thoughts about how the investigation would or should proceed, in spite of the fact she had a major role in it.

When the time finally came, she was relieved when introductions were made and she told her story, what little of it there was to tell.

Detective Lugano was middle-aged, average height, build, and dressed in jeans with a dark sports jacket over a light blue shirt, the least likely looking policeman she could ever have imagined. Not even his hair gave hint to his profession, being a little long and in need of a trim and those were just the obvious, external clues. His behavior was even less police-like. Slightly shy or awkward, soft spoken and not displaying any machismo, he conducted the interview in an objective, almost disinterested voice. Marsha knew from the way he observed her, that he was anything but disinterested and that when the facts were all on the table, the questioning would take another line; it would get personal. She often used the same tactic.

"So you don't have any explanation for the assault on the Reynolds woman, Dr. Coleman?"

"No Detective, I don't. I've told you everything I know, which is basically what I have been told by others."

"Would you care to speculate on what caused this?"

"Speculate?"

"Off the record, Dr. Coleman, completely off the record. Not that we won't follow up on anything you have to offer because we often do, and occasionally with some success too, but it won't come back to haunt you... that's a promise." It was a conciliatory statement. Logano was pretty sure Dr. Coleman wouldn't spread gossip or innuendo, besides, the Chief made it abundantly clear he would get all the cooperation he needed to put this thing behind them as quickly and as fairly as possible. Plus, she would cooperate because Fielding promised the Chief she would cooperate fully and all he wanted in return was a quick and fair investigation, mostly quick.

The Chief made one more thing clear: 'No witch-hunt Lugano and I don't care how many witches you find along the way. Get in quick, get out faster.'

From the first moment Marsha heard about the assault on Julia, she had done nothing but speculate. It was all she could do. Marty Sorenson wasn't her patient and ever since the incident with Brita Black in the day room, weeks ago, he hadn't said more than a couple of words to her, avoiding her completely whenever he could. Not that he had ever been particularly chatty and she only ever got anything out of him by digging for it, but his behavior had definitely changed. This was also noticed by the other orderlies who found Sorenson's preoccupation with certain topics to be rather out of character. What did Steve say they started calling him? Born again Norwegian? That didn't make sense either.

"You might want to talk to Steve Walker, he knew Sorenson better than anyone else did." Marsha didn't want to speculate but not because it was speculation; she just didn't like the quality of her thoughts.

"I've done that, Dr. Coleman. Has anyone else said anything to you that might be helpful?" he asked, half thinking about the case while the rest of his thoughts were on her. She didn't fit, didn't belong to the same club as all the other shrinks he had ever had the pleasure, or the frustration, of interviewing. Over the years, he had met his share of them and he never expected to meet one like her.

Lupo Logano, Lupo being the Italian nickname which stuck to his Italian surname. Lupo, the wolf, was assigned the Reynolds' case because he was assigned every case like it. Anything which was bizarre, twisted, bent, weird, crazy, insane or psychotic landed on his desk. Anything which looked like it had an insanity plea hanging on its coat-tails and they called for the wolf. Sometimes he was called after-the-fact, when an insanity plea was the defense's last resort but that wasn't the situation here. An orderly attacking a patient in a mental hospital ensured his involvement; the brutality and spontaneity of the attack guaranteed it would be his case before anybody meddled in it and after that decision was made, no one would come within ten feet of it.

"Not really, detective. I have talked to everyone who might know something and I don't have any explanation for what happened, not even a worthwhile speculation."

"A random event, is that how you would classify it?" His un-patented trick question. Irresistible for any therapist, key word being random. Every last one of them took it as an insult to their expensively framed high-priced, gold lettered, wallpaper. Not that they all had the same response because they didn't, but they all hated the word because by implication it was the one word that could exclude them from practicing their profession. Random doesn't need analysis and can't be cured.

"I'm not sure that I could ever classify an episode like that as random, Detective Logano but I'm sure you know that already."

She was on to him already. Was it his reputation or was she really that clever? "How so, Dr. Coleman?" He asked, wondering how she would counterpunch to protect her degree, her career, her very own personal, sanitized definition of reality. She responded more quickly than he thought she would.

"My guess is that you have done this before, many times before. Is that right?" she asked, looking for the truth in his words, not the words.

"It is." Fifty-fifty but he'd guessed wrong. He figured, based on her age, she would jump on the pulpit and explain to him why random wasn't random. It was really just very poor planning and even if things didn't go as vaguely planned or completely in the opposite direction, that still didn't make anything random. To them, it was all a matter of timing, just ask enough questions after-the-fact and then nothing looks random because the questions are logical so the answers, by default, attain a degree of logic as well; ergo, end of random. Anyway no big deal if she decided to play head games with him. If that wasn't their first pick, they got around to it pretty quickly.

"Then I'll tell you right up front, detective. If I can be of any help to you, I will be. This hospital may not be the average place of work for the average person but it isn't a medieval torture chamber, nor is it the complete and utter chaos most people imagine it to be. In many ways it is very predictable. What happened between Sorenson and my patient was very unusual."

Dr. Coleman was deviating from the norm and Lupo liked it. She was playing one-on-one with him. Mano-a-mano. Shrink to flatfoot. If there was another game in the background Lupo couldn't sense it, but he knew better than to trust that instinct too damn fast. "But you are curious about it?"

"Curious? No, not really curious. I wish it had never happened in the first place but I would like to know how to prevent it in the future and that means I need to know something about it. I think you feel the same way."

Lupo was taken aback, silenced by both the intensity and honesty of her answer. *'I think.'* Reality testing from a psychiatrist. Now that is unusual.

Before he could say anything Marsha took control of the silence he was using to restore his control.

"Yes Detective, I said, 'I think.' Personally, I find it upsetting. No matter how many times I see such destructive behavior, it is upsetting. I would be just as happy if it never happened at all than to know why it happened and not have done anything to prevent it."

For the second time in a matter of minutes, she made complete sense. She was real. But how real would she be? "You referred to him as Sorenson, not Marty or Marty Sorenson. I take it you don't like the man."

"No, I don't like him."

"Do you dislike him?"

"They're the same thing. Yes I dislike him."

Not to most people they aren't. Most people claim neutrality at that point, including several murderers who he could remember. They were completely neutral when they blew the person's brains out. No motive whatsoever. Just felt like it that day. 'Naw, Lupo. I didn't dislike her. Didn't like her either; didn't even know her. It's just this thing in my head.' Before he could finish his thoughts and frame his next question, she started answering it.

"Sorenson believed he ran this hospital. He and a small circle of the orderlies who, for reasons I can't begin to understand, believed he was in charge. He took liberties with the patients and the system. Either personally or he allowed others to do it."

"Liberties?"

"You know exactly what I mean, Detective Logano, please don't play dumb with me."

"Sorry Dr. Coleman, it's a bad habit." He meant it. When doctors played head games with him, it pissed him off royally and he was doing the same thing with her. Maybe it's human nature. Maybe it's wolf nature? He tried a smile and it probably looked hideous. She didn't react at all to his attempt at humility which he figured must have taken some real effort on her part because he felt like a complete asshole.

"More likely a habit born of necessity, Detective. It's your job to try and uncover the truth. Mine too." She smiled at him, hoping to relieve his discomfort, a little surprised that he showed it. The situation was quite hopeless, it really didn't matter what she said so the sooner it was over, the better.

The Director had made that point clear with his early morning briefing, also known as Proclamation of the Party Line. There wasn't a single course of action which was any better than any other. An insane orderly in a mental hospital was just as bad as a sane orderly committing such an atrocious act. Either way they were going to get sued and either way, they would lose. 'There are no heros in the courtroom so let's just keep our losses to money, okay? Occupational hazard, that's the party line. No sense in going any deeper than that, no one is to blame so don't blame anyone and that includes blaming yourself. The guy will get what's coming to him, insurance will pay, justice will be served, end of story.'

"For what it's worth, I think Sorenson did experience some changes over the last while, over the last weeks. Nothing overt or negative until this happened, in fact with me it was almost a positive change. He…I'm not sure how to put it…he stopped being such a pain in the ass."

"He stopped contesting your authority." Lupo corrected. The discussion was changing from interview to conversation and he was happy for it. Dr. Coleman would make a lousy expert witness. He didn't doubt that she knew her stuff but she also readily admitted to what she didn't know and that was just the kind of weakness the other side prays for. The bigger the expert's ego, the better they witness, without exception.

Suddenly, being put in the same company with people who fight for authority and control made Marsha feel petty and small. She didn't glorify her authority any more than she glorified her appearance and that pretty much summed up her attitude on power and authority. She hadn't won the contest of wills with Sorenson because she outranked him, or because she outfought him or outthought him. She won because he gave up.

"He just seemed to give up. Like it didn't matter anymore." she said a little contritely because that was how she felt.

"Was he at all friendly? Considerate? Did he acknowledge defeat?"

"No, he avoided contact as much as he could."

"That's not good."

"Isn't it?"

The conversational mode was still intact even if the flow of questioning was reversed. She was interested, he sensed it. He also sensed she was pursuing her own line of thought, one related to the incident but with a lot of 'ifs.' associated with it, the last of which was, as ever, 'if I tell the detective'.

"We see the same thing in prison. Inmates fight the system, the guards, other inmates, fixtures, the bars, walls, you name it. A few of them never give up but most of them, particularly long timers, eventually have to accept their situation. Then they become cooperative. Not overtly cooperative but you know that you can turn your back on them for a couple of seconds and they won't take it as an opportunity. But a few of them just quietly withdraw from the fight and those are the dangerous ones. Those ones become part of the woodwork and you take them for granted until it's too late and they've got you on the floor. Point being, when they withdraw, they don't fight with other inmates, fixtures, the bars and walls because they're hiding, they're waiting for a chance at somebody in charge. They want to win back what they have lost; they want some command and control and they attack anyone in authority because they think that's how to get it back. Maybe not quite the same here but that's how it starts because it's human nature in these kinds of occupations."

"You worked prisons?"

"For a while, then I decided to work on this end of the spectrum."

"Why? Didn't it work out?"

The question seemed honest, even if it was personal. It was also a diversion from the topic at hand. If psychiatrists had a bedside manner, hers was pretty good. He decided a little friendliness wouldn't create a conflict; if somebody had to take the stand, it would be the Director, he definitely had the ego for it.

"Why is pretty naïve. I figured that we were putting some people away who really didn't deserve it, that we were making things worse because that's what happened by not putting bad people in prison with people who were really bad. But no, it didn't work out. What I didn't understand then was that people on the outside are not the same as when they are inside. A reasonably decent inmate inside can be hell on wheels outside when they don't have anything, or anyone, to hold them in check."

"Interesting. Sorenson may be like that. As far as I know, he didn't have much going for him in his personal life. No family life to speak of and even his hospital friends, if you can call them that, didn't associate with him outside the hospital. His life was pretty much here, the only place he was in charge of anything, this was his identity."

She was back on topic as if they had never left it. "So he ran the place like a petty dictator, anybody inside the circle was on his protected list and could, as you said, take liberties while everybody else was frozen out."

"Yes. Whether they were stealing drugs or molesting patients, they certainly wouldn't want to get caught at it. They covered each other's backs and he covered everybody's back, everybody in his inner circle, that is."

"I can raise some hell with them if you like. Throw a little fear their way if you think it will do any good." Too late and he remembered the Chief's no witch-hunt regulation and then just as quickly rationalized it. He rationalized by thinking it might protect Dr. Coleman and then by reasoning that throwing a little fear in somebody's path was a whole lot different than burning them at the stake, ergo, no witch hunt.

"It can't hurt but, honestly, Detective Logano, I don't think it will change the system."

"It seldom does, Dr. Coleman, but that's my job." The conversation was getting warmer, at least it felt that way.

"Call me Marsha, Detective..."

"They call me Lupo, Marsha. Not my real name but I'm so used to it that it might as well be."

"Lupo, the wolf?"

"Right, but not like in Red Riding Hood, not the Big Bad Wolf. It's because...because I prowl a case. I'm a stalker, in the legal sense of the word of course – well, most of time it's legal." he risked the joke.

She took him seriously: "I see. Others investigate but you hunt. You must be very good at it."

"I am – but to tell you the truth, it really is stalking. Unfortunately that's usually what it takes, just waiting for them to make a mistake and me being there when they make it."

Marsha noticed right away the lack of pretense for either modesty or ego. Because the job was tough, his pride came from doing it, not talking about it.

"Would you be willing to assist our shrinks with Sorenson's evaluation?" A spontaneous idea which he immediately regretted, especially calling her a shrink but a second later and he changed his mind. It was actually a brilliant idea to have someone like her around the department's standard insane expert-witness crime buster head-shrinkers.

She paused and thought: "I'd like that, Lupo." Then paused and thought again, "but it might be better if I was an observer, an unofficial one." She watched for a reaction but didn't quite get the reaction she expected and decided to explain. "I haven't always been complimented for my team work. Occupational hazard, you know?"

Her honesty and backhand joke elicited a nod from him but he kept his eyes hidden from hers.

She realized he was every bit the stereotypical cop but it was just as obvious a heart was beating in his chest. He was a human being and more than a little cautious to show it. Not macho but masculine; definitely the kind of man who could throw the fear of God into the orderlies if he decided to get tough with them. She sensed he would do precisely that. She sensed he would prowl around long enough to change somebody's behavior, maybe even send a few of them to jail, if for no other reason than they might get something positive out of being on the receiving end of the abuse they seemed to enjoy handing out.

"I'll make the arrangements, Marsha. Right now Sorenson is isolated in holding. But everybody wants to get to him 'yesterday' so I won't be able to give you much notice, could even be today but most likely tomorrow." He started to get up, half a dozen questions still forming in his mind but they could wait, he would see her again and next time he planned on being more himself and less of a Lupo.

"That's all right, Gail will move my schedule around as necessary. Where should I go?"

"I'll send a car for you, if that isn't a problem."

"Not at all. I wish I could have been more help."

"One piece at a time, Marsha. That's the way it works. Not very often that we get to the bottom of a case like this without lots of digging." He winked at her as if winking and digging belonged together. They didn't so he shrugged his shoulders as if that would correct the mistake, maybe erase it. One thing for sure, he would put plenty of muscle between Sorenson and Doctor Marsha Coleman. If she wasn't the fuse, she was the detonator and Sorenson was ready to blow. No doubt about it, he was a sleeper of the most dangerous kind.

The hair on the back of his neck bristled as if it had just received a big charge of static electricity. He hated that feeling. It came from a place he didn't understand and he didn't care to understand.

The wolf understood it and that was enough, more than enough.

* * * * *

Jesus Christ, Gut Vik, look what you've done. All these years I've never been caught for anything and now look at all the shit I'm facing. Where the fuck are you Gut Vik? Where are you now that all your shit has hit my fan?

'Sonovabitch.' Marty muttered to himself.

All of sudden and life sucked. Sucked big time and that's what he was looking at. Lots of big, long, degrading time. Shit, shit, shit. He was pretty sure Julia was still alive but maybe that was just wishful thinking. Damn near 48 hours of wishful thinking with about that many months of sentence, if he was lucky. Unless she was dead in which case numbers wouldn't matter, just throw away the key. His hand hurt like hell. Across his knuckles, the marks from her teeth were plain as day and still oozing a little blood and clear liquid. No friggin' hope of denying that he'd hit her, several times, and damn hard too. He? He hell, it was Gut Vik but how was he going to explain that and, even more importantly, would Gut Vik let him explain it? Talk about being between a rock and hard place, if this wasn't it, then it was just two mighty big fuckin' rocks.

What a helpless, out-of-reality feeling. Like watching himself in a home movie was about as close as he could come to describing it. It was him all right, but then again it wasn't, it was an imposter from another time. An imposter who beat poor Julia and beat her mercilessly without killing her, he hoped. Challenging Gut Vik to a showdown was a bad idea.

The bastard could come and go as he pleased with absolutely no consequences. Putting his own thoughts forward, spouting his own words and now, evidently, he could take complete charge whenever he wanted to and Marty couldn't do a thing about him, couldn't even lift a middle finger in protest. But the real mistake was denying his presence for so long and now being totally ignorant of just what...make that who, Gut Vik was...make that is, not to mention the lack of a single shred of useful detail about what he wanted.

Then again, that's the way it had always been with everybody in Marty's life, so he couldn't exactly be faulted for making that mistake. All he ever really knew about anyone was how to push their buttons, how to manipulate them, how to screw them over or how to intimidate them. When to wait and when to act was his method, his only method. And now he was on the receiving end of it. Now the shoe was on the other foot and it was kicking him right in the ass. Just like dear old dad said would happen, how the fuck did that stupid old man know that?

He was dead for almost twenty years but Marty still thought of him, quite a bit lately.

If the old fuck had told him 'don't do that' once he'd told him a million times. One time, he even tried to figure it out, counting the number of times he was told for an entire week and then multiplying it by all the past weeks in all the past years he could remember. It came to pretty big number but the number of 'don't do that's' waiting in his future was even bigger so that was the problem. A problem that was resolved when dear old dad was crushed under the car with an oil filter wrench in his hand. 'Don't touch that jack, Martin.' Funny part was, he wasn't even thinking about it until the old man mentioned it.

Unfortunately, if that was the good news, the bad news was that Marty never really learned how to get to know people let alone how to get along with them and now, it seemed, that minor social ineptitude was coming back to haunt him. Haunt him? Good choice of words because that was the feeling, exactly.

The fog was gone and now he knew he shouldn't have feared the fog; he should have feared what was hiding in it because he sure feared it now. He needed help in the worst possible way but all he could relate to was all the times he had been asked for help and taken advantage of the situation. Fuck. No sense asking that question.

One way or another, he had to convince the cops he was mental. Temporarily mental. Preferably not criminally mental, chances of getting killed in that ward were even greater than getting killed in jail. Benignly mental would be best, with a little luck he would even be committed back to his old hospital where the guys could look out for him. Maybe Doctor Marsha would be his therapist. Maybe he would get better. With a little luck and some help, he could have a long, long life.

Never-Ending.

Not now. This is not the time.

That's what you think.

Shit, Gut Vik. Are you trying to get us killed?

Not us.

What do you mean? That made no sense at all. How the hell could there be a single survivor? Silence.

I can hear you think.

So what?

You'll find out.

Find out what?

You will see.

No, no please Gut Vik. Whatever it is don't do it. I'll behave, I will. Just let me handle this.

"On your feet, asshole."

"What?" Marty knew from the voice it wasn't Gut Vik but it took him by surprise for a moment. He realized just how distracted he was becoming and that he had better smarten up if he had any hope of survival on his own terms.

"I said on your feet. If you gotta piss, do it now."

"I don't."

"Then get over here, put both hands through the opening, one hand above the other and don't even think about fighting it. I don't give a sweet damn about when you're delivered or what condition you're in when you get there. In fact, I don't care if you get there at all."

The sonovabitch was as big as a house and he wasn't alone. Three of them all dressed the same, like football players, line backers, without their helmets but heads shaved so close he could see every wrinkle, ridge and a lot of scar tissue. Julia must be dead. For both our sakes, Gut Vik, don't start anything with these guys. Let me handle this, please!

Two corridors down, one elevator up two floors and another corridor later, the final destination was exactly what Marty expected. Plain, dirty, off-white walls with a one way mirror on one wall, a steel oval table in the middle of the room with five chairs, three on one side of the table and two on the other side facing the mirror.

Who knew how many people back there were watching him but he hoped some of them were really curious. He was led around the table.

Facing him were a man and a woman, both of them over sixty and seated on two of the three chairs with a single page in front of them. His life probably. Doctors, no doubt about it. Sanity hearing, thankfully, his best chance.

With a linebacker on each side and one behind him, he was wedged into one of the chairs facing the doctors and the mirror. What with the cuffs on his hands and feet and a chain connecting them together he didn't have any choices. Same for moving the chair which must have weighed four hundred pounds because it was probably welded to the floor like the table was.

The cop who had done the talking in the cell reached under the table, pulled out another chain, ran it through a ring on the ankle bracelet and another ring on his right hand then back under the table where it made a metallic, jailhouse clank. Satisfied that he couldn't move anything more than a foot or two in any direction, the cops left the room without looking back.

"I am Doctor Basscurt and this is Doctor Jorgenson." said the older man without looking up.

Sanity hearing, he silently repeated to himself and hoped Gut Vik was listening. He tried to ignore them and look detached but the woman, Jorgenson, was staring at him like he was some kind of rare bug. A rare bug which was still moving and she wanted to put a pin through its thorax.

A pin through the thorax?

A spear though the heart?

Just like bloody Eric Black?

Bloody Eric Black? Is that where all this came from, Eric Black's blood? Could that be it? The day he had a fit and sprayed blood and corruption everywhere. Is that where Gut Vik came from? For the first time in a long time, something, however improbable, was starting to make sense.

"You are Martin Sorenson?" asked Basscurt in half question, half statement.

"I am."

"Do you know why you are here?"

"I killed my father." The words came out at exactly the same time they registered in his head, like in a movie or a joke where you figure out the punch line at precisely same instant it is delivered.

"For Chrissakes. Shut up, Gut Vik!"

"Gut…Wick? What is that?" Basscurt wasn't surprised by the murder confession, obviously intended to form the basis of his insanity defense and just as obviously false, but he couldn't quite figure what the second part had to do with it. Not that it mattered much because one way or another he knew before he walked into the room he had to find his way past the masquerade and prove, without reference to fact, the prisoner knew what he was doing when he committed the assault. Those were his orders, but details mattered. Loose ends were tolerable in a hearing but in courtroom they were fatal.

Jorgensen, on the other hand was totally surprised. Her Norwegian was still as fluent as her memory of ancient Norwegian folklore was clear. "Gut Vik." she corrected. "When you kill fadder?"

"A long time ago. He was under the car and I let the jack down. Crushed him like a bug."

"Why you did this?"

"Why not? He was a bad father."

"How old were you then?" asked Basscurt.

"Twenty-one."

"Had you thought about killing your father before then?"

"Ja." The word drooled out of Marty's mouth like it was full of something detestable that had to get out.

"And now, now you want to confess?" Jorgenson asked without much interest in her own question but her eyes riveted to his.

"Ja."

Behind the one way mirror, Marsha put one and one together and came up with four. "Took A-Look." came out in a soft breath.

"Took A-Look?" repeated Lupo. It was all too bizarre and he'd seen plenty of bizarre. More than enough to know that when three psychiatrists share the same baffled expression, any hope of a conviction was as good as gone. They had one for the journals and not even a team of wild lawyers would be able to rip it away from them. Damn. By the time they're finished with him he'll be about as indictable as a tree stump. But unlikely that harmless. The hair on the back of his neck tingled and he knew it was standing straight out like little radio antennas. He absolutely hated that feeling, didn't know where it came from but knew something bad was waltzing down the path and into his life. Something he couldn't change, couldn't stop and wouldn't see coming until it was too damn late to do anything about it except clean up after it was done doing what it absolutely, unstoppably had to do. He even knew the color of the mess, crimson with some grey spongy material splashed in it.

* * * * *

Julia had never been so happy. It felt so good, it almost hurt. Finally she had someone to talk with. Someone who understood. Someone who finally made some sense and who cared about her, who actually cared for her. It was wonderful, simply wonderful.

I do so love your name. Oost Roven.

No, I won't keep Reynolds. I don't think I'll go back to Bloomquist either. I've been thinking…

Really, really, you don't mind? Julia Roven. It is pretty isn't it? Yes, exactly, very strong. No, of course I won't tell. I can keep a secret, you know that, don't you? What shall we talk about today? Not Lawrence? Okay, anything but Lawrence. He's not too terribly mixed-up, is he? He's still such a little boy. I know, just like his father. But that can be changed, can't it?

Surely something can be done. You will think about it won't you Oost? I know you want to meet him and then you'll see what can be done.

Of course it was an accident. Lawrence knew better than to play with fire. He was just careless, that's all.

Yes, we'll see about that when you meet him. Of course I believe you. Your thinking is so present, I swear sometimes you could predict the future with it.

My husband? He hates me, you know. Says I'm forever talking. Never-Ending you say?

Yes that's much better. I couldn't agree more.

Yes, we'll see about him too. Indeed we will. Just as soon as we leave this place. It's high time he told the truth. I know I deserve it and this time I'm going to get it.

CHAPTER 20

"Doctor Masters, that was the most interesting talk. If I had one criticism though, it would be that it wasn't nearly long enough."

"Very kind of you to say so, Mrs. Arnheim, and no one accepts that criticism with more regret than me. I wish I knew more but there is so much to do, so much more to be learned." Market research had long ago confirmed that you don't beat around the bush when you are asking rich people for money. They knew why they were invited and appreciated candor when it came to their charity. Dance around too long with what you knew and what you didn't know, or postpone the topic of money for too long, or be too shy about it, and you'd be lucky if you cleared expenses.

Market research had also spent a lot of time, money and energy trying to figure out how to maximize the return on his post speech mingling. Seating arrangements were analyzed, introductions by old wealth to new wealth and vice versa were evaluated, confidential surveys probing for questions that might go unanswered in public because rich people didn't want to look stupid yielded nothing predictable just like all kinds of variables were studied without producing a single, positive correlation that improved contribution efficiency.

It was time, energy and money wasted because in the end, the rich and powerful had a very well defined and carefully observed pecking order (excluding trophy wives whose actions were mostly unpredictable). If he had time for ten conversations, they would, with alarming frequency, be in that order of wealth.

When Roland stepped away from his podium, he observed the protocol and went directly to Mrs. Arnheim's table and introduced himself. He was expected and knew within seconds that her interest in the Legacy Gene was not just an idle curiosity of the rich. Market research got that right, just as they accurately predicted there was nothing even idle about her.

Her dress, make-up, posture, expression and smile were all business. Not a single chestnut hair was out of place. Not a second of hesitation in her brown eyes or a moment of doubt in her firm but feminine handshake. She was as warm and engaging as the pale yellow diamond pendant necklace with perfectly matching marquise cut one caret ring were rare. If there wasn't a royal pedigree in her past then she was wearing it.

"It must be fascinating to work with mysteries, doctor. Particularly one like this. Who hasn't wondered what they might have in their heads, some ancient skill or knowledge, something from the origin of the species?"

According to the profile developed by marketing, she wouldn't be asking any detailed questions because while she would part with some of her money, it was only after all her questions had been answered, with a process she would control completely.

The Legacy Gene Foundation had been established with opportunities that catered to such wishes. For a million, a hospital wing with the benefactor's name etched on a brass plate of founders was common, but it was not an offer by him. He offered something more exclusive, a gene with the Arnheim name on it. That was like buying eternity and much more unique than sharing wall space and brass plates. He could pitch that because he had dedicated his life to it and it was also where he where he would put his own money.

"Genetics is a fascination, my only real regret is that I have to specialize within it. Of course the Foundation keeps well abreast of all research and development but the field is huge and, truth to tell, this mystery is best investigated by a lot of independent research with highly specialized areas of interest. It just so happens my obsession is with the Legacy Gene." Translation: this is a competition, sooner or later and all the good genes will be gone.

"No else is looking at that area?" she asked with little concern for the subtle innuendo she had clearly heard. There were lots of ways to play that game, she knew all of them but that was irrelevant. Games were for children, not business. She watched him as carefully as she listened to him. Talking about his competition could easily reveal something important that his carefully prepared patter was intended to disguise.

"I can't really say that. After all, the area holds tremendous fascination… and potential…but we are the clear leaders in Legacy Gene research and that gap will continue to increase over time." he said with un-pretended, well-practiced modestly.

"So you don't publish your results, share the wealth, so to speak."

"Of course we do. We share results with our Foundation Members, who also have a say in research direction and we share findings with our Foundation Patrons but, at the patron level, there isn't any participation in setting strategy. We also publish some results publicly but our methods, apparatus, detail test results and so on are not for either the public or the Foundation Contributor domain, unless of course, they are protected by patent. The Legacy Gene Foundation is private and will always be private. I could have someone send you more details on how it operates, if you wish." Roland knew she got part of the point he was making: it was an exclusive club and if market research was correct she would be happy to hear that the club had a very special place just for her.

"Perhaps you can explain it over supper at the ranch when we can have you all to ourselves, doctor. Does Tuesday at around eight work for you?" Mrs. Arnheim knew all about the Foundation and if he had answered any differently, or with any less modesty, she would have introduced him to one of the other ladies and left with her check book unopened.

He accepted graciously and that was the end of discussion. She wasn't interested in sharing anything that might be overheard by people she barely knew let alone people she knew too well.

Roland knew it too, market research had stated she would set the agenda. An agenda specifically tailored so her husband could hear the promises before he would sign the checks that would make absolutely certain everybody knew exactly what role Lucy Arnheim would be playing. That was how things got done in her life. This was not her first rodeo.

"Perfect, Doctor. My driver will come to your hotel at seven, it's a bit of drive I'm afraid. Pack a bag if you would like to stay overnight, we'd love to have you. Now, may I introduce you to my friend Mrs. Abigale Mayerthorpe? Of the industrial Mayerthorpe's, the banking branch of the family is in Geneva this time of year, more to do with snow banks than the other kind, I would wager." The dry wit of her introduction served to acknowledge a true friendship.

He chuckled politely. The two women were well rehearsed. It happened all the time.

"How do you do, Mrs. Mayerthorpe."

"I should ask you that question, shouldn't I?" chirped the impeccably dressed, early thirtyish looking woman who was probably ten or fifteen years older than that.

Direct, penetrating eye contact which only a complete idiot would take as flirtation, in spite of the fact that that was its origin. Mrs. Mayerthorpe was on the Boards of Directors for the family's industrial and financial conglomerates but not because of her pretty face. Almost as wealthy as her friend, number two in the room if statistics were current and correct, no small feat in the churning turbulence of the decade's economic climate.

"If I had a million dollars…" he flirted back innocently.

"For every time you've been asked that question." she interrupted and finished his thoughts, never taking her eyes from him. "Somehow, doctor, I suspect you have managed to get your hands on much more money than that for a little barbecue beef dinner." Her eyes brightened with the game and showed the tiny laugh lines around her eyes that she permitted to stay there.

Definitely flirtatious but by no means an invitation for him to play. Those women knew their scientists. Stroke the ego but leave the rest alone. "Unfortunately, a million dollars just isn't what it used to be." he quipped in return. No beating around the money bush; shy won't get you a dime.

"Isn't that the truth. If you have to be rounded up to a billion, you just don't count anymore. Tell me doctor, if you had to put your money on what these legacy genes mean, what they do, where would you put it?"

He sized the question thoughtfully, concluding that it wasn't a deal maker or deal breaker but getting there fast and without any foreplay. "Personally, I think all the possibilities are equal. Anything from a second spleen to an immunity reaction to an extinct bacteria."

Another tactic on which marketing had been right. Recognize the down-side as soon as possible; rich people knew all about snake oil because they were the first to make and market it.

"You aren't afraid of finding anything bad?"

"Not according to theory. Self-destructive material would never have been propagated. It would have become extinct itself. Nevertheless, we take every precaution."

"Yes, you mentioned that earlier and I understand a little bit about the theory of natural selection. Key word being theory isn't it?"

"It is Mrs. Mayerthorpe. But it's also a theory to which most geneticists agree. Nature it seems, isn't much of a housekeeper, if things get too messy, she seems to prefer a scorched earth policy - just burn it down and start over." Roland looked for any hint that his violent and uncaring metaphor might have offended her and finding none continued:

"Who knows, perhaps the opposite is true, after all, a few extra genes here and there don't use up very much space so…so as long as they are not expressing, they get carried along. Just like the excess, redundant or unsubscribed nucleotides have been carried along. I mentioned that but I didn't mention the possibility that this unsubscribed DNA is just inventory, building blocks for future requirements. That, however, seems to imply some planning which is more of a spiritual than scientific nature, but nothing can be ruled out."

"Is that also your area of interest, doctor?" She had been through this before and wasn't about to spend another million with an old scientist who couldn't keep his scope under control or his microscope in focus.

"Excess nucleotides within a gene sequence for potential manipulation?" he replayed the science side of the question, receiving a nod in reply. For him, genetic engineering was an interesting but a dangerous and sometimes detestable topic.

"Interest yes, investigation, no. Redundant nucleotides along the gene sequence which is responsible for, say, kidney functioning, is really in the investigatory domain of those who are doing kidney research. When it comes to genetics, even the simplest human function, and by no means do I include the kidney in that category, becomes a very complex area of study. It takes a huge amount of investigation and very specialized training to discover how even a small part of a functioning gene works and that presupposes the most current knowledge in the organ under the microscope, so to speak." He was pretty certain she approved of his answer but wasn't given a chance to confirm that as her next question was in the air before he could read her reaction.

"Thank-you, but you still haven't answered my question when it comes to the Legacy Gene."

He understood. She had heard it before, probably right before she accepted the dinner invitation, probably from a geneticist and most likely from one of the Foundation's competitors. And the competition was fierce. Every ailment known to the human species was laid out like sparkling diamonds in a solid gold display case. Just waiting for the right buyer to come and put their name on the ailment's genetic cause along with the genetically designed cure.

"No, I suppose I haven't. So let me get to the heart of the question. We have reason to believe that Legacy Genes are not mistakes and that they were, once, fully functional. The average individual has about 20 of the 300 which have been discovered to date and these genes are blocked by what is called a regulatory protein. In a sense, that makes them no different, functionally no different that is, than any other gene which is turned on and off by what can be called a regulatory protein switch. The only thing missing is that we don't know what condition is required for the regulatory protein to move aside and allow the gene to express, that is, to become active."

"Nor do you know what will happen when it does become active and you still haven't answered my question." she said teasingly. She knew scientific hedging when she heard it and was quite comfortable with inserting her probe a little more deeply under the scientist's skin. Words like 'average individual' or 'discovered to date' were nothing more than bait on his hook and she knew it.

"What we are hoping to do, is to unblock a Legacy Gene, to allow it to express. What do we expect will happen when we are successful? We expect what is called a lac operon to occur, that is, a tandem multi-gene system which is under the control of a single promoter to be activated. It is kind of domino effect, one that might even cause the redundant, dormant nucleotides in other genes to become restarted, if they do in fact have a purpose. In other words, we believe that unlocking a Legacy Gene could become the catalyst to the expansion and expression of brain functions which have, through evolution, become suppressed."

"So you think that there is a whole system of DNA functioning which is untapped, perhaps one which has been established for future development of the human race."

The key question on her mind, at least the half of it she could speak in public.

"That is a provocative question. The future may very well be written in the past. Where we have been might tell us where we are going. Like charting the solar system led to the big bang theory, the explanation of the origin of matter as opposed to the origin of mind."

"Very compelling doctor, very compelling indeed. The possibilities are indeed great." Mrs. Arnheim interjected.

She too had received some expert guidance, unlikely by the same experts but together the two women had mounted a rather straightforward joint frontal attack. They knew their scientists and, not unlike promoting or blocking a new entry to their country club, they kept their personal motivations well hidden but were otherwise forthright with their wants. Research for the sake of research didn't interest them, if they didn't know where they were going, they wouldn't buy the ticket.

"It promises to be quite an adventure." he concluded honestly. Time was running out and he had pockets to pick.

"I look forward to hearing more about it on Tuesday. Now, we had best let you attend to your other guests." Abigale Mayerthorpe smiled vivaciously, her eyes twinkling and invoking a past memory which he couldn't quite place. It happened all the time, so many experiences were connected to so many triggers that it was really quite normal, albeit always a little curious when memory failed to cooperate with familiarity.

The space vacated at the top of the money list was soon occupied by the next. Evidently not nearly in the same bracket because the Foundation's Donation Manager, Sally Brisbois, took her customary place on Roland's left. By the end of the evening Sally would be on a first name basis with the lesser wealth. She would probably never meet Lucy or Abigale and certainly not their husbands but she would be on a first name basis with their lawyers. Rich and powerful lawyers whose main claim to fame was their client list but Sally would mine them; efforts that more than paid her annual salary, monthly.

Roland had heard it all before but treated each and every question as if it was posed to him in his own personal examination room. When it came to fund raising, the MD behind his name made a huge difference compared to Ph.D. scientists, most of whom were openly pathetic with getting a decent part in their hair let alone with the fine art of parting money from those who treasure it nearly as much as life itself. Roland figured MD made that difference because his clients assumed the role of patients who were programmed to disclose, not hide, the truth from good old Doc Masters.

"My grandmother was something of clairvoyant, a mystic, she was very good at it, everyone came to see her. The Gift came to her when she was about fifty and became more and more powerful as she aged. Lately, I've been getting odd sensations, déjà vu and that sort of thing. Do you think that one of my legacy genes is being turned on; I'm just entering menopause, in case that matters."

"Could a Legacy Gene be responsible for acute hearing, you know, like a blind person's hearing is so much better than a sighted person? Could those two things be connected?"

"Do you think that Legacy Genes will tell us about our past lives?"

"I'm sure that the redundant nucleotides are left over from previous reincarnations, as we moved up the ladder of divinity. Has anyone checked to see whether or not those redundancies are in other animals? That would explain everything and prove reincarnation at the same time."

"How can I find out which Legacy Genes are in me? Maybe I have a new one or a very special combination of them."

"Do you think that diet has anything to do with Legacy Genes? What if we ate a frozen mammoth from the Arctic or some old grain from a pyramid? Could that get things started?"

"Is it possible to track everybody who has a particular Legacy Gene to a specific place, like Peru where they have the extraterrestrial landing sights? Maybe that's where they came from? Why not, stranger things have happened, we don't know everything, do we?"

"Could Legacy Genes hold the key to eternal life? You know, stop the bio-degradation of the cellular structure or jump-start a repair function like a computer can diagnose itself and make repairs?"

"Our son is a genius when it comes to solving weird puzzles, a real whiz when it comes to computer games. Maybe he should get involved in this type of work. Who should he talk to, could you meet with him?"

"Suppose you find a Legacy Gene which has great humanitarian potential. Would the donor of that gene get anything for it?"

"Is this like cloning? I mean, suppose I don't have a particular Legacy Gene in me that I want, can it be cloned into me?"

"When you turn on a Legacy Gene, will you be able to turn it off?"

CHAPTER 21

As a long time student of human behavior, Lupo considered himself to be in the top quartile of the class, a standing that he attributed to three qualities, none of which were superior intelligence for in that department he was just average and knew it. His understanding of the human species was the combined result of hard work, ordinary run-of-the-mill common sense and the head-strong, stubborn determination of a bull dog with a bone between his teeth. When put together, not only could he dissect almost anything but he could remember every detail of a six hour interview, right down to the body posture that accompanied each lie. Then, if that didn't crack the suspect, he would feed all that detail to his bone-crushing logic until he worried and gnawed his way to the marrow, the truth. But most of the time, in most of his cases, he would just shake the suspect apart with question after question, relentlessly separating the lies from the truth like he was pulling meat from the bone.

Sorenson was not that kind of suspect. For reasons beyond imagination, the fool had confessed to murdering his father and, wilder yet, he had signed the confession and the waiver of attorney privilege as if he was doing himself a favor. And it wasn't just Lupo who was reeling in disbelief, the three psychiatrists now sitting in the briefing room were just as bewildered. It was something he had never before witnessed and was pretty damn positive that jointly bewildered psychiatrists was not the sign of an open and shut case, regardless of how it looked at the moment.

"Well that pretty much sums it up." stated Basscurt with utmost finality. "The attack on the woman......what's-her-name......was simply a precursor event. Anybody or anything could have triggered the behavior, so it isn't really important what did it. Basically, he realized that he'd never get caught for the murder so he did the next best thing and found a way to confess it. Too bad about the woman but at least he didn't kill her, probably because he didn't have to but still too bad for her, wrong place at the wrong time, clearly."

Basscurt was pushing his weight around, and he had plenty of it to push. Built like the wine barrel that his red nose and ruby cheeks suggested he was all too familiar with, he also had enough years, ego and sufficient lettering behind his name to be the state's leading expert witness in the crazy case department. Whether he was trying to start a fight or trying to avoid one was anybody's guess but Lupo figured on both. He wanted Jorgensen to roll over and show her belly and he wanted Marsha to say something so he could bark at her like the top dog he wanted everyone to believe he was. He had a full head of grey hair but Lupo knew better than to ascribe wisdom to white hair. Besides, he'd worked with Basscurt lots of times and knew the man's enormous ego was directly related his insecurity, a matching that can make a person mighty defensive so they compensate for it with preemptive offensives.

"A professional opinion, Dr. Basscurt." Marsha replied without putting any emphasis on her words. Nor was there any courtesy, compliment or contradiction evident in either her face or her voice. Five words that meant what the words meant but without any other clues they were also open to almost any interpretation. They did, however, stop Basscurt dead in his tracks as he tried to figure out if he'd won a battle of intellects without firing a single idea or if he had just been placated like a baby with a bottle.

Helluva good way to shut up the old fart, thought Lupo as he reasoned how any response to her words would work against him. If he took her words as agreement and he didn't shut up he would have to start an argument with himself. If he took her words as implied dissent but they weren't she could simply repeat them and he would end up looking like a spoiled child who had got his way but didn't know what to do with it. Either way he would look like an idiot so he shut up, his best, though least preferred, defense.

"Dr. Jorgensen, you mentioned…Gut Wick?" Marsha asked, neatly side-stepping Basscurt while making full eye contact with her, obviously measuring and assessing her but in a friendly, open way. Jorgensen had to be in her mid-fifties, hopefully beyond the age for obsessing over a published patient pathology and therefore open and approachable.

"Gut Vik. No, the patient…the prisoner mentioned it. It is an old Norwegian name, what you might call a legend."

Basscurt's crossed arms telegraphed his outrage with his sudden demotion to third-ranking shrink in the room. "Is this relevant, even in the slightest? I remind you, we have a confession." he blurted in frustration. "We have a confession and there is no doubt about it being given free of duress. What is the point of this unnecessary questioning, Dr. Coleman?" As his words took on some heat, the few patches of Basscurt's face which weren't already red joined those which were permanently in that state.

That Basscurt's silence lasted mere seconds bothered the hell out of Lupo. Gut Wick, Gut Vik, or whatever/whoever, was mentioned shortly before Marsha had also muttered the odd word-name, Took A-Look, and Lupo hadn't cleared up his questions surrounding that muttering let alone the introduction of this Gut Vik character. Both names had aroused his curiosity, an occupational necessity but when accentuated by his personal interest in protecting Marsha, which now included protection from Basscurt, Lupo wanted answers and not ego-centric interruptions. Basscurt had trespassed on this imperative and Lupo felt like giving him a good thump on the nose. A nose which was standing out so brightly it was fairly begging for it.

It had only been a matter of hours since he had first met Marsha but those hours had left her mark on him. He had replayed their conversation a number of times and remembered her mannerisms, her smile and the keen, somewhat fearless intellect which she possessed. But it was the way she tried to make him comfortable, even after she had given him hell for the head games he was playing that really stuck to him. She had a heart and she wasn't afraid to show it. That was the draw which piqued his curiosity and so for reasons he didn't completely understand, but didn't need to understand, he thought she needed protecting because that was something he did well.

"You are correct, Dr. Basscurt, it isn't at all relevant to this…situation. Simply a matter of curiosity on my part. I'm sure you have better things to do. I'll follow this up privately if you wish. It was very nice to meet you." Marsha replied calmly.

She didn't stand, offer her hand or put anything into her words which could be construed as compliment or criticism but there wasn't much doubt about who was in charge. Basscurt actually lost some color, remarkable considering that the small wine soaked veins on his nose and cheeks were so close to the surface that Lupo could practically see the blood coursing through them.

A situation which was about to explode into a down and dirty psychosis slinging contest was just as quickly deflated, along with Basscurt's ego. One more thing Lupo now knew about her; she didn't start fights, she ended them and she definitely only needed protection against things physical, not metaphysical and for damn sure not just words.

"Gut Vik?" she repeated to Jorgensen, once again bypassing Basscurt's returning anger by inviting him to stay, if he chose, but without actually issuing the invitation. Jorgenson wasn't given the option to leave, Marsha's eyes had her pinned to the chair but she didn't seem to mind, she simply returned the eye contact and nodded.

Lupo noticed the gold specks in Marsha's eyes, gold specks he hadn't noticed before. They fairly danced, no, more like they floated. Floated? Maybe so or maybe not but definitely to do with the sea. Like when the wind picks up a little, the sun is at just right angle, and all of sudden there are colors and patterns you couldn't possibly imagine but are certain you are imagining because they are just too fantastic to be real.

Little wonder that Jorgensen relaxed with the beginnings of a smile. She was at ease with Marsha and anyone walking into the room at that moment would have thought them to be the best of friends, maybe even family. Not that there was that much physical resemblance with Marsha's features being more Mediterranean compared to the fair, blond, blue-eyed Nordic features of Jorgensen but they were both trim and somehow Lupo saw them both as being survivors. He didn't know where that impression came from but he trusted it to be right.

"Ja, Gut Vik. An old legend from the far north of my country. I was surprised to hear the name, not a well-known tale outside of the villages."

"It is a fable, a fairy tale?" asked Marsha. Lupo wondered if she was trying to keep Basscurt quiet or prompting Jorgenson to the telling. He hoped so, but not so much because he cared about fables, he just liked the idea of listening to a story and not dissecting the confession he wished he had never heard. Jorgenson will talk, he figured, who wouldn't? Obviously she felt the same way.

"No, not a fairy tale, a most tragic history. Some say that the famous Shakespeare borrowed from the story of Gut Vik. Who knows? The truth may be mixed with some fable but it is an old history still told by the old women to the young girls. Do you want to hear it? Ja? It goes like this. Always told at night, a clear night with the moon and stars watching down from the sky. At the time of darkness when what you call the Northern Lights, begin their dance. That is how it starts, the story of Gut Vik, told by the oldest woman, her crackle voice, the breaking waves and the call of the Arctic wolf the only companions to her story." Jorgenson's eyes misted over, distanced and then cleared as she fell into a part she obviously knew very well and that still moved her.

"'See the heavens dance.' starts the old woman to the young girls at the time of entering their maidenhood.

Dancing like the body thrusting in love with the mind in rapture so high and far away it can touch the stars. Not touch them with fingers but with eyes so yearning for explosion that they pull the little lights inside, deep, deep inside and imprison them there forever like babies who are waiting for the seed. Spinning and whirling, clutching and grasping, pricking and teasing, tiny bright collisions of desire, sparks from a fire so hot and consuming that it licks with pain and pleasure indistinguishable from each other. Dancing in a body making love with a mind so hot and consumed with rapture that not even the stars can cool it.

See the colors so bright; see the dance so firm, so bold. Hear the rhythm so wanting with desire that it pushes and pulls like a raging sea until it builds so high and strong that it explodes on the rocks with a crack of thunder. Colors fly against each other with such fierce competition that all life is held between them like the silence between one heart beat and the next. Life. New life from old. See the dance, feel the heat, pleasure the moment, pleasure yourself in the making of life. Know it is ancient but forsake all memory because that is the moment of creation and the past has no part, no sense, no place.

Feel the prong of life between your legs, the urgency of creation pushing you down, pulling you up, urging you on, pulling and pushing beyond your imagination, your dreams, yourself, your inner being, your outer being, your whole time of existence. Feel a creation so strong that it sucks the wind from the air and pulls the stars from the heavens while it sings sweetly in your mind. See creation as red as blood, as blue as sea and green as the spring pine bud.

Feel it, touch it, taste it, let it draw and spin but know its strength, know its power, know its danger for if you let it, creation that is as white as mid-winter snow will become as dark and black and heartless as the curse and the omen that is the man, Gut Vik. Remember it when you dance that dance, when the flames heat your belly and your passion reaches for the stars. Remember that Gut Vik lives in all men; do not be aroused by him and never arouse him for to do so is to risk death.

Gut Vik once lived as a man and now forever lives on in man. He is remembered in the image of a sailor with long blonde flowing hair, fashioned by the cold north wind into which he sailed. Tall and lean, brave beyond courage, he was sculpted by the very forces he challenged. His features chiseled by gale and storm, hardened by the sting of ice salted sea and bronzed by sun. Hands cut and callused by frozen sail, limbs as straight, strong and knotted as the weathered spar of the pine masts that held his sails. Legs as sure on shifting deck as on the weathered rocks of his village or their slippery green cousins on the shore. Loins as broad and pleasing as the manhood which grew from them. Gut Vik, himself, forever leaning into the wind like the bowsprit of his ship as it rose in defiance of seas as great and fierce as the gods chose to send at him. Gut Vik, himself, as strong and set as the monsters in those seas when they felt the need, the desire or the folly, to put his courage to the test.

This is the tale of Gut Vik the Warrior, the legend of Gut Vik the Explorer and the curse of Gut Vik the Man.

Gut Vik, the warrior, was born from Gut Vik the boy at sixteen summers of age, the year he dealt death to the Saxons. They were merciless unholy hoards from the south who held as little fear of death as they held value for life. It was not the first time they had plundered our villages but it was the first time they had met Gut Vik and the first time they were defeated. A defeat made possible by their own history and their mistaken notion that they could repeat it because their victims would repeat their fate; their destiny. But Gut Vik did what no one expected him to do. That was to become his way and it became the way of certain defeat for all his enemies.

The Saxon's always came from the south. Into some of the villages, they sailed their warships and many would escape to the woods but for their attack on the villages around Gut Vik's home, they anchored their ships in the cove called the Cauldron, for that was its shape. A deep, dark hole in the fjord, surrounded by cliffs but with a small beach and inland trail to the massacre, if the surprise could be held which this time, it could not.

This time, Gut Vik arrived first and waited until the hoard had left their ships with only a small guard of old, crippled or drunks to protect them. Under the cover of dark, ten men and boys from his village rowed small boats to the sleeping fleet and with barrels of fine whale oil, set them ablaze.

Only the mother and father of Gut Vik believed he would return, believed in his courage and his strength. They knew their son. At least at that time they knew their son for he had their blood in him and like every father and mother they knew and trusted their own flesh and blood.

After that, it was a battle never fought or won when Gut Vik left his village with one hundred men, most of them warriors with scars as deep and black as the memories which caused them. None looked back, for to do so was believed to curse their return. The women wailed and the children hid. The old men prepared for death.

Gut Vik also had death on his mind, but it was not his own death, although as his feet moved toward the battle, he thought of it enough to understand that he was unafraid of dying and he would, if he survived the day, forever be that way. That is what he thought, and it was true.

As true as the words: 'Beware Gut Vik, the Man, do not be aroused by him and never anger him.' Some things are so and have always been so. But that is the tale of Gut Vik, the man, not yet told, and this is still the telling of Gut Vik, the warrior.

Gut Vik knew the way of the Saxons because when it came to butcher, it was always the same way, knowledge which was to become their fate, not his. He knew the beach where they camped, where they sharpened their knifes and heightened their desire for the rising screams or ebbing moans of torture and death. He knew they would follow the stream through its cracks and crevices, up though the steep, narrow gorge which would deliver them onto a short barren valley, always swept clear by winter avalanche and spring flood. From that valley they would follow the same path to his village as the one beneath his feet. A path littered with the evidence of past defeats, piled with cairns for graves, a pathway growing lush from the tears of widows mourning husbands, fathers and sons. Head bowed, he passed with respect just as others would walk past him if it was his fate to be interred in one of those piles of stones.

But he would not fight there, he refused to fight surrounded by defeat.

He met them where the gorge emptied onto that fateful, futile little plain like serpent's tongue. A gorge that never saw the sun, that was dank and dark and full of spirits from the underworld and which spilt onto the plain around a high rock pinnacle, itself deeply scarred and sparsely treed. That was the place for his battle, he knew it by the feel of the air, the voice in his mind and the crawl on his skin.

He waited and they came, not in the rushing wave they preferred but in a line pinned on each side by rock walls. He was the first to stand; his arrow went through two men.

After that, it was slaughter made easy by the pile of corpses and the slip of blood.

In the time it takes for a shallow pot on a raging fire to reach the boil, more than half the Saxons were dead or dying and Gut Vik hadn't lost a single man. They ran with the gods they had sacrificed to, chased by Gut Vik and his warriors. They ran from slaughter in the gorge, to slaughter down the inland trail to the open space of the beach, the open space where they preferred to fight. Preferred to fight when they were two or three or four against one. Any less and they preferred to run and now, outnumbered, with their backs to the sea, they clustered together like the beasts of their own nature and screamed their death chants, mortally afraid with no ships for escape and no more land to run.

Gut Vik drove them into the water and then called an oath for the seas to rise. One after the next, the waves rose and carried Saxon after Saxon onto the swords, the spears and the daggers of Gut Vik's men.

He lost not a single man and this was the beginning of Gut Vik, the Warrior. Never again were the Saxons to visit the shores of Gut Vik but the opposite could not be said as Gut Vik then became the horror to them that they had once been to him.

This was the beginning of the blood which flows through all our veins. Beware the man Gut Vik, do not anger him for his revenge is calculated and death is certain. Do you understand this now, young women?

At this question, the old crone would pause and wait for the night air to chill the sweat. Sometimes she would moan, sometimes she would chant but always she would look into the eyes of the young women. Always would she look for those who would heed her words and those who would be tempted to test them. It was their choice whether or not to join the names of those who had failed to listen or obey.

Some girls could not resist the knowing. Whether it be their loins or the loins of Gut Vik, they could not resist the arousal, the heat and the fire. She would say the names and tell of their fates and yet, for some of them, this only incensed them more.

'Listen well, young women, for you are entering the realm of the stars, the time of thrusting and grinding, the slip and the slap of sweat and passion. Listen well, young women, or you may arouse Gut Vik as she did. Are you ready? Are you ready to hear this?

It was at the end of his twenty-third summer, summers which he spent in conquest and to the devastation of all in his path, that he met the virgin Elsa, who he later called his orchid, like the flower, Fjellkurle. She, in her fifteenth summer and in full blossom.

Like all the young women, and many whose bloom was fading or even completely spent, she wished to share her nectar with Gut Vik. For some this yearning was driven by the sheer magnificence of his body and the presence with which he carried it. For others it was driven by the size and shape of his manhood, the bulge in his loins and the promises it hinted when emerging, wet and tight against the cloth after bathing in the river or large and languid after sweating in the sauna. Some craved the knowledge of that member for all the sweet, secret places which it had been, whether invited or otherwise. Young or old they all wanted to know the secrets of Gut Vik's bed because every woman who had wound her legs around his back had kept silent and secret the most intimate details of their thrusting. Elsa was no different; she wanted to know those details just as badly as the others. Indeed, she wanted it so badly that at times she could think of little else.

But to Gut Vik, Elsa was as different from all the other women as a bird is different from a fish. Almost as tall as himself, she was perfectly sculpted for the pleasure of a man's eyes. Clear and clean, her lightly bronzed skin was soft and supple. Golden hair framed a face as finely featured as could be found in any village. Her mouth was wide with full, red lips like a luscious flower eagerly beckoning the bee to enter.

Her shoulders were almost square so when she walked with a firm and determined pace, it was not unlike the manner of Gut Vik when he leaned into the wind as he cut through the waves. But her walk had more purpose and intent than that mere appearance. It was perfectly calculated to push her breasts forward and with just enough sway and canter to allow their size and shape to be appreciated, her own appreciation included as the rubbing on her nipples filled her pleasure.

Pleasure imagined by anyone with thoughts riding the mount just as she imagined it, and imagined it quite accurately for while she was still a virgin, few of her friends were and they could talk of little else. Talk which ran wet and hot when it came to Gut Vik and the women who were, to their regret, still virgins to the dance with him.

Elsa practiced the positions which they described and while careful not to be too obvious about her interest in them, she was just as careful to get all the details so she knew what pleasures each position gave, or denied. It was a challenging time for no one seemed to agree on all the details or experiences save one. The first time was, without a single woman saying otherwise, a bitter taste of a cake which looked so sweet. Whether too fast or too slow, too wet or too dry, too rough or too gentle, not one of them had opened the gift which their imagination had promised for that occasion. Every one of them had a reason, all that is, except for the one who Gut Vik had taken for the first time, and she maintained her silence. A deafening, maddening silence which no one could penetrate.

Elsa practiced with herself until she was as certain in her own pleasure as she was in the pleasing vision which her body, in various attitudes of recline would provide. In this she had no shame, for her own curves and valleys, nooks and crevices were frequent topics of discussion with her friends and Elsa was generally held as having the finest of those curves, the most lovely of valleys and all her nooks and crevices were perfectly formed. All agreed that when it came her turn to ride or be ridden, she had everything she needed, everything a man could desire, to make it an unforgettable experience.

Her uplifted breasts were perked and pitched as if sitting on a ledge but not flat underneath, containing instead a delicate curve that extended gracefully and purposefully to display the raspberries at their peak. Hardly a crease where her breasts met her body and not a line, crease or dimple save the ripple of her ribs interrupted the flow from her breasts to the slender, toned waist before fanning out again at her hips. Not an angular line like her shoulders but a long, smooth, flowing curve which made no attempt to disguise the power or potential of those hips. Not even a slow walk could disguise that hidden pleasure and it was no different whether seen from the front or the back.

Where her hips turned to her backside, they revealed buttocks which were every bit as perfectly formed as her breasts, but without their jiggle or bounce. Exquisitely formed like the breasts of a grouse they joined to her back and her legs without a single moment of flat where a curve should be found. When she stood naked facing the sun, a small bright triangle of light could peer through the opening at the top of her legs, although no one but herself and her few friends were allowed to witness that intimate wonder.

Those same few had seen the run of her belly, mostly flat but sloping in from the bones of her hips and down from the slim waist to the mound of intimacy which rose from between her legs like earth being pushed up by spring growth. It was not present when she walked for her strong, muscular thighs protected it from sight but when lightly clothed or when wet from the stream, her mound was so wonderfully risen that the temptation to run a hand over it was as strong as the desire to admire it with the eye. For those lucky enough to see her naked, it came with wisps of golden hair that radiated down the mound, gathering force and density until it parted to reveal the lips of her intimacy. Pouting, moist lips which she kept constantly aroused with her walk and the way she bound and knotted her underclothes.

As expected from the legs driving it, her walk had a spring to it but few were the men who held that thought when they could be thinking of the wrap of those legs around their back. Men she could have any time she wanted, but she wanted only one man. That body and all its pleasures were destined for Gut Vik. It was her desire and she would not deny that desire even as she denied herself the feelings and sensations she could not truly experience by her hands alone. Still, she tried and, with the help of her friends, came close to understanding just what she might expect and how she might make her first experience everything she wanted it to be. Friends who would tell her what she wanted to know and some who would show her as she peered between trees or through the crack of a door or a window to watch their demonstrations. Demonstrations which fully inflamed passions that had, up until then, only been aroused.

She watched them in all manners and methods of stroking, grasping and kissing. Positions and motions, cries and whimpers, passive and not, fast or slow. She set the order of the experience she intended with Gut Vik so many times and in so many ways that in the end she finally acknowledged that if she couldn't have all of it, she didn't want it at all. She had to have all of him in all those ways and she had to have it the first time she made it to his bed, if she even made it to his bed before having him for the first time. She thought that unlikely but perhaps he would have the patience that she did not.

He was alike and unlike every other man and she knew of the differences and the similarities. Leaner and stronger than any other man in the village, he was created to be on top of a woman. The image of his tumescence as it hung between his legs made her shudder. Like the rest of him, his loins exuded power and control but for entirely different purposes than his arms or legs. Arms which could hold her waist and legs which would steady and guide that organ into her intimacy with such long, firm stokes that she imagined it coming to the back of her throat where her cries would build until they emerged in a scream of ecstasy. Alone in the woods, she had practiced that sound until she wasn't even aware she was making it.

She would have Gut Vik until he wanted no other woman because he would be incapable of rising to anyone else. She would conquer the conqueror because she wanted to experience the feeling.

But first, he had to want her and she believed he did. His interest was growing and she provoked that interest but she did it slowly, a little at a time, for she wanted him mad with desire for her. When she had the opportunity, opportunities she often constructed, she provoked him with innocent conversation, part girl and part woman, part yes and part no, always later, sometime soon, teasing and pricking, pricking and teasing. She used the shift of her clothes and the brush of her hand against a breast or her belly to incite his imagination. The bending of her body to pick up a stick or a stone and display her curves from this perspective or another.

Gut Vik knew the temptation she was presenting. He had known it from the first moment of her bloom but she was different from all the others. Elsa was a creature for years, a creature from all eternity and not one for a single night of pleasure. Her proportions were so natural that he didn't think of her as being the same as the other young women who constantly surrounding her. She had purpose and determination. She had a realm of her own but not as a queen or a princess but with such control and presence as to make either of those blush with jealousy. He had to have her but he had to have her completely, she would be his only possession if it came down to that condition.

He spent many nights thinking about what to do with her, often while in the arms of another, a most inconvenient distraction from pleasure. He knew he could wait because not a man in the village would lay a hand on her, let alone anything else, unless Gut Vik himself gave away that right. He was seeking a woman for his bed and a mother for his children and all knew that choice was his right and he hadn't given it away.

Those were his thoughts as he left the lodge of his brother, in the late summer night, when the flames from the cooking fires had died down and the glowing embers shared their essence with the stars. Quiet around him, just a faint breeze off the sea carrying nothing particular to his senses. Nothing that would invoke a memory from all the days and nights he had spent on those waters. Waters which now churned like he did, each wave its own destiny with no two the same. He would be alone that night, the least of his concerns for he was used to being alone even though he seldom was. That was his thought as Elsa came out from the dark.

She had decided. That game was over.

Coming up to his side, she allowed her hip to touch his before moving her body a little closer to him. His arm moved out of her way; she entered the space it created, her hand falling casually between his legs, just barely touching him. Not a word said, none of the promises she had made to herself required words. Many promises and she knew where she would start. Falling into pace with him as if they had always been together, without looking at him, she licked her lips.

CHAPTER 22

Jesus Christ, Gut Vik, what have you done?

Confessed.

I know that for Chrissakes, for Chrissakes, I know that. We're screwed, you know that, do you know that?

We?

Yeah we. What the hell do you think they're going to do, who the hell do you think will get screwed now?

You.

And you too, for Chrissakes. You think you're going to get out of this, is that what you think?

Who wants out?

Shit. What a mess you turned out to be. You hear me? You hear me? Do you understand anything you've done? Apparently not. Little bloody wonder. Christ, what a mess. A signed confession. Totally logical all the while. And for what? For my old man telling me 'don't do this and don't do that.' What a waste, what a stupid waste.

Maybe I should tell them more.

Go ahead, for Chrisakes, it can't get any worse.

Don't count on it.

"Fuck you."

"You talking to yourself, Sorenson? You better be."

The big cop with the big arms.

Gut Vik was right. It could get a damn sight worse. Correction, it was going to get a damn sight worse. No doubt about it. Jesus, how much time did he have before time ran out, before Never-Ending started or whatever it did when it did it. He had to act and act fast.

"I want to see Doctor Marsha Coleman, she's up there, I know it. Tell her I've got something important to tell her, tell her I have to see her right away. This can't wait."

"Yeah sure. Anything else you'd like as long as I'm here? A little room service, tea and toast, maybe?"

"It's important…it won't take long…tell her right away. Please."

"Don't work yourself up Sorenson, you aren't going anywhere."

He actually wished that was true.

CHAPTER 23

Lupo shook his head to clear the images that Jorgenson's tale had put in it and he wasn't alone in that spell. Basscurt and Marsha were also deep in thought, probably doing the same thing he was, working out the ending based upon the story line they had heard so far. Then again, maybe not, maybe that was just for detectives. For sure it wouldn't be a happy ending, all those warnings about angering Gut Vik had to mean something horrible was going to happen. Anyway, they would all know pretty soon as Jorgensen picked up with the same story-telling voice as before.

"It is a story always told at night with the sound of waves and the call of the wolf and then the old woman would ask, 'Are you ready to hear the story about Gut Vik, The Man? Are you sure? Are you sure you want to see the past reflected in your mirror as you brush your beautiful hair and get ready for your warm bed? Are you sure you want to feel it mount you in the middle of the night like a stranger with a hollow eye and a voice from the dead? Are you absolutely certain you want to know this man?

They all wanted to know but for some the time was right and for others it was not. The old woman would put her head back and stare at the stars as if trying to recall the exact words, trying to get the details of the dance to flow from the heavens and into her mind. The girls who could not bear to hear the rest would sneak away in the shadows to the safety of their beds but one or two of them would always hide where they could hear without being seen. The buds of those flowers were still tightly wrapped and as much as they were curious of the form they would take, their color or their scent, they knew that not all flowers are desired and were afraid that theirs might be one of them.

The old woman's head would drop slowly, her eyes searching the stars for as long as they could before finally coming to rest on those who dared to hear the tale of Gut Vik, The Man. So complete, so detailed is the telling told, that no young woman ever asked a question nor would their eyes leave those of the crone. Her voice, whether hoarse or cracked, high or low, sweet or bitter, became slow but not flat. A voice that came not from her lips but from deep inside and all watched the eyes dart and dash, quiver and shake as if those old orbs actually watched the tale as it was leaving her lips.

'In the arms of Fjellkurle, his orchid, Gut Vik, the warrior gave way to Gut Vik, the man. It began that night and before the sun had finished its rest, Gut Vik, the man was born just as surely as a babe leaves his mother's womb. She had satisfied him completely and he was just as certain that he had satisfied her but he also knew she had many more curiosities of the flesh to satisfy. Happily, it was the future he desired and he wanted nothing more than to be with her.

And so it went the entire winter, the long nights of darkness suited her appetite just as well, sometimes even better than the short hours of winter light. She had him when she desired and was equally disposed to please him whenever he wanted, however he wanted. She stroked his passion as expertly as she stroked his mind, hearing his tales and conquest. Hearing of the women with whom he had been and all the seas on which he had sailed. With each tale she urged more detail, more description and more intimacy with his feelings, his thoughts and his history. What he liked and what he didn't. This woman compared to that one. Favors which were given to him freely and those which he took while blood still ran hot from his sword. Everything she could learn until she knew him completely. Knew every inch of him and how it moved, what it felt like and where it wanted to go or what it wanted to become. The more she knew about The Warrior, the more she became one. The more she knew about conquest, the more she wanted to conquer.

And, as in many misfortunes of knowing, the more she knew about Gut Vik the man, the more she wanted men. That was inevitable. She had trained herself too well for it to be otherwise. He was just a man and now that she knew him completely, she wanted more. Perhaps he knew this too, perhaps he decided to leave so he could return to please her, to once again arise her interest in him but whatever the reason, he told no one of it.

He left in the spring. Some thought he wouldn't be able to leave his Fjellkurle but others knew the open water was in his blood, blood which ebbed and flowed with their tides and their season. He could no more resist the wind in his sails than he could plant his feet in the ground and become a tree.

For him it was time of rare conflict. The urge to conquer was spent, perhaps because he had himself been conquered. Or maybe it was more simple than that. Perhaps there was another nature to him that needed light, that needed adventure so he could be re-born into Gut Vik, the explorer.

He kissed her goodbye and set his sails to follow the sun to its setting. At dawn, under fair wind, four strong ships of pine and square sail, disappeared over the horizon and ceased to exist for those who were behind it.

Under steady winds they sailed for days which turned to weeks. They were guided by the setting sun and the night stars, often setting their course by instinct, no rhyme nor reason to each day. Sudden squalls would break on them but those were nothing more than foolish tests of their courage and conviction by a force of nature from which they were bred and born to survive.

Time became an endless horizon in every direction, they were at once in the center of it yet also lost in it. No references, no point of light or feature other than one wave which might be greater than the others until, not even at the edge of the summer solstice, the call went out. "Land." A brilliant flash of light from a white peak, to the north.

They sailed to that light, only to find an iceberg the size of a small island. And then another and another until they were surrounded by them, all manner and sorts of huge, white, bleached skeletons of monsters floating around them, surrounding them, threatening them with their deadly crush. There followed perilous, but thankfully, short nights after long, bright cautious days, each filled with betrayed hope that a peak in the distance would offer them more than an interesting shape and a challenge to their navigation. When land came, they hadn't even sailed for it, thinking it to be just another false hope in a sea thickly schooled with ancient trickery.

They found a land of rock and ice, melt water, harbors and bays which were most often surrounded and protected by high cliffs, not unlike their homeland when seen from the horizon. But except for the seas which were abundant with life, it was a useless discovery. From one end to the other, not a single tree in sight, but here and there a trunk or a root or a weathered branch lying on a beach or thrown into the rocks from somewhere else. Nor any land animals except for mice and small foxes so wary and shy they could only be seen by the contrast of their color against snow or rock.

With nothing to guide him, no reason for choosing one direction over the other, Gut Vik sailed into the wind, following his nature by honoring its challenge. At times he hugged the shore and at other times he sailed far out to sea, looking at the vast, barren expanse from a distance. Day after day, he surveyed his discovery and its deceptions. Green forests at distance yielded only meadows or rock colored with lichen. Time and time again was he fooled, were all of them fooled. Gut Vik laughed at his discovery, such a useless monument to history. In the midst of watery nothing, he had discovered its solid form.

The days just before mid-summer were carefree and easy. The seas were calm and the wind was steady and westerly. A most uncommon time without snow or gale as it stretched forward, day after day, timeless and empty but there was no fear, no superstition or ominous prediction from the ships of Gut Vik. They were always within sight of safe harbor, the seas provided in abundance and the stocks of whale oil for the cooking cauldrons were ample. Even if they were not, not a day passed without seeing a dozen or more of the huge creatures which provided their fat for fuel.

Gut Vik's warriors, men who absently missed the blood and the battle which Gut Vik denied them, were content to roll on the waves or lie in the sun. Sooner or later, they reckoned, and a village would be discovered. No land could possibly be completely uninhabited for no land had ever been found which was and then, they reasoned, Gut Vik the warrior might return to his old ways.

It was close to midsummer, the time of perpetual light when the first inhabitants of that barren, monotonous land were discovered. A most peculiar sight as there seemed to be people but no village, no huts or dwellings growing anywhere on the wide, sweeping valley which led to the rocky beach. The valley rose high into a mountain, protected on both sides by tall ridges which dropped down to the sea like arms open for a greeting. The peak was shrouded in cloud. It was as if the inhabitants on the beach had been dropped from the sky.

As the ships of Gut Vik approached the beach, the inhabitants lined the shore. Men, women, children and a few dogs whose ancestry was clearly the wolf prowled about, all watching something new and unknown. Some of the boys and men held spears but they were long and slight with primitive, slender bone or ivory tips, used for hunting seals, not for war. And not held that way either but to the side, like a man uses a staff for walking and not holding it in readiness for a thrust to the chest or the belly.

"It is curiosity looking in on itself." muttered Gut Vik. The sight of his ships and all the sailors who leaned over their sides was something they had never witnessed as their interest in the ships was just as great as their curiosity of those who sailed them. Sailors who were warriors first and explorers second and only then because Gut Vik had not given them a choice in that decision.

"They have nothing." Echoed from man to man as the distance between ship and shore shortened and more details could be observed. No bronze or iron, certainly no gold. "Where is their village?" Not a question of curiosity so much as a hope that something valuable might still turn up.

"Lapps." said another, the common thought of every man who had challenged the north wind and found the nomadic people who lived where no one else could survive, at least not survive a winter.

"Of a kind." answered Gut Vik, knowing that all were wondering if they had missed a star or been blown in a circle back to their homeland by a storm that none of them could remember. But Lapps would not have been so curious of the sight before them, a sight they had seen before. No, not Lapps but they were of the same tribe. Short and stocky, dark hair and eyes which seemed to be half-closed from staring into blinding light or into the black of night. Weathered skin but unlike that of a sailor which is deeply creased at a young age because only the old were featured like that, the young had clear skin, stretched over high cheek bones and broad brows.

The ship of Gut Vik edged to the shore, a pebbled beach which showed no signs of having ever seen a storm, but which knew ice and snow as well as a mother knows her child. A few of the inhabitants came over and touched it, as if its wooden planks had to be felt in order to be real. Others turned and left, their curiosity satisfied or with something more important to do than see what had never been seen and if they left their curiosity behind them it was certain that Gut Vik and his men took it up. It was too strange a behavior to leave unquestioned.

They seemed not to have a leader for no one greeted them or attempted to engage them in any formalities of welcome or otherwise. No one except for the children who were free to do as they pleased and were soon among them, touching and jabbering in a language with no seeming start or finish to it. They displayed no fear and received no warnings as they grasped at daggers, clambered aboard the ships or stared deeply into the eyes of the warriors like they were searching for an image, an identity, someone or something they knew.

Gut Vik watched as they moved about, some to small, over-turned boats that were covered with dark skins that blended with the rocks. The same skin covered their dwellings, some using rocks for their sides and some using the bleached rib bones of whale, ancient skeletons draped with a foreign skin. All the dwellings were the same with nothing to distinguish one from the other, or show the presence of a leader, a sorcerer or a healer. Just as there were no differences in tools, spears or clothing. No orders or commands from one to another as if each person was alone and because of this, a curious society, and a peaceful one.

Gut Vik ordered his men to secure the ships. He would stay until his curiosity of these strange people and their customs was satisfied. Unlike conquerors who reach the end of a battle, the curiosity of an explorer is never satisfied, something Gut Vik did not know at the time or fully appreciate in the days which were to follow.

Even when the first bite of winter winds came down from the mountain, he ignored the warning just as he ignored all his men who casually observed it but who were not inclined to acknowledge their real concern. He ignored the ice which formed on the streams and in shallow ponds, refusing the warning that his ships could soon be locked in a grip so tight it would break them to pieces. He stayed through the first snow and the second, each day bringing him more knowledge and understanding of the people and their ways. One curiosity answered and another revealed, he could not leave.

From the children, he learned their tongue, from the men he learned the ways of their survival and from the women he learned about their society and how it operated. All of them were as free to come and go as the nomadic life they lived. Some bonds between men and women were short-lived and others were constant. This was as true with his men as with their own; as if the two worlds had come together because they were destined to come together and no one took issue with that destiny. If any of their seed took root, the next time anyone found these people they would know they were not the first. Not if the blond hair and blue eyes found their way into the mix. Not if the wisps of a red beard showed on an otherwise hairless face, or on a face that was a head taller than the others. He hoped that was all they would leave behind, and not their own quarrelsome nature.

If there was disagreement over a woman, it was always a disagreement between his own men. Disagreement over anything whether it was a boat which no one seemed to own, a piece of meat or a place by the fire. But in the end even Gut Vik had to admit that most of this was caused by winter's approach, the shortening days and the thoughts of sailing through ice-packed seas. Still, it was not that which made him set his sails.

On a day which dawned no differently than any other, and without warning of any kind, the decision to leave was made by the gods and with a vengeance and a fury that Gut Vik had never before been handed."

CHAPTER 24

"Doctor Coleman? Sorry to disturb you but the prisoner, Sorenson, insists on seeing you. He says he has something important to tell you." The cop shrugged his shoulders like he knew that it was a bullshit request but he had to deliver it anyway. Delivered reluctantly because psychiatrists never did anything except confuse things but he reasoned that when a case started in an asylum, safe was better than sorry. Word of Sorenson's confession - to a murder for which he wasn't even a suspect - an old, cold accident, was already circulating so who knew what else to expect? Maybe the shrinks were doing something positive for a change.

"Like I didn't see this retraction coming." fumed Basscurt, happy that he could get back on his professorial podium and away from brutal but sexy Norwegian fairy tales. "I'm just surprised it took him so long. Crazy, hell. Crazy like a fox. Anybody want to bet that we'll hear how much he loved his dear old Dad, was supposed to stay away from the jack but accidentally hit with his bicycle...et cetera, et cetera, et cetera." For good measure, he pronounced his concluding words in pretty good Italian: 'Eh CHAY-trah. Eh CHAY-trah, Eh CHAY-trah.'

Lupo caught Marsha's eyes searching his face but his mind was blank. Gut Vik, Eskimos and Dr. Basscurt's Italian had swarmed his consciousness. He had no idea what she wanted from him and the last thing that came to him was Eh CHAY-tray so he shrugged his shoulders. It was pretty good Italian, maybe that what was she was asking.

"Please bring him up, Sergeant...unless you think I should go to him." she said, but continued to watch Lupo. After all he had done that day to keep her safe from Sorenson, she was a little surprised that he didn't have anything to say about this spontaneous request.

"Bring him up. Follow the procedure." Lupo said with authority, silently reminding himself to get his shit together. Sorenson couldn't be trusted and that wasn't a mere fact of recent events; that was an instinct from deep in his guts. Guts, hell, his testicles tingled like he was looking over a cliff.

"Just so you know, folk tales notwithstanding, we have a perfectly good signed confession and it's going to stick. No debate, no exceptions." Basscurt's ego was showing the bruising it received from Sorenson's request to see Marsha and not him, not to mention her unspoken request for permission from the lowly detective and not him. They just didn't get it, he was in charge here and besides, how the hell did Sorenson even know she was here – she was behind the one-way mirror during the entire confession?

"While we are waiting, please continue with the legend, Dr. Jorgenson." Marsha used the unfinished story to bypass Basscurt's ultimatum for analytical closure, sane or otherwise.

Jorgenson hesitated then replied: "Maybe first we see what he has to say. Ask him why he left the people. See what he has to say. Best if the question comes from you, that it comes from a beautiful woman who he insists to see."

The hair on the back of Lupo's neck tingled and he hated that feeling, rare as it happened, but three times in two days had to be some kind of record. What the hell would cause something that you hardly ever felt, like neck hair, to react like that? It had to be something really bad, like when damned dangerous meets up with shit out-of-luck.

CHAPTER 25

Hey Took A-Look, you see that one? Yeah, I know I said that before but that was when we first got here. That was when we first got back to your Arctic home, and I thought I saw a polar bear because that's what you want to avoid and once that's on your mind you aren't avoiding it any more, are you?

Yeah I know, I know it wasn't a bear, that's just what was on my mind so that's what I thought I saw. Sure it was a fox but even you said it was a big fox, right? What do you mean you've changed your mind? It was a big fox before and it's still a big fox. You think this is the same big fox?

What do you mean, a bear? No way it's a bear. No I don't want to go check it out. Okay, fine then, it's a bear but I still think it's a big fox, just like before and all you are doing is trying to trick me.

Yeah, it sure is quiet. Don't tell me you miss her?

Yes, that was a joke. She sure put up a stink didn't she? Her and that lawyer of hers. Mean son-of-a-bitch. What do you mean you liked her? Oh, sorry. You liked it. You liked the part where she got more money than she deserved? What a curious thing for you to say, Took A-Look, why do you feel that way? Interesting point, the more money she has the more unhappy she will be when she loses it.

Interesting, but what makes you think she is going to lose it?

Seriously, 'because when you lose the truth you lose everything?' How can that matter when she wouldn't know the truth if it hit her in the head? It is going to hit her in the head you say?

You are right about that, you definitely are, no one gets out of Never-Ending, that's the truth and there is only one word and one meaning for truth. Once Never-Ending is in her head, the truth will also be there and then all her lies will fall apart. I never thought about it that way.

And it's already started, you say? Also interesting but not easy to understand Took A-Look, especially when you say it like that. I'm still not used to your language, only one word for truth but so many words for snow. Why not just snow and an adjective and leave it at that?

Because is not an answer and you know it. No, we're not going to go and see the bear, it's just a big fox. Okay fine, it's a bear, a little one. Want to go over to that outcrop over there, I see a little glitter. You do? Okay.

Arlene wasn't too happy either was she? For a while there I thought she was going to pop the lawyer right in the teeth and give her a couple of thumps on the nose just for fun. Yeah I know I should have done it too but you know where that would have landed us, don't you? No, not the hospital, someplace worse. That's right, bear trap, not seal country by a long shot. Do you miss your seal and her gold specks? You do? You are being very agreeable today Took A-Look, I appreciate that.

Yeah, I like it here too. This is pretty close to where we met, isn't it? Right. Right over that mountain and down the valley on the other side. The one that looks like two arms reaching out to the sea. Nice beach too, tons and tons of polished black rocks, all different sizes. Nobody around for a thousand miles, I bet. Not for a thousand years either, I bet. Longer you say? No kidding. Never-Ending too. No kidding again.

I'm happy too. You think Arlene is happy? Yeah, you're right but she'll find that out herself.

Yeah, sure it could be a dog. Not a big fox or a little bear but a dog. There must be somebody around. Do you want to go see? You do? Why are you being so agreeable today? No it's not a crime. Just unusual.

No I don't think it will be anybody you know. No, not likely. No, not likely is not just another way of saying not possible. The same as twenty words for snow are all different even they all mean snow. Because it isn't, that's why. Well it isn't. Fine, maybe it will be somebody you know. What's got into you lately? First so agreeable and then you argue over every little thing. What is preoccupying your thoughts, if you don't mind sharing them.

No, I never liked Sorenson. No, I just didn't like him. Well just because I don't hate him like you do doesn't mean that I liked him, I just didn't like him. Sure, that might be the same as not likely isn't the same as not possible. Or is it? Are you trying to confuse me, Took A-Look, is that what you are doing?

Now I don't believe you. I thought so. Yes that was pretty clever, using lots of words to hide the meaning of things. Why did you do that?

So what? So what about Sorenson? You say he is doing that, he is hiding something. Did you say something or someone? Which? Fine, now you don't want to talk about it. All of sudden your own topic isn't worth talking about after you've said what? Nothing except the subject which now doesn't have a verb, that's what.

Fine if spears are your next topic then go ahead and sharpen some but it was a just a fox, not a dog.

He pokes at a cloud which I hadn't noticed before and a huge polar bear jumps out, mouth wide open and showing all his yellow teeth, growling and mean as hell and extremely frightening. My heart skips a beat and then jumps straight into overdrive even though I know almost immediately that it's a Took A-Look trick. 'Tee Hee' he goes as he disappears around a cloud at the back, 'Tee Hee' like it's stupid to be afraid of polar bears because they wouldn't eat you which it definitely isn't and they definitely will.

Lately, starting practically when we got off the float plane and onto the tundra, Took A-Look has been very talkative. Still pretty bossy but at least I could get a conversation started and, except for little jokes like that one, he leaves the clouds alone. Plus he's been pretty informative which is new. Mostly little things like another word for snow but they seem to be important to him so I ask questions and listen. Yes, fair to say it's been a lot better, even better than it used to be, before he made the clouds his number one priority and me his number eight priority. But he's still messy...

...and still not listening...highly unusual but happening more and more all the time. He'll disappear for hours and hours, who knows what he is up to. Remember Who Knows? And what a great question it is? This might be an exception to the rule. Then again, maybe eventually he'll say something about it. At least it's got Never-Ending constantly off his mind. Probably because we're in it again.

It was a good decision to leave the hospital and an even better decision to leave her. She was driving both of us crazy, some people have a way of doing that and she was at the head of the class and not first class. No such thing as solitude in her world. Like the only way she could keep breathing was if she talked the air out of her lungs. Talked about anything. About every drink she ever drank or what the weather was like at this time last year. If she was afraid of anything in the whole of Never-Ending, it would have been silence. Silence would be the death of her but not just anybody's silence. We tried that. She just kept filling the space until it didn't matter if they were her words or not, just one huge pile of not going anywhere or meaning anything. Confusing doesn't describe it because the end of silence cannot properly be described by a single word, not even a very good word like confusing. She will never understand silence because she has to talk about it in order to think about it.

But all that ended and we came here, that was the deal with Took A-Look. We came back to the tundra, the Arctic desert, the plains and the mountains. Arlene thinks we're prospecting or maybe that's just what she wants to think. We didn't talk about 'it' but after a few days she settled down and stopped looking for anything that didn't seem quite normal and came to the justified conclusion that everything, meaning me, was as fine as it ever was. And all because Took A-Look and I made a deal to share parts of now with parts of Never-Ending and even she sensed that. At least when she dropped us off at the airport she didn't say good-bye like she'd never see us again so maybe she knew that peace had been declared and that we were moving steadily forward without a destination or a plan to get there. You have to be happy when people accept that, don't you?

Marsha called a few times, which was surprisingly pleasant. Not a hint of therapy in her voice, not a mention of Took A-Look but when she said 'you' it was obvious he was included. Nice friendly chats, five minutes at the most; she spent a little longer with Arlene and probably heard everything she had to hear but nothing she wanted to hear. Marsha is an inherently peaceful person, which is probably what attracts Took A-Look to her. Peace runs in his blood, at least as long as he isn't disturbed, it does. Disturbed is different but you know that.

She knows that peace doesn't just come, peace is made. People get that wrong all the time, they think that peace is the absence of conflict, which it isn't. Peace is the absence of a lot of things but that still isn't what it is. Peace is what is left when all those things are gone and peace is declared in their absence. That's what Took A-Look believes. Fights must be finished before they get started, that's the only way, the way of his people. It takes a lot of inner strength to get things out in the open before peace can be undeclared which is why there isn't a lot of peace in this world. The people who run it into war don't have the inner strength to stop conflict without conflict. They don't really care about their people. That idea takes a lot of getting used to, just like the first few days of being here, being in Never-Ending without a watch or a map. It takes some getting used to.

Being completely isolated requires some adjusting. First comes the 'what if' syndrome. What if I break my foot? What if I get sick? What if I fall down that crevasse? What if a bear comes into camp and destroys it? What if there's a nuclear war and the plane doesn't come back before the last big freeze of winter? What if the plane crashes and nobody knows to come looking for me because they assume I went down with it? What if that ice isn't as thick as it needs to be and I go through it?

It takes a while to get over 'what if? because death is the only answer to 'what if' and death is to be resisted at all cost. Fortunately, 'what if' is nothing more than a huge circle of fears who eventually scare each other away but it takes time to go through the process.

But it's a process with a good result because once the fear stops it makes you careful where you put your feet. It makes you think about tomorrow but not like the fable of the grasshopper and the ant where the ant runs around storing food and getting ready for the worst. More like the grasshopper who sits in the sun and sings. Preparing for tomorrow is taking good care of today, that's how it works up here. There are no good tomorrow's without a good today, especially after the big freeze, trust me on that one.

And that introduces the next big hurdle; getting time sorted out. For most people time is too short. So many days or months or years in the future and so many of the same measures looking backwards. They use the moment they're in to think about the ones to come or the ones which are gone, which is a waste. Hardly ever are they actually in the right time and to cover up that mistake they blame time and call it too short, which is pretty insulting.

Here time stretches out to the horizon and goes all around it in a big circle connected in all directions and up and down. No need to go forward or backward in time because it's everywhere so no matter where you are, you are right in the middle of it. There is simply no point measuring how long it will take to get to this ridge or that stream because two steps or two hundred steps later and time hasn't budged a bit. That's just counting.

I could walk clear across New York City and not see a thing, not even notice the time I've wasted. You can't do that here. It's impossible to waste time when it's part of everything, when it reaches into your heart and makes your mind beat in tune with it.

Which is the next big hurdle, mind and matter. Large and small doesn't matter. Deep or shallow doesn't matter. Black and white doesn't matter. Things are what they are and putting words on them is just window dressing without a window. That's just man-handling the senses and giving them something to do by providing with them with nouns and adjectives and adverbs. Like saying this rock is big and black and round and that rock is small and gray and sharp. What did that accomplish? Every rock is different from every other rock so what's the point? If that's the sort of thing that makes you feel better, you'll go crazy up here. You have to dump relativity because all it does is make you feel too big or too small or too wrinkled. Where's the good in that? It didn't help the rock.

Once relativity over mind and matter is dispatched to the non-existent, Never-Ending trash can, it's time for the purpose discussion and once that discussion is done, adjusting is justing. Why am I here and what am I doing? Tough questions almost anywhere else in the world but not so tough here because the options are endless, not pointless. Mainly because there aren't any contradictions or any arguments. If you want to walk to the ridge, you do. If you would rather walk to the stream, you do. If you start for the ridge and end up at the stream, that's fine. Just like a mouse or a fox. They don't think about why they are here or where they are going. They know. It's in their blood. It's in everybody's blood, if only they paid attention. Walk around New York City for a day and see what you remember. Walk around up here and see the difference. It's easy to remember things that make sense, they have no choice but to be what they are so you remember them because that is how you find your way around. They matter.

Turns out the dog isn't a dog at all, which doesn't come as a big surprise. Chances of anybody being within a few hundred miles are really slim and if there was anyone closer than a hundred miles, I'd know it and so would they. There would be a sound, or a wisp of smoke in the air. Maybe a little glint from a piece of metal and then a speck of movement would head towards you and keep on coming. That's when you know, when it keeps on coming toward you. Nothing else does that, just people. Bears circle around, most everything else runs away, hides or isn't curious.

Here, people will travel for two days just to find out who you are and then if they don't like the way you put your feet on the earth, they'll leave, sometimes without even saying hello. After that, anybody within a thousand miles will know you are here and avoid you because if you don't belong to the land you aren't worth a visit.

Marsha would like it up here. Her need for peace is the give-away to that conclusion.

Took A-Look is worried about something and it has something to do with her. He keeps changing the subject, even when he starts it. Most of the time he changes it into Sorenson and that turns into a one-sided argument with Took A-Look trying to convince somebody who isn't me that Sorenson is up to no good. Just when it starts to make some sense, he changes the topic.

He's on to something but he won't say what and he won't let go of it either. Unusual.

Not that he won't say what it is, or that he won't let go of it, that's not the unusual part. It's unusual because it is firmly in the past and Took A-Look doesn't dwell on the past. Not unless the past and the future are about to collide but that's different, plus it has to be squarely in the jurisdiction of right now and how Sorenson could ever fit into that territory is beyond my imagination. And what he could possibly have to do with the future, now that he is in the past is hard to reconcile, least of all mention being way outside of right now. But something about Sorensen is bothering Took A-Look, that's obvious because for one thing, it's starting to bother me too.

What? You finished sharpening those spears already?

He has the bent twig spear with the too much leather wrapping in his hand, like that's going to be the next topic of discussion. He must have made that one when he was three years old.

I know you sharpened everything yesterday, there's bits and pieces of bone and tusk and wood shavings all over the place. Are you going to clean it up sometime or do you like it that way? You do? No, it doesn't bother me at all. No, not bother is not the same as don't care. Because it isn't.

No, it wasn't a dog. I know a dog would have barked, that's what they do. They bark and then they run straight toward you for a while and then they run back to whoever they belong to and back and forth. I know that's not what people do, they keep coming. You think I forget everything you tell me?

What outcrop? Oh that outcrop. Sorry, I forgot. Are you sure we checked it out before?

Really, way back then? We saw it from the other side, before going up the mountain with the ridges reaching out to sea and the stone beach, you say? Well, you would know. Yes, I know you know and no, no reason at all, I just happen to be going this way. No it's not an accident that I'm going this way, I'm just going this way but for no real purpose. Do you mind? No? You're back to being agreeable again, how come, did you have a nap or something?

No, I haven't been thinking about the seal and her green seas with dancing gold specks. He throws the bent twig spear at another cloud I hadn't noticed before and out pops a picture of Marsha, the real, not seal, version. The time when she was sitting on the bed looking out the window at the horizon and telling us about still studying and I was thinking that a really hard test was coming her way. It's her profile and a pretty one too, much better than when it actually happened. Her nose has little uplift to it that I hadn't noticed before. High cheekbones too but not the long face which usually accompanies that feature. Nice chin; lovely neck. It's a nice profile, very delicate, but not the kind of delicate you are afraid will break but delicate like you want to protect it. Thanks Took A-Look, I really hadn't noticed how very pretty she is.

He goes over to the window and checks out the scenery. This is one of his favorite places in the whole world, this side of the mountain. A vast expanse of timeless horizon that doesn't need relativity because even when something is bunched up into a concentrated state it still belongs, still sits in balance with everything else. Always the same, always completely different every time. Like rocks are rocks until you hold one in your hand and then it isn't what it appeared to be but it isn't just the sense of touch that does it, you know that.

Rocks. I've spent my whole life with them and have never seen the exact same rock twice, unless it was the same rock, of course, I've had lots of those. That's how things fit up here, just like that but we've had that discussion already, see how it doesn't matter?

Sure, if you want to. Something for me to do? What is it? Okay.

We head down to a stream he wants to see then to a point where it flows around a bend before widening out, not quite forming a pond, just shallow, rippling water, bordered on one side by a little beach of small stones and pebbles but cut deep into the bank on the other side. Just a few inches deep at the deepest part, not even half way up my mukluks, I see the stones he wants me to find. Ten of them lying in black sand where they didn't belong. The sand is hard packed but I put my feet down gently, leaving just the slightest of footprints; they won't survive for long, no more than a year, after the next melt.

With three stones in one hand and the rest cupped under the other arm, I back off the sandy bottom, not stepping in the same place twice. It's a small thing, but Took A-Look appreciates it as I place the wet stones back with their brothers and sisters on the little beach, one here and another there and I don't throw them.

The stones are all are about the same size and shape, about the size and shape that fit nicely into the hand of a small child who is learning to throw.

I don't ask any questions. Why am I here and what am I doing have already been answered to my complete satisfaction.

Yes I'm sure I haven't been thinking about Marsha. Why don't you make yourself useful and clean up your mess back there? Spears and shavings, arrows and stone chips, are everywhere.

Say what you want to say about Took A-Look but don't say he's neat.

No it doesn't bother me.

Because it will give you something to do, that's why.

I know, you've got plenty to do without cleaning up. Fine, now Marsha is on my mind too. You win.

He leaves the window and gives the seal cloud a little nudge as he goes past it, he's already completely forgotten about the house cleaning comment. Out she pops, looking at me with those huge dark liquid eyes. Not the playful ones, the sad ones. Apparently I haven't finished thinking about her so I sit down on the little beach. It's a pleasant topic and sitting down is the best way to enjoy a pleasant topic, no surprise there although sometimes the thoughts can surprise you.

The first time we met her was a Monday. Took A-Look was a bit wrecked after the 'this won't hurt a bit' needle. I was stuck in cement. The one with the big mouth was there and Marsha was asking her questions; she was lying through her teeth, as usual. Strange but all I really remember is what Took A-Look saw, the green seas and the dancing gold specks. That was the first time he shot an arrow into the seal cloud. It wasn't much of first impression, not at all what first impressions are supposed to be; that first minute or less when you know, somehow you know, whether or not you will like that person. A decision that pretty much sticks to you forever after that. No, it wasn't that much of a first impression at all, at least not for me. But Took A-Look got a really good first impression, like he knew her right away, he knew she was a seal person right from the very first second he saw her. He just didn't bother telling me, probably wouldn't even talk about it now.

Then Tuesday came along and Marsha came with it, just after the crush. The cement was gone but I still couldn't move much, I was in the bear trap. Marsha knew about Took A-Look, the mouth had taken care of that, she had made certain of that because whatever the plan, that was part of it. That's when Marsha sat down and introduced herself. Very nice and without any presumptions. She talked about getting to know people and them getting to know us and studying.

That was the picture Took A-Look just showed me, her profile, something I hadn't really noticed before...there's something about that cloud, the one with Marsha inside it...Took A-Look knew just where to find it... strange. Strange but then again, he knows his clouds...but whose cloud was it? Mine or his? I try to find it but can't.

Say what you want to say about Took A-Look's messy housekeeping but for sure his curiosity is behind a lot of that. He loves to hide things just as much as he loves to find them so it must be his cloud.

Later that same day she came in to check on the wrecked arm. She talked to Took A-Look, not to me. He liked that. He even let a fast little beam of his own light out the window for her to see. Did she see it?

Then, I remember the part when she touched me, she put her hand on my head, touched my cheeks, very seal-like. I can still feel it, that cloud is definitely mine. She was one sad doctor, I do remember thinking that.

I also remember thinking she would never be a friend to Took A-Look. That turned out to be completely wrong. He liked her right from the very beginning, right from the first moment he saw those green seas and gold specks. Anybody else looking for him like that and he would have harpooned them right off the bat, good presumptions or otherwise.

I should have figured that out before but didn't and can't blame myself for that. I didn't get a first impression, he did and, after all, we were in state of undeclared peace so I had other things on whatever parts of my mind that weren't being shared.

Wednesday, mashed potatoes and Took A-Look wasn't talking. She walked right by, like she knew she shouldn't stop and talk. Again the next day, when we were in the garden and we could feel her looking at us but couldn't see her doing it.

Then Friday, first thing in the morning, she came in for a visit. Came in for a normal conversation which was what followed and then a couple of hours later there was another visit in her office, that time with Arlene.

Took A-Look had seen all he wanted to see of hospitals, parrots, line painters, pale blue, green and pink. I couldn't have agreed more which was a good thing because it was up to me to talk our way out of there.

It was all business, just another meeting with the Chairman in the boardroom. A little vague, a lot detached. That was the plan and it worked fine. Marsha was pushed into a corner from which she didn't fight back. What she didn't know, what she couldn't know, was that the fight was over before she could even think about ending it. Certain decisions had been made and peace had been declared. Clouds would be honored and consequences would be shared. That was the deal. Our first real, honest agreement with each other in a long time. Even if I never learn all the words for snow, I know someone who does and that's worth a lot. We share and because we share all the obstacles to peace have been removed and it now has a place of its own. When peace is invaluable to both parties, it tends to stay declared.

Took A-Look watched my memories float by and didn't say anything to interrupt or correct them. Not directly and even now he is only just hinting that something might be missing. Something is going on, just like with Sorenson. Something he isn't sharing. I guess we don't share everything.

A puff of bored, Arctic wind made the water in the little stream shiver and that sucked all the reflections beneath the surface. Maybe that's all there is to this talk about Marsha, just some reflection, just a momentary distraction like a rabbit taking one trail then running across another and deciding, why not follow this one? see where it goes? why not indeed? off we go, hippity-hop.

Still, even without a first impression, I now know I knew I liked Marsha right away. Come to think of it, who wouldn't? For someone in the unreal business, she was dyed in the wool as real as could be. Calm, intelligent, curious, even a little humorous. Pleasant to be around, easy to be with.

She was like Shelley, Arlene's mother. Only Shelley had a wild side, an impetuousness, an urgency to inhale as much life into her lungs as they could take for as long as they could take it. She died too young to savor the essence of who she was.

What a strange thought. Was that you, Took A-Look? No? No it wasn't you or no it isn't a strange thought? Both? Now that you mention it, I suppose it isn't that strange a thought. No, that doesn't make it your thought. Of course it's a compliment. You're welcome.

Marsha would really like it up here. Probably wouldn't even bring a book, which is not a mistake. Books don't make sense when everything in them is completely alien to everything around them. Like trying to read Russian when you don't speak it. Not even the alphabet is the same.

What are you up to, Took A-Look? Are you missing seals that much? Do you want to go over the mountain, down the arms to the sea? There are lots of seals there. Do you want to go there?

You do?

Sure, right now is fine, but why the hurry?

What do you mean this is the time? Does that mean there is no other time? Of course Never-Ending is Never-Ending, what has that to do with anything? Are you trying to be confusing Took A-Look? No, this time it is not a compliment.

No, Took A-Look, I am not being confusing, you are.

You are too.

Fine, let me know when it's not, not time anymore and we'll leave slightly after that but just in time for Never-Ending, Okay?

Something is bothering him. No doubt about it.

CHAPTER 26

Brita sat staring down the street in the direction of La Bastide where her most recent troubles started and they were, without question, five-star troubles.

Her small balcony was barely wide enough for the rusty bistro chair and even then it had to be sideways or her legs would have hung over the edge. She wore a loose, aquamarine hausefrau dress, cheap slippers and sunglasses with the largest lens she could find. No hat and her hair had a very slept-on look. She hoped no one would recognize her, especially the police.

It was a horrible irony. She had over a million dollars in the bank but this was all she could afford and her cash was running out. When that happened she would be destitute. She was hungry but not for the canned sardines which were to become her supper just as they had been her lunch.

She was stuck and there was no way out. After two days in jail, the police had taken her passport and she wasn't about to get it back. She didn't dare talk to them; she didn't dare talk to anyone. Not a bus driver, not a waiter, nobody. Her mouth was a huge liability.

The problem was obvious, she couldn't stop the lying. About everything. She lied about the color of a flower, then she lied about it being a flower and then she lied about lying.

She lied about being a doctor, a model, a princess and the Consular Director of an African country nobody had ever heard of. That's when they threw her out of La Bastide.

She had a big bill to pay so she went to the bank to cash a cheque and then she lied about who she was which really created problems because if there's one thing banks really care about, it is making sure that the person getting the money is the person who owns it. She even wrote the cheque to the person she was lying about and, the French police being completely obtuse when it serves their purpose made a big deal about one of her identities paying the other one. Like that should bother them when all they ever did was have affairs and call it joie de vivre.

Okay, she made it worse, that she could admit to herself. With every question they got more lies, good ones. Even the same question was answered differently every time. They had a lot to check out and weren't about to let her go until they got the truth, which for the first time in her life she really wanted to tell but couldn't.

She did a really first class job of convincing them of every identity except the one she needed to get at her own money. In the end, they clipped her passport and started the search for the real Mrs. Brita Black, warning her that if she tried to leave town she would go back to jail. Like leaving town was even an option when it wouldn't solve a damn thing anyway, just like even if they proved she was who she used to be, she would have to deny it.

If the truth will set you free, then it was pretty obvious what was in front of her.

She couldn't get help because she couldn't ask for it.

Whatever was in her brain was hell bent on self-destruct.

Or was it?

Suppose she stood on the railing, suppose she jumped.

Would that be a lie?

Didn't it have to be?

Why believe your own brain when you know it is lying to you?

Seriously, jump.

No, don't jump.

Dive.

CHAPTER 27

Here we are, Took A-Look. There are the bones, just like years ago. Should I set up camp first? The same spot as before? How long ago was that? Almost twenty, I bet. Very funny, it couldn't have been that long? No camp? Okay. Then what next? You want me to do what with the bones? Why? Fine, don't ask questions, just do it. Why are you so bossy all of sudden?

I know that's a question but it's not the same question as the bones, is it?

I know that's another question but it's different too. Not all questions are the same are they?

Yes, that's another question. The first question was on bones, the second was on bossy and the third question was on questions. There, are you happy now?

That's right, that's the fourth question you won't answer. Never-Ending, that's what you are. And that's not a question.

Fine, I'll deal with the bones. Was that so difficult?

Never-Ending yourself.

* * * * *

Okay, that's all I can find.

I've already looked over there, twice. Now what?

Walk out on the left arm and throw the bones into the sea? I understand, walk all the way to the end of the arm, then to the end of the hand and then into the water for a few paces. Yes, I see from the color where the sea drops like a steep cliff. I know, throw the bones as far out as I can. No, I won't go too far and fall in. Trust me on that one, I don't feel like a swim.

Far up on the mountain's shoulder, hidden by boulders and tucked into a twisted crevice, the three elders watched. They had been in disagreement for the last two hours and each of them had changed their opinions at least once. Mostly they argued about whether or not the white man had seen them or if he knew they were watching him. That he was going to die was never in dispute. That in spite of the fact that killing was never the way, not the old way or the new, not even killing a white man, not even when they deserved to die, which was most of the time. But forbidden meant forbidden and there was no question about the penalty for breaking that law. White or not, he was in the forbidden place and he had to die, and that couldn't be negotiated, reconciled or changed. Not ever. Death was death regardless of Never-Ending. Anything else and forbidden couldn't exist; nothing good ever came from that. No exceptions.

Not even as they watched him gathering the bones in the forbidden place. Not even when he walked out onto the hand, then onto the pointing finger and then into the sea. Not when he threw the bones, one at a time, into the depths of the abyss. Not even the second time a handful of white bones made a white splash but on the third trip to the edge of the abyss they weren't so certain. It was the old woman who was first to change her mind and it was clear to the two old men that she wouldn't change it again. "He has a guide." she said with certainty.

The old men could scarcely argue that point. In all the seasons and all the generations of all the elders who had lived those seasons since it was first forbidden to go down there, human feet had only walked on that beach once. That was many years ago when a white man, like the one they were watching, found his way, the only way there was, up the mountain and down the other side to the elbow of one arm, crossing over to the other side and then down to the protected beach between the palms of the rocky, weathered hands. But that white man had died, he had become sick and killed by the spirits who lived in the camp so long ago abandoned that it was only a legend. Not that anyone had seen him die or seen his body or bones but they had waited and watched, from the very spot where the three elders stood, until the ice filled the bay and neither survival nor escape were possible.

Yet the white man they were watching had gone to places that none of them had ever been and he had gone with purpose. Quiet, unhurried but moving with defined, deliberate purpose as if he knew what to get and where to find it. Bones. Bleached white. Large and small, he put them, unhurried, calm, with respect, dignity even, on a blanket he had spread for that purpose, right in the center of the beach. Actions that were most unlike a white man whose steps were always hurried and whose head was always turning with fear and suspicion of a nature he didn't, or couldn't, understand.

The elders could not go down nor could they let him leave. If the spirits didn't kill him, they would kill him themselves. And then, by law, they would go down to the camp where no one had been for as many winters as there were people or tribes or memories of them. They would go down between the arms of never-ending and ever-lasting to die a death for which there was no memory. Forbidden meant forbidden and to touch one who has touched forbidden, which they most certainly would have to do in order to kill him, meant they too had broken the law. No matter. Their old eyes had already seen everything they wanted to see. Death would come quickly, of that they were certain, of that one thing they were in complete agreement.

Except now they weren't so certain that the white man had to die, not after the fourth and last trip to the edge of the abyss, so clear from above where the sea turned from emerald green to black as though a line had been drawn through it. So black was the abyss that they could see the silver-white splash of each bone, each bone thrown with such purpose and care into the abyss from which it could never come back and from where it would never again be touched by a human hand. Thrown with such purpose, with such care, that he had to have a guide.

To kill a white man was one thing, to kill a guide was another thing completely. "He has a guide." repeated the old woman. The old men on each side of her nodded. It was the only explanation for such behavior.

The spirits had made their decision and nothing the elders could do would change that any more than they could change the past and all that was written in it. Nothing and Never-Ending were all part of the same thing, common knowledge.

So they watched him like their old eyes watched the village, the babies, the young, mothers and fathers; all their seed, just as they had been watched by those who seeded them. The white man with the guide, unhurried and calm in a place which was anything but that. Walking around and between the arms, looking for more bones, like he belonged to the place or like it belonged to him. From time to time the white man stopped and looked out to sea or into the sky but never to the crevice where they hid.

"The guide knows." the old woman murmured. The silence from the old men was agreement enough for her to continue. "We will honor the guide, he will tell us what do. He will tell us if we are to kill and by doing so meet our destiny, our timeless time."

"And how will we know?" asked the old man to her left, the one who was closest to death and therefore most prepared to die.

"The guide will tell us what to do." she repeated. "Then you will know because he knows." She knew they were thinking about death and how close it was to them. She also knew death for a woman was no different than death for a man, even if they thought otherwise. Only a woman can bear life so she can accept the ending of it more readily. Once again, the old men's silence signaled their agreement. She stood and moved into the open. They followed her like shadows, slightly out of step, but shadows nevertheless. Each foot rose to the air and fell to the ground until they were standing where they could be seen without meaning anything other than being seen.

How long have you known they were there, Took A-Look? How long have they been waiting for us?

Forever? Forever is a long time. What do you mean, not so long? Forever is…forever, and that's a long time. No, no, I'm not surprised you have six words for it. Is it time to go? Why are you so sad? Are you concerned about them? Okay, I'll mind my own business.

The white man placed his foot with care, always choosing the stone or the ground onto which he stepped. Now and again he would stop and turn, nudging this rock or that pebble back to the place from which he had dislodged it, sometimes moving a rock which he hadn't touched, as if changing the stone's position would put it to a peaceful rest that it hadn't known for a thousand years.

He said nothing, his exertions didn't tire him and he carried himself upright at all times, never fighting the slope but leaning into it, like he belonged to it, like a rock would stand on it. His eyes were blue and sharp, as clear and intense as one would expect from a man with all the seasons he possessed. The color was not at all unlike that of the abyss when the wind rippled the water over it.

The elders waited as only elders can wait, calm and peaceful, the past and future embracing each other until they are forced to separate into the horizon. Time and words were no longer measured or counted because there were so many more important things to think about including what little was left for each.

Do you want to talk to them Took A-Look? You do? Good because all I know are a few words for snow and there isn't enough of it around even if I could figure out which snow belonged to which word.

Sure it's okay with me, why are you being so agreeable? Fine, you aren't being agreeable, there does that make you happy? Good. I think the old man, the really old one, wants to talk to you. He's not so old? He sure looks old. You think it's the old woman who will do the talking? Because of the necklace? Are you sure? I bet it will be the old man.

"Are you a spirit?" she asks.

You win Took A-Look.

"I am guide." Says Took A-Look who hasn't spoken a word for twenty-six years.

Say what you want but it's always interesting to hear words coming out of your mouth that you don't make yourself. It's been a long time since you did that Took A-Look. Say, how come I understand them? No kidding, it's that cloud up there. I always wondered what it was for. Who would have thought? Okay, nobody except you, sorry, sometimes I ask questions that I don't expect you to answer. You do know your clouds, that's for sure. What's next? Wait? Okay, I'll wait.

"You come in peace?" she asks.

"I go in peace. Forbidden returns to forever." Took A-Look says.

All three nodded.

What do you mean we can go now? That's it? That's the whole conversation? I could've done that. What do mean I would have got us killed? Oh, you don't say. You don't say? One word? That's all it would take? Sure I'll keep quiet. No problem with that. The old guy's spear looks pretty sharp. You don't say? It would have been that little knife in the old woman's belt? You don't say?

The old woman was staring into my eyes like she was trying to see the cloud behind me.

"Took A-Look? Are you Took A-Look?" her expression matched the question like the whole universe was being asked to explain itself and it had better deliver a single, solitary answer for absolutely everything, perfectly, or else. Like one rogue wave coming in between those outstretched arms would be too much or not enough and only she would know the difference. Like a seal popping its head up from the abyss and holding a bone in its mouth would change everything for all time. Like when death ceases to be a concept and becomes a reality, the exact moment when that fearful word finally loses its power over every cell, over all thought.

Tricky, and more than slightly uncomfortable to be asked such an easy but possibly impossible question for which the consequences would be so serious. Fortunately they would be Took A-Look's consequences this time, however that happened, which probably explains why he never explained any of this before. Seriously, how can you explain this? Surely not with something so primitive as words.

"I once was Took A-Look and will forever be but am not now. Nothing is lost on the path to Never-Ending. The beginning will start where the end is finished. That is the meaning. Say my name until you understand; stop saying it until you know."

"Safe passage Took A-Look." said the oldest man. His eyes were sharp with lots of beams of light radiating from them. Like he was laughing with a child while playing a funny game together.

"Go no further. Forbidden in this place has one meaning." said Took A-Look.

"Forever, Never-Ending, Took A-Look." they said in unison and moved aside for us to pass.

They followed us to the top of the mountain and part way down the other side until they went one way and we went the other. Took A-Look was so quiet I didn't even know he was there. I wondered if maybe he wanted to talk to his people some more. I wondered if that was why he was sad. I wondered if he would rather be with them than with me. I wondered if he had something else for us to do but no matter what I wondered, he didn't answer.

There is simply no place for wondering like the high Arctic. That's when I figured he was doing his own wondering and letting me do mine. The best wondering is always done alone and shouldn't be shared until it's over and then who cares about sharing because when wonderment is done it loses its majesty.

It didn't matter to me that we'd come all this way to throw some old bones into the sea. It was damned odd though, the oddest thing I've ever done or felt. The feel of a human skull in your hands as you throw it into an abyss is something you can talk about with words or think about without them but you can never truly feel unless you've done it. A human skull, the vessel of life, pitched into the ocean, don't think about it, it won't help.

It didn't matter that Took A-Look hadn't said a thing about it until we were right there, right where we first met, so long ago. No, not so long ago, he would correct that notion in a hurry. Anybody with six forevers in their dictionary wouldn't give that tiny bit of history, measured in mere years, the compliment of 'long ago.' Anybody who had been there and back, twice, wouldn't call a few thousand sunsets long ago by a long shot. No, it didn't matter that Took A-Look hadn't said anything. He could keep his feelings and his thoughts and his wonderment to himself if that was what he wanted to do because it didn't matter.

Nothing matters when everything is in its rightful place. Or is it when everything is at peace with itself, when the rocks are where they belong, when the sea is spilling with waves and the birds can sweep through the sky, free to soar and dip and turn with the wind. Places change but not your place in them. That's where peace is found, nowhere else. How could anything matter after that? How can anything matter when it is attached to everything else before it falls into time from which there is no escape because there is nothing to escape from?

I went back to the little stream with the rock strewn beach. Everything was still in order. Was it ever truly out of order? Perhaps. Perhaps a small boy threw stones into the water in a rage or a temper tantrum and it was his way of making peace with himself by undoing what he had done. If only everything was that easy.

Maybe it is that easy, maybe that's how it makes sense. Maybe that is the job of the past. It is there to make everything else fit because being dropped into the future without it would short circuit everything. Dropped into the future without having just one day before and the whole passage of time toward it would cause Never-Ending to disconnect from itself. Then again, maybe it doesn't make any sense because it really doesn't have to make sense, maybe that's just a human reaction to something for which words haven't yet been invented.

The little stream rippled over the shallows casting shards of light back into the sky where they belonged. Where the water deepened, it darkened, becoming a mirror. I understood why there were six forevers and figured this had to be one of them. For that wonderment, I received a little nudge in the clouds, a pleasant little nudge from you-know-who.

Had a little nap, did you? No? Me neither, nice of you to ask. I was just wondering, that's all. You too? What were you wondering about?

He sent an arrow up between two clouds which I didn't think had enough room between them for anything bigger than a really narrow, fast beam of light but the arrow squeezed past and flew up high, over a cloud in the back, missing it by a mere hair, hardly any room at all for error. Once it reached the crest of that cloud, it seemed to hang there for a second or two and then it began to drop, not straight down but you could tell that would happen pretty soon and if it didn't hit something soon that arrow would go behind all the clouds where arrows hadn't yet been invented and be lost for good. But it didn't, it hit the seal cloud instead.

Great shot, Took A-Look. When did you move the seal cloud?

Out she came. Pretty as ever. Big, watery eyes as full of life as the dips and curves, bobs and weaves of her joyful, carefree swimming. In and out, around and between the blocks of ice, a splash of her flipper and then one from her tail. Full of life. Plumb full of life. Except for the dark speck behind one of the big blocks of ice behind her, the only life around, but her absolutely joyous. Dark speck? Dark speck with a long spear pointed straight at our favorite seal?

What are you trying to tell me? Who is that? Really Took A-Look, who is that?

Is it someone you know?

Fine, I'll never mind, who cares if I know what's going on, not you, that's for sure. Thank you, an explanation later will be just fine with me.

Later? Later? That doesn't make sense? Why not now?

Because what? Because why?

Because we're leaving? Oh. Because no time like the present? That's an odd thing for you to say, Took A-Look. Would you care to explain that?

No, you don't care to explain that, not in the present?

Maybe in the future if you see then what you think now? How long have you been working on that thought, Took A-Look? It's a tricky one.

"You can cut the chit chat orderly, you don't know half of what you think you know." came out of my mouth. It was exactly as I had spoken it the first time but this time it meant what it meant.

So that's what you've been thinking about.

No, I'm not thinking about it. We're on our way.

The same way as before. A walk to the base camp then into the boat for half a day and then another walk to the landing site where we wait for the float plane. Yes, we wait for the plane. Maybe half a day if the plane isn't already flying somewhere and if the pilot is sober and if the weather is good. Sure, we can radio him from the base camp and tell him to meet us. Maybe he will and maybe he won't, who knows?

Because they don't like to be waiting on the ground in the middle of the Arctic with their engine getting cold and their wings getting icy, that's why. That's why he wants us to be at the landing site before he will fly, that's the way it works. What difference does it make?

The seal was looking at me. She couldn't see the speck behind her or the spear in its hand. Those pretty, full of life, joyful eyes would never see what hit them.

I got it.

HE WILL WAIT FOR US, Took A-Look, I'll pay him so much money he will wait until spring if he has too.

CHAPTER 28

Marty Sorenson couldn't figure out who was in charge, let alone in charge of what. He knew he had his own thoughts and was in control of those thoughts but he also knew he wasn't the only person in his head with those abilities and that was about the extent of his understanding. Sometimes his own thoughts were spoken when he didn't want them to be and sometimes the words which were spoken weren't his thoughts but he became responsible for them. Like when Gut Vik took command and confessed to the crimes of Marty Sorenson. Talk about double jeopardy and that wasn't even to talk about jail where losing control of your physical and mental capabilities took on a whole other meaning. It created the vulnerability he had never experienced from a victim perspective. He had heard that story many times before but nobody said it like this.

Like this? No fucking way anybody talked about this, nobody ever said anything about somebody inside doing more damage than he was doing outside.

Ultimately, Marty decided, and he was pretty sure about it, he could make a decision, as long as it pleased Gut Vik. Not that he was getting any clues about what pleased or didn't please Gut Vik but it was the only solution that made sense. Then, following that logic to its only logical conclusion meant that maybe, just maybe, if there was conflict between him and Gut Vik, things would probably get really weird if not dangerously fucked-up. And that meant somebody might declare him insane, and odd as it was in his upside-down world, that was a win. At least in a hospital he, or Gut

Vik, could go around telling people to fuck off without getting the crap beat out of themselves, CIW not included in that sentence. In that ward you could get the crap beat out of yourself for breathing somebody else's air. Somehow he had make sure that it didn't go that far, that he didn't end up in the Criminally Insane Ward.

He tried to figure the odds on Dr. Coleman seeing him and figured that he had a better than even chance she would. After that he tried to figure the odds on being able to tell even part of his story without interruption but couldn't come up with anything that made any sense because that was when he realized he really didn't know very much about Gut Vik except there was no way he could fight him and win. His only chance was that the bastard also wanted to survive and the best place for that was the hospital.

Absolutely the best place to be, he repeated slowly to himself and anyone else who might be listening. If Gut Vik didn't care about dying then all of this was a square box in the middle of a circle. Try explaining that to someone who doesn't know the geometry of thought.

On the bright side, he thought to himself and anyone else who might be listening, all those years at the hospital could turn out to be very valuable. At least he wasn't really afraid of losing his mind because at the end of the day, territory was more important.

Plus, he knew his way around the place and the orderlies and what they were thinking so if he played his cards right, he wouldn't have to take any of their crap. All he needed was a little luck…and with little help from Gut Vik, things could end up just fine. It seemed like a good deal, even with a little craziness from time to time, it would be fine. As long as people listened when it got a little tough, he could manage it. Just as long as they listened, he repeated silently.

"If you gotta piss, do it now. They're waiting for you."

"I'm ready." He went over to the bars, spread his legs and put his hands into the tray opening, one above the other, just like before. The handcuffs went on one wrist then the other, the cop using only one hand to do the job, keeping the other hand on his baton, ready to deal with the slightest attempt at resistance. When the handcuffs were secured, he felt the jab of the baton, turned and put hands behind his head while another chain was threaded through the ankle bracelets through the belt loop and up to the handcuffs.

"Okay. You're done. Same procedure as before, one dumb move and you won't need ankle bracelets anymore." The cop tapped the baton on Marty's kneecap. Even Marty knew it wouldn't be the kneecap that got busted first and didn't object to the procedure or the humiliation that went with it. He'd done worse.

With Lupo standing and the three doctors sitting across the table from him, it was as close to a trial as Marty hoped he would ever have to face. He waited until the cop finished chaining him to the chair before making eye contact and then only with Dr. Coleman. It was a damn odd moment of complete familiarity mated with total estrangement because all of sudden he didn't know how to start. Turned out, that didn't matter because he wasn't in control, not even remotely and Marsha sensed it immediately. She didn't exactly know Marty Sorenson but she knew with certainty he wasn't the man staring at her. She also knew that where Took A-Look wouldn't speak, this one would.

"Tell us what happened. Tell us why you left the people at the mountain with the arms that reach into the sea." she asked, not blinking at the brutal, penetrating glare that her question evoked with such suddenness it made Lupo reach for his gun. If ever a pair eyes had witnessed death in all its forms, those eyes had. Brutally cold and uncaring with no more remorse for killing a person than an ant. The chains under the table rattled as if to tell everyone in the room that they wouldn't be there forever and then look out. His eyes never left Marsha which wouldn't have mattered anyway because she was the only person capable of maintaining eye contact with him.

For a moment Lupo wondered if she was incredibly brave, absolutely fearless or if she was seeing something no one else was seeing, like she was in another world and as if to confirm that, the telling started again, only this time it came from Sorenson, or whoever was speaking on his behalf.

"Three of them, all old men, died in the night. First the sweat, then the legs went numb, starting at the toes and working up, hour by hour, with a pain like the legs were being chopped off, one bit at a time. When it reached the groin, the insanity of pain started the minds to wander. One of them poured oil on his belly and put a torch to it, trying to kill the pain, after a while, he died. The other two screamed for death but no one would do it. I watched, a new death is always interesting.

When the sickness reached the chest, the pain stopped but there was no feeling below. A knife would draw blood to bone without complaint. Then they became calm, not the calm before the heart stops beating, because they didn't talk of death, they didn't see that in their mind. But what they saw, what they thought, no one knew, for their words were not in a language which anyone understood. The words were spoken in tongues from animals, some we knew, others distant and strange but animal, that much was clear. Grunts and howls, they jabbered in tongues which the two old men remaining seemed to understand of each other when no else could.

Words and sounds were said in calm the likes of which is on a face that searches the horizon. Looking for land or storm, a bird or a sail then finding it, but finding it as a surprise, not as if it was expected to be found. At the end of that surprise came curses and threats from lips which twisted, nostrils that flared and snorted with burning sulfur and ears which moved and fluttered like a fox listening for the sound of a mouse beneath the snow. No one understood their search and no one wanted to know what they found. Native or Norse, all agreed by that.

Then, came the blood. From arms and legs and body. Fingers, toes, front and back as if stuck with pins. No cuts or holes to explain it, just a red smear like the sweat of fat melting from a pig turning on a spit. Wiped away, clear clean skin. A moment later and it would be crimson with thin blood abandoning the body, a corpse not yet dead.

In the end, the face became rigid, so rigid that even after death the eyes could not be closed, frozen into rock. But not frozen in pain or in the final, thankful relief from torture no longer felt, but into a crude, stone carving. A poorly made image of an old man, disproportionate, barren of intimate details, like a piece of weathered root looking like a face but with all kinds of mistakes on it. Something missing or something there which shouldn't be there. So poorly carved were those faces that they couldn't be known for who they once were.

It was an omen, a curse had taken root on the land and all those who lived under the bleached whale bones and the hides which covered them. A most unnatural death, that much was in every mind, Native and Norse. The message was clear, escape and don't wait.

They had never seen such a disease, such a death and neither had we but all knew, though none said, it was the mixing of blood which gave the curse its birth and its power. Blood of my men with their women or blood spilled by accident of rock or spear when hunting, hook or line when fishing, or cutting the catch, the finger, the toe. Blood mixed because it always does when men work together or when men and women live together.

We didn't bury them. Perhaps that was native custom or maybe the old men became so foreign and wrong in appearance that they were treated like enemies who are left to rot in the place they fell.

Under orders which no one heard or saw, they left. Men, women, children and dogs, taking little from their camp and moving up the mountain between the two arms until they disappeared into the clouds from which they must have come. No one believed they would ever return to that beach, nor did any of us Norse want to see it again."

Sorenson, or Gut Vik, whoever was responsible for the narration, paused, seemingly for recollection, or perhaps searching for a detail which had been overlooked but which was of some importance to the telling.

Whatever was going through in his mind could not be read by the expression on his face or in the eyes that stared at Marsha like they were trying to see inside her mind, or perhaps open a pathway into it. Lupo tightened his grip on his revolver, an involuntary reaction which startled his thoughts back to the present. His finger was on the trigger and while he knew the safety had to be on or he would have shot himself in the leg, he checked it anyway. If Jorgenson's tale had been interesting dialogue, the words from Sorenson were real, recognizable, understandable and far from being a story. This was the truth, the exact present truth hundreds of years later, however ridiculous that was.

"And so you returned to Nor...to your homeland?" asked Marsha.

"We set sail by mid-day. Sailed straight into the horizon, not the most direct course but the wind was at our back and it multiplied the distance from that beach at the fastest rate. We stayed that course all the night and to the exact hour of the next day when the first one died just as the old natives had died on that condemned beach.

The next morning five more crude and unrecognized carvings were dumped into the sea. Four ships became three and three became two. Half the men died while the other half watched and listened to the scream of pain. But it was not the screams which caused the still living to be thrown over the side. It was the last moments, the sounds of animals and the words from foreign tongues, the eyes of strangers meeting the eyes of those who had known them for all their lives. One by one, slippery with their own blood, they were thrown over the sides to the sharks which followed, day and night, lured by the blood, satisfied with flesh only they did not fear. Other fishes, whales and the porpoises which were always racing the bow, were nowhere to be seen, as if they understood the dying on the decks and in the holds and wanted no part in it, as if they understood the curse and feared it with their own lives.

We had delayed our leaving too late but that saved us. One storm after another pounded our ships and covered them in ice so thick it threatened to sink us. Day and night, ice formed on spar and sail, sides and deck and all who were not sick had a club or a knife frozen in the hands to break and battle. A worst enemy or a better friend we never found for certain it was the cold that ended the sickness. Those who fought the ice did not catch the sickness, though many of them died too."

"Did anyone who caught the sickness, survive?" Marsha asked. Something told her she knew the answer and the same thing told her she needed to have that confirmed.

"Only one who caught the sickness lived through it."

"Gut Vik." said Jorgenson. The telling was accurate, at least as accurate as all the old women who had ever recited the legend had told it.

"Ja, Gut Vik himself was the only one who caught the sickness and defeated it." came out of Marty Sorenson's mouth and he listened to it with impartial but almost flattering interest.

So far, things were going better than expected. The detective was ready to jump out of his skin and the fancy-pants doctors were being held hostage by Gut Vik and his tale of woe. It couldn't have been better if Marty had scripted every word of it. Barring the minor detail that it was Gut Vik who got him into all this shit in the first place, Marty would have been thankful to him. Any second now and he would jump in and cement his non compos mentis defense.

"And then Gut Vik, the Barbarian was born." Jorgenson wasn't sure how long the story would last, how long it could last, considering what she knew of the ending.

"Barbarian!" shouted Gut Vik. "A barbarian is one who kills for pleasure, who eats the heart of his enemy while it still beats! Barbarian? You call Gut Vik a barbarian? You dare to call Gut Vik such a name?"

"Very true, it was then that Gut Vik, the man was re-born." Jorgenson quickly corrected herself. Barbarian was a relatively recent interpretation, addition really, of the events that followed. Civilized people sometimes chose to deny their own bloodthirsty roots, clean up their act posthumously, so to speak. Every serial killer since the dawn of time had the same evil spawn as Gut Vik and none of them thought of themselves as barbarians. Quite the opposite. At worst they considered their actions to be normal and natural to the circumstance, not sick or abnormal because the common reaction to brutality is often more brutality. Perfect logic, a death sentence for a death, what's barbaric about that?

"Ja. Gut Vik returned to the village and the village was happy to see his ships. Happy to see even two of them return but Gut Vik knew before the first man walked to shore. Gut Vik knew they were not happy to see him. Gut Vik knew from the way they looked at him, not in his eyes but at his feet. They had shame to hide. Shame to hide from Gut Vik and the source of that shame was his Fjellkurle. She was there, belly ripening with child, with your child my husband, she lied."

Damned interesting, thought Marty before a torrent of anger, stronger than any emotion he had ever felt, imploded his inner being like water hitting molten steel. Shards of red hot liquid metal exploded and penetrated everything and went everywhere in anger so red with fury and driven with such force that it simply couldn't be contained, couldn't be reasoned and certainly couldn't be understood. Anger which was so focused, resolute, uncaring and unyielding to every other thought except for destruction, brutal destruction. It completely obliterated all reason and thought until he became rage incarnate, his entire self was sucked into the emotion to fuel it and then become it.

The chains under the table snapped with such force that the broken ends flew up and penetrated the wood. He lunged across the table, his manacled hands aiming straight for Marsha's throat, fingers clawing at the air, sizing themselves to the dimension of their slender white target, greedy for the snap of her neck and the sensation of a windpipe being crushed beneath his thumbs.

"She lied to you?" repeated Marsha, in order to restart the telling.

Marty cowered behind the apparition which Gut Vik had sent him. His heart was racing and he couldn't catch his breath, so certain was he that it was real and not simply another invasion of his thoughts, another trick. He tried to concentrate, had to think and when he realized it was an apparition, he knew his heart wasn't racing and his breathing wasn't racing. He also knew he was losing more and more control because when he tried to move his toes, he couldn't. Fear happened. All his brain could do was ask a simple question. What is happening to me? A stupid question because he knew there wouldn't be an answer.

"She lied and said the bastard child was mine but it could not have been. I had been gone for too long and it was too little in the womb for it to be mine. All the eyes told me was a lie. She had disgraced me and then, she decided to die.

She told them that it was I, I Gut Vik, who could not please her and that she longed for a real man between her legs. She confessed to one man, then another and another. One at a time or several at once, with each act she spit the names like poison and told of the length or the depth or the position of their act with such relish of desire that her telling dripped with greed and bled vengeance. All this in front of the village that I had saved, all this with the boys who had grown to manhood so they could take pleasure with her. All this and worse.

'No more.' I shouted to her. 'You crave the sword, you shall have the sword.' My rage was as sharp as its edge and so strong that each blow I delivered only fed my rage. She spread like a puddle which was Fjellkurle and her bastard child until there was nothing left to know her by. Just a mess of rendered flesh and blood. The village watched as my rage joined force with my need for revenge and then I sought out those who had wronged me.

My brother, my poisoned Fjellkurle's proudest conquest, the deepest wound she delivered to me, was next to feel my sword. His blood, mixed with hers, dripping from the blade in front of my mother and father, my love for them turned to hatred. They were next. 'All this time you allowed this shame to be done to me. To be seen and spoken by all in the village? All this time when you could have put a stake in her heart? All this time and you just watched?'

They could no more answer that question than they needed eyes to see what they chose not to see. I blinded them and then to the mast of a ship which had returned with me, I tied my father. To the rudder, wedged tight so it would steer straight into the sunset, I tied my mother. That was their fate. Not knowing where they were going or what wave would break the ship or what fish would tear at their limbs, they sailed. No matter, only by half was my rage satisfied. The rest was to be my life's work for as long as that life would last."

Marty Sorenson could still feel the rage, even diminished by half it left him with the uncontrollable desire to hurt something, anything, anyone. No reason, no justification, no thought required. Just lash out and do as much damage as possible. Perfect because other than having to deal with that incredibly brutal impulse, Marty concluded that Gut Vik was doing beautifully.

He really couldn't have asked for more. Gut Vik had become the killer. Gut Vik had kicked the switch on the car jack and watched it ratchet down on dear old dad. Someone would have to deal with that, starting by getting rid of Gut Vik. Surely they could do that. For once they would have to earn their money; this was a serious psychological problem.

"And you started your revenge?" prompted Jorgenson.

"Ja. I did. As punishment for all who fell to the temptations of my poisoned Fjellkurle and all those who watched in silence, I became their conscience of revenge. I took the women whenever I chose and however I chose. Mothers and daughters, women and girls, with no thought to their pleasure or concern for their pain. If they resisted, I broke them. If a man complained, I put the sword to him and then spent my revenge on their women even as the tears of grief still flowed from their eyes. For days and days I feasted on their anguish.

The village was in shame and they had to hide it for the name of Gut Vik was still as powerful as before, perhaps even more so because of all those who were cursed with the sickness only Gut Vik the Conqueror, had survived. I was a god and they had to hold their tongues in fear and shame. No one would share the seas with such cowards and they knew it, so they suffered my rage in silence. The more they suffered, the deeper the silence."

"Until the end." said Jorgenson.

"Until someone found some courage, if that is what you can call it when a sleeping man is beaten with a club. It had to happen, I knew it would happen. Every hour, I waited for it, at first to fight back but when it finally happened, it was without caring from me when or by whom. My rage was worn and the fear and pain which fed it had lost strength and purpose. It mattered little, by then the seed of Gut Vik had been sown, I would live on, generation after generation. Such things are known by great men like me.

Ja, it had to happen; I wasn't even surprised that it was her. Not even fourteen summers of age when I took her. Like so many of them, I took her so brutally she would never again look at another man with desire. One by one I was taking my revenge on all the men who spoiled my Fjellkurle.

No, I wasn't surprised that it would be a young girl, especially that one. I had taken her mother and her sister before I took her. She had plenty of reason to do what she did, so much so that when she didn't fight me, I thought her too young and too afraid to do anything so I slept. But she wasn't young or afraid, she planned to be taken. She knew what she was doing and for that I can forgive her because she was brave. But for what happened next there is no forgiveness. She should have killed me, after the first blow she could have done it easily but she chose instead to conquer me.

I awoke lying on the deck of my ship, bound to heavy pine spars on each side, branches and cut wood piled around and on top of me. Sails set and winds strong, the leather pots soon burned through and the oil ran across the deck, lighting the pyre. It was not the worst of deaths."

"And so began the practice of sending a warrior, a Viking Lord, to Valhalla in a burning ship. The village saved itself by making the murder of Gut Vik into a ritual of respect and honor." Jorgenson completed the telling.

"Is that so?" said Gut Vik.

"And what became of the land with the arms reaching into the sea?" asked Marsha.

"No one should ever go to that place." he answered.

* * * * *

Lupo couldn't recall the last time he had been in a room with three psychiatrists and the silence had lasted more than five seconds. Had he ever been in room with three psychiatrists? He had, but that was in court and the judge had to keep reminding them to shut up. Anyway, at that moment they were quiet and it was an odd quiet, as if everyone was waiting for something to happen or trying to understand an answer or come up with a question.

Marty Sorenson wanted to break the silence, wanted to do it in the worst way, but he couldn't get anything to work. All he could think, all he could figure was that someone had disconnected the TV from the cable and every channel he tried produced a lot of grey fuzz. Over and over again, just fuzz. Click - fuzz, click - fuzz, click - fuzz, just like that.

Never-Ending flashed somewhere in the background and he knew that to be truth because that was where he was, in the background of his own life so as crazy as it seemed, it made perfect sense. Click – fuzz; Never-Ending.

Never-Ending he repeated to himself, grateful that the thought loop about cable TV and fuzz had been intersected. With a little luck, maybe something else would get connected and he could resume his normal programming.

Don't count on it.

"Any questions?" asked Marsha, breaking the spell, the silence and the tension born of inertia and exhaustion.

Without thinking, Basscurt responded, "Any point to them?"

"Take him away. Put him on suicide watch." Lupo told the guard, who didn't react very quickly. Probably something to do with deathly primordial sickness, burning ships, rape, pillage and dismembering pregnant women in front of the whole town. Some things always stop traffic.

The three doctors watched as Sorenson was unchained and half carried, half-dragged from the room. They watched the display like a bunch of teenagers watch a smutty movie, eyes vigilant for intimate detail and memorizing every move for replay at a future date, but for the moment, seemingly emotionless and joking about any serious involvement or interest with the show.

Lupo watched the watchers, one in particular. Marsha was so highly concentrated on the performance, he could almost read her thoughts.

She was doing the math, adding it all up, comparing this with that, deleting the superfluous and identifying the common denominators with all she knew about Sorenson and all the others she knew who were even remotely like him. Barring something unseen or some random combination of the bizarre, Lupo figured hers would be the most accurate opinion. She had the background which neither of the other two possessed and that was just the least of her advantages, particularly over Basscurt. It didn't take a genius to know that the longer that one kept quiet, the faster they would reach consensus.

"Sorenson is pretty familiar with catatonics and with multiple personalities, isn't he Dr. Coleman?" Basscurt asked without trying to hide the intent behind his question. He had learned a thing or two about her and wasn't about to increase her credibility even more by starting a fight he was destined to lose.

"Twenty years or so but I'm not sure how to best define that experience. Maybe a little bit of everything, academic, practical, tutorial, theoretical. He wasn't very disciplined about it unless it served his own purposes." She replied without a lot of interest in her own answer.

Basscurt was stuck with the ball in his court, again. "Absolutely bizarre." He uttered.

"It is." she agreed and this time it sounded like she meant it.

Whether or not that agreement had been expressed on the same topic didn't matter to Basscurt, who decided to take his chances with a comment to the entire group. "He might be able to fake the condition for a little while, but not for long. On the other hand, he might even be able to fake recovery, but that I seriously doubt. We should commit him for observation before making a final decision."

The middle ground, the safe ground but for a change Lupo agreed with it. It made sense, at least as much sense as you could make out of a mental condition based primarily on a Norwegian folk tale that was initiated by a brutal, unprovoked assault in a mental institution which at this exact moment was looking like a petty misdemeanor. But there was more to it and there was bound to be more to come. There just had to be. He would wait, sometimes that was the only way to catch something that was running; just wait until it runs out of breath. "CIW and nowhere else, no exceptions and no changes without my written permission." he said firmly.

"Very smart thinking." Jorgenson's compliment was sincere.

"I'll handle the commitment personally. That way it won't be open to interpretation, by anyone, anyone who might think they are doing Sorenson a favor." said Marsha abstractly.

"No contact without my permission, Okay Marsha? No contact by anyone." Lupo gave the order as best he felt he could possibly order Marsha in a facility he didn't control and she didn't run.

"I understand. It will be in the file." she agreed without contest.

Basscurt considered his options. He had asked for observation and got it but wasn't in charge. It seemed perfect. He sensed Marsha's eyes on him and nodded his agreement. Besides, she would tear his dissent apart, on or off the record and then he would look like an idiot. Case closed. He nodded his assent again then rose slowly and left like a doctor who needed some of his own medicine. A nice Merlot…no, maybe a well-chilled Pinot Grigio would be better. A red just didn't seem to be appropriate after all that bloodshed.

Jorgenson followed Basscurt out the door, but her stride, once she passed him, was long and quick.

"Sorry to be so insistent with Sorenson's…conditions." Orders were Lupo's first choice of words but he tempered it to conditions out of respect for Marsha. He wondered if he done the right thing and added: "He could be dangerous."

"You are right to be concerned, Lupo. He is dangerous." She didn't seem to be in a hurry; he wondered if she ever hurried.

"What did you think?" she asked.

Not flat like she had talked to Basscurt but interested, engaging him with a simple smile and leaning into him slightly.

"It was quite a tale. If I didn't know better I'd think that Jorgenson and Sorenson had rehearsed this little performance."

"That passed through my mind too." She wondered if the detective was always suspicious, if everything was viewed in terms of motive and opportunity. Probably, occupational hazard, just like her job had exactly the same hazards. Detectives in jail and doctors committed to the ward might suffer differently but they suffered equally.

“There is a problem though, a break in the logic…” It had bothered him at the time and he couldn’t find a way around it.

“A break in the logic?” she asked.

“Is that so? That’s what Sorenson, Gut Vik, whoever, said when Jorgenson talked about the Viking ritual. You know, the funeral pyre at sea.”

“Yes, that’s what he said.” she remembered.

“If he knew the story so well, why didn’t he know the ending, the moral of the story if you want to call it that: ‘Is that so?’ he asked, like he had never heard about a Viking funeral before, about the cover-up to his own murder. And, just to confuse it more, Viking lords were usually buried in their boats, not burned in them, but he was pretty definite about that: ‘It wasn’t the worst of deaths’.”

“Maybe he hadn’t heard that, maybe the tradition changed. But that isn’t a break in the logic, unless…” her words trailed off with fresh thoughts. It changed her view of Lupo’s suspicious nature into one of natural curiosity served up with a generous helping of common sense. He wanted all the puzzle pieces to fit and had found one which wasn’t quite cut properly.

Lupo finished her sentence, keeping to the topic, extending it to see what she would say. “Unless he couldn’t have known about it because it happened after his death and that, to my way of thinking, makes it just a little too neat, just a little too much like a courtroom tactic. Could Sorenson have met Jorgenson, or could he have known her reputation through hospital gossip? Some way he could have known that just a couple of words, ‘Gut Vik’ would get this show on the road?”

“It’s possible but I don’t find that very credible. Sorenson kept to his own side of the fence, if you know what I mean.”

“Didn’t fraternize with the enemy? Didn’t like head doctors?”

“That’s pretty much it.”

“Didn’t want to know the enemy?”

“Or didn’t want the enemy to know him.” She strayed back into her thoughts. How could she have missed conflict like that? All the times she had talked to him, coached him or told him what to do. How could she have missed that big a secret? Was it always there and if not, when did it start?

Who cares? She missed it. "He stayed on his own turf and he had that turf pretty neatly cut. He imagined, and not too wrongly sometimes, that he ran the hospital. Like I said before, he was a long-term orderly, twenty years in the making and he wasn't going anywhere, his career had definitely peaked as had probably occurred in his life. I don't think he knew Jorgenson and I don't think he would have cared about her as long as their paths didn't cross. Who knows, maybe it was just coincidence that he said Gut Vik and she picked up on it. Maybe he figured that even if she didn't know, someone else would, or someone would look it up." Marsha realized that not only was she talking about Sorenson in the past tense but that she was also thinking of him as dead.

'Or didn't want the enemy to know him', Lupo repeated silently. She's made up her mind about the situation, her prognosis is in, neat or otherwise. Too bad but not unusual. Most people, doctors included, stop with the most convenient answer. If a piece doesn't quite fit, they either ignore it or hammer it into their theory. It's especially easy to do when the starting point is crazy. Then, with very little hammering required, everything can be made to fit because everything fits anyway once norms are options and exceptions cease to be questioned.

"Is that so?" she said innocently, catching him in his thoughts. She wasn't about to let him come to any old conclusion about herself or what she was thinking when she was still undecided. That was familiar territory to her but she didn't resent him for treading on ground already well trampled by others. Having to fight for everything that was ever important to her made her a pretty formidable opponent.

Her question 'Is that so?' didn't distract him.

Nor would he let it. Rule number one in the detecting business was to keep your own hand from being seen and not just from the suspects. From everybody, absolutely everybody until the thing was nailed down so tight it couldn't get up again. "Is that so?" he sent back to her.

"Check." she said.

Trying to read another person's thoughts by reading their eyes and body language then extrapolating your opinions of their logic was as old as time. Before Viking funerals, even. The irony of it made her smile.

Green seas with dancing gold specks crossed his mind as he dropped his detecting role and smiled back at her. He couldn't have resisted the impulse to be friendly…no, not friendly, more like familiar, like family, if he had wanted to. She knew him and he knew it. He just wasn't certain if, or what, he knew about her.

"Multiple personality disorder?" He expected a yes but as the silence grew he decided it had to be no. He had seen some pretty convincing acting by criminals who could lie so well that even they didn't even know when they were doing it. But he had never experienced the real thing so either Sorenson was one helluva an actor or he'd just had the pleasure of witnessing the actual phenomena.

"The official diagnosis?" she asked.

"Not required at this time." he said. She had already answered him. Officially no, unofficially don't know.

"It's strange, very strange. But then aren't they all?" she muttered unconsciously.

"Anything I can do to help?" It was only polite for him to ask. She would say thanks but not at the moment. Then she would say she would call if she needed help, but she wouldn't call even if she did. She would smile, he would nod. They would say goodbye and he would cook up some reason to drop by from time to time, for reasons professional but with motives somewhat more personal, like family.

"Yes Lupo, there is something you can do for me. Given that you are going to drop in from time to time anyway."

CHAPTER 29

"Is that so?" muttered Jorgenson as she left the police station, repeating it again as she turned the key and started her old Volvo. She could feel the fame of a real case study resting on her shoulders and knew the boost it would give to her career and her opinions. She had always thought that the feeling of responsibility would be heavy but it was the exact opposite, it gave her momentum and from that came an unexpected confidence. All she needed was the right partner, the right set of complimentary credentials to corroborate her findings and then she could leave the backwater of expert witnessing that had become her career and enter the bright lights of the erudite.

She mentally searched her network for the right partner, eliminating one after another for the same reason: they were too greedy. They would want to co-author and take an equal share of credit. She couldn't afford to share this find with just anyone because even the nice ones would rip it out of her hands and run with it. It had happened too often for her to believe it wouldn't happen again.

Finally, she was left with two choices, Dr. Anil Singh who was too old to care about the glory and Dr. Clifford Basker, who was quite brilliant and desperately in need of even the most meager of publishing or research credit in order to jump-start his career. Marsha Coleman wasn't under consideration. Authorship by two women was bad enough but if one of them came from a state hospital it was bound to put a curse on the findings.

Standing in the wings, in third place of partnering this momentous opportunity, academically unqualified but with financial and research clout that neither of the others could begin to match, was Roland Masters. He was an enticing possibility which would ensure both timely publication and enormous amounts of publicity. Findings which, if they turned out as she hoped they would turn out, would take the mental health community by storm; a devastating one and that was a huge advantage in Master's favor. He didn't give a tinker's damn about devastating the mental health system and they knew it.

As far as most of the serious shrinks were concerned, not only was he unqualified in psychiatry but he was practically a GP outcast to boot. Of course, some of that detest was jealousy of his ability to get attention, meaning money, for his cause. That and some sour grapes of benefactors who paid healthily without getting the return they expected for their philanthropy but that was the least serious of the criticisms which were leveled at the man.

If Masters had his way, the study and analysis of human behavior was in for a major shift in direction, a shift in the same direction the medical community was following, namely, genetics, the molten source and principle cause, action and reaction to everything under the sun. And that volcano, if it erupted on the study of human behavior, or at least a sizable chunk of it, would rain hot ash on a lot of soft leather couches and expensive degrees.

CHAPTER 30

Oost, Oost, are you there? Of course, of course you are there. Where else would you be? I've been thinking…yes, about that. Yes, about that some more. I know we have discussed it to death but I still have my doubts. You know how stubborn my husband can be. Yes, I know you know. Yes, I know you will be right here with me.

Oh dear. Too late to discuss it now, here he comes, her comes Sam. Yes, Oost, I'll try, I really will.

"Hello Julia."

"Hello Sam."

"Doctor Coleman told me what happened. What a terrible thing. How are you feeling? How is your jaw?"

"They have it wired up. I can barely talk. Why didn't you come yesterday, when it happened?"

"I was busy. They told me on the phone that you would be fine."

"On the phone is not the same as in person. I'm still your wife you know, you could have visited me even if they told you I was going to survive. What would you have done if they said something else, what does it take to be treated like a human being by you, Sam?"

"I just couldn't make it. Are you in a lot of pain?"

"They gave me something for it. It's not too bad. I want to go home. I don't want to be here any longer." There, it's started, I've said it, Oost.

"I'm sure you do Julia, but you know that's not possible. You're not better yet, are you?"

"Yes I am. I am perfectly fine and I want to go home. I want you take me home, right now."

"Julia, you know that isn't my decision; I can't do that. Dr. Coleman won't agree with that, as much as you may want it…as much as you think you are better, you still need some more time. Time and therapy. Think about it…you're just frightened because of what just happened but you needn't be. It won't happen again, that's been taken care of, the orderly is in jail. Doctor Coleman said so."

"Sam. I know what's right for all of us and I'm telling you to do it. Do it today Sam. I know what I'm saying and that's all you have to think about."

"Today, Julia, today you know what's right. What will you know tomorrow? Have you thought about that? What will be right for us tomorrow? The same as it was before you came here? Is that what I have to look forward to, for every tomorrow for the rest of my life?"

"No Sam. Tomorrow will be the same as today. You know I have to see my son, I've always wanted to see him but you keep coming up with excuses. It's not fair. It's just not fair that you get to make all the decisions like I don't exist anymore. Just a few minutes of your time every Wednesday, is that all I mean to you? And what about Lawrence, what do I mean to him when I don't get to see him at all? Answer me that. If you can."

"All right then. I'll talk to Doctor Coleman today and I'll talk to Lawrence. Maybe he can come for the next visit. We have to be very careful about this, Lawrence is still getting adjusted to the way things are."

"No. No. No. No maybes. Promise me that you will bring Lawrence and not for the next visit but tomorrow. Promise me that. You owe me that. You owe me at least that."

"Julia…"

"Promise. Promise on your mother's grave that you will do that."

"My mother isn't dead, Julia."

"It's just an expression, Sam. Stop being so damn difficult. Promise me. Promise me that tonight you'll talk to Doctor Coleman about my release and tomorrow you'll bring Lawrence for a visit."

"He has swimming tomorrow."

"He can miss it. For Pete's sake, he can miss swimming in order to visit his own mother. For crying out loud, Sam, I haven't seen him for six months. He must think I don't love him anymore."

"He doesn't think that..."

"Promise me. Tomorrow night, no matter what. Believe me Sam, I'm serious about leaving this place, with or without your help, so promise me that you'll bring Lawrence tomorrow or one way or another I'll find a way to see him myself."

"Okay, okay, I promise."

"On your mother's grave."

"On my mother's grave. Christ, Julia, I'd better go talk to Doctor Coleman before she leaves."

"You do that. I'll see you and Lawrence tomorrow. Tomorrow, that's your promise."

"Fine, I'll be here tomorrow. Now try and get some rest."

"You will be here tomorrow with Lawrence, that's settled. And you will talk to Doctor Marsha now, that's settled too. Good night, Sam."

"Good-bye, Julia."

I did it! Just like we planned. I love you Oost, you are so smart. I'm sure he will bring Lawrence tomorrow, aren't you? You are? Good. Yes, our own flesh and blood. I'm dying to see him too. Yes, I can hardly wait to introduce him to you. I hope you don't see anything wrong with him, I really do, but whatever you see will be a big help to me, and I will believe you. I trust you. And Lawrence had better be on his best behavior or he'll regret it. I'm so excited!

CHAPTER 31

"Good evening, Roland."

"Mrs. Arnheim, it is a pleasure to see you again."

"Just plain Dorothy, Roland. There are no formalities here at the ranch. You remember Carmen?"

"I do, very nice to see you again." And a bit of a surprise as well, he thought. Marketing must be a little out of step with current events, the wealth gap between first and second place seems to have closed, hopefully due to success and not failure. For reasons that he still couldn't fathom, going from a net worth of 20 billion to a lousy 15 billion made a big difference to these people.

"And this is my husband, Conrad and Carmen's husband, Oliver – of the industrial side of the Mayerthorpe's, or at least that is what he wants us to believe." Dorothy quipped.

Hand shaking and eye contact completed the introductions. First impressions taken which were a natural reaction for anyone except these people acted on them. A bad first impression and you would be lucky to get away with your hat. Someone had once told Roland that the true meaning of brutal consequences came with the first billion and not a penny before. Whether true or folklore didn't matter, Roland knew the game and came to win. He was already working on his second impression; he knew his place and wasn't about to create problems with an unforced error.

Conrad Arnheim could have walked right off a page of GQ. A little portly but if his firm handshake was any indication of his physical condition his extra weight had some real muscle behind it. His hair was thin but his complexion was ruddy, like he had been riding all day on a fox hunt with the result being English squire and not American billionaire. His friend, if they were friends, Oliver Mayerthorpe was in complete contrast. Tall and thin, he looked like he would be more comfortable on his yacht. He was tanned and extremely steady in posture and gaze, like he was rounding the Cape of Good Hope under fair winds.

Neither man bore visible signs of ego or the ostentation that frequently came with the rich, especially the newly rich. The two men shared matching wives; both of whom obviously knew their way around a financial statement. Always best when old money marries old money.

“How was your day, Roland?” Conrad asked pleasantly and with sincere interest.

Interest which wouldn’t last long if he didn’t work damn hard to keep it; he was the evening’s entertainment and knew full well he could leave with a handshake or a handful depending on his performance.

“Most unusual.” he tossed into the conversation like he was in the company of life-long friends. “Not that I don’t get my fair share of extraordinary speculation about Legacy Genes, because I do, but this report was so bizarre that if it hadn’t come from a reputable psychiatrist, I’d have thought someone was pulling my leg.”

“A psychiatrist?” echoed Conrad. “I thought you were personae non grata in that circle, Roland.”

“Only because I am.” he said slowly, playing his existential joke with subtle humor.

“You must tell us more, Roland. Unusual for you is a command performance that we can’t ignore.” Carmen chirped. “You aren’t under some kind of vow of silence are you?” she teased some more.

“No, not really. Dr. Jorgenson…perhaps you’ve heard of her? No, well, of course she is looking for some research assistance so she doesn’t want to let the cat of the bag too soon, but she didn’t put a gag order on it. Even if it turns out to be a complete hoax, it is a most interesting story. A kind of mythical Norwegian folk tale, if you can believe that, for a starter.”

“Let’s get a glass in your hand, doctor. What would you like?” Conrad extended the offer brightly, his evening entertainment off to a good start. Listening to a good tale was one of the greatest pleasures of life and he knew Masters would be able to spin a yarn with the best of them. He knew it because he knew the man’s numbers and that kind of success didn’t happen to anyone with just average story-telling abilities.

“A little bourbon and branch, thank you, Conrad.”

With Dorothy on one arm and Carmen on the other, he was guided past the living room and into a library the size of a small auditorium. The sense of shock or wonder with the environments and personal appointments of the unspeakably rich had never before affected him but that changed the moment he walked through the door. The room was wild with contradictions. The scent of cigar smoke blended with the citrus of wood polish and leather saddle soap but the dry, musty scent of old paper was the undercurrent. The heavy, ornate, antique desk which was the command center of every personal library he had ever been in was absent yet he knew, immediately and without question, it didn’t belong there anyway.

The room was bathed in light which had been so skillfully created that it looked natural in spite of the fact there wasn’t a window or doorway to the outside. It was a light that tricked the senses into believing they were experiencing the rain forest environment of the mahoganies and teaks which made up most of the room’s floor, walls, shelves and furniture. The light came in shafts and streaks, opening up meadows here and there but creating dark intimate pockets where predators and prey could play hide and seek. Like the desk, absent by design, the computer and monitor of the modern library, were, thankfully, either hidden in a cabinet or banished to some other room.

The sense of contradiction was reinforced by the two women at his sides. Dorothy’s firm grasp setting the pace and moving him forward while Carmen’s gentle touch, no heavier than gravity, slowing him down, relaxing him. The peaceful engagement of contrary states simultaneously filled and lulled his senses; the scientist chanting to the spirits and the shaman looking into the microscope, quintessential states in harmony even when in opposition.

As the butler handed him his drink and his escorts drifted away to their places on the sofa, their mates took their spots on a sofa facing them. If he wanted it, he had a large armchair positioned between the two sofas from which he could begin the evening's entertainment. Otherwise, he could stand or walk around.

Everything had been arranged. Everything from the introductions to the choice of rooms had been evaluated and considered in advance, just as he knew it would be, just as he had prepared his entertainment for them, just as he knew he would stand. It would be a mistake to sit down, this story had to be narrated, not told.

"This…" he began in a slow monologue which was not the way he intended to tell the story but which, once the first words were out of his mouth knew was the only way it could be told. "…this is the story of Gut Vik."

CHAPTER 32

My, my Oost, look at that. Look over there…isn't that? Isn't that? It is! It's Marty Sorenson they are bringing in! No, I'm not scared, not with you by my side, I'm not. Besides, he is out there and we are safe in here. We can watch from this corner and he probably won't even see us.

Yes, he does look different. Of course he should look different being all strapped up like that. I wonder how he likes it. Not very much I'll bet. Where do you think they are taking him? You're right of course, he belongs up there. Maybe someone will do to him what he did to me. Wouldn't that be justice? No, I don't mind going a little closer. He isn't going anywhere, not with all the orderlies and the police and being restrained like that, he isn't going anywhere, he certainly isn't.

How's that? Good. Still, I hope he doesn't look this way. I wouldn't like that, not at all. I think he's full of drugs, don't you? He's so quiet, like he doesn't care anymore. You don't believe that? It doesn't matter. Pretty soon and it will be all over for him. Once they go up there, they never come back. If they aren't crazy when they go up, they soon will be. No, I don't want to go any closer. Yes, he does look different, his eyes are completely different, so wild and brutal, like when he was hitting me.

"Okay Marty, you know the drill. Nice and peaceful, nobody needs to get hurt and you don't want to go to CIW with a head full of sedation do you, buddy? You don't want to go up there stoned to the gunnels, you know what could happen to you in that condition, don't you? We can't watch out for you every second, you know that too, don't you? You're going to have be careful. Good man, Marty, just relax. Take it easy."

Steve didn't know quite what to believe. Marty hadn't been himself lately but he never expected him to go ballistic without saying something to someone, not even make the slightest attempt to get his back covered, regardless but especially for something that violent. That was the way things worked, at least for most of them it was. If things got a little tough at home or out of control on the personal front, everybody pitched in and took an extra shift or made way for some light duty until things were back to normal. If a patient got the worst of a bad day and it sometimes happened, most of the time it was simply because it wasn't easy working in a place like this. But Marty wasn't just having a bad day and now he was headed upstairs. CIW, Criminally Insane ward, absolutely the worst place to work and that was to work. Living there was something else altogether. Living? Hell, you couldn't actually call that living, more like existing. No, not even that, it was survival the noun, not even the verb, survival or not, that's the most that could be said for being around those crazy bastards.

Steve waited for some kind of a response from Marty but didn't get one which increased his caution in dealing with his old friend and mentor. It made sense that Marty wouldn't do or say anything, after all, going upstairs for a few days was his best defense but at least he could give him some kind of signal without the cops seeing it. Something that said he was okay, not to worry, nothing to fear. Just a simple signal, a wink of the eye would do it.

"That's it Marty, take it easy. Everything will be okay in a couple of days. You've just been working too hard and need a rest. Don't worry, we'll look after you."

Still no response, not a twitch. If he was faking it he was doing a damn fine job. If he wasn't, he better look out when he got upstairs because no matter how much they tried to look after him, sooner or later one of them, if not several of those hop-head crazies would get to him. It happened all the time up there. It was a friggin' zoo. A survival zone and not survival of the fittest but survival of the meanest and most cunning. Marty could be in for a real shit-kicking. Bad enough to be a stranger up there without any friends but to be an ex-orderly surrounded by the enemy? They'll probably kill each other just to get to him.

"We'll put him in isolation for a few days." There was no such order on the admitting papers but Steve would fix that later. Legitimately or otherwise, he'd fix it. It was the least he could do; it was also the most he could do; the rest was up to Marty. Steve's hopes for a signal were fading and with that his hopes for Marty were also fading.

Not quite certain what propelled her feet into movement, Julia stepped out of the corner, right up to the window in the door which framed her face like a portrait. Still plenty far enough away, a good twenty feet away, and with a closed, locked door between herself and him she should have felt safe but didn't and for good reason. Marty saw the movement behind the glass as Julia's face came into his line of vision. It was close enough for him to focus firmly on her eyes. He hoped he'd see some pity but didn't get any. He knew Gut Vik saw her too, saw right into her eyes just like he had.

Oh Jesus, No! No, Gut Vik, NO!

Steve no more sensed it coming than he saw it coming. Neither did Phil Teck who, with only three months of experience, was standing behind Sorenson. He had a decently strong grip on the strap around Sorenson's waist but it snapped out of his fingers like it was attached to a bull elephant, not a man. The two cops, one standing idly at the admitting desk and talking to Ruby Jackson and the other behind Phil Teck, weren't paying much attention until they heard the crash of Steve's body hitting the wall.

Gut Vik caught Steve standing bolt upright with his legs apart and went straight into him, pushing him backwards until there wasn't any backwards left and slammed into the wall. A full contact body blow sucker-punch with more to follow. With the wind knocked out of him, Steve bent over to catch his breath, putting his head directly into the path of Gut Vik's right knee. That blow spun him sideways so violently that he hit the wall with the other side of his head, leaving an impression of his right eyebrow in the wallboard.

"Get him! Stop him! Tackle him!" Ruby yelled at Phil who was looking at his hand like he had never seen it before. The cops were already moving, nightsticks in hand.

Gut Vik spun on his heels and made a charge for the cop who was nearest to him. The cop braced for the charge which didn't materialize as he turned sharply and bolted straight for the door behind which Julia was standing, stock still, like she was waiting for him, like she was baiting him.

"Get him!" Ruby yelled. It didn't make sense and that frightened her. Marty Sorenson would know that door was locked just as he would have known it would take an elephant to break through it but that was exactly what he was about to try. If he wasn't stopped, or at least slowed down some, at the very least he would hurt himself. It just didn't make sense. What frightened her even more was the thought that he might actually break it down. He looked like he believed he could so maybe he would.

Julia watched Marty Sorenson's eyes get closer and closer to her. Intrigued, when she should have been scared to death. Angry when normally she would have felt sorry for herself. He was practically at the glass, within an arm's reach when he began to tilt downwards but all the while he kept staring at her. It was just before his eyes slid below the bottom of the glass that she saw it.

Fire was dancing in his eyes like it was trying to burn through his pupils. Like a match held beneath a sheet of paper, the black hole of his pupil being slowly surrounded by flames. Anger and hatred so fierce that she could feel the heat of it right through the door and feel the rush of cool air at her feet as it was being sucked under the crack of the door to feed the fire. Fire which was intended for her, no doubt about it.

Oost! Oost! Why does he hate me so much? What have I done? Good God, what have I done to deserve this?

You! You are the one he hates? How can that be? Why? Why, Oost, why would Marty Sorenson hate you so terribly much? How could anyone hate you?

You can tell me. Yes I can keep a secret. Please, Oost, please!!!

CHAPTER 33

"Is that so? replied Gut Vik."

Roland noticed the untouched drink in his hand and automatically glanced at his watch. Forty-five minutes had passed but that didn't make sense, like the length of a dream doesn't make sense. The subconscious doesn't deal with time the same way as the conscious does, which measures it linearly and allocates each segment to an activity, records it in memory and counts down the clock. Not so with dreams that can take only a few minutes to construct but can pack in a week or more of dream reality so convincing that sometimes the dreamer doesn't remember what day or month it is when they wake up.

"Is that so?" came from one set of lips after another, led by Conrad Arnheim and finished by his wife, Dorothy. Carmen and Oliver Mayerthorpe's responses were wedged in the middle; Roland hadn't noticed which of those two was first to mumble the words. 'Is that so?' told him all he needed to know. They saw the gap, the contradiction, the opportunity, that was all he wanted them to see; all it would take to get their minds started down the cow-path he had so carefully paved for them. Next, he was certain, they would fight it.

"It seems like fertile ground for investigation." Conrad stated, causing Roland to wonder if there was a pecking order for commentary like there was a pecking order for after-dinner-mingling chit chat. He used the time to gather his own senses, starting by trying to remember the order of the Mayerthorpe's responses. Carmen's 'Is that so?' came to him, followed by her husband's. Somehow that didn't surprise him. Oliver Mayerthorpe was the grandson of The Mayerthorpe who built the wealth and that made him the generation most likely to squander it. Carmen was the safety catch in a marriage which was probably arranged by Oliver's grandmother. The territorial imperative of wealth was pretty straightforward. Don't share it if you don't have to but if you do have to share, pick your partner carefully. Oliver's grandmother had done a good job; she could depend on Carmen to expand, not expend the inheritance.

"There are so many questions." Carmen said, almost to herself.

Almost to herself, Roland knew. She was the least likely person of anyone in the room to talk to herself. That woman had more secrets than a Mafia Don, no doubt about it, and she'll keep them to the end, no doubt about that either.

"Questions there are indeed. I'm glad you found the story interesting. It made my day, that's for sure." It was an offer to change the topic if anyone wanted to do that. His expectation they would fight the obvious conclusion was wrong so he abandoned any further attempts to predict the direction of their thinking. Besides, he told himself, it was a damned interesting little puzzle. Damned interesting, he repeated to himself, and then wondered why he had done that followed by the logical extension of thought 'had he consciously done it or was his mind echoing itself?'

"I suppose, years ago, this would have been put down to a case of multiple personalities." Carmen stated the obvious but without displaying her own thoughts, her actual agenda, if she had one, and Roland strongly suspected she had at least one.

"I don't think we're talking that many years ago, Carmen." Dorothy entered her correction gently, obviously avoiding any challenge to her friend's statement. The two women were closer than Roland had originally thought. When it came to admitting or refusing entry to their country club, they didn't use strategy and tactics with each other. They owned the place, yes or no came to them in a heartbeat and they respected each other's vote without debate.

"Point and set, Dorothy." Carmen's eyes flirted with everyone in the room.

'Fertile ground for investigation' came to Roland's wandering attention and he immediately understood what the rest of them knew all along. If the

performance met expectations, Conrad had pre-approved the 'investment' before the shaman had even set foot in his rain forest library.

'There are so many questions.' Carmen wanted a piece of the action.

'*Point and set, Dorothy.*' replayed in Roland's memory. Control had also been decided which supported what marketing had said all along. These people didn't let go of their money. But marketing hadn't figured it all, they never did. Roland was facing a team, a well-organized, well-practiced team and that could be a problem. Research was a funny thing that way. You don't always find what you are looking for and have to be careful not to miss other opportunities along the way because your focus is set too narrowly. Sometimes you don't find gold but you damned sure don't want to leave a pile of diamonds for the next guy.

"Why don't we talk about this after dinner, Roland. I'm sure you have some concerns about how the research will be managed and we should get those out of the way before the evening is over." Dorothy said in a very business-like fashion. "But don't let that ruin your dinner…you will find that we are quite used to spending money on research and, if your marketing boys haven't already confirmed it, we are pretty well respected patrons."

Roland nodded slightly and smiled honestly. It was the safest reaction. In fact marketing had had one helluva time trying to get any information on how the Arnheim's or the Mayerthorpe's worked with others. Scientific secrets of the first magnitude were easier to obtain than any information on the management of the Arnheim-Mayerthorpe patronage money which discovered them. His heart skipped a beat, a telling sign of his own enthusiasm with being sworn into that secret order.

Anticipating his confusion, or perhaps reading his thoughts, Carmen clarified the issue. "Where do you intend to start?"

"With a blood sample." he replied spontaneously. That was always the starting point and sometimes the ending point as well.

"Let the search for an active Legacy Gene begin." Oliver Mayerthorpe raised his glass in toast. One by one they touched glasses. Roland couldn't suppress the image of a fox being released and the sound of the bugle signaling that the hunt was on. Now his heart raced with the anticipation. The answer, an answer, could be weeks, months at the very most, away. An answer which would create a scientific avalanche the likes of which had never before been witnessed. The past, the present and the future fully exposed on the operating table for all to see.

One way or another, an active Legacy gene was going to be discovered and a whole lot of questions about the past were finally going to be answered and all the naysayers were going to have shut their traps, once and for all time. Maybe this Sorenson/Gut Vik person was just the clue he had been searching for and by the sounds of it, he might even be pretty cooperative. But, cooperative or not that clue was going to be dissected until there wasn't a molecule left to be examined. Having a living subject was certainly more interesting but it was by no means a necessity.

CHAPTER 34

It took a while before Steve caught his breath but when he did his words were ready: "Sonovabitch, the bastard tried to kill me. Screw isolation, he can look after himself. Or not, who cares, maybe somebody will beat the sense into him." He knew he was lucky not have been badly hurt but the possibility of getting hurt wasn't responsible for all his anger. Being caught being stupid to ever trust a patient, any patient, provided the real heat.

Ruby didn't much care whether Steve left Sorenson high and dry with the other crazies in CIW but she had a gut-wrenching feeling that it wasn't a good idea for anybody and not just Sorenson. And if it wasn't enough that he still seemed to want nothing more than to get his hands around Julia Reynolds' neck, the look that woman's face sure wasn't the look of an angel. Unless it was the angel of death. Something very unusual was going on.

Of course there were always easy explanations, patients and orderlies often had their disputes but she didn't see this violence coming and that was bothersome to her. Buttons were being pushed and she couldn't see it happening but had no intention of ignoring that reality. Just like she had no intention with participating in whatever happened next. "It's just one big random event." she said softly to herself.

* * * * *

When his name was needed, which meant someone was telling him what to do, they called him Ernest, never Ern or Ernie, that was too friendly and he had no friends. Behind his back they called him Boston, Boston Carver. Boston after the city and Carver after his father's hunting knife, sort of. As usual, dear old Paps got in the final word, this time, from the grave. Pap's knife had connected him to four murders; nobody knew about the other six plus one in county and one in maximum security but those didn't really count because he used his hands, not the knife. Big hands connected to strong arms coming from a big barrel chest. As usual he was half naked so everybody could see the muscle, the tattoos and the scars. He kept his hair short because some of the best ones were there. Lotta head-butts, lotsa scars, that's what it takes. Busted nose that was never fixed and never would be because he liked it that way.

No matter, he liked the knife and his father's memory, so maybe the combination of Boston and Carver was meant to be, born to be, so to speak. Regardless, he'd had the name for a long time, it wasn't going anywhere and neither was he.

About as long as he had heard the voices inside his head. Voices that were just like the ones on the outside, always telling him what to do, when to do it and how to do it and on and on. Sometimes they were damned annoying but, unlike the voices outside, most of the time they weren't too bad. Most of the time those voices were telling him to do the exact opposite of what he was hearing from the outside. 'Don't go out in the rain' became, 'Screw'em, do whatever you want.' so he did because he had to listen to somebody and the inside voices were usually more fun.

The hospital was no exception to the rule, although there were fewer people telling him what to do and hardly anybody cracking him over the head with a baton if he didn't do what he was told. Regardless, fewer people still meant the same thing, namely the stuff you weren't supposed to do was really just stuff you weren't supposed to get caught doing. Outside if you got caught they threw you in a place like CIW but when you got caught doing a bad one here, they filled you so full of dope you couldn't think in a straight line even if you wanted to. Then you were vulnerable, and then a bad one would happen to you and then you'd have to get even with that sonovabitch with an even bigger bad one and the whole thing would go round and round, faster and faster, like a carnival ride surrounded by stainless steel razor wire and stupid painted clowns until you got throwed off and if the razor wire didn't get you, the clowns did.

And no friggin' doubt about it either, the orderlies knew exactly what they were doing. One false step and the next thing you knew it was next week and you couldn't even remember your own name. They weren't no different than the screws in jail except in jail everybody wanted the dope but in the hospital you avoided it like the plague 'cause it wasn't, by any stretch of the imagination, the feel good kinda of dope. They knew it, that's how they kept order, except when they wanted a little chaos and frenzy for their own personal amusement. Screws, orderlies, bosses, inmates, all the friggin' same. Just a pile of rotten meat waiting for Carver to slice it open so the flies could get in and the maggots could get out.

The voices outside were all saying the same thing. 'Go get the fancy pants orderly, Boston. Teach'im a lesson.' The voices inside were saying the opposite. 'Stay away. Don't touch.' No big deal to Boston, the voices were always disagreeing but that didn't make one right and the other wrong. Boston Carver did what he damn well wanted to do, when he damned well wanted to do it, to whoever he damned well wanted it done.

But the best part of doing somebody was them knowing it was comin' and watching them waitin' for it. Once he got the scared shitless part started the inside voices would change their tune, sure as glory they would. Once the fear started, those voices would come around to his way of thinking. Sure they would, just like sure as glory he'd get away with it like every other thing he'd done since he'd made the common room his home territory. It wasn't much, just a few tables and chairs, no windows, two doors with spyholes in them like everywhere else, but it was his and it was more than anybody else had so that made him the head honcho and everybody got what was left-over, which wasn't much.

For a virgin, Sorenson didn't look too bad. Not doped to the back teeth which was good 'cause if that was case, he'd forget the threat in a second, if it even got through at all. Nope, he looked like he'd get the message and remember it. Then maybe whatever dope was in him would work on the threat and make it worse, make it bigger, nastier, uglier. 'Course if it didn't work out that way, the threat could always be repeated. Hell, it would be anyway. Best if the clown was scared to death before the really nasty stuff got started. That usually made for weird fight, but a fast one.

Like all virgins, he was sitting alone, staring at the wall, pretending to mind his own business when really his radar was on everything in sight and whatever it could pick up that was hid. Who was where, what they was doing, that kinda thing. 'Course he wasn't exactly a virgin, being kicked down from a high and all-mighty X-orderly and all, which probably explained why he didn't pick a spot with his back to the wall, figuring he still had some say-so. And he didn't have his hands on the table, which is more defensive, but had them crossed against his chest like he owned the place. Which he might have once, but no more, welcome to Boston Carver's personal domain, are you ready to get X'd again, smart ass?

Boston knew the crew was watching him as he sauntered over to the virgin. Not watched like they were watching TV but watching out of the sides and backs of their heads. They wouldn't come near either, no matter what happened. One little picture on that video tape and before you knew it, bang, you're into next week with nothing to show for it including the memory of how it all got started. No sirree, the little virgin was all alone and nothing was gonna change what nobody can change which is what Boston wants and the virgin don't. Nothing would change what can't be changed, not even if they put the virgin in isolation. Sooner or later, everybody gets out. Sometimes, depending on the orderly, it was even possible to get in. That could happen, that could happen with this one. This one didn't have any buddies looking after him and that meant he had to have some enemies, somebody who might want to watch through the peephole. Hell he probably had more enemies than you could shake a dink at. Isolation was a great place to do a bad one. Lotsa time with no interruptions. Yessir, a great place, providing, naturally, you were doing and not gettin' done.

The virgin must know its comin'. He doesn't even turn around to see who's comin', probably already pissin' hisself. Everybody turns around, at least a little bit, but not this one, just sittin' there with his arms crossed and his back ramrod straight like he's listenin' to the preacher at Sunday school. Just waitin' for somebody to whisper some sweet nuttin's in his ear.

"Hey Big Shot, I get the first dance. Get it?" Boston growled out of the side of his mouth, their heads almost touching. It felt good to start the fear. It always did but with that little virgin it was extra fine, sittin' buck straight up like that and payin' attention like he was. Like he was trying to suck up to Boss Carver and maybe cut hisself a break.

Gut Vik's right hand moved so quickly it was blur. So fast that Boston couldn't have seen it until the last inch or two and then he didn't have time to focus on it, not that it mattered. With the pointer finger shoved into one eyeball and the index finger plunged into the other, focus didn't mean a goddamn thing. The fingers dug in fast and as far as they could go.

Boston felt the pain before the shock of the aggression came to him. Instinctively, he tried to pull his head back but the fingers clenched down like a couple of hooks until they got a solid grip on the inside of his cheekbones and pulled him forward again, pulled him back over Gut Viks' shoulder, just about where he started, their heads touching, cheek to cheek then the left hand got a firm grip on his throat and starting squeezing. Carver's arms flew out like a bird trying to take off and stayed like that even as the fingers released their grip on the cheekbones, straightened up and poked right into his brain, grabbing and digging away like little swimmer legs. When they weren't pushing in and out and sideways doing the frog kick, they flipped up and down with a fast, crazy flutter kick.

"Ja, you dance first." came past the sound of churning water and the mass of confusion which the fingers were creating. Incredible, paralyzing confusion on the inside of his head. No voices, just spasmodic, uncontrolled blitzes of wild consequences until a blinking red light and a low buzzing hum signaled the end to the overload of messages being sent by Gut Vik's fingers to Boston Carver's brain. It was all over in a few seconds, most of which had nothing to do with time because for Boston Carver, time had been stretched completely out of shape and was no longer a concept worthy of consideration.

Holding Carver's head steady from the inside of his cheekbones, Gut Vik eased off the chair and pulled the unconscious body onto the seat beside him. Then he retracted his fingers from the eye sockets, holding Carver's forehead in his bloody palm before dropping it onto the table. He wiped the blood and tissue from his fingers on the man's back like he had just gutted a fish.

Boston Carver's blood flowed onto the table, pooling around the eyeballs which were hanging out the cavities they once called home; one orb crushed like a split grape but the other intact and laying on the table, looking back at the crew and into the closed circuit TV. He would never again be a threat to anyone. Just another vegetable that had gone past its Best Before date.

Jesus Christ, Gut Vik. What the hell did you do that for? We'll get ten years for that. Marty knew better than to be critical and was actually trying to be helpful.

Ten years is not so long.

What? Not so long? We're screwed!

In all his life, Marty Sorenson realized for the very first time he had quit on a lot of things, a lot of times, and he wanted nothing more than to quit again but couldn't figure out how to do it. No doubt about it, he finally concluded, Gut Vik was there to stay and he could do whatever he wanted to do, whenever he wanted to do it. How do you give up on something like that?

You don't.

What do you mean you don't? You mean I can't. I can't give up because there is nowhere I can go and nothing I can do, absolutely nothing. You won't even let me help and this is going from bad to worse.

You can die.

Die?

Ja, die. Get used to the idea. It could happen anytime.

If nothing else, for the moment at least, his, Gut Vik's, attack resulted in him, Marty, being locked down in the bubble room where he was safe even if that wasn't why the orderlies did it. That was just a spin-off benefit to a decision which actually had the safety of everybody in CIW, particularly the orderlies, as the primary objective.

The bubble room was like being inside a dimpled, not quite square balloon and that was all there was to say for it. No distinguishing features whatsoever, like the inside of a golf ball. The corners at the floor and ceiling were all molded together so while you could more or less see where one flat plane met another, it just curved into the side and top or bottom, completely destroying any perspective of distance, slope or dimension. No toilet, sink, bed or amenities of any kind. No windows of course. All covered with an indestructible foam, semi-hard, semi-soft. Like the whole thing had been extruded into an outer space machine, that was how it looked and with it came the feeling of being in a totally foreign place, like being the last person on the planet. Except he wasn't alone, no matter how much he wanted that, Marty wasn't alone.

Gut Vik stopped communicating but that meant absolutely nothing. He was most definitely in charge and that sensation was growing. It was a sensation the exact opposite of what was happening to Marty and he understood that. He understood that he was, in true grit reality, shrinking smaller and smaller while Gut Vik grew larger and larger. Being pushed into a corner like so much garbage and with less and less responsibility for anything, less and less control over anything. He couldn't make an arm move or an eye lid blink unless Gut Vik let him. Before, when Gut Vik did those things, at least he used to know they were happening but now even that awareness, that feeling, that essential tie to his own physical existence was disappearing and disappearing fast. No doubt about that either, Gut Vik was in charge and Gut Vik wasn't about to share a damn thing, not even the knowledge of what his own body was doing. All Marty could do was think and he wondered how long he would be able to do that.

It occurred to him that his symptoms were very much like ALS, Lou-Gerhig's disease, and for a moment he felt relieved with that as a possible explanation for his condition. Then he remembered that there wasn't a cure for ALS, just a conscious mind trapped in an unresponsive body until the end came, until the lights went out for good. Plus, his logic told him Gut Vik had to be responsible for what was happening, that was as undeniable as it was inescapable. It was a problem surrounded by questions. How the hell is he doing it? When will he quit? Will he quit? If I can't talk to the doctors then I can't tell them what's wrong. If I can't tell them what's wrong they can't cure me. If they don't cure me, I won't be able to talk.

Like the room, all the corners of his questions curved into each other and went around and around, up and down. If Gut Vik didn't talk to him, he was sure to go completely insane. What a complete hell this had become. He thought of Gut Vik's last words.'You can die. Ja, die. Get used to the idea. It could happen anytime.' Maybe he was already dead. Maybe this was death. How the hell do you know?

Did somebody just turn out the lights?

They weren't supposed to do that in the bubble room, the lights were always on, dim sometimes but always on!

Gut Vik! Gut Vik! What have you done now? For Chrissakes, turn on the lights!!! I can't see a thing! I can't feel anything! I can't do anything! I'm completely in the dark! For Chrissakes, Gut Vik, don't leave me like this! Do whatever you want to do but don't leave me in the dark!

Oh no.

This can't be it.

Don't do this to me.

I'll be good, honest I will.

Leave me something, anything. I don't want to die. I'm afraid, really afraid.

I'm…

I'm losing words…

I'm losing thoughts…no…

* * * * *

One floor down, a 45 second walk north into the administration wing and Director Fielding was trying to determine Marty Sorenson's future. The consummate budget wrangler, bare-fisted legal expert and self-proclaimed scion of the institution, he looked the part. Always in a dark suit, white shirt and plain dark tie, his easy smile was as polished as his black, brogue shoes. In his job, he had to look organized, in control and unafraid and he did; not a hair out of place and two shaves a day if a late meeting demanded it. This one didn't.

"I'm not sure that continuing your role as lead therapist with the Sorenson case is a good idea, Marsha." He had taken his usual posture with the issue and presented it with semi-open words but the closed body language which, to anyone who knew him, telegraphed he had already made his decision. He chose that approach because it never hurt to hear what the other side was thinking, if for no other reason than it made their future actions more predictable. In a mental hospital, there is no such thing as too much advantage.

Marsha knew the tactic, it was one of the first things she learned about him. It had taken her a couple of tries, a couple of debates over this or that therapy or diagnosis, she couldn't remember the exact details of those decisions, but in the end she understood how the system, how Director Fielding, worked. He had made his decision and would take some input from her but unless she came up with something earth-shattering, she was off the case. Way off the case. At the very best she might be able to review findings, read the reports and maybe get an invitation to the occasional meeting but other than that, she might as well be on another planet. Unfortunately for her, at the moment, earth-shattering was a commodity in short supply. Then again, she wondered, maybe she should consider herself fortunate.

After his brutal attack on Boston Carver, the case received a rather large dose of administrative spin control with Fielding managing the joy stick. Not too much rotation because the brutality of the attack, bad as it was, wasn't completely uncommon in CIW but not too little because the dust had hardly settled on the previous attack on Reynolds woman, a patient, not a prisoner. Any judge worth his/her salt wouldn't give a fiddler's fart about what happened to Boston Carver but settling with Mrs. Reynold's broken jaw was a whole other problem. Orderly, X-orderly, plus this, minus that, multiplied by the rest equaled a strategy which required close management from a distance.

Marsha sensed she was part of that distancing and didn't have a single fact that she could use to wedge the door open, however slight the opening left to her. Her findings from the interview at the police station hadn't yet been typed, that might have given her some editorial opportunity but too late for that now because Fielding had listened to the audio and come to his own conclusions, the first of which was that he didn't really need her. Not that her editorial license would likely have changed his mind anyway because unlike most doctors at the hospital, she didn't keep her records in some bizarre form of personalized, academic shorthand with obscure connective phrases that only the narrator could understand and from which they could take any desired, or deniable position they needed at the moment. Her reports told the truth as she saw it and right now, the truth was that the only earth shattering commodity available was residing in Boston Carver's head.

"I understand." she agreed, but decided to include her request for continued involvement before the issue was permanently closed and she was on the wrong side of the door. "Would it be possible for me to act in consultation capacity?" She was prepared to negotiate all the way down to mere file privilege and be thankful if she got that. Consultation was damn near as good as being in charge. She would have a say in the analysis methods, another say in the written conclusions and have basically unrestricted access to everything other than the patient himself. Director Fielding, she told herself, is a reasonable person and she hoped she was wearing an expression which communicated that compliment as she waited for him to reconsider his unspoken decision.

Fielding read her expression correctly and accepted the implied compliment with a smile. As clever as she was, she still had a thing or two to learn. The question in his mind was whether or not this was the time to give her a lesson in the real world of politics and ambition. He decided to risk it, actually he had already made the decision, he simply advanced the timing of its announcement. Timing was his specialty.

"Marsha, I wasn't going to say this now but here it is; this is the lay of the land. I've already received a call from Dr. Jorgenson. She is making a lot of noise about taking control here, and she doesn't even know about last night's…incident. She didn't come out and say it directly but she might as well have. You and I both know why…the bragging rights to this Gut Vik personae are pretty damned enticing." He stopped for a second to assemble his thoughts. The situation was already complicated and he'd been around long enough to know that it would get worse before it got better. And that was without any more help from Sorenson a.k.a. Gut Vik. If that crazy mother's son got around to killing somebody and that meant anybody at this point, there wouldn't be enough protective cover for a part time janitor let alone the hospital's full time, big cheese, director.

"I'm going to assign the case to Peter Wheeler…"

The outburst he expected from her didn't materialize, her trusting expression didn't change and the gold specks were still sparkling in her eyes. He couldn't help but smile at her and she returned the smile. Maybe she didn't have as much to learn as he thought.

"Wheeler?" she asked with feigned disbelief. Talking about colleagues was always a delicate issue, even when those colleagues had significant shortcomings and even more significant personal problems. The only reason Peter Wheeler hadn't checked himself into a facility was because he was already in one. He was like the team mascot, always around the bench, seldom allowed to sit on it, and only allowed on the playing field after practice. "Jorgenson will eat him alive."

"Precisely. Peter will probably get yanked off the stage before he's done much of anything...well, never mind that, that is neither here nor there..."

"...Precisely. So...So you actually do want me in a consultation capacity so that..." she stopped herself.

In her excitement with the possibility of staying with the case and in an attempt to make it easier for him, she had jumped into the conversation without bothering to make certain that she had all the right words to finish what she had started. Jorgenson, she understood, could very well seize the lead role from Peter Wheeler but once a consultant had been put on the file, they almost always stayed with it. It was a classic case of sacrifice, Peter Wheeler being the lamb. Oddly appropriate. No big loss to anyone, not even Peter who likely wouldn't figure out what happened even if he spent the rest of his career in analysis of it.

"So our backsides are covered until Wheeler gets the boot and anything that happens after that is on Jorgenson's head, shoulders, degree, whatever?" he finished what she couldn't politely phrase.

When she didn't flinch with the sacrifice, he continued: "All true but that's really just strategy isn't it? We want to maintain our involvement for the same reason that Jorgenson doesn't want anyone else involved."

It was a game and Marsha knew there wasn't any sense in beating around the bush, not with Fielding clearly hiding behind it. It was also the hard, cruel truth. Jorgenson wasn't wrong in trying to seize the opportunity but she was dead wrong if she thought no one else saw the case potential or that they wouldn't put up a fight for it. Plus, she knew that Gut Vik's rampage was hardly satisfied and the next time he blew up, if Jorgenson didn't have her psychobabble in a row, she would end up as collateral damage. Then the whole bloody works would fall right back into Fielding's lap, right where he wanted it.

"Makes sense." she lied. A harmless little white lie, she told herself. After all, her motives for continued involvement weren't much better than his. Her need to satisfy her intellectual curiosity wasn't a whole lot cleaner or more humanitarian than his desire for fame and recognition. A desire which was so common in the profession that no one really bothered trying to hide it, even if they tried their damnedest to hide their patient until the psychosis was perfectly analyzed, documented and published.

"Kind of you to say so." he replied, sincerely.

Might as well get on with it, she thought. "What do you want me to do?"

Whether she was ready for it or not, it was too late for her to back out. Fielding hoped she remembered what Sorenson had done, what he had become, because that was just a fraction of the hard, cruel truth coming her way. Sometimes the operation was a success even when the patient died, sometimes it was even better when they were dead, autopsies can be damned useful.

It's all a matter of timing. Timing and optics that are management responsibility; sacrifice and physical risk, on the other hand, are worker territory. Everybody is dispensable, everybody except Sorenson who would either lay pure gold eggs or get himself cracked like one. You didn't have to be genius to figure that one out.

"We won't have a lot of time…" he began.

She listened intently. Two years of hospital politics had taught her to keep quiet and reserved. As long as your name wasn't Sorenson or Jorgenson or Wheeler what he said made some sense but if she didn't want her name on that list, she had to be damn careful of him.

CHAPTER 35

Dr. Jorgenson's day started on a positive note and improved steadily until mid-afternoon, when it leveled out. That was fine with her, she had a lot of work to do and needed all the time she could get in order to properly plan it out.

The day started with a call to Doctor Fielding, the Director of the hospital and she received a fairly warm reception to her inquiries on the subject, meaning the patient, Sorenson. Warm enough for her to mention that the assessment of the patient's state of mind was not quite finished, regardless of what either Drs. Basscurt or Coleman might have said. Not surprisingly, Basscurt hadn't said a thing, contrary or otherwise and it was unlikely that he would. His cereal box diploma might be good enough in a courtroom but in the real world of academic and political psychiatry he'd be flayed alive. And that was if his drinking problem was ignored, which it wouldn't be. No, if that one didn't stay completely in the dark, he should definitely keep to the shadows with the other nickel players. As to Coleman, well, she was the Director's problem and if he wanted to get anything out of this, he would have to take care of her, which he probably already had. And that left the rest of her day clear to plan the future, her future to be specific.

Unlike the snail's pace which the rest of the world moved, including the world in which Jorgenson once lived, there wasn't a second to waste in the world of Doctor Roland Masters.

Their meeting had been brief.

"I know you aren't in this for the money, Dr. Jorgenson, none of us are, so let's get that out of the way first."

It was only a one year contract but it was four times her present salary, plus expenses which didn't seem to exclude anything, so there wasn't much to negotiate. Title, copyright, patent and all results from the research would be owned, forever, by the Institute and that point was non-negotiable but publishing credit, prestige and recognition was included with the appointment so there wasn't anything to argue about there. Unfortunately the Foundation made every decision on publishing but that too was non-negotiable so she just had to take his assurances that the Foundation did research in order to publish and not to keep secret what they discovered. Facilities, equipment, staff, consulting, whatever was at Research Institute, just ask and it will be delivered. No sense in spending money foolishly but no point in being preoccupied about it either.

"What about Sorenson, the...patient?" she asked, uncertain whether or not to disclose her thoughts on the discussion with Dr. Fielding. She thought not, given that Masters had pretty much scripted the entire conversation the night before.

"A day or two at the most and he'll be delivered." said Masters.

"How? What do I have to do?" Jorgenson suddenly feared the implications of the contract she had just signed. Fast was great when somebody else was doing it but a whole other matter when they were looking over your shoulder and telling you to hurry up.

"Lawyers, politicians, the chief of police, it doesn't matter. We aren't asking for much. He'll be delivered. What you need to do is work up the program for him. I'd like to see a draft of it by tomorrow morning, is that a problem?"

Translation: It had better not be a problem. "Tomorrow morning..."

"In my office, your Admin or your Research Assistant can give you a tour of the place. Your identity card is coded with all your privileges: building access, room access, purchasing, file privileges, network access, that sort of thing. Has your Admin explained this to you yet?"

"No."

“He will. Along with all the calendaring for meetings which will include this one, tomorrow, nine o’clock in my office. You know what we want, don’t you?”

“I do.” She confirmed, but he was half way out the door.

She turned the page in her notebook and titled it: ‘Tests, Physical’. The preceding three pages were a reasonably comprehensive list of ‘Tests, Psychological.’ Yes indeed, it would be a very rough ride, bone shattering, eventually. She wrote that on the last line of the page, just so she wouldn’t forget about it.

CHAPTER 36

Oost, Oost, are you as excited as I am? Lawrence is coming today! Our little man is coming for a visit! What should we wear? Something colorful would be nice, wouldn't it?

Why are you always thinking about him? There's nothing we can do about him now, you heard what the orderlies said at breakfast. He's in isolation, in the criminally insane ward.

I know he's bad, of course I know that. But he is precisely where he belongs, can't we just leave it at that? Aren't you the least bit excited that Lawrence is coming for visit?

Don't be silly Oost, that can't possibly happen. Why would anyone, even someone like Marty Sorenson want do such a terrible thing? Guts what?

Gut Vik? Who is he?

Oh my. Oh my goodness. Why didn't you tell me this before? How could you keep such a terrible secret from me? We must be very, very careful. If anything should happen to you, I would just die, really, I would.

* * * * *

Dr. Peter Wheeler's day started as normal, with Patricia yelling at him when she wasn't yelling at the kids who were spinning around the house like two little tornadoes. He had slept in fits and starts. When he wasn't sweating like a race horse, he was freezing. The unwelcome prospect of another day at the human zoo was always in the background, like a rash that didn't itch all the time but when it did, it took over completely. He wasn't expecting things to get any worse, just another shit day on the wards and he was surprised to receive the call from the Director's secretary, whatshername, for a one-on-one meeting. It was a toss-up, either his day was going to get better or it was going into the can, probably big time.

He figured on the can, rationalizing it was better to be prepared for the worst than hope for the best but also because he knew his moon was seriously on the decline and there wasn't much he could do about it unless he got a break.

And then, miracle of miracles, that was exactly what happened. Fielding offered him that little ray of sunlight he needed to unthaw the frozen turd that had become his career. Lead therapist to Marty whatshisname. It was totally what he needed and one way or another this time they would have to listen to Dr. Peter Wheeler. If this case wasn't already a classic, it would be by the time he finished with it and thank heavens Fielding picked him because the man didn't seem to be too sure about what to do next. Typical administrator.

Peter half listened and half planned the changes he would make to Fielding's office once it was his.

"Take your time with him Peter, this is important, you know that. Marty Sorenson is experiencing a lot of conflict and, while the source of that conflict might come to the surface fast enough, we don't want to jump to conclusions or rush into therapy until we are sure what we are facing."

"I understand. What is the legal situation with his attack on the patient, whatshername?"

"Julia Reynolds. That situation is being handled separately, Peter. What is important right now is for you to develop a good, solid plan for analysis. The sooner we get some sound, persuasive diagnostics on Sorenson, the better."

"Sure it is. Who is handling the legal case? I'm only asking in case they need information."

"I am handling that situation, together with the lawyers, of course. For the moment, everything on that issue will go through me. I'll let you know when that changes but for now, I want you to keep everything strictly confidential. Okay?"

"Sure. What about the other one who Sorenson attacked, the socio, whathisname in CIW?"

"That's Ernest Mulgrove, also known as Boston Carver. That shouldn't be a problem, he doesn't have any family or any other personal relationships that we know of; he's never been visited since he arrived here, two years ago. You can look at the video tape and come to your own conclusions but it was Carver who approached Sorenson, who was probably just defending himself."

"So no chance of that one going to court?"

"No."

"And what about Marsha? Didn't she go with the police after the first attack on the woman, whatshername Reynolds? What's Marsha's involvement in the case? Do you want me to take over the Reynolds therapy too?"

"No Peter, let's leave the Reynolds therapy where it is for now, I don't want you distracted from Sorenson's treatment. And we'll let Marsha complete the first phase of her work with Sorenson along with the outside experts on the initial assessment, it's almost finished anyway, then she will simply consult. There isn't much doubt that Sorenson will eventually be committed but that isn't important right now. What is important, is your analysis approach and your assessment. Both must be very thorough."

"I should probably meet with the lawyers, see what kind of questions they will ask at trial, what kind of report they need, right?"

"Not yet, Peter. Get the approach started and then we'll talk about next steps, okay?"

"I hear you. But if the attack on whathisname…Carver, was self-defense, there isn't much to do is there? I mean, Marsha has already handled the first episode and the second one is just a normal reaction to a threat so maybe we should have a strategy for dealing with the lawsuit first. Then I can just dove-tail my findings into that so everything fits. Do you know what I mean?"

"I do and maybe that will come later but before then, we need a professional, objective assessment. You can do that can't you, Peter?"

"Sure, sure, I can do that. I'll get Marsha's notes and talk to the police and the other experts first. See what they think, that sort of thing. Then I'll take it from there, make sure that everything fits nice and tight, right?"

"No. No talking to outsiders. Not at this time. Your assessment must be completely objective, no outside influences."

"No outside influences?"

"No. I don't want to speak badly of anybody who isn't around to defend themselves, but the fact of the matter is, most of the time these outside experts jump to conclusions. Not that they have a lot of choice, being given so little time to do a proper job and all, but the fact is, they are motivated by the legal system and not medicine, not mental health, not the real issues. You understand what I mean?"

"Sure, sure I do but I still think it would be helpful to know what they have done…just so I don't go down the same path again, right? Maybe we should get them and the lawyers all together in one room and see what damage has already been done. Then I can, independently, develop a plan to mitigate the risks on the legal, medical and what's the other one you mentioned, oh sure, mental health. Anyway that might be a big help to me."

"It's a little too early for that. For now, just work up your analysis plan and remember to keep everything strictly confidential. We can work around the other details later, when we know what we are up against. Remember Peter, confidential means no one but you and me. Okay?"

"It's bound to be millions, isn't it? At least it always starts that way, doesn't it? But an orderly beating up a patient is going to be damn tricky, isn't it? What is our approach for dealing with the media?"

"We'll take of that when, and if, it becomes necessary. Right now, the media isn't involved and we should do everything we can to keep it that way. Okay?"

"Sure, sure, I couldn't agree more but don't you think we should develop a contingency plan for that event? Sooner or later it's bound to surface. As soon as the lawsuit is filed. We should be ready for that, right?"

"We will be ready…"

"Maybe our best strategy is a preemptive strike. You know, make our own announcement so we control the spin. Something like we're dealing with it, Dr. Peter Wheeler is working with the patient, blah, blah, blah, legal language, you know. Something similar to that so it doesn't get out of control right off the bat. Right?"

"I'll give it some thought, Peter. In the meantime, you have to get started with the plan for Sorenson's analysis. We don't have a lot of time."

"Precisely. I'll start working on a draft of the press release. Do you want your name mentioned? Director Fielding appointed Dr. Peter Wheeler... that sort of thing?"

"No, not yet, we'll hold that back for the time being. When will you see Sorenson?"

"After lunch, no, make that about four o'clock, I have a group session from one to three. In the meantime, I'll work up a draft of the press release and leave a paragraph or two open for first impressions...nothing too clinical you understand, just some subtle messaging that the situation is in control, in good hands, that sort of thing."

"That will be fine, why don't we meet at, oh say, six o'clock. That will give you a couple of hours with the patient and we can discuss your preliminary findings. Is that enough time for you?"

"Could we make five? Jeremy has a soccer game tonight and I'll get skinned alive if I'm late for it."

"Five o'clock. You know he is in isolation in CIW, make sure you follow the process, restraints, support staff and so on. The man is dangerous. If you have any questions, call me."

"Sure, sure, I'll take care of it. See you at five."

Eventually, Peter concluded, it was just another dumb shit case. Fielding was going to stay permanently in the spotlight and Peter Wheeler was going to do all the work. It was obviously a scam. Sorenson had been around forever and a day, everybody knew him and everybody was surprised when he flipped out with the patient. But that sort of thing happened in the human zoo, happened more often than most anybody suspected and damn sure more often than it was ever reported.

It was cover-up time, no doubt about it.. Analysis paralysis my ass. The important thing was damage control. A few days of rest and Sorenson would be right as rain, if he wasn't already. Damage control was the key, no matter what Fielding thought to the contrary and that's what separated the men from the boys. That's also what would separate his past from his future, starting with his press release..

The wording had to be just perfect. Keep it positive, no accusation because that meant guilt somewhere, a little vague on the actual incident... still under assessment, a little vague on the cause which is still under analysis...a very complex issue...the human brain blah, blah, blah...Dr. Peter Wheeler, foremost in the field...working night and day...

* * * * *

As far as Gail was concerned, if Detective Lupo had ulterior motives, he was setting himself up for a disappointment. Marsha was one pretty package and he wouldn't be the first, or the last, to try unwrapping her. But he was in the wrong movie in the wrong era. He was black and white and she was technicolor. Not that he wasn't a catch in his own right but he didn't belong in Marsha's net. As if cued from off-stage, he walked through the door.

"Good afternoon, Detective. No appointment, I notice...but then I suppose in your business you don't need one do you?" she mixed her professional and personal greeting so that it came out warm but not suggestive.

"Actually, I usually make one...unless I'm serving a warrant, then it's not such a good idea." he said. Any boss who was decent and competent had a protective and competent administrative assistant looking out for them, and this one was doing that job effortlessly. Lupo accepted her control because he knew swimming against that tide would be downright foolish. Even with a warrant he'd have a tough time getting past her if she decided to put up a fight and he sensed she could and would be good at it.

"I'll let you get away with it this time." she said as if reading his thoughts.

"I'll remember that. Is Marsha in...does she have some time for me?"

"She's in but you'll have to wait a few minutes...she has a patient... anything I can do?" Gail kept eye contact with him. She didn't know any detectives and was surprised at how quiet and humble he was. Television, she reasoned, had set her expectations too dramatically and too wrongly, as per usual.

"No...well...yes, perhaps you can. Marsha asked for some background on Sorenson. I've done a little digging...it's all in the file, she can call me if she has any questions. There isn't much to it and I don't expect we'll find much more."

Gail took the envelope from the detective before he could place it on the corner of her desk. "A mystery man, is he?" She didn't expect a reply and wished she hadn't said something so trivial and common. She was a little surprised the envelope wasn't sealed.

"Pretty normal actually..."

"My name is Gail." She took the chance for an introduction.

"I'm Lupo, Gail. Like I said, it's the usual background stuff. Most people think we can find out everything with the push of a button but unfortunately, not so. Most of the time the criminal needs to get caught doing something they don't want anybody to know about and then we know where to start looking. That's the key to it really, getting a good starting point so you know whether you should talk to drug dealers or the PTA. Believe it or not, it's usually the criminal who gives us the starting point ."

"Which he has done." she finished his overly long explanation of some pretty common behaviour.

"Which he has done." Lupo repeated for no other reason than to keep the channel open, something was going on and he was curious about what it might be. The cassette from Marsha's tape recorder and the freshly typed transcription of it were sitting on the far corner of Gail's desk. Sorenson was an open book to the secretary, she probably knew as much about him as anybody did. But that didn't explain her tone or the steady gaze as she maintained eye contact so he gave her a ten second id. Nice eyes, nice eye shadow, a nine to five woman but smart and dedicated, no wedding ring, nicely dressed but not a fashionista, has a dog or a cat, probably a dog, definitely neat, hands, fingernails, hair, office, desk, what you see is what you get, she hadn't laughed yet but she had the laugh lines around the eyes so she was probably a family person, friendly for sure.

"Will Marsha be Sorenson's therapist?" he asked. Not the question on his mind, but on the way to it.

The question seemed to have only one level to it but Gail suspected there was more to him than that. He asked too casually, waited too patiently. He wore a disguise which was too obvious not to notice but too good to see through. "No, she won't be."

"That doesn't seem right."

She recognized her own tone when she mockingly chastised him for failing to make an appointment. It was friendly...and professional...but not suggestive. This isn't a game! Dammit Gail, Sorenson is dangerous.

"Detective...Lupo...the wolf?"

"In sheep's clothing..."

"Somehow, Lupo, I doubt that. I doubt that very much, anyway, Marsha is consulting on the case..."

Gail told him everything and answered all his questions. The alphabet on consultation and why she suspected the Director had assigned the case to the incompetent Peter Wheeler and why he kept Marsha firmly on the sidelines, for as long as it suited his real agenda, which could be anything but which was primarily for the sole and exclusive benefit of the Director, as usual. She didn't elaborate on Sorenson's attack on Boston Carver and it was the only time that Lupo interrupted her.

"He put out his eyes?"

"Out yes, removed no, at least not right then, but they're gone now. There's a videotape of the episode...at least there was one, who knows if that's still around. Somehow I doubt it."

Lupo was more than familiar with Boston Carver and while he didn't feel any pity for the man, he understood the extent of the malevolence that could actually inflict such damage on somebody so used to being on the sending end of that brutality. Like so many of the Boston Carver's of this world, they didn't lose very often but when they did, they lost big.

"Maybe I should look in on Sorenson."

"You mean on Gut Vik." Gail corrected him like it was after-dinner conversation.

"Do you believe that story?"

The question startled her. She hadn't thought about it in terms of belief or disbelief. Years and years of typing transcriptions, like the one she had just finished, had left their mark on her - if that's what they thought, that's what they thought and also what you should accept if you want to have a conversation with them. Of course some of it was pure nonsense but most of it was just different. Like some people's hobbies were really obsessions but no one ever admitted it.

But this one was different-different. For her. In that instant she realized that she knew it was true, she knew every last word of that Norwegian tale was true, and she knew that Gut Vik existed and Sorenson probably didn't and that scared her. She looked the detective in the eyes and nodded.

The hair on the back of Lupo's neck bristled. He hated the feeling.

* * * * *

Peter Wheeler's group session went pretty much as it always went. Basically, nobody ever listened to him. That much was always obvious from the group's individual and collective contributions to the day. Some people, he figured, were beyond help but no point in getting all wound up about that right now when he had his own problems to deal with.

Composing his press release had not only stroked his ego but had also put the entire issue of Marty Sorenson into a perspective which he hadn't seen at the outset. In the beginning, it looked like more work for very little recognition but now, for the right person, it was looking like a golden opportunity. At last, at long last, it was his turn. Almost everybody else had had a good case opportunity - something worthy of publication, and now it was his turn to stand at the lectern and preach. Providing, of course, that Sorenson lived up to his end of the bargain and was truly sick. Sure, it was a good starting point, a long term orderly running amuck in the asylum held some decent potential for the long term effects of this and that, the consequences of funding and management and this and that over the years. He already had the title. The Politics of Mental Health, Anarchy in the Asylum. Damn catchy, if he did say so himself. Thanks to the group session taking over control and running late, he didn't have a lot of time to see Sorenson before meeting with the Director. He hated being rushed, much preferring to put that shoe on somebody else's foot.

He went up CIW like he owned the place, even though he hardly ever went there but most of the staff rotated and he recognized them so it wasn't too strange. Besides, he figured, by now everybody in the hospital knew he was Sorenson's therapist and he was pretty sure that a couple of orderlies looked relieved to see him on the job so quickly. Somebody had to protect them, make sure they didn't get the blame for Sorenson's breakdown and that somebody was him. He straightened his back and went through the day room where Boston Carver had been blinded but didn't see any blood on the table or floor and reminded himself to watch the video later when he had some time.

Through one secure door which opened to the patient's rooms, nobody called them cells but that was what they were, and then through another secure door, this one closed, he would go into the isolation ward which had two cells on one side faced by a service closet and a full bathroom on the other side. At the end of that was a security station, basically a double door hatch, like you would see on a space station. As he entered ISO he saw an orderly looking through the small, reinforced glass window of the first cell. He cleared his throat.

"Steve, isn't it?"

"That's right Dr. Wheeler." Just like on the name tag where you read it. Like most staff, Steve was neutral on Wheeler's appointment to the case. Neutral because Marty Sorenson didn't necessarily deserve anyone better but also because he was unlikely to be harmed by Wheeler's therapeutic approach, such as it was. It would be harmless for as long as it lasted and, on that issue, the staff were in complete agreement - Wheeler wouldn't make it through the week. If he didn't screw himself out of the job, the Director would swat him like a mosquito. The only person who was blissfully unaware of that fact was Peter.

"How's the patient?"

"This isn't my ward, Doc. I just came to see how he is doing. We used to work together." There wasn't much point in telling the truth, either of them. Truth was, Marty Sorenson was a total train wreck but orderlies didn't do diagnosis so best just to shut up and listen. Truth also was that Steve wasn't there for a visit; he wanted to make sure the orderlies in CIW understood just how dangerous Sorenson had become. Turned out that was unnecessary. If cleaning up Boston Carver's eyeballs hadn't convinced them of the danger, the video tape had.

"So, did this episode surprise you?"

"You could say that." Steve replied but managed to keep the distain from his voice. Like would you be surprised if one of your friends smashed you against the wall and then tried to kick your face through the back of your head? Or maybe if he pulled the eyeballs out of your sockets and laid them on the table so you could look up your own nose, would that be a surprise, Doc? Or are you asking if the guy is really, really sick because then it won't be a complete waste of your time, is that the real question?

"Well, I might as well get on with it. Confront the beast, so-to-speak." Peter didn't have much time, or talent, for chit-chat.

"Uh, Doc, are you sure you want to go in there? He isn't in restraints, you know? No sedation either. Aren't you supposed to be accompanied, no matter what, by two orderlies, plus restraints of some kind?"

If he walked in there alone, he was just as crazy as the person he was going to visit. And the aftershock of that logic doubled for anybody stupid enough to witness such stupidity. "I better get back to work. I'll send a couple of orderlies down here right away." CIW was on the third floor, the top, but everybody still called it 'down there' or 'down here' even when they were on the floor.

Wheeler checked his watch and compared it to the wire-caged clock, high up on the wall at the end of the hallway. It was already four-twenty, he had to meet the Director at five and it would take ten minutes to get to Fielding's office from CIW. A preliminary diagnosis in thirty minutes was stretching it pretty tight. "Sure, send them down. I'll be okay for a couple of minutes."

"Uh, Doc…that's not regulation in this ward, nobody goes anywhere alone, especially not into isolation…that's dangerous, seriously dangerous."

"I thought you said you had work to do? You want to go in there with me?"

"No Doc…I'll send a team…on the double. Wait for them, seriously, wait for them." Steve practically shouted while turning to run. Regulations were broken all the time, half of them were just plain stupid to begin with but not that one. Breaking that one was just plain crazy. Crazy, stupid with unimaginable consequences. They didn't put anyone into ISO for fun. "Wait for them." He broke into a trot, then picked up the pace.

Wheeler had one hand on the door lever and was fishing with his keys for one that would open the dead bolt above it. Most of the place ran on a computer card system but the ISO cells were an exception and he wondered why.

The orderly was out of sight as the dead bolt slid smoothly back and he put his hand on the lever to open the door. He stood there for a few seconds, hand stuck on the lever, wondering what he would find on the other side. Then he was struck with a strange premonition that he shouldn't go in there alone. Not why he shouldn't go in, or that he might find something he didn't expect to find, just that he shouldn't go in there alone. Damned annoying and with no more time to waste thinking about it, he pushed the lever down.

CHAPTER 37

Here we are, Took A-Look back in the big city, back in the line-ups, back in the hustle. Time has started again, do you think we lost any?

Time, what did you think I was talking about?

We were away and now we are back, so did we lose any time? Yeah, that was an expensive plane ride but no, I'm not talking about that kind of time, not the time is money kind of time. I know you don't care for money, but we aren't talking about that. I know it's a stupid concept. I'm glad you're happy we're not talking about it. Did we lose any time, that was the question. You are the expert in that field, aren't you?

How do you lose time? Well, if you fly from New York to Paris, when you get to Paris its five o'clock in the afternoon but its only noon in New York so you lost five hours. No, that isn't gaining time. I know it sounds like that but it isn't. It's lost time because it's gone, because you got older without getting the time. I know five hours isn't older where you come from, that isn't the point. You asked me how time got lost and I told you.

It didn't go anywhere.

That doesn't matter, it's still lost. Yes, if you go back to New York, you get it all back, that's when you gain time. I know you'd hide it better than that. Anybody with six forevers in their dictionary would hide it where no one would ever find it, obviously.

No, that's not the case here, nobody actually hid it.

It's just that we've been away. Sometimes when you are away you feel like you've lost time because things have happened, maybe things have changed. Lost time is just one way to say it.

That's right, it's not the same as going to Paris, that's just a way of explaining why we change our watches, that's physical time.

Sure we could change our watch right now but that isn't the same thing. No one would understand that.

You don't either? Fine. We've lost at least a minute having this discussion, would you agree to that? You would? Good, no more talk about time.

Look at all the people, this is one busy airport, isn't it? I don't know why they are in such a hurry. No, I don't think it's because they are all going to Paris and are afraid of losing five hours. That was a joke? Not a very good one, Took A-Look.

Are you going to tell me why we threw the bones into the sea? Not now?

No that isn't another time question. Because it isn't, that's why. It was just a question, it had nothing to do with time. What do mean, that's what I think? You are confusing today, Took A-Look. Take it any way you want. Fine, then take it as a compliment. You're welcome.

Should we call Arlene or go straight to the seal, I mean, Marsha?

Okay, straight to the hospital. Are you going to explain that or is it a surprise too? No? You'll explain it later...you'll explain it to her too? That is a surprise, Took A-Look. Are you sure it's a good idea?

I'm sure seals can be trusted but still...she might not understand...we could end up you-know-where. Why is it so important that she knows? I know you said you would explain it later but this is a different question. Oh, I see. The answer is the same so the question is the same. Sure, I can go along with that.

You want me to leave the luggage but take my hunting knife, is that what you said? Yes, I thought that's what you said, I was just checking, that's all. And I suppose you'll explain that later too? I thought so.

CHAPTER 38

I know it's a little early, Oost, but I'm so excited. We've been ready for hours, so why not go down to the door leading to reception and wait for Lawrence there? You don't mind? Oh good, let's go then.

* * * * *

The latch handle was fully down when brute force the likes of which Peter Wheeler had never before encountered came from the other side. The bottom of the door which was cut high because of a raised sill so the room could be sealed up like in a submarine, caught on the top of his shoe and immediately wedged it to the floor. The foot stayed put for a another second or two before another violent push slid it back, crashing the door into his shoulder and head, toppling him over backwards. A third violent blow, a full-on body check with a running start, broke three toes as the door rode over them then shattered his ankle as the foot was telescoped into the shoe. It all happened so quickly that Peter's brain registered the event, the pain it caused and Gut Vik's eyes staring down at him almost simultaneously. At that, he fainted.

Gut Vik stood in the empty hallway, something he hadn't expected but immediately appreciated. With one hand on the belt of the unconscious doctor and the other grasping the white lab coat at the collar he pitched the body into the cell, removing Wheeler's security card and keys from his coat pocket. The door closed automatically behind him but he didn't bother locking the deadbolt; Peter Wheeler wasn't going anywhere and Gut Vik had no time to waste.

He turned and fled in the opposite direction to the one taken by Steve. Not even Gut Vik, The Warrior, could fight his way through all the doors, the orderlies and the idiots who were in the CIW just waiting for something or someone to do.

He passed a barren therapy room and an open area with a couple of chairs and a table that served as an orderly station. There wasn't anything on the table or walls that could be used as a weapon. After that was a security hatch leading to the stairwell.

Using Wheeler's security card he entered the hatch, one steel door with a small glass reinforced window entering a closet with a full steel door on the other side. Locked, painted red and stenciled on the other side:

EMERGENCY ONLY

ALARMS WILL SOUND AUTOMATICALLY

Conveniently designed for the express purpose of escape, he went through the security hatch into the empty stairwell, immediately filling it with the high pitched ringing of fire bells. Soon enough and the entire wing of the hospital, top to bottom, would be in chaos and confusion; the elements of battle which had always worked to his advantage. Gut Vik appreciated that some things are too good to be changed by the mere passage of time.

Real warriors are always calm and reserved, qualities which contribute as much to their ultimate success in battle as any physical abilities. It is that patience, that unerring confidence which worries and whittles at the enemies' mind and resolve before the first arrow takes flight. It is a time when the experienced warrior thinks not in the heat of battle but coolly explores his enemies' weaknesses and finding one, strikes without warning.

He didn't race down the stairs and when he reached the ground floor he waited just outside a fire door like the one he had opened to begin the chaos. He waited and listened to the budding, building intensity of panic on the other side of the door and for the sound of pursuit on the stairs above his head. Too much waiting and someone would discover the alarm was false, turn off the bells and then the panic he needed for his escape would quickly subside. If he moved too fast he would be trapped in the very chaos upon which he depended. Some things never change, he thought, as the tempo of pounding feet on the other side of the door increased and then focused, as he knew it would, toward the only escape, out the front of the building. That was the tide he wanted to ride.

"Shut down the alarms, we have an escape from CIW. It's Sorenson." echoed from the third floor. "You two go down and stop him. I'll call reception for a perimeter lock-down. For Chrissakes, be careful." Steve expected the worst. He expected to find Peter Wheeler lying dead in a pool of blood, he expected Marty Sorenson would escape and he expected to be fired. And if that wasn't bad enough, he knew that was probably the best case. He had seen the tape of Boston Carver's defeat and what details the camera had denied him, he had also seen what was left of Carver's face and his imagination filled in the blanks. Whatever Marty Sorenson had been in the past, not all good to be sure, it was pale and benign by comparison to who, or what, he had become. Free that evil onto an unsuspecting, ill-prepared world and nobody would be safe. Fear mixed with guilt.

Gut Vik waited until the sounds of pounding feet were on the second floor before he pushed the fire door open and bolted through it. The organized chaos that he wanted, the confusion he needed for his escape, instantly surrounded him. All kinds of it, coming and going in every direction with varying speeds and reactions to the bells and the shouting. But instead of being carried along by the crowd toward the front exit as he expected, sometimes he had to fight against it. There seemed to be just as many people who were interested in going toward the danger as there were those who were afraid of it. It was ridiculous and completely unexpected but that wasn't new to him, nor was he lacking the resolve to conquer it. He pushed when he had to and pulled when he could, lunging from one open space to another on his way to the exit. It was far too slow; what he really needed was his broad sword but he would settle for anything.

As if in answer to that unspoken request, an old man in front of him was hobbling toward the door, poking at the floor and those around him with his cane. Gut Vik grabbed it and shouldered the old bag of bones against the wall, breaking his will to protest and his grip on the cane at the same time. The implement was light with only a dull, flat rubber point but it was sturdy enough and in the right hands, when applied to elbows, kneecaps, jaws or temples it was effective enough to produce pain and pain reduced resistance. Pain and death would have been much better but he hadn't the time, or the weapon, for that.

Swinging the cane from one target to another, the cries and curses he produced did half the work of clearing the path in front of him; pushing and shoving did the rest. But he knew it also worked to clear the path for the two orderlies behind him and they were gaining on him with every blow he had to make, every back he had to push, every neck he had to punch out of his way. Not that he feared the orderlies, Gut Vik would never fear two men and it was detestable that he had to run from them like a coward, but he had to get away before two became three and then four.

And, he also had to go down the hall to the doors leading into the hospital's main reception before the crowd which was holding those doors open could be pushed back and the doors locked shut again. Beyond those doors was his freedom, trapped behind them and he would soon enough be back in the cage from which he had just escaped. When he finally reached the front it was at least 15 people deep and all of them were trying to get out.

So thick and packed were they that he couldn't fight his way through them without being caught from behind. Nor would they move aside with shouts or threats they probably wouldn't hear, perhaps not even understand. He couldn't go through and he couldn't go under so he launched himself onto their heads like a fish cresting a wave.

With one hand he grabbed at heads and shoulders to keep himself aloft. He used the hook end of the cane to grapple arms or necks, and pull himself forward. His feet kicked backwards and his knees spiked heads, shoulders and bodies, propelling himself forward, little by little. He was getting closer, close enough to see his next hurdle.

Standing just outside the doorway were two orderlies, although they had little to do. Somehow they, or someone in a panic, had put a table inside the doorway and it was wedged against the door jams. The barrier had become a death trap as the crowd from behind pressed the ones in front hard against the table. Unless the door frame gave way, those in front would be crushed to death, slowly but steadily compacted as every space that opened up, each arm that moved up or to the side was occupied by another arm or leg, a hand or a head, from behind or beside, all trying to inch forward and taking any space available like sand filling cracks in the rocks.

Julia Reynolds was one of those trapped in the corner where she had been watching through the window beside the door for her husband and her son when the fire bells sounded. She should have moved when she had the chance but didn't and now she was unable to get past everyone trying to escape. Still, she reasoned, she was one of the lucky ones because she had a corner to her back and, with her hands at her chest and one knee up, she could push back, diverting the energy of the crowd to the helpless ones pinned at the table. She felt bad for them but she had to save herself. Lawrence was coming to visit her, it was still the only thing on her mind. She would survive because she had a reason to survive and because of that she had the strength and the will to keep from being crushed.

When she saw the man she had known as Marty Sorenson scrambling over the heads of the crowd, she feared for her life but when she locked eyes with the man she knew to be Gut Vik, her fear was gone because she knew she was going to die.

"Gut Vik! Gut Vik the barbarian who can please no woman, no matter how old or how lonely." came from her lips, unbidden and un-thought. She marveled for an instant at the curiosity which that sound, her own voice, made. How quickly it occurred, how right were the words but how strange they sounded without any suggestion of her own reason or logic behind them.

She watched the fury build in his eyes until it consumed his thoughts. Veins throbbed in his temples, lips pursed so tightly they became a straight, thin line pointing back to the round, hard muscles of his clenched jaw. She heard the grinding of his teeth and felt the steam of heated breath as it came to her with his words.

"Gut Vik, who does as he wants with a woman!" With two sharp kicks, both of which found the flesh and bone of someone's head behind him, he was within reach of her. Another sharp thrust of his knee and the fingers of both hands found their place around her neck, the cane dropped.

She was helpless.

Oost, I am not afraid. For the first time in my life, I am not afraid of anything. Thank-you Oost, thank you for that. I only wish we had met sooner. Good-bye, Oost, good-bye.

The fearless eyes of the woman mocked the warrior, the conqueror and the man. They mocked him until they sparked and fluttered with the pressure around her throat, then jumped back in their sockets with the snapping of her neck. When he released his grip, her eyes fell back for their last moments of sight. Her head rested sideways on her shoulder, her body held upright by the crush against it. He knew she could still look at him, she still had a few moments left for that and he wanted her to take that last look and see his victory over her but she refused. She refused him that satisfaction, knowing that if he tried to take it from her he would lose his chance for escape.

He felt fingers grasping at his kicking feet and had to get away before they got a grip and pulled him down.

Oost, is there anything I should do? Is there anything I need to know before the end? Yes I'm listening. You don't say? Really. Who would have thought? Who would have thought? Is that why Lawrence set fire to the house? I should have known, I really should have…

With one hand pulling on the door jamb, Gut Vik launched himself over the last few heads on the chaotic side of the door and landed, kicking and punching, on the orderlies standing on the other side. They crashed to the floor just as the bells stopped ringing, momentarily suspending all thought and action for those who wondered at the silence and tried to make sense of it. Gut Vik didn't wonder. He didn't hesitate; he was free and he ran.

No one stopped him, he wasn't even questioned when he walked past the gate. Why should they? Some knew him and for the ones who didn't, he wasn't wearing pink or blue or green so they ignored him. Just as they always ignored Marty Sorenson. But that was Marty Sorenson and those days were over.

* * * * *

It only took one interview to figure it out but Lupo didn't feel like a genius because of it. The physical events were absolutely straightforward. Peter Wheeler, obtuse idiot who he is, explained, rationalized and whined his way past his own blatant stupidity with opening the door. After that, the trail was easy to follow. Down the fire escape stairs, through the hall to reception, pausing only long enough to break a neck, over the top like a surfer, out the door and long gone.

Maybe ten minutes before it happened Lupo had walked past the spot where Julia Reynolds was murdered. A mere one minute later, and he might even have been able to stop it. For sure he would have stopped the escape and he knew it would have been a kill shot because that was absolutely the only positive way to save the next victim. And there would be a next victim. No doubt about that.

The political motivations which led to the escape were also beyond reasonable doubt and he didn't need the interview he had with the director to know that. Putting an idiot like Peter Wheeler on a case only ever meant one of two things: either somebody was trying to get rid of the idiot or the idiot was a scapegoat for an agenda which had yet to be disclosed. Director Fielding's agenda was wrapped with ribbons of greed and tied with bows of ambition. A good case study, like a good bust, was enough to warrant the sacrifice of common sense.

"A most unfortunate turn of events, Detective. Wheeler will be fired and so will the orderly. How long will it take you to find the patient?" It was the time of getting worse before it got better which Fielding had, he remembered, so accurately predicted. Not quite the kind of worse which he had anticipated but more than bad enough to warrant an immediate sacrifice or two.

Even if Lupo hadn't had all the background he did: the Sorenson interview at the jail, the discussions with Marsha and her secretary, Lupo wouldn't have fallen for the line of bullshit the Director was spouting like he was reading straight from the Old Testament. In truth, he rarely had as much background as this and it filled him caution. Like he couldn't be truly objective because he had prior knowledge of the event in question, like he was investigating himself, so he did what every perp does, he shut up.

The crime scene guys were just about done, so too were his interviews which normally would have taken a lot longer but in this case didn't. Few of the many witnesses were reliable and putting them on the stand would likely result in the commitment of the arresting detective, and deservedly so. Such is the case in an asylum.

Gut Vik was free. He'd be hard to catch but easy to follow. Just connect the corpses. Enough of those and the cops would ultimately bear the brunt of the blame that Fielding deserved.

* * * * *

"Dr Jorgenson is here to see you, Director Fielding."

"Damn it. I forgot about her. Show her in. No, wait. Put her in the meeting room and get Marsha. Tell me when she is there and I'll join in." He hoped Marsha would take her time, he needed a game plan and a damn good one. Was there a positive anywhere in Sorenson's escape?

He knew Jorgenson didn't know about it yet or she would have come straight in, breaking down the door if necessary. It's what he would have done. She will be mad as hell. As will be her connections, whoever they are but including the Chief of Police who was part and parcel of setting up this meeting. Was there anything positive in that? Not likely.

The whole thing might go away when Marty Sorenson is found, and eventually he will be. Until then, the Chief of Police can take the heat so maybe that's a positive.

Maybe that's also the plan. Play dumb and line up some more sacrifices, just in case they're needed.

"They're waiting for you."

"I'll be right there."

Marsha wasn't sure what to expect, but the post haste meeting with the Director wasn't a surprise. Jorgenson wasn't really a surprise either. Maybe she did know what to expect. Then again, the day had been nothing but one surprise after another. For sure listening seemed like the best idea for this meeting because for sure she had nothing to offer.

"Director Fielding, I presume."

"Dr Jorgenson, nice to make your acquaintance…hello Marsha."

"I am here to pick up the prisoner, Sorenson. You know about this, I am certain?"

"I do. Unfortunately there has been an incident. Sorenson has escaped."

"Escaped? Escaped!!! How could such a thing happen? Did you not know he was dangerous? How could you let this happen? This is terrible."

"It was a most unfortunate accident but I'm sure he will be re-captured soon. The police are investigating, they were practically here when he got away. I'm sure they will catch him before too long."

"The police were here to pick him up?"

"No, perhaps Dr. Coleman can explain, wasn't the detective here to see you, Marsha?"

Fielding sat back in his chair, arms folded across his chest. Jorgenson was on the edge of her chair, keeping her balance with her elbows on the table, wringing her hands, looking at Marsha and hoping for answers that would save her two day old career.

Marsha eyed Fielding and knew she had to be careful. "There isn't much to say. The detective came by with some background on Sorenson."

"Background?" asked Jorgenson. "What kind of background?"

"Criminal records, personal history, family, that sort of thing. I thought it might help…with the analysis."

"What did he find?"

"Sorenson didn't have a criminal record, it wasn't much help."

"What about family, brothers, sisters, anybody?"

"He was an only child."

"Parents? What about them?"

"Both dead…you know about his father. The mother died two years later."

"Does he have uncles or aunts?"

Jorgenson's interest in the patient's genealogy was not necessarily unusual but the timing of it was. Then again, maybe not, Marsha had looked for the same details. "None that are known."

"Blood. Did you collect any of his blood?"

Genealogy be damned, thought Marsha. Jorgenson is up to something else entirely. Blood? Why would she care about that?

"No, no blood samples were taken." said Fielding. "Unfortunately we were just beginning his analysis when this…unfortunate incident occurred."

"What? You didn't…"

"There wasn't time, doctor. We have more than one patient at this hospital…"

"Ridiculous, this is ridiculous. Incompetent, completely incompetent. What have you cost? What have you cost?"

"Now see here, doctor, you watch what you are saying. My staff does the very best it can with the extremely limited resources they are provided. The very best it can. There is no call for you to attack them."

"You don't know what you have done, none of you. You don't know what you have cost. Where are the police? Where is someone who knows something?"

"On the first floor, by the...by reception, you can't miss them." The door hadn't completely shut before Fielding was standing beside it with his hand on the latch. "I suspect that's the last we'll see of her."

"And Marty Sorenson too." said Marsha.

"Probably." He said over his back as he left the meeting room.

"And Marsha Coleman will probably make the list next." she said to the closed door. Explain this Marsha. Explain that Marsha. That would be the strategy and there wasn't anything she could do about it. Explain the escape, explain the murder, explain all the patients who were bruised, broken or crushed. Then explain what that does to their mental state, to their recovery. Peter Wheeler was just the first to be sacrificed. She was doomed and her career was...well, her career was past tense, at best.

Her career? What about poor Julia Reynolds? Attacked not once but twice and with Boston Carver thrown in between for an excellent, brutal side bar to the lead story. That wouldn't be overlooked. More like emphasized along with the rest of the brilliant findings from everyone who could get their name in print by dumping on her. What a lousy way for it to end. The only real question was whether or not she should bother hanging around until the end.

So many questions and so many people chasing answers, all of them wanting to mine Marty Sorenson's psychosis until the last nugget was sluiced from his brain. Fielding and Jorgenson were the same and when all motives, not just career ambitions, were included, she had to include herself in the tribe. Her bloody curiosity with what she didn't understand. The only one who seemed content with this whole mystery was Eric Black, and he was the biggest mystery of all. And long gone at that. According to Arlene, he went back to the Arctic. 'He's back to his old self, Dr. Coleman, prospecting up north. I'll call you when I hear from him.'

Back to the Arctic. Quiet and peaceful, where everything made sense because all the pieces fit together. The ocean and the mountain with arms that reached down to the sea. Now why would that come into her mind?

More to point, when had it come into her mind? When she was watching the tiny light in Eric Black's eyes, that's when. The loving face of a parent with the arms of comfort, that was the first time she had the vision. Correction, that was the only time. Sorenson, or Gut Vik, had just talked about the place but Eric Black, or more specifically Took A-Look, had, somehow, shown it to her. Somehow? Not a very scientific answer, about as scientific as intuition or...what was that other thing?

...instinct? like a dog? 'James wouldn't hurt a fly. Earl got bit. The dog's got instinct, it's in the blood.' Something like that. Ruby's words.

In the blood?

In the blood, in every cell, the genetic fingerprint. Is that what Jorgenson was up to? A genetic explanation for behavior?

In the blood, a sound method for a viral or bacterial transport between individuals. Something that might unlock a code and start a function, an intellectual one? From Took A-Look to Eric Black to Marty Sorenson to Gut Vick to Julia Reynolds; all connected by blood? Could that be?

If so, were Eric Black's blood samples still in the lab, still waiting the testing she had ordered and then cancelled? Two vials of his blood which just might, if she was right, satisfy her curiosity, perhaps salvage her future, perhaps give her a future?

Just a little past five o'clock....No one would be in the lab.

CHAPTER 39

You want to do WHAT, Took A-Look? Are you serious, now you want to talk to Sorenson? Isn't it crazy enough that we followed him to his home? Shouldn't we go back for Marsha, shouldn't we protect her, isn't that why we came back?

This is dangerous, Took A-Look. I know you aren't afraid but your curiosity could get us killed. No, I'm not afraid. What do you mean I should be? You aren't making any sense and until you do, we aren't going anywhere.

Then let it be too late, too late for what? What has that got to do with Never-Ending? Everything is not an answer. Tell me why you have to look in his eyes. Because your name is Took A-Look is not an answer. No it isn't.

It is? Really, Took A-Look, this isn't one of your jokes is it? No? Dead serious? Absolutely dead serious? No time? What do you mean no time, there's always time, Never-Ending says so. Not this time? Just one last time, you want me to trust you just one last time, is that right? Then you'll do anything I ask? Really?

This must be awfully important for that big a promise. Sure, I'll do it. Should I knock at the door or just waltz right in? Just waltz right in, okay. I sure hope you know what you are doing. Yes, I trust you. Yes I have my knife, you know I do. You bet I'll keep it handy. Are you going to do the talking or do you want me to? Depends on what you see. No, you don't have to explain that to me. Why start now?

It's called sarcasm.

I'm not surprised you don't like it. There he is, get a good look because he's standing right in front of us and he doesn't look at all friendly. Doesn't look at all like Sorenson either, for that matter.

"What are you doing here?"

"We met a long time ago, don't you remember?" Took A-Look asked. Eyeball to eyeball.

"I remember. You are the little boy with the crooked teeth. What do you want?"

"The same as before. I want you to go back to where you came from."

Face to face for only a fraction of a second but more than enough time for the knife blade to slip between his ribs, tilt upwards to find a heart-beat and then a hard quarter-turn twist to lock the blade between the ribs. All the while Gut Vik was watching Took A-Look's eyes for a sign that something was going to happen and that was a mistake. All he saw was the blue, just the sea.

Took A-Look managed the move with ease, just like the old woman on the mountain would have done. It wasn't until we stepped back and Gut Vik felt the pain that he knew what had happened.

He pulled at the knife buried in his chest but it was locked in his ribs. He pulled harder until he figured out what was wrong, turned the blade and pulled it out. A gush of bright red blood followed the blade out of the hole. As if trying to catch his balance before lunging at his attacker, he rocked forward and back then to side to side before falling to his knees, gasping for air that could get to his lungs but with a hole in his heart, not to his brain. "Gut Vik killed by a child. Ridiculous." he said before toppling face down.

Dammit Took A-Look, we've killed Sorenson. Why? Why did we do that?

Marty Sorenson was already dead? We killed Gut Vik? Who is Gut Vik? No, this time you won't explain later, you'll explain now. This is serious Took A-Look, do you have any idea what will happen to us now? What do you mean, nothing?

I understand that, nothing will happen to us if we don't get caught, but that's all I understand and it isn't enough.

What do you mean that's enough for now? No, it isn't enough. For Pete's sake, we've just killed a man. What do you mean he's been killed before and if we don't do something he will kill again. That doesn't make sense. You have to explain, you have to. After what?

Burn the place down? You must be kidding, burn the place to the ground and then go and see Marsha. Are you crazy, Took A-Look. Is that why you want to see her? No? And there's absolutely no time for explanations?

Actually, I do believe that.

Of course I'll do it. It's the only chance we have. But then you will explain, then you have to explain all these secrets. You promised, remember? You also promised you would do whatever I said, and that includes going back to where you came from, back to Never-Ending if I ask you to. Good, I'm glad you remember.

I heard you the first time, burn it to the ground and don't leave a trace, not even a bone.

* * * * *

"What do you think, Chief?" Like Lupo didn't already know the answer.

"Arson, no doubt about it, Detective. By somebody who knew what they were doing. It took almost an hour for the gas company to shut it down at the main and it had been burning for quite a while before that. Not that half an hour here or there would have made any difference, the place went up like a tinder box but somebody made damn sure that it burned to smoke and ash."

"And then some." said Lupo. What was left of the house was in the basement floating in a foot of water and there weren't enough pieces to build a raft big enough to float a dog. In the middle of it all was a charred and half-melted, heavy metal workbench. "Looks like a regular Viking funeral." He said absent mindedly.

"Viking funeral? Oh I get it." said the Chief.

"He's in there? You think Sorenson's in there?" Jorgenson interrupted. She had followed the detective from the hospital and came up from behind him.

"It's his house and somebody, or somebodies are in there. Can't you smell it?" said the Chief.

"Is there anything left of him, anything at all?" she asked plaintively.

"Not much more than some damn well charred bones, if you're lucky. Nothing that you could use for id, that's for sure. Like I said, somebody knew what they were doing. Assuming they didn't go up in flames themselves."

"Why do you say that, Chief?" Lupo asked.

"Well, as near as I can figure, the gas was shut off at the meter, you can see what's left of it on that wall?" he pointed.

"Then the supply line to the furnace was disconnected at the regulator, turned at that elbow over there and pointed at that metal workbench, right at the middle where it's melted. Basically what we've got is a one inch blowtorch with an unlimited supply of air and gas. Then the gas was turned on and somehow, with the gas on full bore, it got lit without blowing everything up, maybe they used a burning rag or something as a pilot light then ran like hell when the valve was turned. We're talking about one helluva torch. Six feet of flame, minimum. Like I said, somebody knew what they were doing. One mistake and whoever put the corpse on that table just joined the barbecue. Light that pyre at the wrong time, or stand in the wrong spot and if it doesn't blow up and kill you then the heat alone would suck your lungs dry in no time at all."

"No explosion?" Lupo figured on no. The debris field didn't support an explosion, everything on site was burned to ash and there wasn't much left on site.

"Probably a good bang but not enough of an explosion to rock the building. Between the gas and all the flammables which were put around that improvised blow torch, see all the paint cans melted around the bench, plus anything else that would burn hot and fast, you name it, this little bonfire was lit by somebody who didn't want it to blow up or get put out. This was a cremation and a damned effective one. Hell, by the time we got here, the only reason we opened the hose on it was to cool the concrete, everything else was already in the basement by the time we got here. All part of a master plan and a good one at that. Good luck with figuring out who did it. Look for somebody smart."

'Is that so?' said Lupo.

Jorgenson couldn't believe it. She had missed a lifetime of fame and fortune by a couple of hours. She would hear those words for the rest of her life and she knew the detective was telling her she was actually lucky to have lost what she did.

He was probably right, she never doubted that the story of Gut Vik was true and knowing more than that just might include something she would forever be unable to erase from her memory. 'For alltid' she said softly to herself. Forever.

THE END?

Marsha's meeting with the Director lasted three minutes instead of thirty. The difference, she reasoned, between who sets the agenda and who has to follow it.

She was more fed up with being a follower than she realized. But that was in the past and she was grateful it was over. As she walked out the front door of the hospital and down the broad concrete steps, her mind became lighter with every step. She noticed the small drop of dried blood from a dark blue vein on her wrist and flicked it off.

He caught her by surprise.

"Hello Marsha."

"Eric, this is a pleasant surprise." Standing one step higher than him, she put one hand on his shoulder and looked into his eyes with interest and passion, passion for life, for knowledge, for a beginning. It surprised her. She felt like a young Italian woman standing on the Spanish Steps looking into her lover's eyes. Dark blue eyes, just as she remembered them, only with an intensity they had regained, perhaps renewed, from somewhere deep, dark and extremely cold.

"Maybe not so much a surprise as it seems." He stumbled with his words but he didn't and couldn't, lose contact with her gaze. He saw the flashes coming from them, just like when Took A-Look and the old man were talking – or not talking – on the mountain.

After that he wasn't so sure how to say what he wanted to say or when was the time to say it. Maybe it couldn't be said or maybe it didn't need to be said. Perhaps she already knew. Those were his thoughts and he was pretty sure, but not entirely positive, they were entirely his own thoughts.

Took A-Look giggled as her gold specks and green seas became his horizon.

When you are finished giggling Took A-Look, maybe you can suggest how I tell her about Never-Ending?

What do you mean there's nothing to explain?

What do you mean, look at her? I am looking at her, aren't I?

That doesn't make any sense. Okay, fine, I'll listen with my eyes.

Gold specks and green seas danced and then fused with Eric's dark blue eyes, and then he smiled as he understood.

You can start, Eric, by calling it Ever-Lasting. That is a much nicer way to say it. And a much nicer way to think of it, too. So from now on it is Ever-Lasting, okay? And that goes for you too, Took A-Look, especially for you.

Tee Hee, goes Took A-Look, rolling around like he is going to bust a gut or something. Calm green seas with dancing gold specks. I was wrong. I should have known better. A friend to Took A-Look is definitely someone I want to know.

ISBN: 978-0-9919688-1-7

9 780991 968817 >